SONG

of

ISABEL

SONG

of

ISABEL

A Novel

BY

IDA CURTIS

swp

SHE WRITES PRESS

Published 2018
Printed in the United States of America
ISBN: 978-1-63152-371-7 pbk
ISBN: 978-1-63152-372-4 ebk
Library of Congress Control Number: 2017956049

Book Design by Stacey Aaronson

For information, address:
She Writes Press
1563 Solano Ave #546
Berkeley, CA 94707

She Writes Press is a division of SparkPoint Studio, LLC.

At the beginning of the ninth century, the Frankish Empire included territory that is now France, Belgium, the Netherlands, Germany, Switzerland, Austria, and half of Italy. King Charles, or Charlemagne, as he became known, ruled this vast empire.

When Charlemagne died in 814, the long reign of his son Louis began. Unlike his father, who enjoyed having grandchildren and encouraged his daughters to bear children out of wedlock, Louis was committed to the Christian view of marriage and became known as Louis the Pious.

PROLOGUE

Narbonne, 817

WHEN ISABEL PLUCKED THE BRIGHT RED flower from the rich soil, she felt an immediate reaction. The ground shook as though Mother Earth were protesting the theft. But that wasn't what made the peaceful meadow quake and thunder with sound; it was galloping horses heavy with the trappings of war.

"Run, Isabel, run!" Emma's voice was shrill with panic as she raced through the brush that bordered the meadow.

Isabel, wide-eyed with admiration at the sight of the giant horses, stood her ground. Her father's farm horses were tame compared with the magnificent beasts racing toward her. She paid no attention to a young soldier who was shouting to attract the attention of the others. Only when Isabel lifted her eyes from the horses did the sight of four soldiers bearing down on her give her pause.

As the riders slowed their horses and circled around her, it dawned on Isabel why Emma had urged her to flee. Both girls had heard cautionary tales of how soldiers mistreated peasant women. But Isabel wasn't a peasant, and she glared at them as they continued to circle her.

"Yo, what have we here?"

"A young, fresh one by the look of her."

"But old enough, I wager."

They leered at the silent Isabel and encouraged each other with lewd remarks. "Look how she is ripening." "A tasty treat." "Time for a little refreshment."

Suspecting it would be unwise to show the fear that was knotting her stomach, Isabel watched for a break in their circle. She knew if she could reach the trees where Emma had disappeared, she'd have a chance to escape into the forest where the horses couldn't follow.

Even as she was planning her escape, one of the men jumped down from his horse and grabbed her arm in an iron grip. Under his helmet, ugly scars marred his cheek, but he smiled at Isabel as though he thought she should appreciate his attentions.

Trying to shake her arm loose, Isabel became furious at his daring. "Release me, you oaf! My father is lord of the manor. He will have you whipped to death for touching me."

The large man paused to study Isabel, but he didn't release her arm. When she attempted to pull free of his hold, he laughed.

"A lady of the manor? Dressed like a peasant and roaming about in the meadow? What do you say, men?"

Another soldier, who appeared much younger than the first, dismounted to have a better look. "Looks too wild to be a lady. I say she be putting on airs." His hand whipped out and ripped Isabel's dress so that it fell off one shoulder. He stared at the small breast he had uncovered. "Looks ready to pluck," he said, making a sucking sound with his mouth.

Isabel's courage fled, and she was suddenly sorry she had insisted on dressing like her friend Emma. With a trembling hand, she managed to pull her dress up enough to cover her breast. Straightening her shoulders, trying to hide her fear, she looked to the first soldier who still grasped her arm. He was older, and she hoped he might be more apt to listen to reason.

"My father is Lord Theodoric." By now her voice had lost its haughty edge. "You will be sorry if you do not cease your abominable behavior."

"Listen to her," the young one scoffed. "Don't she talk fancy?"

At her words, the scar-faced soldier released her arm and pulled back. "She sounds educated to me. Maybe she *is* the lord's daughter."

When the older one retreated, Isabel saw her chance. Dodging past him, she started running for the woods. There was a loud protest close behind her, and she feared the younger one was running after her. She hoped he would be too burdened by heavy armor to catch her, but then she realized another rider had come to his aid. The man on horseback cut her off, and when she had to slow down, the one on foot caught her by the hair.

Isabel's hair was thick, and it felt like he was pulling out a large chunk of it. Effectively imprisoned, she tried to blink away the tears of pain and frustration that leaked from her eyes.

"That's better," the soldier panted as he pulled her around to face him. "I'll share her with you, Roul."

Realizing her only chance to break free was for him to let go of her hair, Isabel went limp and waited for the soldier to loosen his grip. Believing she had given up, he said, "Now, that's better."

As Isabel had hoped, the soldier released her hair to tear at her dress. Isabel grabbed his hand as it ripped her sleeve, biting into the fleshy part at the base of his thumb until her teeth hurt. The soldier screamed and tossed her away from him. Before she could regain her balance and run away, a heavy blow to the side of her head knocked her to the ground.

Groggy, Isabel tried to crawl away from her attacker, who suddenly cursed. She thought his words were for her, but she heard a different voice shout, "Get away from her!"

"She bit me," her attacker whined.

"You'll get more than a bite if you're here when Malorvic arrives. You're supposed to be scouting the area."

Isabel heard horses riding away. She rolled to her back to see if she was alone. Although her hair, as well as something warm and sticky, was blurring her vision, she felt a presence nearby. Blinking, she tried to sit up, hoping her rescuer was someone she knew.

"Just lie still while I see how badly you're hurt." His voice was kind, but unfamiliar. "You took a hard blow to your head," he said as he leaned close and arranged her torn dress to cover her.

His touch was gentle and Isabel did as he asked. She felt him moving her hair. "His wrist leather broke the skin, and you're bleeding. Can you see me, little one?"

Struggling to see his face, all Isabel could make out was a golden light. She kept blinking and trying to focus.

"There's a bright light," she whispered.

"Sorry, little one. It's the sun that's blinding you. Is that better?"

He must have moved his head between her and the sun, as she could now see the dark outline of his face surrounded by a golden light. Isabel smiled up at him. "You're an angel. I can see your golden halo." Relieved by what she saw, she gave in to her need for release.

CHETWYND LEANED OVER TO MAKE SURE THE GIRL WAS still breathing.

"Is she dead?"

He turned to stare at another young girl standing above them. She looked much like the injured girl, but her dark hair hung down in neat braids. He almost laughed at her blunt words, but managed to answer seriously, "No, she just fainted. Are you her friend?"

"Yes. You saved Lady Isabel from the soldiers. I saw you chase them away."

"This is Lady Isabel?" Chetwynd was stunned to realize that the slip of a girl lying on the ground was the daughter of Lord Theodoric and sister of his friend Justin. "What was she doing out here?"

"Isabel and I were picking flowers. I ran when the soldiers came, but Isabel loves horses. She wasn't afraid."

"Well, she should have been. What's your name, girl?"

"Emma."

"I need your help, Emma. I know the manor is some distance away. Is there a cottage nearby where I can take Lady Isabel?"

"Our cottage is not far. I'll show you. My mother has healing skills."

By this time, there was a large troop of soldiers in the meadow. A few slowed and made smutty remarks when they saw Chetwynd carrying the young girl. Lord Malorvic, recognizing one of his most trustworthy warriors, stopped and listened to Chetwynd's explanation.

"Damn. I had hoped to spend the night at the manor, but I don't want any trouble. It's best that we move on. Are you sure she's Lady Isabel?"

"I don't doubt the word of her friend. Besides, she showed a spirit that reminds me of her brother. I'd like to stay and make sure her wound is tended, my lord."

Malorvic nodded. "Catch up with us when you're done," he said, clearly eager to be off.

At the cottage, Chetwynd sat crossed-legged by Isabel's pallet and watched as Emma's mother stitched the long cut above the unconscious girl's left eye. He had often observed wounds being repaired, and had even done some of that duty himself. But the young age of the patient troubled him. He prayed she wouldn't wake up until the woman was done, and his prayer was answered.

After Emma's mother had secured the last stitch, she turned to Chetwynd. "Saints preserve us. It's fortunate you came along when you did. From what Emma told me, you saved Lady Isabel from ruin."

Chetwynd stared down at the small face that appeared pale despite her sun-darkened complexion. "Will she have a scar?" he asked.

"No doubt. But she has enough hair to cover it. Perhaps the mark will remind Lady Isabel to be more cautious in the future," she said, although Chetwynd could tell by her smile that she was fond of Isabel and meant her remark only as a mild rebuke.

"I promise you the men responsible will be punished."

She shrugged, clearly not confident he spoke the truth. "You said your troop has already left. It's best that news of what happened not get back to the manor. I will keep Lady Isabel here."

"Won't someone be looking for her?" Chetwynd asked.

"It's not unusual for her to stay with us a few days. There is no reason to upset her father or her betrothed."

Chetwynd understood that, despite Lady Isabel's innocence,

such an incident might cause gossip and ruin her reputation. Since her father held a large and valuable property, he wasn't surprised that she was already betrothed. Still, looking down at her small form, she seemed too young for marriage.

As though responding to his thought, Emma's mother said, "Lady Isabel is already twelve and will be married this summer. She hasn't met her betrothed yet, but I've heard he has grandchildren."

Chetwynd couldn't help grimacing at the thought of the young girl married to a man old enough to be her grandfather. It happened all the time, he reminded himself as he started to rise.

Suddenly Lady Isabel moved restlessly on the pallet and murmured, "I saw an angel, Emma."

Chetwynd grinned. If only she knew, he thought. Then he took his leave before Lady Isabel became fully conscious.

CHAPTER ONE

Narbonne, 825

*A*T THE SOUND OF POUNDING HOOVES, Isabel fell to her knees and crawled behind the nearest thicket. She made it a habit to walk at the edge of this particular meadow where there was plenty of brush to hide her from view. Cautiously she raised her head just enough to peer through the branches and watch the muscular legs that shook the ground beneath her. She enjoyed the precision and rhythm of the horses especially bred for the warriors of King Louis. Their long legs pounded the earth, and their power never failed to excite her.

Despite their size and energy, Isabel had no fear of the horses. It was the soldiers riding them who made her cautious. She'd never forgotten the feeling of helplessness she'd experienced in this same meadow when other soldiers had overpowered her. Eight years had passed, but the incident still haunted her.

Rolling onto her back, Isabel stared at the patches of blue sky visible through the branches of the trees. The memory of that day was not all terror. A glimmering image stayed with her, a bright recollection that warmed her heart. It was associated with the warrior who had rescued her from the clutches of her would-be ravishers.

After the attack, it frustrated Isabel not to be able to recall his face. "What did he look like?" Isabel had asked her friend Emma.

"Beautiful. He was beautiful. You thought he was an angel," Emma had replied with a giggle.

"Men aren't beautiful," Isabel protested. "Tell me exactly what he looked like."

"Tall, I guess. No beard. Maybe younger than the others. They seemed to respect him and backed off at his words."

"What else do you remember, Emma? He carried me. He must have been strong," she prompted.

"I suppose. You don't weight much." Emma shrugged. "Mainly I remember his golden hair. It was long and curly. That's why you thought he was an angel. Everything happened fast. That's all I remember."

Although Isabel had asked her friend many times to repeat the story, Emma had never been able to give her the detailed information she sought. Frustrated, Isabel would close her eyes and bring to mind her own memories of her hero. There was the mellow, soothing sound of his deep voice as he spoke kind and reassuring words. When he adjusted her ripped clothing to cover her breast, his hands had been gentle, although she recalled feeling hard edges on his fingers. She imagined the calluses on his hands, as well as the scent of his body, resulted from controlling a magnificent war horse. Over the years, the memory of his touch had progressed from gentle contact to caress.

Shaking her head, Isabel cleared away the memories she had stored away and revisited many times. The meadow was quiet. No doubt the soldiers would seek shelter for the night at her father's manor house before continuing north. Isabel knew it would be the first of many stops they would make on their route from the barrier against the Moors on the southernmost boundary of King Louis's empire. Charlemagne was dead, and King Louis was doing his best to protect the Holy Roman Empire his father had ruled after being crowned emperor by Pope Leo III in 800. Since guarding against invaders along the Spanish March was a desolate tour of duty, the warriors would be happy to be headed for one of the king's palaces in the north.

For a few years after the vicious attack that had left Isabel with a thin scar below her hairline, she waited for her champion to return. Unwilling to face visiting soldiers, any one of whom could be her attacker, she often hid behind a convenient tapestry in her father's great hall and searched the assembled lot. Although frustrated that she didn't have a better description, Isabel was certain her golden hero was never among them.

When all the warriors had passed her hiding place, Isabel ran through the woods to her favorite refuge, a secluded pond that few people knew existed. She peeled off her slippers, vest, and heavy gown. Heated from her run, she found the pond especially inviting. Wearing only a thin shift, Isabel waded into the cool water.

After paddling about quickly to give her warm body a chance to become used to the chilly water, Isabel relaxed. Floating on her back, she squinted at the sun filtering through the trees. Although she was not the first to discover it, Isabel thought of this place as her own. Many years ago, her older brother, Justin, had laid claim to the secret pond on one of his frequent journeys of exploration through the thick forest on their father's land. The children had been warned against such jaunts, but Justin had been fearless and Isabel tried to emulate him.

She had been but five years old when she followed the brother she adored as he slipped away from the manor. When he discovered her, Justin tried to send her home. But by that time, they were already at the pond and Isabel kept jumping into the water. Justin realized he had to teach her to swim or watch her drown.

The only children of Lord Theodoric, Justin and Isabel spent a great deal of time in each other's company. Their mother had died shortly after Isabel was born, and their father never remarried. Once Isabel was able to swim, Justin ignored the fact that she was a girl and treated her as an equal. Being included in his many adventures was one of her happiest memories.

But when Justin reached his twelfth year, everything changed. Since it was the custom for young noblemen to be trained on estates much larger than his, Lord Theodoric arranged for his son to enter the household of Count Jonas. Justin would begin his education as a page, serving in the great hall. If all went well, he'd advance to learning how to ride and handle weapons, skills necessary for a knight who would serve the king.

As the servants packed the things Justin would need on his journey, Isabel wailed her protests, insisting that she be allowed to go with him. No matter how hard her grandmother tried, she could not convince Isabel of the justice of the tradition that sent male progeny off to be educated while females stayed with their families.

After Justin left, Isabel missed him terribly and in rebellion refused to learn any of the household skills her grandmother tried to teach her. It was summer, and Isabel continued to roam the forest and swim in the pond that she had shared with Justin.

Isabel's loneliness ended when she met Emma. The

daughter of one of her father's tenant farmers, Emma turned out to be a kindred spirit. Isabel initiated Emma into the pleasures of the secluded pond, and before long the two girls became inseparable. A few years later when Emma married, she showed her husband the secret pond and taught him to swim. Isabel had tried not to be jealous, but it was hard to lose her exclusive relationship with Emma.

Even in the cool water, Isabel's face flushed when she remembered seeing Emma and Derek together. She had never told her friend she had happened upon them one hot summer evening. As she watched, the swimmers emerged from the water. Both were naked, a fact that surprised Isabel as she and Emma always kept their shifts on when they swam. When Derek began to caress Emma's breasts, the sight made Isabel's own breasts tingle with longing, and she had fled.

Although Isabel hadn't watched for long, the scene had made a lasting impression. The memory returned as she stretched out her arms and twisted her hips to propel herself slowly across the pond. Loving the freedom her body possessed in the water, she closed her eyes. Touching her own breasts, she tried to imagine what it would feel like to have a man touch her the way Derek had touched Emma.

A shadow suddenly alerted Isabel that someone was near. Lifting her head, she gasped at the sight of a soldier looming above her on the shore. His face was shaded from view because the sun was behind him, but his hair was lit from behind. A halo seemed perched above his golden hair.

Struggling to secure her footing on the sandy bottom of the pond, Isabel lost her balance. The deep water closed over her head. When she resurfaced, her hair covered her eyes. Quickly pushing it away, she searched the shore. In the few seconds it had taken her to clear her eyes, the vision had evaporated.

Fear quickly replaced her excitement. Perhaps it hadn't been her champion. Was a soldier hiding, waiting to spring upon her?

Not eager to tempt fate, Isabel leapt out of the water and grabbed her gown. She pulled it over her wet shift and was already running as it fell into place. As she rushed toward Emma's cottage, she tried to reconstruct what had taken place so quickly. She hadn't had a chance to see his face, but she was sure the outline of the figure she'd seen had a sword hanging at its side. She had no doubt it was a soldier. Remembering her movements in the water, she bit her lip. How long had he been watching her?

Lifting her long skirts out of the way of her bare feet, Isabel pushed herself to run faster. In her haste she had left her slippers and outer vest at the pond. By the time she reached Emma's open door, she was panting for breath. Unable to speak, Isabel flopped down on the straw pallet in the corner of the one-room cottage.

"You shouldn't be running in this heat," Emma chided absentmindedly. Accustomed to Isabel's sudden arrivals, she continued settling her babe in his cradle in a dark corner.

Although Isabel was the daughter of Lord Theodoric, and Emma the wife of a tenant farmer, a stranger would have trouble telling which was which. Most of the time, Isabel adopted peasant dress and left her hair free of the head covering her grandmother insisted was proper attire for a noblewoman. Only her thick, long dark curls and delicate features suggested her noble heritage.

"Emma," Isabel gasped out between pants. "Listen. At the pond . . ."

"You went swimming without me?" Emma's eyes narrowed. "Why didn't you come fetch me? I could have brought the babe."

Ignoring her words, Isabel pushed her wild hair away from her heat-flushed face and blurted out, "There was a soldier at the pond." She was satisfied to see that her words had captured her friend's full attention.

Quickly pouring Isabel a cup of water, Emma sat beside her on the pallet. "Just calm down. There was talk in the village. I heard a company of soldiers arrived today. How could one of them find the pond? What happened? Are you all right?"

Isabel noted the worry lines on Emma's forehead. It was clear her friend was remembering the day the soldiers had surrounded Isabel.

"Nothing happened," Isabel assured Emma. Her heart slowed and she took a long drink. "I was swimming when something caught my eye. A shadow over the pond. When I looked up, I saw an outline—nothing more, as the sun was behind him. It was a soldier with a golden halo."

"Saints preserve us," Emma declared in a disgusted voice. "Not that again." She began to stand up, but Isabel grabbed her arm.

"This was no silly imagining. I really did see him, Emma. But, just as last time, I didn't see his face."

Shaking her head with resignation, Emma settled down again. "Isabel, your obsession rules your life. If it was a soldier, it's good that you ran away. But it could have been anyone."

"I know that, Emma. No obsession rules my life," she protested.

Emma narrowed her eyes. "Eight years ago, you sent Lord Frederick away."

Isabel interrupted before her friend could continue. "He was old, Emma. You have a short memory. At the time, you thought I should discourage the match."

"It's how you discouraged it that worries me. You let him believe the soldiers defiled you."

Isabel shrugged. "He noticed the scar and asked what happened."

"You could have hidden the scar. Or you could have told a tale. You don't usually have problems in that area."

"I don't lie, if that's what you mean. Sometimes I embroider the truth."

Emma gave a snorting laugh. "It's the only type of sewing you know how to do."

"You sound like my grandmother. When did you become so righteous?"

Emma sighed. "It's not some little incident I'm referring to, Isabel. You spoiled your chance to wed by allowing Lord Frederick to believe you had been ruined."

"He jumped to conclusions. I didn't encourage his belief. I just didn't correct it." Isabel shrugged. "I was young and didn't want to marry. It seemed an easy way out of the match."

"What was easy about it? Your grandmother was so angry I thought she'd burst a blood vessel. Her eyes were actually bulging when she discovered what had happened."

Isabel tried to hide her grin.

"Don't laugh. Your father threatened to send you to a nunnery. You promised to wed another suitor. But then—surprise—he too heard about the attack. How many times did that happen?"

"Don't pretend you condemn my behavior, Emma. If any of those suitors had looked like Derek, I might have been tempted."

Emma smiled at the compliment to her husband. "Keep your eyes off Derek."

"Why are you bringing all this up now? You've always sided with me."

Emma nodded. "What you say is true, Isabel. But it's gone on too long. The vision of a soldier you saw for a few minutes is ruling your life. You're waiting for him to return, but that's not going to happen. It's time to move on with your life."

"Emma, I swear on my mother's grave that I saw a soldier at the pond. He had golden hair."

"It could be some other soldier with fair hair. Lots of soldiers from the north have fair hair. Does that mean he's your angel?"

"No, of course not. That's why I ran away."

Deflated, Isabel lay back and stared at the rafters that supported the thatched roof. For many years, Emma's cottage had been a sanctuary for her, a place to hide when soldiers stopped at the manor or she had a disagreement with her grandmother. Perhaps she had imagined the soldier with golden hair. When he appeared, she had been thinking about how her champion would touch her when he did come back for her. It could have been anyone, or no one.

Emma's sympathy for her friend was evident on her face. "What are you going to do, Isabel? You're the lady of the manor. Are you going to hide behind the tapestry and search for your champion?"

"I gave that up years ago."

"Now you usually wait here until the soldiers move on. Maybe you did see this hero of yours today. Why don't you join your family for supper and have a look?"

"You don't really believe me, Emma. You just want me to face my fear of confronting a troop of soldiers."

"It's time."

Isabel lifted her eyebrow. "My grandmother would be surprised. She has been more than happy to assume the role of lady of the manor."

"She's just filling the role you refuse, Isabel. Instead of learning the skills you need to run the manor, you spend your time studying Latin with Father Ivo."

Isabel sighed. "Lord Theodoric is pleased with the way Lady Winifred runs his household. My father wants me to enter a convent. Maybe I should do that."

"Be serious, Isabel. You like your freedom too much for that. There must be other things you can do."

Lately Isabel had been thinking the same thing, but she had been reluctant to approach her father. To marry or enter a convent were the traditional choices for a noblewoman. And her father was steeped in tradition.

"Father Ivo has taught me to read and write. He's fond of history and geography, so we study that in addition to reading holy works. Perhaps Justin could find me a position at court. He's a minister to King Louis, after all. He should have some influence."

Emma rolled her eyes, clearly not impressed with the idea. Pushing herself to her feet, she began to straighten the kitchen area. "You often talk of joining Justin at court. But first face the soldiers, Isabel. There are a lot of soldiers at court. Either do it or accept one of the matches Lady Winifred manages to unearth."

"I'm twenty years old. You know as well as I do that my chances for a desirable match have dwindled. Men want to marry maids of twelve, not twenty. If I didn't like the choices before, imagine what they'll be like now."

"You are playing an old tune, Isabel. You're waiting for your champion to return."

Isabel stood up and poured another cup of water. "Maybe he has returned. I swear to you, Emma, the soldier at the pond was tall and well shaped. Isn't that how you described him?"

"Enough, Isabel. A lot of soldiers are tall and well shaped. As I said before, you're obsessed. It's like one of those tales you told me. Remember what happened when Apollo was obsessed with Daphne, chasing her through the forest day after day? In the end, Apollo caught nothing but a handful of leaves when Daphne turned into a laurel tree."

Isabel shook her head in disgust. "I should never have told you those tales."

"It was a fair exchange," Emma said, adding slyly, "I gave you lots of details about the marriage bed."

Isabel giggled as she thought about the stories they told each other. Her contributions were based on the erotic tales of Ovid that she was now able to read in Latin. But Emma's were based on reality. "You're right, Emma. It was a fair exchange."

When the baby cried, Isabel lifted her out of the cradle and soothed her until Emma had freed her breast to nurse her.

"Do you really think you saw a golden-haired soldier, Isabel? Or were you just dreaming? You think of him a great deal."

LATER, WALKING TOWARD THE POND TO RECOVER HER slippers and vest, Isabel wondered if she were beginning to imagine things. The golden vision had disappeared quickly. Perhaps it was a trick of the sun on the water that had inspired her to see what she desired.

The pond was isolated and almost impossible for someone to stumble upon. That fact was the best reason to doubt a soldier had appeared. Isabel moved to the spot where she had seen the vision and searched the ground. Breathless, she fell to her knees. At the very edge of the pond where the earth was soft, there were two large footprints. Someone wearing boots had stood in this very spot.

CHAPTER TWO

WHEN LORD CHETWYND ENTERED THE manor's great hall to join his men, he saw they had already made themselves comfortable at the lower tables. He was annoyed at missing his opportunity for a swim, and the warm air and boisterous noise in the hall did not improve his humor. He held back to observe the scene.

Chetwynd easily identified the solidly built man seated at the center of the high table as the lord of the manor. Theodoric, his full head of white hair shining in the light, was clad in an elaborate purple mantle trimmed with fur and silver ornaments. Chetwynd's own unadorned black doublet was spartan in comparison.

An older woman sat beside Lord Theodoric, but a quick glance along the table revealed no sign of the water nymph who had kept him from his anticipated swim. He had followed Justin's directions to the pond, only to find it occupied. At first he had hoped to join the swimmer, but when she looked up, her startled eyes had been exactly like those of her brother. Lady Isabel's movements in the water made it clear she awaited a lover, and he suspected she wouldn't appreciate being interrupted.

Chetwynd wasn't sure what he expected, but discovering that Isabel had matured into a shapely, sensual woman had been a shock. He remembered an innocent slip of a girl who had called him an angel. There had been something unbearably sweet about young Isabel. Of course, he had never been an angel, but for some reason her mistake had touched him.

He remembered other things about the young Isabel. Though small of size, she had boldly stood up to the soldiers who were tormenting her. The bite she gave one of her pursuers had been deep. It caused the young soldier great pain when it later became infected. Chetwynd's face softened at the memory of the struggle she had put up before being struck on the head. Her courage had given him time to reach her before the soldiers could overcome her.

According to Justin, Lady Isabel had not been untouched by her mishap. Chetwynd knew that she had not married as expected. He had assumed that leaving her with Emma's mother would prevent the incident from becoming common knowledge. Surely a small scar that could be hidden by her hair would not be enough to discourage a suitor.

For all that, Lady Isabel had appeared happy enough as she moved sensually through the water. He frowned as he imagined the couple frolicking in the pond after he rushed away. Her involvement with a lover could very well hamper the hope Justin had of bringing her to court. Chetwynd regretted seeking out the pool Justin had described, upset that he had neglected to mention that Isabel also swam there.

Finally pulling away from the wall he had been leaning on, he made his way to the high table to greet the lord of the manor. Chetwynd wondered how much Lord Theodoric knew about his daughter's activities. Perhaps he shouldn't be surprised at the change he found in Lady Isabel. He had grown up on a secluded farm manor himself, and knew that country life encouraged lusty appetites. Yet, he couldn't help preferring his memories of an innocent, courageous girl to the reality of the sensual woman he had encountered at the pond.

When Chetwynd introduced himself by name, Lord Theodoric smiled and rose to indicate that Chetwynd join him at the table. Theodoric spoke loudly to be heard over the noise of the great hall. "Welcome, Lord Chetwynd," he said as he indicated that others make room for his guest. "We meet at last."

"Your hospitality is appreciated, my lord."

"Sit, sit." Theodoric motioned to the servants, indicating that food be passed to Chetwynd, and urged him to fill his trencher.

"Your reputation precedes you, Lord Chetwynd. My son Justin has often spoken of the time you spent training together with Count Jonas."

"It seems a long time ago now. Although our training often pitted us against one another in mock battle, we still managed to become friends," Chetwynd replied, remembering those carefree days.

"Justin says you are one of King Louis's most favored warriors. I congratulate you on your success."

Chetwynd tried not to grimace at his host's words. Lord Theodoric had no way of knowing that his favor at court had plummeted of late, or that Justin no longer held him in high regard. Instead of answering, he took a bite of the joint of meat on his trencher.

"I hope you will enjoy your stay at Narbonne, Lord Chetwynd. Was this your first assignment on the Spanish March?"

"It was my first assignment in the region with my own soldiers. Many years ago I served Lord Malorvic when his troops guarded the border."

Chetwynd wondered if, after all these years, Theodoric might connect him with the injury to Lady Isabel. Perhaps she had told her father what happened at the hands of Malorvic's men.

"I heard about your campaigns against the Saxons, Lord Chetwynd. Your success at besting the heathens is legendary. You're young to have had such an illustrious career. Perhaps after your meal you could entertain us with some tales."

Chetwynd's military prowess was well-known. Shortly after his first success against the Saxons, King Louis had rewarded his efforts by making him a knight and granting him a benefice. Aquis, located near the king's palace in the north, was made up of rich farmlands and a thriving vineyard. The purpose of the grant was to provide Chetwynd with the means of raising enough funds to outfit his own troop.

"I'm not much of a storyteller, Lord Theodoric."

Chetwynd knew it was the custom to hear the exploits of warriors after a meal. The *Song of Roland*, a heroic tale about Charlemagne's most famous knight, was often recited. But Chetwynd was not one to indulge in boasting of his military accomplishments, and after his experience at court, he was even less inclined to talk about himself. His success on the battlefield had not kept him from disaster at court. Flattered by the attentions of Queen Judith, he had acted in a manner of which he was not proud. King Louis was an old man who spent most of his time on religious retreats, while the young queen was lonely and in need of someone to confide in. Or so he had thought.

Chetwynd's growing involvement with Queen Judith had shocked Justin, who accused him of being ruled by his loins rather than his head. It was true, of course. It hadn't taken him long to realize that the beautiful queen was using his reputation and influence for her own purposes. When gossip started to circulate, Justin had proven his friendship by arranging for Chetwynd to be assigned a tour of duty on the

Spanish March. The assignment at the southernmost boundary of the empire had given Chetwynd some much-needed time away from court.

Chetwynd had no intention of entertaining his host with stories of his service to the king. When Theodoric realized he was serious about not reciting tales, his face lost its eager expression. Theodoric shrugged his shoulders and turned to the small but imposing woman seated on his other side. She, too, was elegantly clad in flowing robes of silky green and white, her head covering rising above her head like a crown.

"May I present my mother, Lady Winifred. Lord Chetwynd knows our Justin and is well-known for his service to King Louis, my lady."

"I have heard all about Lord Chetwynd," she replied, a sly smile on her face.

Her words gave Chetwynd a jolt, and he prayed they weren't true. Though advanced in years, Lady Winifred had alert eyes that examined him closely. As though coming to a decision, she left her seat and moved toward Chetwynd, impatiently waving for the person beside him to make room for her.

"It's about time we finally met, Lord Chetwynd. I'm eager to hear the latest news of my grandson."

"I'm pleased to meet you, Lady Winifred," Chetwynd replied, standing to help her settle in her new seat. "It has been a while since I last saw Justin, so my news will not be timely."

Lady Winifred waved away the servant who carried her trencher, indicating she was finished with her meal. However, she did accept a goblet of wine.

"When exactly did you last see him, Lord Chetwynd?" she insisted.

"During the Spring Assembly at the king's palace in Aachen. We spent some time together there."

The king held many assemblies throughout the year, and the Spring Assembly was devoted to planning military operations for the summer months. The widespread empire was in constant threat from encroaching tribes that did not share the Christian faith of the Franks. Chetwynd's army was only one of many armies employed by King Louis to protect his kingdom against the heathen aggressors.

"Justin has mentioned you many times. I know he regards you as the brother he never had. He does have a sister. Perhaps he mentioned Lady Isabel."

In fact, they had had a long discussion about the lady, Chetwynd recalled. Justin believed Isabel was unhappy at Narbonne. Chetwynd had hoped to do him a good turn by bringing Isabel to court, a plan that now seemed to be ill-conceived. He had no intention of mentioning it to Lady Winifred until he decided how he should proceed.

"It's true Justin is like a brother to me, my lady. As pages in the household of Count Jonas we ate, slept, and trained together. Natural brothers could not be closer. But at court we have taken different paths. Justin has made a reputation for himself as a minister to King Louis. I admire Justin's skill as advisor to the king."

Chetwynd's words were meant to please Justin's grandmother, but that didn't mean they weren't true. There were many times when he envied Justin's diplomatic skills. Lately he had discovered how valuable they were in keeping peace at court.

"Oh yes, Justin is talented in that way. I believe he takes after me. We are both skilled at reading people."

To keep the twitch at the corner of his mouth from betraying his amusement at her words, Chetwynd looked down at the tray of fruit being passed along the table. He could only hope she wasn't as good at reading people as she thought she was.

Although the noise in the hall made it unnecessary, Lady Winifred leaned closer to speak in confidence. "Do tell me the latest news from the palace. I fear Queen Judith courts disaster with her demands for the infant Charles. I support her ambitions for her son, of course, but she must be more cautious. I was a second wife myself and know the problems involved when there are children from a previous marriage. The king's three grown sons seem unwilling to give up any of the territory they rule. Tell me your opinion. Does the queen have a chance to prevail?"

Chetwynd wasn't surprised by the lady's knowledge of court politics. The queen's struggles to establish a substantial inheritance for her son were widely known and discussed. But he didn't like the direction the conversation was taking. Although he was in a position to know a great deal about the queen's maneuvers, he wasn't eager to talk about them.

"Queen Judith has many supporters," he stated in a clipped manner, hoping to end the discussion.

Lady Winifred ignored his obvious unwillingness to speak of the matter. "She must be careful of the clergy, Lord Chetwynd. The church fathers were instrumental in dividing the empire so that each of the king's three sons rules a portion. Making his oldest son, Lothar, co-emperor with the king ensures there will be a strong emperor in place once Louis is gone. Of course, the bishops have their own reasons for protecting the integrity of the Holy Roman Empire."

Lady Winifred was warming to her subject. She shook a finger at him as she continued. "Lothar is the son who poses the greatest threat to Queen Judith. Beware of Lothar. The man has a nasty temper, and he jealously guards his right to the title of emperor. It's said Charlemagne was reluctant to assume the title bestowed upon him by Pope Leo III, but his grandson has no such reservations. He will not give up any of his power without a struggle."

Although Lady Winifred had asked for news, she seemed content to display her own knowledge of royal history. She was well-informed and had a clear understanding of the issues. Chetwynd was content to listen to her talk while he poured himself more of Lord Theodoric's excellent wine.

As if she suddenly realized Chetwynd wasn't contributing to the conversation, Lady Winifred took the direct approach. "What about you, Lord Chetwynd? Do you support Queen Judith's ambitions for her young son?"

Playing for time, Chetwynd took a long drink of wine and struggled not to choke as the strong liquid coated his throat. Lady Winifred was an intelligent woman whose probing questions threatened his peace of mind. She waited patiently for an answer.

"I vowed to stay clear of the conflict between Queen Judith and the king's grown sons," he finally managed to say.

It was a recent vow. Earlier Chetwynd had fallen under the influence of Queen Judith. But he had realized his mistake and made the vow to Justin.

Lady Winifred studied his face as though trying to read meaning into his answer. Clearly impatient with her inability to elicit information, she abruptly changed the subject. "Do give me more personal news of Justin. Has he found a wife yet?"

Chetwynd almost sighed with relief. "Not yet, my lady. But there is someone he has been courting. I think he is quite smitten with Lady Lilith, a young widow with two children."

"A widow, you say. Does she have a large estate?"

"Yes, I think you'd call her estate large."

Chetwynd looked down to hide his grin at her satisfied

expression. When Lady Winifred was suddenly quiet, he realized he had lost her attention.

"Praise be to God," he heard her whisper as he followed the direction of her wide-eyed stare.

Chetwynd echoed her words in his mind. Lady Isabel stood at the entrance from the family quarters. She stared at the soldiers, color draining from her face. He had seen stone statues that looked more alive.

CHAPTER THREE

HEN ISABEL STEPPED INTO THE GREAT hall, a wall of noise brought her abruptly to a standstill. Boisterous male voices, sounding much like the taunting laughter she had heard eight years ago, carried her back in time.

She stared at the soldiers at the lower tables. At first just a few heads turned in her direction; then others followed suit. Leering faces that looked eerily alike filled her vision as jarring laughter changed to whispers. The hush that fell over the hall caused a shiver to pass through Isabel's body. Eight years ago, she hadn't known enough to feel fear. It was as though her body were making up for that mistake.

Frozen to the spot, she prayed her wobbly legs would continue to support her. She told herself that she was in her father's great hall, not a secluded meadow. Before she could gain enough control to move, her grandmother was at her side. Lady Winifred grabbed Isabel's arm in a painful grip.

"There's no turning back now, my dear. For heaven's sake, pull yourself together." Lady Winifred's whispered words were a firm command. "It's about time you behaved in a manner appropriate to your station. Come along and take your rightful place at the head table."

Isabel managed to pull her arm free, but at least her

grandmother's presence dispelled her nightmare. Taking a deep breath, she concentrated on putting one foot before the other. Her father stood as she approached the high table, and her grandmother followed close behind. No doubt Lady Winifred wished to block any possibility of retreat.

When Isabel reached her father, he extended his hand and gave her a smile, the first she had received from him in a long time. "Good of you to join us, my dear," he said looking her up and down.

Since Isabel had no clothing appropriate for the great hall, her handmaid had found her a gown from a trunk of her mother's belongings. Isabel had often searched through her mother's chest when she was a child, wondering about the woman who had died before she could know her. Now she wondered if her father would recognize her mother's gown.

Lord Theodoric's eyes widened as he examined the low-cut garment, but if he recognized the formfitting, sky-blue dress as belonging to his dead wife, he gave no indication. Although he was no doubt surprised by her appearance in the hall while soldiers were present, he didn't comment on it.

Isabel had only nodded at her father's words of welcome, and the familiar faces at the high table watched their exchange. Vaguely aware of her father's chief steward and several merchants, the only person Isabel was really conscious of was the one she refused to look at directly. After seeing the footprints at the pond, she had rushed home, determined to search the hall for a golden-haired soldier. Out of the corner of her eye she had caught a glimpse of a visitor with flaxen hair. Was he the stranger who had startled her at the pond? She realized by his position at the high table that he was no common soldier.

Again her grandmother took her arm, this time more gently. Isabel allowed herself to be led to a place beside the stranger. As he stood at her approach, Isabel gathered enough courage to look at him. His tresses were not as enchanting without the sun illuminating them, but they appeared thick and soft, a contrast to the harsh lines of his tanned face. She had imagined a softer visage, and his stern expression surprised her. Although she was sure he had been at the pond, he appeared nothing like her gentle champion. Surely it was only a coincidence that this soldier had somehow found her pond and the sun had lit up his golden head.

Suddenly aware that she had been studying him far too long, Isabel lowered her eyes. She had vowed to seek him out, but hadn't expected to come face-to-face with him so quickly. Her neck flushed when she remembered how she had been swimming and touching herself when he had come upon her at the pond. Despite her embarrassment, she had resented the interruption.

She realized Lady Winifred was making introductions. "Isabel, this is Lord Chetwynd, a knight in the service of King Louis. He and his army are returning from duty on the Spanish March."

When the silence between them continued, Lady Winifred looked from one to the other and then spoke directly to Isabel. "You will be pleased to hear Lord Chetwynd is acquainted with your brother, Justin." Her grandmother nudged Isabel's arm, urging her to reply.

It seemed to be a contest to see who would give in and speak first. Isabel finally surrendered, but only to mutter, "Lord Chetwynd."

In reply, Chetwynd nodded. Isabel knew why she felt uneasy, but she wondered why he seemed so cold.

Frustrated, Lady Winifred waved her hand at her seat. "Do take my place beside Lord Chetwynd, Isabel. I know you are eager for news of Justin," she prompted. With these words of encouragement, Lady Winifred pushed her granddaughter toward the seat.

Reluctantly, Isabel settled herself on the bench, and Chetwynd sat down beside her. Determined to ignore the warrior, she accepted the goblet of wine her father offered and busied herself choosing from the food trays passed to her by servants.

The quiet that had descended upon the troop at Isabel's entrance dissipated as the diners returned to the loud chatter that accompanied their eating and drinking. Isabel watched the soldiers tucking into their food. Their faces no longer appeared alike, and she saw they were a variety of ages. Although the men stole glances in her direction from time to time, they didn't stare for long. Her confidence grew as she noticed the high degree of deference with which she was treated.

There was one exception. A lad with a cheery face smiled boldly at her. He was too young to be frightening, and the open admiration she observed in his eyes amused her. She could not help returning his winsome smile.

Forgetting her intention to ignore the silent lord, Isabel asked, "Who is that young lad, Lord Chetwynd? He does not look old enough to be a soldier."

Chetwynd frowned at the young lad as he answered Lady Isabel. "That's my squire, Jerome. He is young and takes liberties." His expression caused the lad to immediately lower his eyes.

Isabel grinned at her success in finally getting the warrior to speak. "How is it you are acquainted with my brother Justin, Lord Chetwynd?"

He paused only a few seconds, as though trying to figure how to answer. "Our friendship goes back many years, my lady. As I told your grandmother, we were pages together on the estate of Count Jonas of Orleans. We began our training in the great hall, serving meals and observing the manners of polite society. Justin and I shared an impatience for these tasks."

Isabel smiled at his remark and nodded, encouraging him to continue.

"Being a little older, I advanced to caring for the horses first. Count Jonas bred the large animals for King Louis's armies. Justin loved the war horses. He spent all his spare time at the stables. Although he was much better at mastering the social skills than I was, and therefore more welcome in the great hall, we shared a love of horses. Before long we were jousting and hunting together."

Isabel's heart twisted as she thought about how much she missed her brother. "I remember the day Justin was sent off to be educated. It broke my heart that I was not allowed to accompany him. I was jealous of his freedom." She paused, remembering her disappointment. "But go on, Lord Chetwynd, I interrupt your story."

"There isn't much more to tell. I became a soldier in the service of Lord Malorvic. Justin stayed with Count Jonas, who later introduced him to King Louis.

"Though he has a great love for horses and jousting, Justin's real talent is with people. His easygoing manner, level head, and ability to deal with all types of men make him a natural diplomat. It didn't take him long to gain the confidence of King Louis and become one of his most trusted advisors."

After his earlier silence, Isabel was surprised at how freely he spoke about her brother. "You have high praise for Justin. And what about you, my lord? Clearly you have advanced in your career. You have your own army and a young squire to serve you." She waved her hand toward Jerome and his other men.

"There is nothing remarkable to tell," he replied, again sounding taciturn.

"I'm sure you're being modest, my lord." She paused as though waiting for him to say more about himself. When he didn't, she added, "It has been over a year since I saw my brother, Lord Chetwynd. I miss him. Thank you for telling me about him."

Isabel looked around, but found no one paying any attention to them. She lowered her voice and asked, "How is it you found our secluded swimming spot, Lord Chetwynd? Few know about it. Did Justin mention it to you?"

Chetwynd's eyes widened and his mouth softened as though he might smile. "Your guess is correct. Justin related many details about his life at Narbonne. He described his secret pond at length and with enthusiasm. Hot and dusty when I arrived at Narbonne, I craved a swim. From his description, I was able to find the pond. It didn't occur to me anyone would be there."

"I guess he didn't tell you I often swam with him."

"No, he neglected to mention that."

"I'm sorry you didn't get your swim, my lord."

The noise in the great hall had increased even more as the men and women slowed their eating and did more drinking and talking. Isabel and Chetwynd had exhausted their talk about Justin and remained quiet. Flushed with the success of her presence in the great hall, Isabel wondered if she dared to advance her plan.

Looking out at the troops, she saw that there were a few women traveling with the soldiers. Isabel turned to face Chetwynd again. She took it as a good sign that he no longer appeared as stern as he had when they met. "When do you leave Narbonne, Lord Chetwynd?"

"We will rest here for a day or two. My men are eager to

return to their homes to help with the fall harvest." He paused and then continued, "I'm headed for Aachen to report to King Louis about our patrol on the border."

Father Ivo had told Isabel that Aachen was the king's favorite palace, and Justin would be sure to be there. Since that's where she wanted to go, she saw no reason why she couldn't travel with Chetwynd's army. "Would you take me with you to Aachen?" she asked.

The shocked expression on his face made Isabel realize she should have prepared him for her request instead of blurting it out. In order not to appear a wanton woman seeking to be one of his camp followers, she said the first thing that came to her mind. "I wish to visit with my brother before taking religious orders."

"You are planning on a religious vocation?" he asked sharply, ignoring her request to travel with them.

Isabel squirmed in her seat. "Yes, my father suggested it some time ago. He is becoming more insistent each day." At least that was true. "I haven't told anyone yet of my decision, so please don't mention it."

His eyes narrowed, and Isabel knew at once that he didn't believe her.

"We have to move quickly." He sounded harsh, and the frown had returned to his face.

"I assure you I can keep pace with your caravan. I grew up riding horses and am quite skilled." Isabel was eager to prove that she wouldn't be a bother on the journey.

"I'm sure you can ride quite well. There must be a religious group from this area that will be attending the Fall Assembly. In view of your planned vocation, I think they would be more suitable companions for your journey."

The sarcasm in his voice when he spoke of her vocation was not lost on Isabel. "I haven't joined a religious order yet, and I may decide against it." She realized how illogical that sounded, even as she said the words. The man was infuriating and forced her to say the most unreasonable things. She couldn't believe she had ever suspected he was her champion.

They were glaring at each other, unaware of the attention they had attracted. Lady Winifred spoke up. "Isabel, why don't you take Lord Chetwynd for a stroll through the garden?" It was more an order than a suggestion. "You can speak more freely there," she whispered into Isabel's ear.

Without a glance at Lord Chetwynd, Isabel stood up. Unmindful now of the crowded hall, she stalked across the room to a passage leading to a doorway. She wondered if he would follow, but told herself she didn't care either way. In the sudden quiet of the garden, she could hear he was close behind. She hurried along the path. The hallway had been dim, but the garden was lit by moonlight.

Chetwynd grabbed her arm to still her flight and roughly turned her to face him. Isabel stumbled against him, shocked at his hold on her bare arm and the proximity of his hard body. She felt angry instead of frightened. Before she could pull away, he backed up and dropped her arm as though it had burned his hand.

"Your bold request took me by surprise," he said. Frowning, he appeared sorry he had handled her roughly, but he didn't apologize. "Your father is the one to make such a decision. Why would you ask a stranger to escort you on a long journey?"

"Since you know Justin and my father, you are not a stranger to my family." She felt defeated and close to tears, but managed to ask in a trembling voice, "Why won't you escort me?"

They were still standing close, and he reached out to trail his finger along the thin scar on the left side of her forehead.

He quickly withdrew his hand, but not before Isabel gasped at his gentle touch. It was the touch she remembered.

"It *was* you who rescued me, wasn't it?" she whispered, wondering if he would admit it.

Before answering Isabel's question, Chetwynd paused, remembering how he had watched as the healer sewed the gash together; then he nodded. He had barely been able to feel the slight mound of the scar. Turning away from her, he sat upon a nearby bench.

Leaving a space between them, Isabel joined him. They had gone only a few steps into the garden, where there was enough light to see each other. But Chetwynd didn't need to look at her to remember how she had filled out the gown she wore to the dining room. The low cut and soft folds emphasized her full, grownup figure. She wore a head covering, but it couldn't contain her thick dark curls, and a few hung around her face.

Isabel finally broke the silence between them. "I've wanted to thank you for a long time. I hope someone thanked you that day eight years ago when you rescued me."

Chetwynd nodded his head again, still a little shocked at his need to touch the small line on her forehead. "Why don't you cover the slight scar?" he asked. "It would be easy to do."

"The scar has been of use a few times," she answered with a sly smile. "It has discouraged suitors who believed I had been ruined. Old men like to believe the worst."

He shook his head at her words. "When they noticed the scar, you must have given some details of what happened in the meadow that day for them to think that."

When Isabel shrugged, Chetwynd changed the subject. "The road to Aachen is long and dangerous, my lady. It's a hard journey for seasoned travelers. I understand you have never been away from Narbonne. I believe you should wait for a group that will take a more leisurely journey." He hoped logic would work better than the anger of their argument in the dining hall.

"You are exaggerating the danger because you don't want the inconvenience of taking me with you. There are several women in your group. I'm sure I can travel as well as they do."

"You have no idea what you're talking about. Why did you lie about taking religious orders?" he demanded, giving up his attempt at logic.

"The only reason I said that was because I was afraid you would believe I was pursuing you. It was clear that my grandmother was pushing us together. She is always hoping to find me a husband. I want to go for my own reasons, and they have nothing to do with finding a husband."

Chetwynd sighed. How had he managed to get himself so tangled up? He knew Justin wished to have her join him in Aachen, and now he was arguing against taking her. But Isabel was an intriguing, beautiful woman, and for this reason he was reluctant to have her on the journey. His experience taught him to be cautious of seemingly innocent maids. He recalled that Theresa had been twelve and of noble birth when she arrived at his father's manor to be tutored with his sister. She and Chetwynd had become involved in some lessons of their own in the woods behind the manor house. In love for the first time, he had believed they were destined for one another. When he went off to be educated, she had vowed her love and promised to wait for him.

Chetwynd was a third son, without prospects of an inheritance. Idealistic as he was, he assumed this would not matter to Theresa. He had been proven wrong. He was unaware that his father also had his eye on the young woman. While Chetwynd was away, his mother died giving birth to her seventh child. Theresa had been quick to accept his father's proposal of marriage. When she later told Chetwynd her marriage to his father need not end their love affair, Chetwynd fled his father's estate to seek his fortune as a soldier.

Isabel was the innocent he had rescued, but he remembered her movements in the water when she thought no one was watching. Her relaxed sensuality as she moved her hands over her breasts was a great contrast to the frightened woman who entered the great hall. Although the lady was wary of soldiers, that didn't mean she feared all men. He knew it made no sense, but the fact that Isabel was no longer the innocent he remembered disappointed him greatly.

Lost in their own thoughts, neither one of them had noticed Lady Winifred's approach. When she spoke up, they were both startled and quickly stood up to face her.

"I followed you because I heard Isabel ask you to take her to her brother," she explained. "It was bold of her to ask, and you were correct to refuse. But I think it's a good idea, Lord Chetwynd. Circumstances have kept her at Narbonne Manor. But it's time for her to leave home and build a life elsewhere."

Chetwynd frowned, surprised at her words. He remembered that his own grandmother was the only person who didn't want him to leave his home. "It would be a dangerous journey for a lady," he replied. Then he thought of a new argument that might work with Lady Winifred. "As she is unmarried, Lady Isabel's reputation would be at risk. I'm sure Lord Theodoric would understand the problem and not approve the plan."

Isabel had either given up her suit or was just opposed to any suggestion her grandmother might make. "Lord Chetwynd is right, Gran-mere. Father will never approve of my leaving Narbonne unless it's to join a nunnery."

"Yes, I understand the problem," Lady Winifred replied. "Your father would, of course, object to your traveling with a troop of soldiers. But I have a proposal that is sure to over-come your father's objections. Lord Theodoric wants to see you settled and safe, which is why he urges a religious voca-tion. He would believe his objective accomplished if you were to marry Lord Chetwynd."

Quiet followed her words. Her grandmother's frank proposal had silenced the blushing Isabel. Just as discon-certed, Chetwynd realized his own words had trapped him. He wondered at Lady Winifred's bold suggestion. Marriage arrangements were usually worked out between the men of the family, although he wasn't naive enough to think that women played no role.

When there was no response, Lady Winifred explained, "Isabel does not have many options. Several opportunities to wed have already been missed. She is past the age to make an advantageous marriage . . ."

Isabel quickly interrupted her. "Lady Winifred, Lord Chetwynd is not interested in my marriage prospects."

Ignoring her outburst, Lady Winifred continued, "Now, what about you, Lord Chetwynd? You are a man of good for-tune, at an age when it is desirable to start a family. I imagine there has been pressure on you to wed."

Chetwynd hesitated, wondering if he should say he had taken a vow of chastity, but that reminded him of Isabel's lie about taking religious orders. He was beginning to have sympathy for Isabel and could understand Justin's desire to get her away from Narbonne. "Yes, it has been suggested more than once that I should wed," he admitted.

"Good, I thought that might be the case," Lady Winifred declared, confident she had made an important point in her argument.

Although Lady Winifred was a slight woman, her shoul-ders rounded by age, she had a strong voice that she used to emphasize her point. "Isabel's father is unlikely to allow her to leave Narbonne on her own, as you both mentioned. But he can have no objection if Isabel is married. Since I sense that you are both reluctant to wed, I believe I have the answer that will suit you both," she said with a satisfied smile.

Isabel looked doubtful, but she remained silent, as did Chetwynd.

"You can marry and live together as brother and sister. Once you reach Aachen, Isabel can live with Justin and the marriage can be annulled." She rushed on before either one could object. "Consider this. Most marriages are entered into for either financial or political reasons, and usually the partners don't know each other. You are acquainted, and you share a deep regard for Justin. There is at least some common ground.

"As a married woman, Isabel will be free to travel without damage to her reputation. Chetwynd will have the satisfaction of knowing he has helped Lady Isabel to join her brother. Think about it, and make your decision," she said. "But you don't have much time. If you decide to do it, let me know tonight and I'll make arrangements with Father Ivo. Now, discuss it and see if you can reach agreement." With an encouraging smile at each in turn, Lady Winifred took her leave.

When Chetwynd glanced at Isabel, she was staring after her grandmother. As if in a trance, she lowered herself onto the garden bench, and after a minute he sat beside her.

"I'm sorry, Lord Chetwynd. My grandmother is determined to find me a husband, and her tenacity knows no bounds. You have to understand that she has her own reason for encouraging me in my desire to leave Narbonne. She enjoys managing my father's estate and playing the role of hostess in the great hall. Her desire to see me wed is not completely selfless," Isabel said, not bothering to hide her bitterness.

Chetwynd nodded his understanding. Justin had been right: It would be best for Isabel to leave Narbonne. He wondered if a marriage would work for him as well. Returning to court with a wife could deflect gossip about his involvement with Queen Judith.

It was a complicated scheme, as he had made enemies at court when he tried to help the queen. Justin hoped Isabel could join him at Aachen, but he would not be pleased to find she had wed a friend whose reputation was tarnished. Chetwynd wondered if Lord Theodoric could be persuaded to allow Isabel to travel without being married, but immediately rejected the idea. At least if Isabel was his wife he would be able to exert some control over her. He didn't need an unwed, headstrong, and extremely beautiful woman traveling with his troop.

"Perhaps Lady Winifred's suggestion has some merit," he finally said.

Shock visible in her expression, Isabel stared at him as though trying to figure out why he would suddenly change his mind. It didn't take her long to come up with an idea. "Would you have something to gain from such an alliance?" she asked.

Chetwynd paused to plan his reply. "There is a reason why it would be to my advantage to arrive at court with a wife." The next part was tricky, but he felt it was important to make it clear that he had no interest in a real marriage. "There is someone with whom I have an attachment, but it can go nowhere."

"Is she married, then?" Isabel asked, making no effort to disguise her distaste at the thought.

"I don't wish to talk about it," he snapped, more sharply then he meant to, then quickly added, "I'm sorry. We have to be open with each other. Do you really need details?"

"No, of course not. It's none of my concern."

"Good, because I don't want to give any. All you need know is that the attachment is over, but the gossip lingers. If you and I do marry, we would, as Lady Winifred suggests, live as brother and sister. We can stay in the marriage as long as it is convenient for both of us to do so."

"That is what I wish, also," she assured him. "But I can see we might have a problem if one of us wants to annul the marriage before the other is ready." Her tone had become cool and practical. "Father Ivo has told me about such matters. I'm sure it will be easy to obtain an annulment if we both approach a priest at the same time."

"You make a good point. I'll agree not to ask for the annulment until you are reunited with Justin and have decided what you wish to do. I'd like you to agree to act as my wife for at least four months after we arrive at Aachen." He figured that would give him enough time for rumors to die away.

"I know you said you don't wish to discuss it, but how will the lady with whom you were involved feel about your returning to court with a wife?"

"That's none of your concern," he retorted. "There was no hope for a marriage between the lady and myself."

"So she is married," Isabel blurted out.

Chetwynd interrupted her before she could continue. "One more thing, Lady Isabel. While acting as my wife, you must obey me in every matter. There must be no suspicion that ours is anything other than a real marriage."

Isabel raised her eyebrows, pausing only a moment before replying, "Of course, Lord Chetwynd. But remember, we both have something to gain by marrying. You are not doing me any greater service than the one I'm doing for you."

Chetwynd knew what she said was true. "It's settled then," he agreed.

CHAPTER FOUR

Since neither Isabel nor Chetwynd wished to linger in the garden after the terms of marriage had been discussed and agreed upon, they sought out Lady Winifred in her quarters. She was expecting them, and invited them to sit while she poured them wine.

Lady Winifred's room was richly furnished with colorful tapestries and cushioned benches that showed to best advantage in candlelight. But the comfortable room did nothing to ease the tension evident in its visitors. Lady Winifred flashed them a satisfied smile as she handed them each a goblet of wine.

Chetwynd drank deeply as though he needed fortifying, and Isabel was tempted to follow suit. Instead, she stared at her wine and took a sip, reminding herself that no one was forcing Chetwynd to take her to Aachen.

"Since you are both here, I assume you have decided to go ahead with the plan I suggested," Lady Winifred said.

Isabel just nodded, but Chetwynd spoke up. "Yes, Lady Winifred, the arrangement you suggested suits us."

"Excellent. I thought it might."

Isabel cringed at Lady Winifred's smug reply. She noted that Chetwynd used the word *arrangement*, not *marriage*.

Paying no attention to Lady Winifred's self-congratulatory tone, Chetwynd continued. "I seek your advice on whether I should approach Lord Theodoric tonight, or wait until morning. My troop is scheduled to stay but two days at Narbonne. There is not much time to arrange matters."

Lady Winifred smiled, clearly pleased that Chetwynd had the good sense to ask her advice. "I think it's best you wait until morning to speak to Lord Theodoric. You can approach him directly after Mass. I feel confident he will approve the match, and once that is done, there will be ample time to arrange matters. My son will want to settle upon Isabel's dowry first thing. Then arrangements for the exchange of wedding vows can be made quickly."

Startled at the mention of a dowry, Chetwynd looked from one woman to the other. "I hadn't thought about a dowry. Considering the type of arrangement we have agreed to, there is no need for one. I received a benefice from King Louis, and it provides me with a generous living. A comfortable estate located near Aachen, it earns enough to support my army and meet all my personal needs. Lady Isabel is welcome to stay there as long as she wishes. There is no need for a dowry, Lady Winifred."

Chetwynd's words surprised Isabel, and she realized she knew little of the brooding man she was about to marry. The fact that he was reluctant to accept a dowry for a sham marriage showed that he had integrity. A promising discovery, she thought.

But Lady Winifred seemed unimpressed. "I'm afraid you don't understand the situation, Lord Chetwynd. My son is a proud man. He might be suspicious if you did not accept a dowry. This is to be a marriage between two noble families, and a dowry is expected. My son would not approve a marriage that did not reflect well upon our family. There is no need to confide the nature of the marriage until it is certain you wish to have it annulled," she advised.

Chetwynd's silence must have made Lady Winifred suspect he was having second thoughts, because she quickly added, "You can return the dowry to Justin if that will make you feel more comfortable."

Isabel knew how Lady Winifred hoped this affair would turn out, and it was not with an annulment. Perhaps Chetwynd was also aware of her grandmother's expectations. Before Isabel could think of a way to give Chetwynd a chance to withdraw gracefully if he wished, her grandmother spoke again.

"I have seen many marriages that began with a lot less chance of success than this one. Most of them lasted a lifetime. It may work to both your advantage to stay together, and I will not deny I'm hoping for that outcome. In any case, you will find out in the coming months whether matrimony suits you. It will be entirely up to you when and if the marriage is annulled. No one can force you to remain wed."

Both Isabel and Lady Winifred watched for a sign from Chetwynd. When he nodded, Lady Winifred continued, "After you receive Lord Theodoric's approval, I will speak to the parish priest. Father Ivo can perform the marriage ceremony tomorrow evening, and you can be off on your journey the next day."

It seemed everything was settled. Lady Winifred stood up to indicate the meeting was concluded. "I'm sure you are eager to be off to your bed, Lord Chetwynd. You must be tired after your long journey. I wish some private words with my granddaughter."

Without another word, a solemn Lord Chetwynd moved from one to the other in a formal manner, taking each of their hands in turn and bowing his head. When the door closed behind him, Isabel gave a long sigh and sank back onto her seat.

"What have I agreed to?" she said with a moan.

Lady Winifred's eyes narrowed and her voice was hard. "You've already sabotaged too many chances to wed, Isabel. Do not dare throw this one away after all I've done to promote it. If this marriage doesn't come off, I swear I'll support your father and you'll be off to a nunnery before you can blink an eye."

Stiffening her spine, Isabel met her grandmother's stubborn expression with one of her own. "I understand what you're saying, Gran-mere. But don't forget, as far as Lord Chetwynd is concerned, this is a short-term arrangement."

"Don't be a goose, Isabel. You're an attractive woman, and attractive women have no trouble tempting men into bed. You can persuade Lord Chetwynd to forget his reservations about the match. It shouldn't be a hardship for you, as he is an attractive man. Once you become heavy with his child, he will want to stay married for the sake of an heir."

Isabel stood up to give her words more authority. "I have no intention of trapping Lord Chetwynd. We will be living together as brother and sister. I won't be bearing his child."

"You are naive, my dear," Lady Winifred replied, shaking her head. "You will change your mind once you discover the advantages of having a husband who has the ear of the king. You will be welcomed at court, plus you will have a manor of your own to manage as you please."

As far as her grandmother was concerned, there was no higher goal in life for a woman than overseeing her own manor. Her fear that Isabel might replace her in that role at Narbonne was no doubt the main reason she wanted her granddaughter settled elsewhere, whether it be with Lord Chetwynd or in a monastery.

Isabel refused to leave without a final word on the subject. "I will not trap him," she repeated, and made a hasty retreat before her grandmother could reply.

Once in her bedchamber, doubts stole any satisfaction Isabel might have achieved by having the last word. She tossed and turned in her narrow bed, repeating the last sentence to her grandmother over and over in her mind. Long into the night, she kept replaying her conversations with both Chetwynd and her grandmother, examining each carefully. She tested the motives of all parties, including herself, and questioned what she had done.

For eight years, she had dreamed of being rescued by the golden-haired warrior. But she was a grown woman now, and Emma was right, it was well past the time when she should have put that dream away. Lord Chetwynd was not the champion she imagined, and he was definitely not here to rescue her. She would have to do that herself.

It was almost dawn before Isabel finally fell into a restless sleep. When her handmaid, Marianna, shook her shoulder a short time later, Isabel awoke with renewed determination. She had been given a chance to leave Narbonne, and she would make the most of it.

Isabel and her grandmother walked to the chapel in silence, as though neither wished to return to the disagreement that lay between them. Chetwynd planned to speak to Lord Theodoric after the service. Isabel wondered if nightmares of Lady Winifred's scheming might not have caused him to flee the manor.

When Isabel spotted him entering the chapel, she couldn't help feeling relieved. This morning his stony expression made her smile a little, as she saw it as a sign of resolve to go through with their plan.

Wishing to hear the news of his interview with her father in a secluded spot away from curious stares, Isabel turned to her grandmother and said, "Tell Lord Chetwynd to come to me at the pond after he has spoken to Father."

"What pond? What are you talking about, Isabel?" her grandmother asked impatiently.

"Don't worry, he'll know what I mean," she assured Lady Winifred, and hurried on ahead of her into the chapel.

The soldiers filled the benches of the small chapel where Father Ivo performed the morning service. He had been both the parish priest and Isabel's tutor for as long as she could remember. As she knelt with bowed head, she thought of his painstaking method of teaching her to read. He pointed out the Latin words in his large, engraved Bible, showing her the verses she heard repeatedly in the chapel.

Her eagerness to learn surprised and delighted the old priest. As a reward for her hard work studying the Bible, he introduced her to the tales of Ovid. The poet had written about the triumphs, tragedies, and tomfoolery of the Greek gods and goddesses. It was with Ovid's stories that Isabel used to entertain Emma.

Father Ivo had suggested she join a religious community, but to be a teacher, not a nun. Perhaps it was her romantic fantasy of being rescued that had made her hesitate, as she would have enjoyed sharing her knowledge. She felt closer to Father Ivo than to her father or grandmother, and wondered what he would think of Lord Chetwynd and their plan to marry.

At the end of Mass, Isabel and her family preceded the other worshipers out of the chapel. She caught sight of Emma seated in the back row. After exchanging a tentative nod with Lord Chetwynd, who walked beside her father, Isabel waited for Emma. Isabel linked arms with her friend and pulled her away from the crowd.

"Let's walk to the pond, Emma. I need to talk to you."

Emma, looking older with her plaits hidden under a head covering, cradled her baby in her arms. Isabel could tell it was all Emma could do to keep silent, but she waited until they had advanced along the path before she spoke.

"I saw the fair-haired soldier walking with your father. Is he the one you saw at the pond?"

"Yes. Did he look familiar to you?"

"No, should he?"

"You mean he doesn't look like an angel?"

Emma stopped in her tracks and twirled around, but Lord Chetwynd was out of sight. "Are you saying it's him?"

"Shush. Not so loud, Emma. Your voice could wake the dead." But Isabel giggled at the startled expression on her friend's face.

"Oh Isabel, he's a well-built man, but I doubt I would have recognized him as your angel. The hair is similar, I suppose, but this man has a hard, proud face. He moved with an arrogant grace that I don't remember, and he fills out his clothes. Your angel was slight of build. This man looks more like the devil than an angel."

"My, you did take notice of him."

"It was hard not to. I'm sure you noticed the same things," Emma replied with a sly smile.

Isabel grinned, amazed at how lighthearted talking with her friend made her feel. "It might interest you to learn, Emma, that the man you just described in such detail is about to ask my father for permission to marry me."

Emma's mouth dropped open, and Isabel had to drag her along to keep her moving. "I seldom see you speechless, Emma. Let's hurry to the pond where we can talk in private."

Neither one said another word as they hurried along the narrow path through the woods. Their fast pace woke the baby, who had slept soundly through Mass. As they sat at the water's edge to cool their feet in the pond, Emma wrestled her clothing open to nurse her crying babe.

Once the babe was suckling contentedly, Emma turned her full attention to Isabel. "Now tell me everything. Leave nothing out," she demanded.

Isabel started at the beginning, describing how she had returned to the pond and found the footprint. She couldn't help gloating. "You see, Emma, I wasn't imagining his presence."

Then she explained how surprised she had been to find him at the high table in the great hall. As she told Emma how she had impulsively asked him to escort her to Aachen, she wondered again at her boldness.

Finally, Isabel related how Lady Winifred had taken over, first suggesting they walk in the garden, then joining them. Her grandmother had suggested a marriage of convenience, and after much discussion Lord Chetwynd had agreed.

Emma's eyes sparkled as she absorbed every word of Isabel's story. Her friend had always enjoyed a good tale. When Isabel was through, Emma pointed out what she considered the problem with the plan.

"And you plan to live as sister and brother with that tempting man?"

"Yes, that's one of the terms of the marriage."

Emma raised her eyebrows in her most skeptical manner. "I doubt it will work out that way, Isabel. You are both mature and well-made, and you are going to be traveling as man and wife. Besides, why would you want to deprive yourself?"

Isabel laughed, realizing she should have predicted her friend's response. "Emma, Lord Chetwynd is not Derek. Your husband can't keep his hands off you, but Lord Chetwynd does not feel the same about me."

Remembering the details of her conversation with Chetwynd, Isabel's amusement disappeared. "There is one thing I forgot to tell you, Emma. Lord Chetwynd is in love with someone else. A woman he is not free to marry. Living together as brother and sister is what he wants. I have no intention of tempting him into my bed, as my grandmother has suggested I do."

"Oh Isabel, what a muddle," Emma remarked. "I don't see how you can not . . . well, you know . . . be tempted just a little. I suspect your grandmother knows exactly what she is doing, putting the two of you together in this way."

"Yes, you're right. She admitted she hopes things will work out between us. But Lord Chetwynd is marrying me because he can't marry the woman he loves. He spoke of it in the past tense, but who knows. No doubt he hopes to use our marriage to disguise their meetings."

"Good lord, Isabel, your story is not supposed to end like this. He is your champion."

"No, Emma, my champion was a fantasy, just as you have told me all these years. Lord Chetwynd is nothing like the gentle soldier I imagined. Most of the time he seems full of anger. When I first asked him to take me to Aachen, he refused and acted offended that I'd asked. There is nothing warm or gentle about him. Even you noticed how stony he appears."

Emma frowned and moved her babe to the other breast. "Lord Chetwynd may have good reason for his anger. Life is not kind to everyone, Isabel, as you know. I'm betting you'll be able to warm him up."

"You sound like my grandmother, Emma. And don't shake your head like that. I know how you think."

"I'm not saying you should trap him. But I think there's a strong possibility that things may work out between you. I agree with Lady Winifred."

"I never thought I'd hear you say that."

"Nor I. Imagine agreeing with your grandmother." Emma

wrinkled up her nose at the idea. "But even if the marriage is annulled, at least you will have joined Justin and escaped from Lady Winifred."

"Yes, that's a definite advantage. She threatened to send me to a nunnery if I sabotaged yet another match."

"The witch!"

Isabel giggled. "Lady Winifred doesn't know the whole story. Not that I think Lord Chetwynd being in love with someone else would change my grandmother's mind. She will have me wed."

The baby had stopped nursing, and Isabel lifted the child away from Emma. Together they sang a lullaby Emma's mother had taught them, and the babe slept cradled in Isabel's arms.

"I'm going to miss you, Emma. Perhaps I'm a bit mad to wish to leave a place where I have such a good friend."

"No, Isabel, you're not mad. I'll miss you, and I'll miss the stories you tell me. There will be a hole in my life. But if you don't go to Aachen, you'll be sent to a nunnery. Either way you'd leave Narbonne."

Emma leaned back on her elbows and stared at the sky. There was a dreamy expression on her face as she made a prediction. "I believe you're destined for a great adventure, Isabel. I hope you will come back and tell me about it one day. What a tale you'll have to tell then."

Feeling a tug of sadness, Isabel looked down at the babe to hide the tears that sprang to her eyes. "You have been blessed, Emma. If I find something half as wonderful as this sweet babe, and your appealing husband, I will be lucky."

"I know you will have good fortune, Isabel. I'll be there when you exchange your vows, but I'd best leave now before Lord Chetwynd arrives." Emma leaned over to kiss Isabel's cheek and held her in a long hug until the babe who was crushed between them began to complain.

After Emma's departure, Isabel moved to lie in the shade of a tree. She wondered how much longer it would be before Lord Chetwynd appeared. Now that she had talked to Emma, she was eager to have things settled.

The warm morning sun made Isabel sleepy. Since she'd had little rest during the night, it was hard to keep her eyes open.

Lord Chetwynd didn't see Lady Isabel when he entered the secluded glade. It occurred to him that she might have changed her mind about the proposed match. As he remembered his first sight of her swimming in the pond, he didn't know whether he felt relieved or disappointed. One thing he knew for sure: Her grandmother would not be pleased if Isabel had changed her mind.

Turning to leave, he spotted Isabel asleep under the tree. Although he and his men were used to sleeping on the ground, he was surprised that Lady Isabel would find it comfortable. But then, the woman had been surprising him ever since he'd met her.

Rather than wake Isabel, he sat beside her and stared ahead at the mirror-like surface of the water. The still pond had a calming effect, and his shoulders began to relax, releasing the tension that had built during his talk with Lord Theodoric.

Their interview had gone more smoothly than he had expected. Although a little taken aback at the suddenness of the proposal, Isabel's father seemed pleased to discover his daughter had a suitor, and he offered a generous dowry. Chetwynd was able to accept the amount by telling himself he would turn it over to Justin as soon as they reached Aachen.

Isabel's father had jumped to the conclusion that Chetwynd and Justin had discussed the possibility of such a match, and Chetwynd did not contradict him. Although Justin had talked of wanting Isabel near him, he was likely to be extremely displeased with the marriage. Chetwynd didn't have his friend's skill in dealing with people, but he told himself he had done the best he could, trying to ignore his own selfish reasons for the match.

His initial guilt at deceiving Isabel's father disappeared when Lord Theodoric began praising him for his willingness to wed Lady Isabel. Chetwynd wasn't sure whether Lord Theodoric believed Isabel's reputation had been compromised because of the number of suitors she had discouraged, or whether he had some idea of her involvement with a local lover. Whichever the case, Chetwynd thought Theodoric displayed a definite lack of loyalty to his daughter.

After meeting Lady Winifred and Lord Theodoric, Chetwynd could understand Isabel's desire to leave Narbonne. He turned to where she was still sleeping. She lay on her side with one arm tucked under her head, appearing both innocent and sensual. Chetwynd grinned, imagining her as a mythical water nymph that had floated ashore and was resting after a long swim.

Isabel's bare feet poked out from the hem of her gown, and he saw they were a good size. As were her hips, he noticed as his eyes traveled up her body. Her long tresses spread out on the ground around her, and there were leaves and twigs caught in her dark curls. Although his fingers itched to untangle a few, he didn't wish to wake her. Instead he slowly lay down facing her, making sure there was a good distance between them. He became aware of her breasts rising and falling with her breathing.

As he admired her natural beauty, he wondered if there was a chance this match could work as they had planned. It was clear there would be temptations, and he knew he would have to be careful. His plans, as well as her own, depended upon them remaining free of emotional entanglements, and his history in such matters was not promising.

~~⹅~~

WHEN ISABEL OPENED HER EYES SLIGHTLY, SQUINTING AT the light, she saw her future husband stretched out beside her. At first she thought he was asleep, but she quickly realized his eyes were focused on her breasts. Heat filled her body as she wondered what to do.

Suspecting that Lord Chetwynd would not want her to catch him staring at her breasts, Isabel closed her eyes and moved a little, as though she were just waking up. Even with her eyes closed, she could tell Chetwynd was quick to sit up. The light changed, and she was in his shadow. When she opened her eyes again, he was staring ahead at the water.

Isabel struggled to sit up. Feeling stiff from lying on the ground, she stretched her limbs to ease them. As casually as she could manage, she acknowledged Chetwynd's presence. "Have you been here long, my lord?"

"No. I just arrived," he said. "You must have been very tired to sleep on the hard ground. Perhaps you did not sleep well last night?"

Isabel laughed softly at his suggestion and was rewarded when a slight smile appeared on Chetwynd's usually solemn face. It was pleasant to experience a simple exchange of understanding without the need for words.

"Did all go well in your meeting with my father?"

"Yes. Lord Theodoric thought the match must have been arranged, or at least suggested, by Justin. You should know I let him believe his assumption was true. It was easier than thinking up another reason for the sudden decision. He wants to talk to you, but he seemed well satisfied with the match."

"Yes, I can imagine he would be."

Her terse reply indicated that she knew her father's feelings on the matter. Chetwynd couldn't help but wonder what had happened to her previous suitors, especially as her many charms were obvious.

"Why is it you never married, Lady Isabel?" he asked. "From what I understand, you had opportunities."

It was because none of her suitors had lived up to her memories of her champion. Her childish fantasies about being rescued were embarrassing, and she had no intention of telling him about them.

Remembering his reply when she inquired about his attachment, Isabel answered stiffly, "I don't think that's any of your concern."

Recognizing his own words, Chetwynd accepted her abrupt reply. He thought of his earlier speculation that Lady Isabel had been awaiting a lover at the pond when he happened upon her. The memory dislodged the companionable feeling that had been developing between them.

"Are you sure there is not a reason why you would wish to remain in Narbonne?" he asked coldly while staring at the pond.

Puzzled by his question and irritated at his tone of voice, Isabel replied, "No, of course not. I already explained why I wish to leave."

Chetwynd stood up. When he spoke, his words were casual and cool. "Fair enough. Our arrangement does not include sharing confidences. Please forget I asked the question."

When Isabel scrambled to her feet, Chetwynd grasped her arm to help. But he withdrew his hand quickly once she was standing.

"Your father and I discussed a time for the marriage. If I were here alone, I could stay longer, but my men are eager to be home. In order to leave tomorrow, the marriage will have to take place either tonight, as your grandmother suggested, or before worship in the morning. Is such short notice agreeable with you?"

"That will be fine. My maid, Marianna, has no family. We can prepare to leave quickly."

"Good. I'm pleased you will have someone to attend you. I think it might be best if we exchange vows tomorrow morning, and then leave directly. If we marry this evening, there will be the expectation that we . . . Well, you know." He was reluctant to mention sharing a bed.

Isabel knew exactly what he meant and answered quickly. "Of course. I'll inform my grandmother of your wish."

The silence between them became awkward as it lengthened. Finally, Chetwynd spoke again. "Since I didn't have a swim yesterday, I'd like one now. Why don't you meet with your father while I do so?"

Isabel nodded and backed away from him. "I think you'll enjoy the pond, Lord Chetwynd." Not knowing what else to say, she turned and hurried away.

It was a few minutes before Isabel remembered she had left her slippers behind. She turned back to the pond and arrived as Chetwynd, his bare back turned toward her, was pulling off his hose. Forgetting her slippers again and hoping he hadn't heard her, she fled, but not before the shape of his muscular body was etched upon her mind. He seemed a great deal larger without his black clothing.

Trying to ignore the vision, Isabel ran along the path and concentrated on the things she had to do. She must meet with both her father and grandmother. When Isabel blinked her eyes, Lord Chetwynd's well-formed body appeared on her closed eyelids, causing her face to flush. Deciding she wasn't ready to deal with her family, Isabel sought out Father Ivo.

The parish priest was in the small room at the back of the chapel where Isabel had received lessons. He looked up from his book, took a minute to focus on the present, and then struggled to his feet.

"My, you looked flushed, my lady."

"I've been running," Isabel managed to say between gasps of breath. Tucking her bare feet out of sight under her gown, she brushed her hair from her face and remembered that she had also forgotten her head covering at the pond.

"I was awaiting you. Lady Winifred has told me the news, and I was sure you would come. I understand Lord Chetwynd is a friend of Justin's, and both your grandmother and father seem satisfied it's a good match."

Isabel nodded, still out of breath.

"But what of you, Isabel? Is it a match which pleases you?" As he spoke, he waved his hand to indicate she should take her accustomed seat on the bench at his worktable.

His question surprised her, and Isabel was touched that he would care enough to ask how she felt. "Yes, Father, it pleases me," she replied.

Although her family life had often been a trial, the hours she had spent with Father Ivo helped fill the void left after Justin's departure. Looking around at the familiar room, Isabel knew she would miss her time spent with the elderly priest.

"I will miss you, my child," Father Ivo said, echoing her thoughts. "In all my years of teaching, I have never had a student who asked such challenging questions. You have brought warmth into the life of an old man."

For the second time that day, tears came to Isabel's eyes.

She felt her control slipping, and she covered her mouth to keep from sobbing.

"No, no, my lady. I didn't mean to upset you. It's time for you to venture forth, and I envy you the opportunity."

Father Ivo patted her shoulder awkwardly, but Isabel couldn't speak.

"You must have a chance to see the empire, Lady Isabel, before the sons of King Louis let it slip away." Father Ivo was a great admirer of King Charles, but had little respect for his grandsons who were destined to rule.

When Isabel still didn't say anything, Father Ivo began one of his familiar tales. "I was there at the beginning, when King Charles was crowned Holy Roman Emperor by Pope Leo III. At first the king seemed reluctant to take the crown, but then he accepted it, as well as the task of safeguarding the empire. He grew into that crown. He was famous for inviting poets and historians to his court, and encouraging his people to learn to read and write. They named him Charles the Great, Charlemagne. What a glorious time that was."

Isabel had heard this story many times, and she would have enjoyed hearing it once more. But Father Ivo abruptly interrupted himself.

"You have listened patiently to my stories, Lady Isabel. Now it's your time. You're to be wed, and I am forgetting my duty. I must prepare you for your role as wife to Lord Chetwynd."

The kindly priest looked thoughtful, as though trying to remember what it was he was supposed to say. Isabel understood Father Ivo's strength lay in his knowledge of literature and history, as well as his heartfelt manner in conducting Mass. According to Emma, his domestic advice was less adept.

"There is no need, Father. I have talked to Emma and am quite prepared."

Not that she needed information, she reminded herself, as she had no plans to be intimate with her husband. The last sight she had of Chetwynd leapt to her mind again. Shocked that such a vision would appear to her in Father Ivo's presence, she blinked and forced herself to think of other matters. "I came to say goodbye in private, Father."

"Well, if you think of any questions about personal matters, please come to see me." Clearly relieved, Father Ivo continued, "You have been the best kind of student, Lady Isabel. One I learned from while I taught. I put aside this small sheaf of poems for you to take with you." He handed her a packet tied together with a string.

"Thank you, Father Ivo." To keep from crying, Isabel hugged the small priest, inhaling for the last time the dusty smell of old parchments that clung to his robe. He was as hard to say goodbye to as Emma had been.

"I will miss our lessons. There will be a hole in my life," he whispered, and Isabel heard his voice crack.

Remembering Emma using those same words, Isabel pulled away. "Father Ivo, there is someone who would love to listen to your stories, as well as learn to read. It's Emma. She never tires of hearing tales and would like to read them. Would you give her lessons?"

His bushy eyebrows lifted. "She is a bright girl. Do you think she'd be interested?"

"Yes, yes, I do. I'll tell her to come see you."

Isabel smiled happily at the thought of the two most important people in her life sharing time together. "Tell her about your adventure with the poet who came to Charlemagne's court from across the waters. I know she'll enjoy it."

"I'll do that. And she can bring her babe. I love children." Father Ivo beamed at her. "You have grown into a kind and thoughtful person, Lady Isabel. Lord Chetwynd is a fortunate man. Go with God, my lady."

His words sobered Isabel. Then the nude Chetwynd stole into her thoughts once again, and she started to laugh. "I'll do my best," she said.

CHAPTER FIVE

*I*SABEL'S MEETING WITH HER FATHER WENT pretty much as she had expected. Lord Theodoric told her she was fortunate to be making such an advantageous marriage and warned her against undermining the match. Isabel kept her annoyance in check by thinking about Father Ivo, who had, in many ways, been her real father.

Her visit with Lady Winifred was even more annoying. Her grandmother was curious about how her relationship with Lord Chetwynd was progressing.

"The minute I laid eyes on Lord Chetwynd, I believed him the husband for you, Isabel," Lady Winifred told her. "He has wealth, a promising career, and is a friend of Justin's. You spent some private time with him. What do you think of your future husband?"

"I think he is an honorable man, my lady."

"Yes, yes, of course," Lady Winifred said impatiently. "But he is also a strong, virile man. Has he shown any interest in you?"

"He seemed pleased that Marianna would be traveling with me," Isabel answered, purposely misunderstanding her grandmother's meaning.

"Don't be so naive, Isabel. Did he touch you in an intimate manner?"

It was difficult for Isabel to refrain from answering sharply. But what was the point, she reminded herself. She wasn't going to change her grandmother. She settled for ignoring the question.

"We talked about marriage arrangements, my lady. We decided to exchange our vows at sunrise. That will give Marianna and me a chance to pack this evening."

This news distracted Lady Winifred from her probing. "But Isabel, I had hoped you would start your married life at Narbonne. If you exchange vows this evening, you can spend your first night together here in your home."

Isabel suddenly had a vision of her grandmother, an encouraging smile on her face, tucking them into bed together. The ludicrous thought cheered her up, but she dared not share her amusement, as she knew her grandmother lacked a sense of humor where the marriage of her granddaughter was concerned.

"Lord Chetwynd prefers to wait until morning," Isabel said. Since men were seldom denied the final say about such matters, Isabel was confident this information would put an end to her grandmother's objection.

Lady Winifred shrugged off her disappointment. "Men . . ." she muttered. Then, after a moment, she changed the subject. "I don't imagine you need any information about the physical aspect of marriage. I'm sure either Father Ivo or Emma has filled you in on the details. Just try not to be cold and stiff. Men hate that."

"Thank you for the helpful advice, Gran-mere." As Isabel expected, the sarcastic tone with which she spoke these words was lost on Lady Winifred.

Her grandmother's attempts at interference gave Isabel reason to be thankful for Chetwynd's plan to exchange vows in the morning. There was no telling how far her grandmother would go to see that they slept together. The sooner they departed Narbonne, the better.

In contrast to her father and grandmother, her time with Marianna had been companionable and pleasant. Isabel had been ten years old when Marianna, two years older, had been assigned by Lady Winifred to be her handmaid. From her first day, she had taken her duties seriously, and her attitude made her seem older than her years. Despite the small age difference, she acted like a mother toward Isabel.

Since she had no family, her personal maid was thrilled at the prospect of traveling with Lady Isabel, and she only complained mildly about the fact they were leaving so soon.

"I'm sure Lady Winifred will help us, if you think the packing is too much for us to do alone," Isabel said to tease Marianna.

As she anticipated, Marianna shook her head vigorously. "We don't need her help. Your mother's gowns and jewelry are already packed, just waiting for you to take an interest in them."

Isabel grinned. "I'm fortunate to have you, Marianna. And I'm fortunate to have inherited a ready-made trousseau. Leave out my plainer gowns for me to wear on the road. Most of my mother's things are much too elegant to wear on horseback."

In addition to clothes, the two women packed bedding, eating utensils, and some herbal remedies Marianna thought they might need. Isabel added writing implements and, of course, the sheaf of poems from Father Ivo. The packing extended late into the night, and when they were finished, Isabel had no trouble falling into a deep sleep.

The marriage ceremony would be a simple affair. Isabel's religion was part of her life, as it was for everyone she knew. Each day started with Mass in the manor chapel. As Isabel had often witnessed the exchange of marriage vows by others, she knew the ceremony was to take place on the porch of the chapel. A worship service would follow so that the couple could begin their marriage with the blessing of God.

At dawn, the residents of the manor, as well as Chetwynd's troop, were waiting inside the chapel. On the porch, the small wedding party stood together while Lord Theodoric gave his consent to the match. Father Ivo prompted Lady Isabel and Lord Chetwynd as they solemnly exchanged their vows. Isabel hadn't expected to be moved by the ceremony, so she was surprised when she had to force her words through a suddenly constricted throat. She fought hard to hold back tears.

Biting the inside of her mouth, Isabel reminded herself that Chetwynd had no doubt already sworn an oath of devotion to someone else. This ceremony was merely a few words that released her from the authority of her father and placed her under the authority of Lord Chetwynd. Looking from the smiling face of her father to the solemn face of Chetwynd, she feared she was exchanging one uncaring master for another.

As Father Ivo led them down the aisle to the front of the church, Chetwynd placed his hand gently on her elbow. The contact eased Isabel's tension. She appreciated the kind gesture from the stranger she was marrying. As she knelt and bowed her head, she prayed their journey together would honor them both.

When they walked back down the aisle to exit the church, the small chapel was filled to capacity. Merchants, tenant farmers, and soldiers were crowded together on the benches and stood at the back. Isabel searched for Emma, and when she saw her, she relaxed and smiled for the first time. Emma returned her smile and wiped away a tear. It was done.

The entire service had not taken much longer than the usual morning worship. A meal was set up in the great hall, and it was eaten quickly. The marriage ceremony was forgotten in the excitement of preparing for the coming journey.

The caravan consisted of thirty-two soldiers, six squires, and a few serving men and women. There were also a few young wives who were allowed to travel with their husbands, as they had no children. Isabel had already become familiar with some of the faces, and she observed how efficiently the group worked together.

The presence of Isabel and Marianna, newcomers to the tightly knit group, gave rise to a certain amount of curiosity and watchful waiting. Clearly the veterans would withhold judgment until they saw how well Isabel and Marianna traveled and whether their presence would slow the progress of the journey. Making good time seemed to be everyone's major concern. After spending the late spring and summer on the Spanish March, the travelers were eager to return to their homes.

Lord Chetwynd had suggested they take a litter for Isabel and Marianna, but Isabel declined his offer. She preferred riding her own horse to bumping around in a litter. She had not been exaggerating when she told Chetwynd that first evening that she was an accomplished rider. Although she enjoyed riding astride as men on the farm did, she also managed well with both legs to the side, a method more appropriate for her position.

Since everyone was eager to depart, the goodbyes were short. Lord Theodoric and Lady Winifred bid the couple a brief, formal farewell. Emma was the only one who lingered at Isabel's side.

"Are you excited, Lady Isabel?"

Taken aback by the formal address, Isabel stared at her

friend. "Emma, I've not changed because I have a husband."

"It's hard not to see you in a different light now that you're married to Lord Chetwynd."

Isabel poked her friend with her elbow and was rewarded with a giggle. "I don't feel any different, Emma," she said, frowning at her friend. "I hope I can live up to the person I'm supposed to be."

"You'll do just fine." Emma glanced over at Lord Chetwynd as he conferred with his second-in-command. "He looks a robust man, Isabel. I predict he will be heating up your bed before many nights have passed."

Isabel's face warmed at her friend's words, and she prayed the others nearby were too busy to notice the exchange. She wondered what Emma would think if she told her friend about seeing Chetwynd removing his clothes at the pond. She couldn't help smiling at what Emma might ask or say about that revelation.

Emma hadn't missed her sly grin. "What?" she asked.

"Nothing. Has Father Ivo approached you? He said he'd give you lessons."

Emma's eyes lit up. "Yes, and he said to bring the babe. I hope it's not too difficult for me to learn."

"When you get tired of trying to follow the words, just ask him a few questions about his days with King Charles. He'll start telling you tales of his days at court."

The friends embraced one more time, and Emma helped Isabel onto her horse. Lord Chetwynd approached them, making it clear he intended to ride beside her. A lump formed in Isabel's throat as she watched Emma move away.

Chetwynd distracted her, explaining the route they would be taking. The caravan was headed eastward to the Rhone River, and from there they would follow the river north.

"The road is in good condition," he said. "It's an ancient

trade route first used by the Greeks and Romans, and later restored by Charlemagne. If the weather is good, and there are no unforeseen accidents, we should reach Aachen in two weeks. We'll spend the first night at a Benedictine abbey near Arles."

Chetwynd noticed that Isabel seemed reluctant to leave her friend, and he wondered if she would be a good traveler. He hoped giving her information would ease her mind. "We'll stop at other monasteries and manors along the way. Hopefully, we won't have to camp under the stars too often."

"Camping out will be an adventure," she replied, hoping to assure him that she would not be a problem.

Lord Chetwynd's eyebrows rose as though he doubted she would find it pleasant; then he left her side to ride at the head of the caravan. He quickly moved out of sight, but Jerome, his cheerful squire, stayed in view and flashed Isabel a smile from time to time. She suspected he had been instructed to keep an eye on her. When she finally smiled back at him, he became bolder and moved to ride beside her as Chetwynd had done earlier.

"You sit a horse well, my lady," he said, speaking with a boldness that was surely not appropriate for a squire.

Eager to fit into the group, Isabel couldn't help but feel pleased at his praise. "Thank you. Your name is Jerome, is it not?"

The young squire eyes widened at her words. "Yes, my lady. How would you know that?"

"Lord Chetwynd told me your name at supper the first night you were at Narbonne."

"There's none the equal of Lord Chetwynd. I'm fortunate to serve him. He uses my given name."

Isabel wasn't sure how other squires were addressed, but Jerome clearly felt honored by Lord Chetwynd's favor.

They hadn't traveled far before Isabel was beyond familiar territory. The caravan moved quickly, and she didn't have much time to enjoy the scenery. Although she was a skilled rider, she was not used to spending long hours in the saddle.

As Isabel began to feel the effects of bouncing about on her horse, she worried about Marianna. She glanced back to see how her maid was managing, and saw that she was conversing merrily with the other serving women. Marianna had clearly made friends quickly, and Isabel was envious. Her position as Lord Chetwynd's wife placed her above the rest, and she knew it would take her longer to be accepted. They had no way of knowing that her best friend and companion for the past ten years had been the wife of a tenant farmer.

But Isabel did not ride alone. Jerome continued to stay close and acted as a self-appointed guide. The lad chattered away about the sights they would see on the journey and the abbey where they would spend the night. Isabel had become accustomed to his constant prattle, and she suddenly realized it had stopped abruptly. Chetwynd's second-in-command, an older soldier she had been introduced to earlier, was approaching them.

Ingram's face was deeply wrinkled, and he scowled at Jerome. The young lad was quick to take his leave, riding ahead to join his master.

"I hope Jerome hasn't been a bother, Lady Isabel."

"Not at all. He's a good companion."

"Lord Chetwynd wishes to know if you need a rest." Ingram spoke in a manner that suggested he didn't like the idea of a delay.

"Tell Lord Chetwynd I'm fine. There is no need to rest on my account."

Isabel was eager to prove she would not be a burden. The

last thing she wanted to do was slow the progress when she knew everyone was eager to reach home.

Her words had the desired effect, as Ingram's face relaxed. "It's not much further to the monastery, my lady." A kindly smile deepened the lines around his eyes as he added, "You will find traveling easier as the week progresses."

Isabel nodded, praying fervently that he spoke the truth. Her backside was sore, and only Ingram's approval kept her from regretting the fact she had refused his offer of a rest. As the day stretched on, Isabel began to believe Ingram had been optimistic when he said it was not much further to the monastery. Even Jerome's cheery company could not distract her from a growing number of aches and pains.

When the twin towers of the abbey chapel finally came into view, rising above the trees in the distance, Isabel could have wept with relief. Her backside was now numb, and she worried about her ability to stay on her horse. Only the realization that they were approaching their destination distracted her from the fear that she would disgrace herself by falling to the ground.

Lord Chetwynd had disappeared by the time Isabel's horse carried her through the gates of the abbey. A porter helped her dismount and took her horse to be stabled with the others. When Marianna appeared by her side, Isabel was clinging to a post, testing to see if her tingling legs would support her. Her maid had obviously found the journey easier to bear.

"Why aren't you as lame as I am?" Isabel asked in a peevish tone.

"I rode astride, my lady. It's the advantage of being a servant."

"Of course. It took all my energy trying to balance. I'll ride astride tomorrow."

Marianna looked doubtful but didn't argue. "Let us go directly to the guest house and have a wash, my lady," she suggested, indicating she had been given directions to the room where they would sleep. "You're to have your own bed-chamber, and I'm to be with the other serving women."

"Oh Marianna, don't leave me," Isabel said, close to weeping. In her weakened state she couldn't bear the thought of being alone on her first night away from home. "Please stay with me."

"You won't be alone, my lady." Marianna spoke the words shyly, with a slight smile.

Isabel tried to conceal the discomfort she felt at Marianna's assumption that she would spend the first night of her marriage with her husband. Since she hadn't confided the circumstances of their union, her maid's assumption was natural. Isabel was sure Lord Chetwynd would make some arrangement so they had separate sleeping chambers, and then she could explain the situation to Marianna. At the moment, she was too tired to say anything further on the subject.

The room set aside for Isabel was located at the end of the guesthouse, affording maximum privacy for visiting no-bles. Inside there was a wide bed, a washing stand, and a long bench along one wall. The rushes on the floor were sweet smelling. Isabel sat down on the bench, groaning a little as her sensitive muscles hit the hard wood. The good news was that feeling had returned to her limbs.

Marianna, still energetic, told her mistress to rest and then disappeared to retrieve some of their belongings. Lean-ing her head against the wall, Isabel stared at the bed meant for a married couple. If she shared the bed with anyone, it would be Marianna, she reminded herself.

Although Isabel closed her eyes and tried to rest, her

body remained tense and her mind active. As the minutes passed, she became impatient for Marianna to return with information about their schedule. She wondered if there would be other guests.

When Marianna finally struggled through the doorway, she was juggling a basin of water for Isabel to freshen up and a bundle of clothes. Isabel jumped up to help and groaned again.

"More guests are arriving every minute, my lady," Marianna said. "You will see for yourself at the worship service. Lord Chetwynd is closeted with the abbot. I was told they are old friends."

Isabel tried not to feel resentful of Lord Chetwynd's friendship with the abbot. This was all familiar territory for him, but everything was new to her. As she washed the travel dust off her face, she grew increasingly uneasy about how she would handle meeting the abbot, as well as the other guests.

"I'm very tired, Marianna. Perhaps I could just have a bit of supper in my chamber."

"Oh come, my lady. You'll feel better after a little walk. We can stroll around the cloister and have a look at the new arrivals."

Not wishing to be a coward, Isabel sighed and pulled a cape around her shoulders. "How is it you are not exhausted, Marianna?"

"I'm too excited to be tired, my lady."

As Marianna predicted, Isabel relaxed a bit as they strolled under an arcade that ran along an inner garden. Across the cloister, elaborately adorned lords and ladies chatted together, clearly renewing friendships. They paraded behind a group of brown-robed monks.

The sight interested Isabel until she realized she should have changed into fresh clothing, as it was clear the other women had. Since the monks were already filing into the chapel, she knew it was too late to return to her room. She feared her casual attire would embarrass Lord Chetwynd.

"I should have changed my clothes," she whispered to Marianna, gripping her arm.

"I'm so sorry, my lady. I didn't think of it. It's my fault."

"No, it's not. We're both new to this. We'll know next time."

"Do you suppose noble ladies travel dressed in silks and velvets? The weight of the jewels must be an added burden for the horses."

Isabel held her head a little higher. "I'm sure they travel in litters, Marianna. Let's pretend we know what we're doing." She spoke with more spirit than she felt.

From the doorway of the church, Chetwynd spotted Isabel and Marianna walking behind the monks. Although he knew Isabel must be exhausted from her long day in the saddle, he noticed she held herself erect. According to Ingram, she had acquitted herself well during the journey, refusing to be coddled. When Lady Isabel first insisted on riding a horse, he had thought her willful and expected her to be sorry for her insistence. If she was suffering from her first day in the saddle, she didn't show it.

Lord Chetwynd's slight smile at their approach encouraged Isabel. He took her arm, and they made their way to the front pews where they joined other members of the gentry. After a brief prayer, Isabel peered about. The setting sun lit the western windows, and light filtered in, giving the otherwise dark interior a muted glow. A chorus of monks commenced chanting, and the service began. Accustomed to Father Ivo and the small manor chapel, Isabel was awed by the power of the more elaborate ceremony in the magnificent structure.

After the service, Isabel whispered to Chetwynd as he led her out the door. "Such a grand church, Lord Chetwynd. A moving service, don't you think?"

Chetwynd nodded, amused by her enthusiasm, and led her to the line where guests waited to greet Abbot Adolphus. When it was their turn, he introduced her.

"Reverend Father, I wish to present my wife, Lady Isabel, the daughter of Lord Theodoric of Narbonne."

There were murmurs of surprise from people around them in the line. By this simple introduction, made in a deep voice, Chetwynd announced to all assembled that he had wed.

Abbot Adolphus held out his hand to Isabel, and for a moment she froze. Then, remembering how she had seen the other women respond, Isabel took his hand and bowed over it. Her embarrassment at her awkwardness was dispelled when the abbot smiled at her.

Chetwynd hadn't expected so many people he knew to be at the monastery. Watching his new wife, he felt her initial panic as though it were his own. He was surprised at how relieved he felt when Isabel relaxed enough to smile at the abbot.

"You have a long journey ahead of you, Lady Isabel. I hope your stay with us will be comfortable," the abbot was saying. "I understand you are newly wed, and I wish you a fruitful union."

Isabel's face flushed at his words. Being careful to avoid Lord Chetwynd's eyes, she answered the abbot. "Thank you for your good wishes, Father Adolphus."

Lord Chetwynd drew her away to make room for others waiting to speak to the abbot. As they proceeded to the great hall, Isabel spoke quietly to her husband. "You seem to be well-known here, my lord." People were still turning to stare at them as they passed.

"Yes," he replied. Chetwynd hadn't expected his marriage to cause such a stir. He told himself he should have known better. Gossip was a popular pastime among the nobility.

In the great hall, the guests were seated separately from the resident monks, and Chetwynd guided Isabel to a place among the lords and ladies. Aware of the continuing attention of several diners, Isabel was too nervous to eat much. One fashionably dressed woman kept staring at her and whispering to another guest. Isabel wondered if the fact that she had not changed her gown for dinner was the cause of all the attention.

Becoming impatient with the scrutiny, Isabel stared back at the woman. "I feel I should have taken more care with my dress, my lord. But that is no reason for people to stare in a rude manner."

"It's not necessary to wear finery when traveling. Don't concern yourself," he replied and followed her eyes. He groaned inwardly when he recognized Lady Pacilla.

"I suspect the lady in the purple gown does not agree with you. Do you know her?"

"Yes. That is Lady Pacilla. Her opinion is of no consequence," Chetwynd answered. He knew that Isabel's gown was not the cause of Lady Pacilla's curiosity. A friend of the queen, she was no doubt eager for information about Isabel that she could pass on to as many people as possible.

Although Isabel longed to ask Lord Chetwynd how he knew the elegantly dressed woman, she held her tongue. Her eyes widened as it occurred to her that the lady might be Chetwynd's lover. She dismissed the idea, as Lady Pacilla appeared curious but not upset. Perhaps she was a friend of Chetwynd's lover.

Lady Pacilla stood up, arranged her purple gown to hang attractively, and headed in their direction. She moved along the tables, stopping a few times to greet people she knew. Finally, the smiling lady headed for Chetwynd. He stood to return her greeting, and after a brief, awkward moment, he turned to Isabel. Chetwynd introduced his wife, repeating the words he had used with the abbot.

Lady Pacilla's expression made it clear that word of Chetwynd's marriage hadn't reached her ear. Her smile disappeared, and she stared at Isabel in silence. She did manage to recover her poise, but her smile did not return.

"Pardon my surprise, Lady Isabel. Our friends at court will be astonished to find Lord Chetwynd wed. Most of us were sure he would never marry." She turned to Chetwynd as though she expected some explanation for his behavior.

Isabel decided Lady Pacilla, for all her finery, wasn't much different from a few of the village women with whom she was acquainted. They, too, were always on the lookout for some tale to spread. When Chetwynd remained silent, Isabel decided to plunge into the waters of social discourse.

"I think Lord Chetwynd rather enjoys surprising people, Lady Pacilla. But that's what makes him interesting, don't you think? Imagine how dull it would be if there were no secrets to learn about a man."

Shivering a bit at her own daring, Isabel smiled brightly. She hoped she hadn't offended Chetwynd. Once she started to speak, the words flowed from her mouth of their own accord.

Although Lady Pacilla seemed at a loss for a reply, Chetwynd had found his voice. "Do give my best wishes to Lord Lassiter, Lady Pacilla. It was a long journey and Lady Isabel is tired. I must see she gets her rest. Please excuse us."

Concluding with a bow, Chetwynd grasped Isabel's arm, pulled her up from her seat, and led her from the hall. Once outside, he released his grip and walked ahead of her in silence.

Isabel rubbed her arm where he had held it. Hoping to head off angry words, she said, "I'm sorry I embarrassed you, Lord Chetwynd. I found Lady Pacilla's manner provoking, but I should have held my tongue."

"You didn't embarrass me," he uttered in a strangled voice. "You did just fine."

It took a minute for Isabel to realize he was struggling to keep from laughing. Shocked, she stared at his twitching mouth and wondered if the man might have a sense of humor. If so, he had kept it well concealed.

"Then why did you drag me away from the table?" she asked.

"To tell the truth, I was afraid of what you might say next. Lady Pacilla is indeed a most provoking woman, and you did well to stand up to her. It's the only way to deal with her."

Chetwynd suspected Isabel was waiting for him to elaborate. The attention their marriage was attracting, as well as her reaction to it, made him realize he needed to confide in her. But he wasn't sure how to begin. He told himself it could wait until he knew her a little better.

The silence between them continued until they neared the guesthouse and Isabel spoke up. "Marianna tells me we are expected to share a room, my lord."

"Yes, I know. I'm sorry. There were many things to do upon our arrival at the monastery, and I was caught off guard by the arrangement. I couldn't think of a reason to request separate quarters. This is something new for me. Having a wife, that is."

It made him nervous to even say the word, and he was glad they were still in the dark. He hesitated at the entrance to the bedchamber, and then added, "Next time I'll be prepared, but I'm afraid we'll have to share the room for tonight. I will walk around outside for a while to give you a chance to settle into bed."

To ease his concern about the matter, she reassured him that she understood. "I am tired, my lord. I imagine I will be asleep when you come back, but I'll leave a candle lit for you." Chetwynd nodded. It had occurred to him that she might be upset at sharing the bedchamber, but once again she seemed to take the situation in stride. When he noticed her pause in the doorway, he spoke again. "Sleep well, Isabel. I will see you in the morning."

The matter seemed easily settled. But although Chetwynd gave her plenty of time, Isabel was still awake when she heard her husband enter the room. Exhausted before she lay down, as soon as she did, she was wide-awake. The bed seemed much smaller than she recalled. To give Chetwynd plenty of room, she moved to the very edge of the bed.

When Isabel heard him moving about in the room, she pretended to be asleep. Thinking of how he had shed his clothes at the pond, she couldn't help being curious about how much clothing he would remove. She listened as he undressed quietly, but with her back turned, she had to use her imagination about what garments he was discarding.

Chetwynd settled into bed with a quiet sigh, sounding like a man with a lot on his mind, Isabel thought. Even after a good length of time had passed, she could hear no deep breathing. She was sure he was having as much trouble sleeping as she was. Instead of relaxing, the tension kept building inside her. Without realizing it, her whole body had gone rigid, and suddenly there was a gripping pain in her leg. Isabel was unable to keep from crying out and rising to a sitting position.

Chetwynd sat up beside her. "What is it?"

"My leg. Oh, there's a fearsome pain in my right calf."

Her agony banished all concern about disturbing him, and she clutched her leg. "It's a big knot," she cried out.

He recognized the problem immediately. "Just lie back and try to relax," he instructed, releasing her hands from her calf and pushing her gently but firmly back on the bed.

Isabel did her best to follow his instruction, but she was anything but relaxed. He was kneeling over her. Even in her pain, she noticed he was wearing a short tunic and nothing more.

"It's a muscle cramp and won't last long," he said. "I'll just try to ease it by massaging the knot. If you can relax, I promise it will disappear."

Chetwynd kneaded her leg as gently as possible, hoping his warm hands would soothe the knotted area. He could feel the muscle respond and relax. When he heard Isabel give a great shudder of relief, he knew the cramp was gone. But he kept massaging her shapely leg, telling himself it would help her stay relaxed. It had been a long time since he had been with a woman, and the one beneath him was exceedingly enticing.

"That feels so much better," she whispered thankfully. In fact, his rough but warm hands created a tingling which spread through her body. Isabel murmured her pleasure at the sensation.

Chetwynd had pushed up the long shift she wore, and with the moonlight streaming through a high window, he could see her shapely legs. Encouraged by her murmurs, he continued kneading the silky leg, moving his skillful hands down to explore her high-arched foot, then back up to her calf. As his own body hardened in response to hers, he wanted more. Ignoring the warning bells in his head, his hands traveled to the tantalizingly soft area above her knee. Her skin was smooth and alluring.

When Chetwynd heard Isabel's sharp intake of breath,

the warning bells began to clang louder. After a slight hesitation, he pulled down her shift. Carefully moving away from her body, he tried to calm his breathing. When he lay down on his back, he saw her turn on her side to face him.

"I was just surprised, my lord." She did not want him to think she had been repelled by his touch. Even now her inner thigh tingled where he had touched her.

With her intriguing smell filling his head, Chetwynd gazed into the face so close to his own. The eyes looking at him were unusually large as they reflected the moonlight that came through the high window. Unable to resist touching her again, he placed his hand on the side of her face and stroked her cheek.

"Your leg cramped because of the many hours you spent on your horse. It's not unusual for even the most experienced riders to have cramps. It's nothing to be concerned about."

While he was speaking, his hand moved to her ear, then into her hair and back to her ear, exploring its small, delicate shape. When he saw she was holding her breath, he leaned forward to kiss her lightly, just brushing her lips and withdrawing. He meant the kiss to break the spell, a way of saying goodnight.

But Chetwynd had not counted on Isabel's reaction. Gently she imitated his stroking, placing her small hand on his face, then into his hair, combing her fingers through his long locks.

"Your hair shines like a halo when the sun hits it, but you aren't an angel, are you?" Isabel whispered the question in her deep, throaty voice.

Her warm breath caressed his lips. A moan escaped from his mouth as he moved forward, kissing her again with increasing urgency, opening her lips with his tongue, and tasting the sweetness of her mouth for the first time.

When Isabel responded by welcoming his tongue and moving her body even closer to his, he knew he was on the brink of losing control. Pulling away, he clenched his teeth and moved back from her.

Shocked by his sudden withdrawal, Isabel saw that his eyes were directed at the ceiling. Since he wasn't looking at her, she was able to study him. His shirt was open at the neck, and she could make out the shape of his chest. Without thinking, she reached out her hand and placed it on the hard muscles, mesmerized by the warm skin. Isabel could feel his heart beating wildly. She was shocked out of her dreamlike state when Chetwynd roughly took hold of her hand and removed it from his chest.

"We can't do this," he growled in a hoarse voice. "It was a mistake to try and sleep in the same bed."

Hurt and embarrassed, Isabel snatched her hand out of his grip and turned away. The thought that she might be doing what her grandmother had suggested made her feel ill. It was only that morning that they had exchanged wedding vows. What would he think of her?

Chetwynd berated himself for his clumsiness. The first night of their journey, and he was doing what he had promised himself, and her, not to do.

"I'm sorry, Isabel. I should have known better. It's hard for a man and woman to sleep together without something happening. It's a natural thing. I should never have entered your bed."

When Chetwynd started to get up, Isabel turned quickly toward him. "Are you going elsewhere to sleep?"

Chetwynd heard the plea in her voice. It was her first night away from home, and he knew she didn't want to be alone. He waited for her to ask him to stay, but she didn't. Instead she moved even further to her side of the bed as though to prove she would keep her distance.

If she had asked him to stay, he might have been able to refuse. But her silent plea was much more effective.

"Go to sleep, Isabel," he said, settling back on his side of the bed.

Rolling away from him, she was comforted at hearing him address her informally. He was not going to leave her bed. Lulled by that thought, she relaxed and thought about what he had said. It was hard for a man and woman to sleep together without something happening. It wasn't her fault, or his. Just something that was natural for any man and woman.

Chetwynd could hear Isabel's breathing relax as she drifted into sleep. He envied her, as he was still vividly aware of her body so close to his. He blamed his wakefulness on the long period he had been without a woman. But it wasn't just any woman who occupied his thoughts and kept him hard. It was the nymph who moved erotically through the water, who slept on the ground with her hair spread around her, who had laid her hand on his bare chest.

Chetwynd finally had to acknowledge that he wasn't going to be able to sleep in Isabel's bed, or even her room. After he was sure she was asleep, he quietly left the bedchamber.

CHAPTER SIX

WHEN ISABEL AWOKE, HER HANDS IN-
stinctively reached to massage her stiff calf
muscle. As she kneaded it, she remembered the
gentleness of Lord Chetwynd's hands, first on her calf and
then on other parts of her leg. The thought of his touch on
her inner thigh brought warmth to her cheeks and a flutter
to her stomach. She turned her head cautiously, but the
warmth disappeared when she found herself alone in bed.

Thinking that Chetwynd had arisen early, she rolled to
his side of the bed and found the smell of his hair still on the
pillow. Even as she breathed in his scent, her sore back and
thigh muscles were complaining at the movement. She wondered how she would face mounting a horse again. Although
tempted to wait for Marianna to come help her get ready for
the day, Isabel wasn't sure how long it would be before her
servant arrived.

Cautiously she dropped her legs over the side of the bed
and pushed herself into a standing position. It was an effort
to straighten up, but she finally managed. Washing and
dressing slowly to minimize motion, she felt better the
longer she was upright. Hoping to find other members of her
party on their way to worship, Isabel opened the door and
squinted at the sunlight. She cautiously moved one leg in
front of the other.

As she rounded a corner, Isabel caught sight of Chetwynd emerging from another room. She was about to say something to him when he turned back to speak to a woman just inside the door. Chetwynd was pulling on his doublet as he walked away.

Realizing what she was seeing, Isabel raised a clenched fist to her mouth to keep from shouting her anger. Instead of spending the night in her bed as he promised, Chetwynd had sought out another woman to be "natural" with. He must have left after she fell asleep.

Unwilling to face Chetwynd until she had gotten her feelings under control, Isabel pulled back to wait until he disappeared. When she rounded the corner again, Ingram stood in her path as though waiting for her.

"Good morning, my lady," he said. "May I escort you to chapel?"

Wondering if Chetwynd sent him to find her, she murmured, "I forgot something in my chamber. I'll find my own way."

Ingram scowled, seemed about to say something, then changed his mind and departed.

Although she hadn't even been aware of his absence, Isabel felt betrayed that Chetwynd had left her bed in the middle of the night. He had promised to stay, but in fact the brute couldn't constrain himself from seeking another's bed on their wedding night.

Instead of following the rest of the guests into the church, Isabel headed in the opposite direction. Desperate for a place to be alone, she kept walking until she found an orchard beyond the stables.

It was a peaceful spot. There were a few late apples left on the dew-covered ground. Isabel picked out one that wasn't too bruised. Sitting with her back against a tree, she bit into the apple and wondered how she was going to deal with Chetwynd.

Isabel knew she was in trouble. She desired a man who was not available. Although he was not the fantasy champion she had dreamt about, in some ways he was much more. He was flesh and blood, and last night she had wanted nothing more than to have him continue to touch her and make her his wife. He must never know how she felt. Clearly, he had just wanted a woman, and since he didn't want a wife, he had found someone else to fulfill his need.

Throwing the apple core into the air as hard as she could, she watched with satisfaction as it flew off into a neighboring meadow. Chetwynd was not really her husband, and she would have to remember that fact in the future. No more wishing for something she couldn't have.

Using caution not to strain her aching body as she pushed herself to her feet, Isabel feared there would be questions about why she had missed morning worship. It couldn't be helped. If she had confronted Chetwynd sooner, she wouldn't have been able to hide her feelings.

As she entered the dining hall, keeping her eyes away from the table where Chetwynd was likely to be, Isabel took a seat beside Marianna and the other servants.

"How was your night?" Isabel asked Marianna.

"I slept as though dead, my lady," Marianna replied. Then she lowered her voice to a whisper. "Lord Chetwynd asked me to attend you this morning, but you weren't in your bedchamber. When I didn't see you at worship, I became worried. Where were you? And why aren't you sitting with your husband?"

In her head Isabel answered, *Because he's not really my husband, and he sought another's bed.* But out loud she said, "I went for a walk. I'm sorry I worried you, Marianna, but I wanted a stretch before the long ride. I had a cramp in my leg during the night, and I woke up very stiff. I thought some exercise might help. And the reason I'm sitting here is that I need to talk to you."

Isabel summoned enough nerve to glance over to where Chetwynd sat talking with Ingram. She couldn't help but wonder if Ingram knew their marriage was not a real one. Chetwynd was staring at her. At the sight of his narrowed eyes, Isabel quickly looked away.

Marianna watched the exchange. "Are you all right, my lady? If something happened last night to upset you, maybe I can help. Sometimes it takes a while for a married couple to . . ."

Isabel interrupted her before she could go any further. "Come with me, Marianna, I need to talk to you and I can't do it here."

"But you haven't eaten, my lady."

Isabel picked up some bread and cheese from the table, knowing it would be madness to travel on an empty stomach.

Marianna hesitated for a minute, and then followed her mistress out of the dining hall. They walked without speaking until they were out of hearing range of any of the other guests.

Finally, Marianna broke the silence. "You are acting very strange, my lady. Lord Chetwynd was staring at you, waiting for you to come to his table. What has happened?"

"Lord Chetwynd can just wait. I'm not going to worry about what he expects of me."

Isabel had spoken sharply, but when she saw the confused expression on Marianna's face, she softened. They were in the covered walkway of the cloister, and Isabel pointed to a bench on the edge of the garden.

"Sit down, Marianna. I should have talked to you about this before we left Narbonne, but there was so much to do, and I had my mind on other matters. Lord Chetwynd and I are married in name only, and we intend to live as brother and sister. He left our bedchamber last night to sleep with another woman. Under the circumstances, perhaps you can understand my reluctance to rush to his side and play the dutiful wife."

Marianna frowned and shook her head. "I don't understand, my lady. Why would he do that? You exchanged marriage vows."

"The marriage will eventually be annulled. We planned it that way from the beginning."

Marianna was clearly shocked. "Why would you make such an arrangement, my lady?"

Isabel sighed. She was beginning to wonder the same thing. "Lady Winifred suggested the marriage as a means of persuading my father to allow me to travel with the caravan. You know how much I wished to leave Narbonne. Lord Chetwynd has his own reasons for agreeing to the arrangement. I should have confided in you sooner, because I'm going to need your help. We have to make sure there is no repetition of last night's sleeping arrangement."

Marianna was clearly struggling to absorb this news. "I know marriages are entered into for any number of reasons, my lady. But I understand that if the couple is lucky, there can be great satisfaction in the match. I think you and Lord Chetwynd are such a pair. I have seen the way you look at each other."

"You are imagining things, Marianna. There is nothing between us." Isabel stood up to indicate the discussion was over, and Marianna followed her along the arcade.

Despite her protest, Isabel began to wonder if she might be looking at Chetwynd in a way that revealed the desire she was beginning to feel in his presence. Last night his touch had excited her to the point where she wanted him to caress her the way Derek caressed Emma. The agreement to live as brother and sister had flown from her mind.

Isabel vowed to be more careful in the future. The last thing she wanted was for Chetwynd to discover how she felt. She sighed at how complicated their marriage was turning out to be.

When they had almost reached the guesthouse, Isabel paused, her hand on Marianna's arm. "I hope you understand, Marianna. Whatever happens, make sure you stay with me at night."

"I will do as you ask, my lady. At least until you tell me otherwise."

Isabel narrowed her eyes at Marianna's smile. "I'm not going to be telling you otherwise, Marianna, so don't give me any of your knowing looks. Lord Chetwynd is in love with someone else. Now do you understand?" Before she had a chance to say more, they saw Lord Chetwynd striding toward them.

"Are you all right, Lady Isabel?" Chetwynd asked solicitously, putting out his hand to take her arm.

Isabel noted that he had returned to addressing her formally, and she couldn't resist pulling her arm away from his hand. "Of course. I'm fine."

Isabel was used to being on her own and felt annoyed that she couldn't disappear for a few minutes without people thinking there might be something wrong.

Ignoring Isabel's brusque reply, Chetwynd spoke directly to her maid. "Marianna, would you see that everything is ready for the journey?"

Once Marianna left them, Chetwynd turned back to Isabel. He was feeling guilty that he had left her alone on her first night away from home. Ingram had told him that Isabel had seen him leaving the bedchamber where he slept. Ingram suspected Isabel thought he was with another woman. He could tell her the truth, that it was Ingram's wife she had seen, but perhaps it was better that she thought he had been with another woman.

But even if she was angry with him, he couldn't have her wandering off. "Why did you not attend worship or join me in the dining hall?"

Isabel frowned. First Chetwynd was giving her servant orders; then he was demanding she explain her activities. Isabel's intention to hide her feelings disappeared in a flash.

"I do not have to account to you for my behavior, Lord Chetwynd. We are not really married, as you made very clear last night." Even as she was saying the words, Isabel regretted her impulse. He was her husband, and she did have to account to him.

"You are mistaken, Lady Isabel." Her flash of temper made Chetwynd wonder why he had ever thought he would be able to control her. The woman was impossible. "You wanted to come on this journey, and I am in charge. It is my responsibility to keep track of everyone, including you. We are leaving immediately. Make sure you leave your childish behavior behind."

His angry speech concluded, Lord Chetwynd strode across the courtyard toward the stables. Isabel watched his receding figure and wished she had something to throw at him. It was not lost upon her that he did not make the argument that she should obey him because she was his wife.

Later, as they were preparing to leave the monastery, Isabel mounted her horse, and this time she sat astride. Her determined look dared anyone to tell her she should ride otherwise. Since her gown had a wide skirt, and most of her legs were covered, she saw no reason for anyone to object.

It was almost midday before Isabel calmed down. Marianna

stayed close and glanced her way from time to time, waiting for some hint that she wished to talk. Lord Chetwynd, at the head of the caravan as he had been the first day, was out of her sight, but not out of her mind.

Ingram rode down the long line from time to time, checking on everyone. He treated Isabel no differently from anyone else, but there seemed to be a kindness in his expression when he nodded at her. She thought he must know about the "arrangement."

Jerome, her attentive companion of the first day, was nowhere in sight. It occurred to her that Chetwynd might have ordered him to stay away from her. She missed his cheery company.

As the scenery changed drastically, Isabel was distracted from her stormy thoughts. The caravan had reached the Rhone River, and it was soothing to travel along the wide, steady flow of water. When they came to some rapids, the roar drowned out the sound of the horses. The sun flickered through the trees, reflecting off the water.

It was an enchanting ride, and Isabel thought of the early caravans that had traveled the same route. The Romans, when their empire was first expanding, used this river to transport goods to the north. She wondered if they had been as captivated by the beauty of the river as she was.

Isabel searched the landscape for any evidence of the period when the Romans inhabited the area. Father Ivo had told her they'd built roads, bridges, and even dwellings that lasted to the present day. When she saw a limestone fortress perched on a hill in the distance, she could hardly contain her excitement. Isabel looked around, wanting to share her discovery. She caught Ingram's eye as he rode near.

Isabel pointed to the fortress. "Ingram, look there. Is that an ancient building?"

"It is, my lady. Are you interested in Roman architecture?"

"Oh yes. Our parish priest knew a great deal about Roman buildings. I have been hoping to see such a sight."

"We are due for a rest. I'll ask Lord Chetwynd if we can explore the fortress."

Ingram rode away before Isabel could discourage the idea. She wanted very much to see the fortress, but she didn't want to ask anything of Lord Chetwynd. He already thought her a spoiled child, and she feared he would not look kindly upon such a request.

When the caravan came to a halt, Isabel was surprised to see both Jerome and Ingram walking toward her. Ingram helped her dismount before speaking. "Ancient buildings are sometimes used by wandering bandits who prey on travelers, my lady. Jerome and I will accompany you up the hill. But if we see any signs of inhabitants, we must return to the caravan immediately."

Isabel thought she could detect Chetwynd's voice giving these orders. Nodding her consent, she exchanged grins with Jerome, who seemed to share her enthusiasm for the adventure. He took the lead, scrambling up the steep path that led to the old building. The ground was dry, and the rocks rolled under her feet as Isabel struggled to ignore her sore muscles and keep up with Jerome.

On the steepest section, Isabel's long gown repeatedly became tangled under her feet, and she had trouble maintaining her balance. When she started to slip backwards, Jerome was quick to reach her side. Although he was no taller than she was, he supported her easily.

"You need a stick, my lady. Stay still."

Within a minute he had found a branch that was a suitable size. "Lean on it with one hand; hold your gown with the other," the squire instructed.

As Jerome became aware of how bold his words must sound, his boyish face flushed red. But Isabel smiled her appreciation, and his embarrassment was quickly forgotten.

Ingram had caught up to them and watched the exchange. "Jerome, why don't you find me a stick?" When Jerome reluctantly left Isabel's side to search for another walking stick, Ingram turned to Isabel. "I think you have an admirer, my lady."

Isabel knew it was true, and it gave her comfort. "I knew squires were young, Ingram, but it's still hard for me to imagine them serving on the battlefield. Jerome can't be more than twelve years old."

"Just turned twelve, my lady, but he has been training since he was ten. He's a good lad, if a little overzealous from time to time. Lord Chetwynd is careful to keep him at a safe distance during a battle. Jerome is devoted to his master."

As Ingram spoke, Isabel noticed that his eyes were scanning the area. It was clear he was alert to his responsibility for her safety. Lord Chetwynd had two fine men devoted to serving him. She was impressed that her husband could inspire such loyalty.

When they reached the ancient fortress, Isabel saw that the limestone structure was still sturdy. Ingram signaled her to wait and went ahead through the large, curved entrance. Then he called, "Come ahead, my lady."

The door was missing, and Isabel peeked into the roomy interior that was empty of furnishings. The building had two stories, and there were stairs at the back. Ingram inspected the signs of a campfire in the middle of the room. He poked the ashes to assure himself that they were not recent.

Although there was rubble all around, Isabel imagined what it must have been like when it was first built. The ceilings were high, and she pictured the walls covered with tapestries.

From the small windows, there was an excellent view of the valley below, which afforded an opportunity to keep watch over the only approach. It certainly would have been a useful defense against enemy barbarians.

As Isabel sat resting on the stone stairs, conjuring up past residents, Ingram came to join her. "It's a sturdy structure. Why do you suppose it isn't being used?" she asked.

"It's a little out of the way. Too isolated to be a safe dwelling." He glanced about as he spoke. "I imagine Roman soldiers were stationed here to act as guards along the trade route. Perhaps a few families lived here as well."

While they were talking, neither Isabel nor Ingram noticed that Jerome had disappeared. Ingram seemed surprised when the young squire suddenly burst into the room. "There are men approaching from the back. Strangers."

Jerome had spoken quickly, but Ingram was on his feet and grasping Isabel's arm before the lad had finished his words. Forgetting her aching muscles, Isabel worked hard not to stumble as she kept pace with Ingram. She knew that strangers on the road could mean trouble. Neither of her companions spoke again, and even as they hurried down the hill, they were careful to be as quiet as possible.

Ingram didn't release his hold on Isabel's arm until they reached the caravan. "You did well, my lady. It was probably nothing to be concerned about, but it's always best to be careful. Bandits are unlikely to attack a caravan of soldiers, but they prey on travelers who separate from the group."

Isabel's heart was still pounding from the rush downhill, and she couldn't speak. She nodded her head, not doubting for a minute that the caution was necessary. She remembered the day eight years ago when she hadn't run away when she should have. The result would have been disastrous if Chetwynd hadn't come to her rescue.

Among the other travelers, there was mild curiosity at the speed with which the trio had returned to the caravan, but the incident was not considered extraordinary, and it was soon forgotten. Only Isabel seemed affected. She looked around her with renewed appreciation for the danger that might be lurking in the beautiful countryside.

That evening the travelers set up camp on the banks of the Rhone River. Fortunately, the weather was mild for Isabel's first night under the stars, and everyone seemed in good humor as they set about their tasks. The men tended the horses while the women built a fire to cook the evening meal. Marianna was already on easy terms with the other women. When Isabel made it clear she intended to do her part, the women accepted her offer of help in preparing the meal.

From the time Isabel was seven years old, her grandmother had insisted on giving her instructions in various household skills. Now she wished she had paid more attention. But she had preferred wandering about with Justin or Emma, and her skills were such that when her grandmother was not around, the women in the manor kitchen were happy to let her escape her duties. As she cut up the vegetables for the stew, she nicked her finger with the sharp knife. Marianna noticed and suggested she stir the stew, explaining that it was important that the bottom not burn on the hot flame.

Lord Chetwynd and Ingram had disappeared soon after the caravan stopped for the night. Isabel understood from what the women said that they were scouting the area, and she wondered if they were looking for signs of the men Jerome had seen earlier. They didn't return to camp until the evening meal was already being served. Isabel was surprised when Chetwynd carried his bowl to sit on a log beside her.

Eager to ease the tension that had begun their day, Isabel

said, "Thank you for allowing me to explore the fortress with Ingram and Jerome, my lord."

"I'm sorry your excursion was interrupted. We found no sign that anyone is following us," he assured her. "But we all need to be cautious."

Chetwynd had spent the day feeling guilty for losing his control the night before and his temper in the morning. Isabel had both tempted and provoked him. The frustration of the physical attraction he felt and could not act upon had caused him to lose sleep. Even after leaving her bed, he had lain awake a long time, listening to Ingram and his wife snoring.

If Ingram was correct, Isabel now believed he left her bed for that of another. In fact, there was no chance he could be tempted by another woman after caressing Isabel's soft, shapely limbs and tasting her delicious mouth.

When he returned to camp and saw Isabel sitting by the fire, she looked like she'd been sitting on logs all her life. He wasn't sure why that surprised him, since he knew she could sleep on the ground and swim like a water nymph. Perhaps he expected her to behave as the women at court did, expecting people to wait upon them and doing little for themselves.

Isabel stole a glance at the silent man at her side and caught him grinning to himself. "Your humor seems much improved, my lord," she couldn't help remarking.

Aware they were being watched by others around the fire, Chetwynd stood up and offered Isabel his hand. "Let's go for a walk, my lady."

Isabel nodded agreement. Because her muscles were still tender, she came slowly to her feet. Chetwynd moved his hand to her arm to give her support and led her away from camp. The ground was uneven and she bumped against him, then quickly found her footing without making a complaint.

"I notice you're walking a little stiffly today, Isabel," Chetwynd said with a trace of amusement in his tone. He remembered that she had boasted that she would have no trouble keeping up with the caravan. "Did riding astride help at all?"

Surprised that he noticed, she answered brusquely, "I'm fine."

Chetwynd didn't reply, but he recalled the remarks Ingram had made about Isabel as they were scouting the area. His usually reticent comrade had a lot to say. When he related the incident at the fortress, he praised the quickness with which Lady Isabel followed his lead. He also commented on her ability to ride and withstand hardship, as he too had noticed the stiffness in her movements. He even spoke of her appreciation of her surroundings and her sense of adventure. All this from a man who by his facial expression, rather than his words, had made it clear he disapproved of the match when it was announced.

It was dark once they were away from the campfire. When they stopped at the edge of the river, Isabel had the fleeting thought that it was the perfect place to bring someone you planned to toss into the water.

"I hope you didn't bring me here to drown me, my lord."

His sudden burst of laughter startled Isabel. "You have an active imagination, my lady. It's no wonder you and Jerome get along so well."

Thinking about how seldom people surprised him, Chetwynd leaned his shoulder against a tree before adding, "No, I have no intention of drowning you. Although you're fortunate we weren't on the edge of the river this morning."

It was Isabel's turn to smile. "Yes, that was fortunate."

"Come to think of it, drowning is not a method I would

consider. I remember all too well how skillfully you move in the water."

Isabel bit her lip at his reference to the first time he had seen her and pretended to be interested in the weeds that grew along the bank. She knelt down to pick a few of the white flowers that she could see in the dark.

Chetwynd stared at the top of her head. "I'm sorry about this morning. I should have handled things better. The only excuse I have is that I did not have a restful night."

Isabel stood up to face him. "You need not be concerned about tonight, my lord. Marianna has set my bedroll in a tent with her and the other women. You can sleep where you wish tonight."

Her tone was haughty, and he suspected she was thinking of seeing him with another woman. "Thank you for seeing to the sleeping arrangement," he said.

Isabel did not want to talk about sleeping arrangements. The subject brought back unnerving memories of the few hours they had shared a bed. That he left to satisfy his desire with another woman still hurt. According to their agreement, he had every right to do as he pleased, but that didn't make her feel any better about it. She sought to return to a less painful subject.

"Traveling through this area reminds me of the tales Father Ivo told me about the Greeks and Romans. Jerome says there are other sights to see along the way. I look forward to seeing more evidence of the building talents of the ancients."

As she spoke, all Chetwynd could think about was his desire to reach out, pull her against him, and seek to discover if her mouth was as intoxicating as he remembered.

Ignoring the impulse, he said, "There is an aqueduct ahead you might find interesting. The Romans built it to carry water from the river to one of their settlements. It's an impressive structure and is often mentioned by people who write about the period."

"I think I know the one you mean. Father Ivo showed me some drawings he made of an aqueduct. I understand the Romans built baths. Will there be a Roman bath on our route?"

Engrossed in the topic, Isabel unconsciously hugged herself. Away from the comfort of the fire, the cool air from the river started her shivering.

"You're cold." Chetwynd was glad for an excuse to wrap his arms around her and rub her back with his hands. Pretending he was doing nothing unusual, he rested his chin on her head and answered her question.

"There are a few Roman baths along the way. An especially grand one is located near Aachen. According to legend, Charlemagne was fond of taking the waters there. I think there may also be a bath near Mainz, which is on our route. I will ask Ingram. He shares your enthusiasm for Roman architecture."

"It would be wonderful to see a bath, my lord." Isabel was speaking into the shoulder of his doublet, as she struggled to resist the urge to wrap her arms around his waist. "I'm also enjoying the countryside. It's more beautiful than I had imagined."

"Are you feeling warmer?" Chetwynd whispered in her ear.

His breath tickled her, and Isabel almost gasped her pleasure. Instead she pulled herself out of his arms. "Yes, thank you." She realized how hoarse her voice sounded and grimaced.

Chetwynd resented the separation and cursed himself for asking the question. He leaned forward and brushed her lips with his own.

Isabel turned away, afraid he might be able to tell how

much she wanted to be back in his arms. She didn't think she could bear a repeat of the previous night. "I'm very tired, my lord."

Chetwynd was tempted to toss caution to the wind and have one deep, satisfying kiss. But he suspected one kiss would not be enough. There were too many obstacles in the way of doing more. He still hadn't explained about Lady Pacilla and the complications facing them once they reached the king's palace. He had no desire to open that topic.

"Of course. It's been a long day," he said.

Chetwynd led the way back to camp, going slowly so Isabel wouldn't stumble. He was careful not to touch her again until they were about to part. Only then did he dare put his hand to her face for a brief caress.

When Isabel closed her eyes at his touch, he leaned forward and whispered, "I should sleep better tonight. I spent last night on the floor beside Ingram and his wife. They both snore."

Isabel's eyes and mouth flew open. Chetwynd grinned and said, "Sleep well." He moved away quickly.

As Isabel settled into her bedroll, she thought about Chetwynd's last words to her. He seemed to be telling her that he had not left her bed for that of another. She wondered if he was telling the truth. He had no reason to lie, and the surprising fact was that he even bothered to explain himself.

Chetwynd might be in love with someone else, but he also had feelings for her, she was sure of it. She remembered Marianna's words about how she looked at Chetwynd, and she suspected it was similar to the longing she saw in his eyes.

Stretching her limbs, Isabel remembered how she had lain beside Chetwynd the night before. She missed him. But if she was correct and Chetwynd did desire her, there was a chance that he would one day again find his way to her bed.

"My lady," Marianna whispered from behind her.

Isabel willed herself to be silent and pretend to be asleep. She was not ready to confide her feelings to anyone, and even if she had wanted to, there were others nearby. The women did not need more to gossip about. She was sure there would be speculation about the fact that she wasn't sleeping with her husband.

But Marianna was not to be put off. "I know you're not asleep, my lady. I learned something today I think I should tell you."

Isabel still did not answer, and Marianna continued. "Don't worry about the other women. They're fast asleep."

The snores and deep breathing around the tent confirmed her words. Isabel gave in to her curiosity and turned to face her companion. "I'm listening, Marianna. What did you learn?"

"Well, it's something I think you should know," Marianna repeated, hesitating now that she had Isabel's attention.

Isabel could just make out Marianna's face in the firelight that came through the opening in the tent. She could see her anxious expression and knew she was stalling.

"You have my attention now. What is it, Marianna?"

"You know how you told me Lord Chetwynd is in love with someone else?"

Isabel felt her heart jump. She was suddenly alert and prompted Marianna. "Yes, I told you that. Have you learned something?"

"I know who she is. The women were gossiping about it. They were saying they thought you are a much better match for him. In their opinion he was infatuated with the other."

"Yes, I'm sure they had lots to say. Who is she?"

"They don't believe it was ever true love, but rather a young man being used by a woman married to an older husband. You know, for the pleasure he could give."

Isabel groaned. Marianna's stalling was driving her mad. She spoke as sternly as she could manage in a whispered voice. "Marianna, tell me what you know about the woman now."

Marianna took a deep breath and said, "It's the queen. Queen Judith."

Isabel was speechless. Could the serving women be playing a joke on Marianna? she wondered. She herself had heard many rumors about the queen. Her incredible beauty was often mentioned. The fact that she was much younger than King Louis made her a prime target for gossip.

Isabel knew that Lady Winifred had certain theories about the royal household that she shared with anyone who would listen. Her grandmother had suggested that most of the rumors about Queen Judith had been made up to discredit her. Isabel remembered Lady Winifred saying, "The queen has many enemies. Her three stepsons and the old bishops are terrified of a woman who is willing to fight for the rights of her son. I'm sure they are behind the scandalous tales."

Was it possible that Chetwynd was involved with the queen? She was beautiful, and the rumors spoke of many lovers. Isabel knew Chetwynd had spent time at court. She could imagine any woman, even a queen, being attracted to him.

"What else did you hear, Marianna?"

"Sarah believes Lord Chetwynd is in danger for supporting the queen. Lothar has a wicked temper and spoke out against Lord Chetwynd at the Spring Assembly. That's the reason that such a fine knight as Lord Chetwynd was sent to the Spanish March."

Her new friends had certainly filled Marianna's ear,

Isabel thought. If Queen Judith and Lord Chetwynd were lovers, it would explain a great deal. He had said more than once that he and the other woman were not free to marry, but refused to give more information.

There was also his assignment on the Spanish March, far removed from the palace. She wondered if Justin had played a part in the drama.

"My lady, are you all right?" Marianna asked.

"Yes, I'm fine, Marianna. You've given me a lot to think about. Now go to sleep."

"The women think you are much better for him, my lady. Henny has known him since he came to court, and she says . . ."

Isabel interrupted her. "Yes, I'm sure she has a lot to say, Marianna, but I've heard enough for one evening. I appreciate you telling me what you heard. Don't concern yourself. Lord Chetwynd was very open about the matter, so I knew there was someone."

"Aye, that's why I told you. You know I'm not one to repeat gossip."

"I know that. Now please go to sleep."

"I didn't mean to upset you, my lady."

Isabel sighed, rolled over, and pulled a blanket over her head. What had she gotten herself into? Not only was Chetwynd involved with the queen, but he had also made a powerful enemy of at least one of the king's sons. It was no wonder that the guests at the monastery were so surprised by his marriage.

Then another thought struck her. She rolled toward Marianna, who had already fallen asleep, and shook her arm.

"What? What is it?" Marianna asked in a sleepy voice.

"Does Ingram have a wife?"

"Yes. Hannah. You woke me up to ask me that?"

"Was she at supper? Did I see her?"

"No. She was tired. Said she was awakened in the middle of last night by an intruder."

Isabel grinned in the dark. "Go back to sleep, Marianna."

CHAPTER SEVEN

HE JOURNEY PRESENTED A NEW CHALLENGE the following morning when the travelers awoke to heavy rains. At first Isabel, still warmly wrapped in her blankets, enjoyed the sound of the steady beat of rain on the tent. If she could have stayed under cover, she would have been happy. But it was soon evident by the moans and groans of the women around her that staying in bed was not an option. Marianna was already digging out what protective wear she could find in the bundles of spare clothing.

Preparations for departure were accomplished with speed and efficiency. The tents were struck only after everything else had been done. Isabel wore a heavy wool cape with a deep hood that shielded her face and made it difficult to move. Jerome, quick to observe the problem, came to help her mount her horse. When she thanked him, she was rewarded with his now familiar smile.

He was the only one in good spirits. The rest of the men and women, no doubt afraid their journey would be delayed by bad weather, wore long faces. As they rode, the pelting rain drowned out all other sounds, and the darkness of the forest enveloped the riders.

The privacy of the rain-drenched ride gave Isabel a chance to think about what Marianna had told her the night before. Queen Judith's reputation had reached legendary proportions. Although the most popular stories were about her physical beauty and numerous lovers, there were also tales that reflected better on her character.

The queen was said to support artists and urge education for everyone. Her efforts were compared to those of King Charles, now called Charlemagne by his admiring subjects. Queen Judith's reputation made it hard to imagine her as a real person. Isabel wondered how Chetwynd had come to be one of her lovers.

The fact that a man loved a woman other than his wife was not unusual. Marriages were arranged to benefit families and provide heirs with little concern given to the compatibility of the marriage partners. But Isabel could not believe Chetwynd would enjoy the notoriety of being in love with a legend. In the short time she had known him, his temper had flared several times when his privacy was threatened. He did not seem a man who would appreciate being the source of gossip.

Deep in thought, Isabel was surprised when Ingram suddenly reined in beside her. He leaned close so that he could be heard over the rain. "Sorry, my lady, I didn't mean to startle you. We are stopping for the night at a manor house outside of Arles. It'll take another hour, perhaps two, to get there. I hope traveling in the rain isn't too difficult for you. Is there anything I can do to make you more comfortable?"

"No, thank you, Ingram. But it will be nice to sit in front of the fire and dry out."

"We're all looking forward to a warming fire, my lady. I think you will enjoy the manor house we're visiting. Lord Herbert and Lady Evaline are gracious hosts, and there are likely to be many guests. Our original plan was to go farther and spend another night camping, but we'll be stopping early because of the rain. Chetwynd is well acquainted with our hosts, and it should be a pleasant stop for you."

Isabel beamed, pleased that Ingram had taken the time to speak with her and tell her what to expect. Each day she felt more comfortable in his presence.

Wishing for a little extra assurance that Ingram was married, she asked, "Did your wife sleep better last night?"

Ingram seemed surprised at her words, then grinned. "I think she did, my lady."

Because of this exchange, Isabel was in fine spirits when they arrived at their destination. The manor was much statelier than the one in which Isabel had grown up, and she had been given a spacious room. The first thing she did was to bathe. Then she relaxed as Marianna dried her hair by the fire, gently brushing the tangles from Isabel's many curls.

"Ingram told me there are likely to be many guests in the great hall tonight, Marianna. Apparently our host enjoys entertaining. I don't want to make the same mistake I did at the monastery. We need to find something appropriate for me to wear."

"I have been thinking about it, my lady. I brought in the parcel with a few of your mother's gowns."

Marianna opened the case she referred to and shook out a forest-green garment, holding it up for Isabel's inspection. "What do you think? Dark green suits you. I can hang it for a spell to get the wrinkles out."

Examining the velvet dress, Isabel frowned, wishing she had more knowledge of fashion. Their home at Narbonne was isolated, and her father entertained few visitors of any importance. She wondered if things had been different when her mother was alive.

"Are you sure the velvet fabric is not too elegant? I'd hate to be overdressed."

Marianna hesitated. "Do you want me to try and find out what others are wearing?"

The gown had a fitted bodice, high waist, and roomy sleeves that were split at the elbow to allow air to circulate.

"No, that's not necessary, Marianna. I like the dress. It will be warm enough to banish the chill of the wet evening. Let's pretend we know what we're doing."

Marianna giggled. "The dress will be beautiful on you, my lady. Now let me do something special with your hair."

Entering the great hall an hour later, Isabel was gratified to notice approving glances aimed in her direction. Her elegant gown was not at all out of place, and Marianna had done wonders with her headdress. She had skillfully braided a creamy silk scarf into Isabel's dark hair, and lifted it above her head. While the scarf held her abundant curls in place, it allowed a few strands to trail down the back of her neck. A thin veil covered her hair without obstructing the view of Marianna's handiwork.

Receiving admiring glances was a new experience for Isabel, and she said a silent thank-you to Marianna. As a finishing touch, her maid had suggested she wear a piece of jewelry from her mother's collection. An ornate pewter cross with a delicate chain hung just above her breasts.

Lord Chetwynd, who hadn't seen Isabel all day, had been watching for her arrival. But even if he hadn't been keeping an eye on the entrance, the commotion she caused would have alerted him to her presence. The evening before, it had seemed as though sitting on a log in front of a fire was her natural habitat. This evening she was a fashionable vision as she entered the great hall. Even her slightly nervous smile was charming. There was little trace of the frightened creature he had first seen entering the dining hall at Narbonne.

Isabel smiled more widely when she spotted Chetwynd, and he strode toward her. Although he had no wish to be married, he was becoming more and more interested in bedding his imaginary wife. Since she had already had a lover, it shouldn't make a difference in obtaining an annulment when the time was right. He placed his hand on her elbow, and it slid through the slit in her sleeve to settle on her soft skin. He felt her shiver at his touch and his mouth went dry, as he knew his hand wasn't cold.

"You look lovely," he whispered.

Chetwynd found it difficult to keep his eyes from the cross around her neck. It sat just above sweetly rounded breasts displayed to great advantage by the low-cut gown.

Distracted by his rough hand on her sensitive underarm, Isabel found it difficult to breathe. She fought to control the shivers his touch sent through her body.

"Thank you, my lord." Her voice sounded husky to her own ears, and she tried clearing her throat. "Marianna was feeling particularly creative."

"She had excellent material to work with." Remembering how her hair had looked spread out around her when she slept on the ground near the pond, he had to clear his own throat. "Come. I'll introduce you to our hosts."

Originally Chetwynd had hoped to avoid stopping at the elegant manor, wishing to avoid a repeat of the scene with Lady Pacilla at the monastery. But they had needed a dry place to spend the night, and he knew their hosts to be kind people. Chetwynd ignored the murmurs of the other guests as he steered Isabel toward Lord Herbert and Lady Evaline. He could depend upon them to contain their curiosity, but he wasn't sure about the others in the hall. Chetwynd feared some of those present might be eager to test Isabel's reaction to palace gossip. He vowed to stay at her side.

Carried along by Chetwynd's guiding hand, Isabel stared in awe at her surroundings. The high ceilings stretched into the distance, and there were so many people she couldn't see the end of the hall. The tables were set with gold and silver that glittered in the bright light from the torches mounted on the walls.

As Isabel observed the gowns of silk and brocade worn by the women present, she knew Marianna had chosen wisely. Even the men were attired in lavish tunics decorated with jewelry. In contrast, Chetwynd's long-sleeved black tunic, although of fine material, was plain and unadorned. But his golden hair and well-shaped form were all he needed to set him apart from other men.

Lady Evaline, tall and elegant in a bright-red gown, welcomed Isabel warmly. "I'm happy to meet you, my dear. Lord Chetwynd has been a favorite of mine since his days in the household of Count Jonas. We used to visit there often. Chetwynd and your brother, Justin, were young pages then. I never knew a livelier pair. You look a little like your brother."

"Thank you, my lady. I'm most eager to see Justin again."

"It pleases me to see Lord Chetwynd finally wed. You are lovely, Lady Isabel, and I'm sure you make him proud."

Warmed by her words, Isabel tried to ignore the unease she felt at the deception she was perpetuating. She couldn't help but wonder what Lady Evaline would think of her if she discovered theirs was not a true marriage. All Isabel could do was smile and thank her hostess for her kind words.

Lord Herbert was shorter than his wife, and not nearly as distinguished looking, but he made up for his rather ordinary appearance with a friendly and open manner. He asked about Isabel's grandmother, whom he seemed to know well. Isabel was startled to realize that her grandmother had, at one time, been a part of this gracious world. Although she knew Lady Winifred had traveled widely in her youth, her grandmother hadn't told her many tales from that period of her life.

The other visitors in the hall seemed well acquainted with one another. As Isabel and Chetwynd moved through the crowd, she clung to his arm for support. People were clearly eager to meet her. They expressed subtle surprise at the marriage with comments like, "How interesting to find you wed, Lord Chetwynd." Then the same questions were repeated over and over. "Did Justin arrange the match? How long have you been betrothed?"

At first Chetwynd answered their questions patiently, and Isabel followed his lead in allowing the guests to believe Justin had arranged the match. But as time went on, she noticed Chetwynd was becoming more and more tense. She suspected the relentless curiosity of those they met was the cause. Isabel wondered how many of those present knew of his involvement with the queen.

Without her realizing it, Isabel's tightening hold on Chetwynd's arm communicated the strain she was feeling. He leaned closer and whispered in her ear. "You're stopping the blood flow in my arm, Isabel."

She immediately loosened her grip. "I'm not used to meeting so many people, and the noise is overpowering."

"You'll have to get used to it. The scene at court will be much more of the same."

His terse answer seemed out of keeping with his earlier attentiveness. Isabel pulled her hand from his arm. She was suddenly .resentful that he had placed her in this position. Chetwynd should have given her enough information to prepare her for the type of curious attention she was receiving. Even if he didn't want to reveal the identity of his lover, he could have at least informed her that his attachment was well-known. She suspected he dreaded the necessity of introducing her at court.

Chetwynd sensed her displeasure. "Forgive me, Isabel. I didn't mean to sound abrupt. You look lovely, and everyone is pleased to meet you. Perhaps it's time we had a talk. I'll come to your room after supper." Then to be sure she didn't misunderstand his meaning, he added, "Let Marianna know we'll need a little time alone."

Isabel nodded, thankful for his change of attitude. She hoped he was going to confide in her at last. Until then, she was determined to enjoy the evening.

There were more introductions and polite conversation during a long meal made up of lavish meat and fish dishes. When everyone had eaten their fill, the tables were pushed back to make room for entertainment. Chetwynd had gone off to talk with the men, and Isabel, surrounded by women, gradually felt more at ease. She was fascinated as the musicians filled the hall with music, and the women began to dance.

Unfamiliar with the courtly promenades, Isabel stood on the sidelines to watch. Soon Lady Evaline appeared at her elbow and urged her to join in. When her hostess insisted, Isabel followed her into the line of women. She managed the reels by watching the dancers in front of her, and she soon found the steps easy to follow.

From time to time she noticed Chetwynd's eyes upon her as he spoke with a group of lords she had met earlier. Judging from their facial expressions, they were engaged in serious deliberations. She wondered briefly why the discussions caused so many to frown, but the music and gaiety of the dancers soon captured her attention.

When the musicians took a break, Chetwynd appeared at her side. "We should retire early," he said. "I want to leave at daybreak."

At the door of her bedchamber, Isabel remembered Chetwynd's request that she ask Marianna to leave them alone. There was no need, as her maid disappeared as soon as she saw Lord Chetwynd. Now that it came time to talk, Isabel was nervous. While Chetwynd made himself comfortable on some cushions in front of the fire, she busied herself pouring the wine someone had set out for them.

Certain that Chetwynd was about to explain his relationship with the queen, Isabel wished to delay hearing his story. "You seemed to be in grave discussions with the other guests, my lord. Is there bad news?"

"You're very observant. There is a matter of concern." He took the goblets of wine from her hands and made room for her to sit on the cushions beside him. "There have been reports of bandits on the road ahead. Ordinarily we wouldn't worry, but there is speculation that the bandits have been receiving information about caravans moving through the area. They probably have spies who report when there is something of value to steal."

He took a sip of wine and said, "The men Jerome caught a glimpse of the other day when you climbed to the fortress may be part of the band. It seems unlikely they will attempt to rob a troop of soldiers, but we must be careful. It is a problem for smaller groups, and the men I was talking to were sharing their experiences."

As he spoke, Chetwynd leaned back on his elbow and stared at the fire. He still hadn't worked out how much he needed to tell Isabel to prepare her for their arrival at court. He turned to look at Isabel. She had settled beside him, and her fragrance, which he was beginning to recognize, filled his senses. In the great hall she had held her own, and he hadn't been able to keep his eyes off her. When she danced, she had stood out from the rest. Even as she concentrated on following the intricate steps, her moves were graceful, and each time she managed a difficult part of the dance, her face lit up.

Sitting close together, Chetwynd had a good view of the thin, white scar on her forehead. They had been different people all those years ago when she had called him an angel.

Noticing that he was staring at her scar, Isabel broke the lengthening silence between them. "Emma told me you stayed and watched her mother stitch my wound. Why did you do that?"

"I was afraid you might wake up and be frightened. I wasn't sure what I would have done if you did, but since you called me an angel, I thought my presence might calm you." He smiled at the idea.

"That was a kind thing to do."

"Why don't you cover the scar? You could do so easily. Emma's mother remarked on that as she sewed you up."

Isabel didn't want to tell Chetwynd that the sight in a mirror reminded her of the hero who rescued her. After the scar had discouraged her first betrothed, an old man she had no wish to marry, it became a badge of pride, or maybe of good fortune.

Instead she replied, "It's nothing to hide. I'm not ashamed of it."

Chetwynd reached out his hand to remove her veil and was disappointed to find that the curls he wished to touch were bound in place. Ever since he saw her sleeping on the ground, he had longed to bury his fingers in her hair.

"Your tresses are tightly bound. Is that comfortable?" he asked.

"Not anymore. I didn't notice the pull earlier, but I do now."

"Why don't you take the scarf off?" he suggested.

"I'm not sure I can. Marianna did it up."

"I'll help you."

Before she could say a word, Chetwynd moved to kneel behind her. He worked slowly so he wouldn't pull her hair. Isabel closed her eyes and sighed with relief as the tightly held locks were set free. She hadn't realized how uncomfortable the arrangement had become until the pressure was gone.

After Chetwynd had removed the scarf, he ran his fingers through her curls, spreading them around her shoulders. He leaned close to smell her hair and suspected it had been washed with lemons.

Isabel closed her eyes as Chetwynd began to massage her neck, sending tingles through her body. "You seem a little tense," he said.

When Isabel laughed in reply, he moved his hands to her shoulders, using his strong fingers in a gentle pattern to knead her tight muscles.

"The summer you were injured, I understood Emma's mother to say that you were betrothed and soon to be married. I was surprised when Justin told me the marriage never took place, and later you told me old men think the worst. Exactly what happened?"

Without thinking about it, Isabel bent her head to one side, allowing her face to touch the strong hand on her right shoulder.

"When Count Frederick arrived, my scar was still new, a red mark above my eye. He questioned me about it. I told him soldiers had attacked me, and when he jumped to the conclusion that more had happened than actually did, I didn't correct him. My father and grandmother were furious at me when he broke off the match."

"It's no wonder they were angry. Why didn't you tell the count the truth?"

"I wasn't sorry he broke off the match. Frederick was an old man, and I had no desire to marry him. He already had four children and two grandchildren."

To Isabel's regret, Chetwynd stopped massaging her shoulders. She had been mentally willing him to move his hands around to the front where her breasts were yearning for his touch. Instead he moved to sit in front of her so he could see her eyes.

"You must have been very willful, even then," he said. "I imagine your father had his hands full trying to arrange another match."

Isabel straightened up at his words, and her eyes blazed. He laughed at the swift change. "Are you going to deny you're willful?"

She couldn't help resenting the fact that he wasn't more understanding of her situation. Did he think she should have been happy to marry an old man?

"I have a question for you, my lord. If you think I'm willful, why did you agree to my grandmother's proposal?"

"It's rather complicated," he warned. "I hope you'll be able to understand."

"I'm not addled. Why don't you try me?"

He sighed, realizing they were getting off to a bad start. Best to just state the truth, he decided.

"Justin knew I would be passing by Narbonne on my way home from the Spanish March. He was instrumental in getting me the assignment." He didn't explain that he had needed to get away from court. "Your brother described you as restless and unhappy. He said you had hinted many times that you wished to leave Narbonne."

Expecting to hear about Queen Judith, Isabel was puzzled to be learning instead of the part played by Justin. Although she knew her brother had been aware of her desire to leave Narbonne, Chetwynd had given no clue that Justin had requested he bring her to Aachen.

"Did Justin ask you to bring me to court? That first night at Narbonne when I asked you to take me along on your journey, you refused."

"He didn't ask me to bring you, but I hoped to please him by doing so. If you really want to know why I refused your request, you had looked perfectly content swimming in the pond. Not at all like the unhappy maiden Justin described. Then in the great hall you boldly asked me to take you along on our journey. I found your request forward and my refusal was instinctive. I guess you could say I rebelled at your impertinence."

Isabel sat even straighter. "Let me see if I understand. You intended to take me to Justin, but because I brought up the subject first, you were offended by my—what—forward request and impertinent manner?"

The sarcasm in her voice tested his patience. "Just calm down. There was more to it than that."

Chetwynd hesitated to bring up the fact that his view of her was colored by the fact that she had just come from frolicking with her lover in the pond. When Justin had mentioned Isabel, Chetwynd had been eager to see her again. In his mind she was still the innocent he had rescued. But he had been unprepared for the grownup, sensual creature he had seen in the pond.

Waiting for Chetwynd to continue, Isabel watched him through narrowed eyes. Impatient, she stood up and began to pace the small room. "All right. I'll assume my request offended your delicate sensibilities. You being such an innocent," she said, thinking about his affair with the queen. "So you allowed me to believe you weren't going to take me along. Even though you hoped to do just that."

As Isabel paced the room, her loose hair swaying behind her, Chetwynd found himself losing track of what he had hoped to accomplish. He had never imagined a woman could be so desirable and provoking at the same time.

"Why did you agree to my grandmother's suggestion that we marry? All you had to do was tell her that Justin wished me to join him in Aachen."

She stopped abruptly and turned to stare down at him. "Wait, let me guess. Would it have anything to do with your desire to have a wife in order to create a cover for your love affair with the queen?"

Chetwynd jumped to his feet. When Isabel saw the fierce expression on his face, she was torn between being happy to get a reaction from him and afraid she had gone too far. Determined not to back down, she stared at him, waiting for a reply.

"I was afraid you might have heard some tales. I did wish to deflect gossip, but not cover a love affair. There is no love affair," he said hoarsely as he stared into her eyes, willing her to believe him.

"If that's true, why didn't you just tell me that? Instead you acted as though I had offended you in some way," she whispered.

Chetwynd looked away for a few minutes; then he turned back and said, "I saw you at the pond. I knew you were no longer the innocent maid Justin hoped to join him. You were a beautiful water nymph, and I wanted to join you. The problem was you were awaiting a lover, and it wasn't me."

Isabel was amazed at his assumption. "I wasn't awaiting a lover."

"There is no need to lie. I saw the way you moved in the water. No innocent maid moves that way."

Embarrassed by what she had been doing when he came

upon her, Isabel wondered how she could make him understand. "I was just imagining a lover. I saw Emma and her
husband once. I've never been with anyone," she said, watching his puzzled expression. "I would not lie about that, my
lord."

Chetwynd shook his head, trying to adjust his thoughts.
Had he been mistaken about her from the very beginning?
"Are you saying you've never had a lover?"

"Yes," she whispered, hoping that was about to change.

Surprise was the emotion Isabel now saw on his face.
"But you're twenty years old," he said.

His tone of voice made it clear he thought she was ab-
normal. "I know how old I am. I'm also unmarried and
haven't been with a man."

He believed her, but her words changed everything. "I'd
better go," he mumbled. His body was still hard for want of
her, but there was nothing he could do about it now but escape.

Isabel grabbed his arm. "You can't run away now. You
already did that at the pond, remember? What is it? Are you
disappointed that I haven't been with anyone?"

"No, of course not. It's just that it changes things."

"Just tell me this. Are you afraid if you stay and take me
to bed, you'll make our marriage real?"

Chetwynd looked away from her eyes and the hurt he
saw there. "I told you I didn't want a real marriage. But I'm
thinking of you, too, Isabel. As a maid it will be easier to obtain an annulment, and your chances of making an excellent
match will be better. I don't wish to compromise you."

"Aren't you the noble one," she scoffed.

"It's late, Isabel. We'll talk more tomorrow. I need to
think this through, and it's hard to do that just now."

Isabel moved in front of the door. "Because you still want

to take me to bed," she said. "You're disappointed to learn I'm a maid."

"Of course not. I've explained that it changes things."

Isabel had never felt so angry. She moved out of the way. "You're right, you should go." As he reached for the door, she added, "I'll see if I can arrange it so I'm not a maid next time you feel the urge to bed me."

Chetwynd stopped, turned to glare at her in disbelief, then rolled his eyes and laughed. "To think I believed I could control you."

His laughter died as quickly as it had erupted. "If you so much as look at anyone in a seductive manner, I'll tie you up and you'll ride in a litter for the rest of the journey. Don't think for a moment I won't."

When Chetwynd closed the door behind him, Isabel sank to her knees. Why did she have to say that? Because Chetwynd was able to reduce her to an idiot, she decided. Physically exhausted from the range of emotions she had experienced, she curled up on the pillows on the floor. Too tired even to weep, she soon gave up and fell asleep.

CHAPTER EIGHT

As her journey toward Aachen and the court of King Louis continued, Isabel settled into the routine of the caravan. Everyone was up at first light, personal matters were quickly attended to, and the horses were packed for travel. If they had stopped for the night at a monastery or a manor house with a chapel, they would attend worship before starting out. Since hearing reports of bandits attacking caravans, Chetwynd sought the protected shelter of a monastery or manor whenever possible. If none was available, they camped under the stars, and guards were posted throughout the night.

Although the routine itself became familiar, the countryside they traveled through was always changing, and it continued to delight Isabel. In one lush meadow, blanketed with late-blooming flowers, she observed small green birds flitting from bloom to bloom. When she declared her pleasure at the sight, she discovered Ingram shared her interest in spotting birds. From that day on, he began pointing them out to her and identifying ones she didn't recognize.

Before long, Jerome noticed their pastime and joined in. Although his sharp young eyes were effective in spotting birds, his loud enthusiasm often scared them away before Isabel or Ingram could spot them. After it had happened a few times, Ingram accused him of making up the sightings, and Jerome's guilty expression led Isabel to believe it might be true.

While Isabel was forging friendships with the two men, Chetwynd remained a distant figure. At first the evenings were awkward, as she waited for some sign that Chetwynd might approach her. He was always polite to her, and even attentive when others were watching. But since he never spoke to her in private, Isabel suspected he intended to keep his distance and ignore the scene that had taken place the last time they were alone together.

Although Isabel considered approaching him, each time she thought about it, she found an excuse to back down. She still felt embarrassed about her outburst that had ended their confrontation. But she also remembered his harsh response and couldn't bring herself to apologize. She was still struggling with the fact that he had assumed she'd had a lover. If he hadn't happened upon her at the pond, matters might have progressed differently. Instead they started off badly, and she wasn't sure things would ever improve between them.

Marianna was clearly puzzled by the situation, but she was protective of her mistress, and tried her best to shield Isabel from the gossip that continued about their marriage.

There was one incident during this time that strained the uneasy truce between Isabel and Chetwynd, and it revealed just how close to the surface their feelings toward each other lay. The caravan had been crossing a rugged mountain when it occurred. The trail was steep, and the terrain posed a challenge for Isabel. Ingram and Jerome stayed close, giving advice and watching to see that she navigated the climb safely.

When the danger of the steep climb was past, the two men relaxed their vigil. The caravan had started downhill, and Isabel was absorbed in the view of the valley below when her horse stumbled. Surprised by the sudden shift, Isabel tried to grab hold of her saddle, but she was too late to avoid falling. The path was narrow and before she knew what was happening, Isabel was rolling downhill, bouncing over rough ground. Instinctively she protected her head with her arms and cape, and her rolling came to a sudden stop when she collided with a tree in her path.

Aware that the downgrade was deceptively easier than the ascent, Chetwynd had been looking back at the long line behind him when it happened. He was horrified at the sight of Isabel losing her balance. Her fall brought her closer to where he was, and he jumped from his horse. Scrambling down the steep grade, Chetwynd reached her seconds after the tree stopped her from rolling farther.

Isabel was dazed by how quickly the accident had happened, but her heavy clothing had protected her from serious harm. Before she could untangle herself from the cape wrapped tightly around her, Chetwynd was kneeling over her.

"Stay still," he ordered, pushing her onto her back when she tried to sit up. He loosened her clothing and gently ran his hands down each arm. By the time he started to do the same to her legs, Isabel had recovered enough to be affected by his intimate probing. Her face had warmed and her limbs were tingling. From her position on her back, she could see that there were many curious eyes trained upon them from above.

"I'm fine," she said, wiggling to avoid the hands that had the power to do surprising things to her body.

Since the night in Arles, Isabel had done her best to forget how her body responded to his touch. Now she was afraid that he might perceive the effect he was having on her. No doubt her reaction would confirm his conviction that she was a wanton woman.

"Stay still," Chetwynd said as she tried to move away

from his hands. He knew his voice sounded cold, but he was too worried to care. "I need to make sure nothing is broken. You could be unaware of a serious injury."

Isabel lay back, holding her body rigid and staring at the sky. She did her best to ignore his hands as they traveled over her ribs and up under her breasts. They were playing havoc with her nerves as they kneaded each new area.

"Does that hurt?" he asked as he gently pushed on her stomach.

"No, I'm fine, truly," she said, trying not to weep. Although her heartbeat was racing and she felt dizzy, she suspected these symptoms had little to do with her fall.

"Is my horse injured?" she asked between clenched teeth, afraid to move until he gave her permission.

Relieved when he found no broken bones, Chetwynd relaxed. "Your horse is fine. He's standing where you fell and is waiting patiently for you."

Chetwynd extended a hand to help her to her feet. Isabel wished she could avoid his hand, but she recognized that she needed his help on the uneven ground. Before she could thank him for his help, Ingram had reached them and Chetwynd turned away from her.

"She's uninjured," he said sharply to Ingram. "Help her back to her horse, and this time keep a better watch on her." Chetwynd moved away abruptly.

Embarrassed by the tears that filled her eyes at his departure, Isabel prayed they wouldn't trickle down her face. She could tell Ingram was only pretending not to notice that she was upset.

"Lord Chetwynd is concerned about you, Lady Isabel. I should have stayed with you," he apologized.

"He has no right to be angry with you, Ingram. It was my fault."

"No, it wasn't. Lord Chetwynd is right. I should have realized the downgrade was as dangerous for you as the rise. Can you climb back to the trail if I help?"

Isabel nodded. By this time Jerome, his young face grimacing, had scrambled down the slope to help them. "I just went to the back of the line for one minute. What happened?" he asked.

"Lady Isabel's horse stumbled and she took a spill. There's no harm done," Ingram assured him.

"I should have been here," Jerome lamented.

Isabel wondered if he meant to help, or whether he was sorry he'd missed the action. Hoping to lighten the mood, she said, "Maybe you can catch my next performance."

When Jerome smiled at her, Isabel sighed, relieved that he was able to see the humor in the situation.

Ingram shook his head and rolled his eyes at their exchange, but he too seemed relieved. By the time Isabel had regained her place in line, she had forgiven Chetwynd for his sharp words. But the incident reminded her of how easily the embers of her desire for his touch could be stirred into flames.

As the caravan drew nearer its destination, there was a definite easing of tension among the travelers. There had been no sign of bandits along the route, and the worry about an attack had faded. Isabel observed the excitement of the soldiers as they approached home territory. They were close enough that three of the soldiers could be dismissed and allowed to head toward homes located nearby.

The fourteenth day of the journey was warm and sunny. Ingram told Isabel that Chetwynd had planned a detour to the site of a Roman aqueduct in the area. Instead of traveling at the top of the canyon, the caravan followed the shallow riverbed so they would have a good view of the ancient structure. Isabel was pleased Chetwynd had remembered her interest and was excited at the prospect of viewing the aqueduct.

Father Ivo, who had made a great number of drawings during his travels, was particularly proud of his sketch of the aqueduct. On parchment it seemed so exotic, with its many arches and levels, that it had been hard for Isabel to believe it was real.

As the caravan approached the giant aqueduct, her first thought was that although Father Ivo's sketch did it justice, the structure was much larger than she had imagined. The banks of the river rose steeply on either side of the riverbed to form a deep canyon. Isabel felt dwarfed as the aqueduct towered above them and filled the canyon. Three layers of arches formed the bridge. The bottom and middle layers were the same size, and the top layer had smaller arches. As she stared up at the amazing structure, she couldn't imagine how the Romans ever managed to build it. Perhaps they'd had assistance from the Roman gods, she thought, beaming at the thought of Jove and Neptune giving them a helping hand.

Marianna was as impressed as she was, and they lagged behind the rest of the group who had seen it before and were only mildly interested. Isabel reined in her horse, letting riders pass by as she studied the graceful lines. Because she stopped under the arch that spanned the river, the sound of passing horses echoed inside the walls of the archway.

The rest of the caravan was already moving out of sight around a bend when Marianna called out that they should be moving on.

"Just another minute," Isabel begged, enchanted by the size, shape, and power of the aqueduct.

When she heard hoofbeats on the rocky riverbed, Isabel was annoyed at the thought that someone was backtracking to hurry them on. It took only a second to realize the sound was coming from behind their party. Five strangers quickly surrounded Isabel and Marianna. One of them grabbed the reins of Isabel's horse, rendering her powerless to move. Another began giving instructions to Marianna.

"Tell Lord Chetwynd to proceed to the Convent of Saint Ives. We will get word to him about a ransom." The leader spoke tersely in a tone meant to discourage argument. It was clear he did not want to waste a minute.

"Release my lady immediately," Marianna demanded.

Isabel could tell by the quiver in her voice that Marianna wasn't as defiant as she sounded. In fact, her defiance changed quickly to terror and compliance when one of the men, without saying a word, pointed a knife at Isabel's heart.

"I'll do as you say, don't hurt her," Marianna pleaded.

The leader spoke again. "If anyone follows us, the lady is dead. Understand?"

Marianna nodded.

"Now get moving."

As Marianna turned her horse to obey him, she wasn't too cowed to shout a warning. "Don't you dare hurt my lady. Lord Chetwynd will have your head if you so much as touch her."

One of the young men laughed, but the leader signaled him to be quiet. "Wait at the convent for the ransom message," he reminded Marianna as they turned to make a quick getaway, pulling a dazed Isabel along with them.

The abduction happened so quickly that Isabel hadn't been able to think of a way to resist. She started to tremble as she remembered a similar attack eight years earlier. This time she'd have to save herself. At the moment, the only thing she could think to do was observe the route they were taking. If she could manage to escape, the information might be useful to find her way back to the caravan.

Wordlessly the men rode up the rocky bank of the river. But when they were sure Marianna was out of sight, they returned to the riverbed where they rode through the water for a short distance before heading up the bank on the opposite side. Isabel realized they were covering their tracks to make it difficult for anyone to follow them.

There was something familiar about the leader. Isabel suspected he may have been one of the many men she had seen at the manor house the night before, but she couldn't be sure. Although terrified, Isabel told herself that if she did what they demanded, they wouldn't harm her. They had mentioned a ransom, and Isabel was confident Chetwynd would pay whatever they asked.

No one said a word to her until they had reached a cave about halfway up the side of the canyon. It was clear they had reached their destination. There was a flat area at the mouth of the cave, and Isabel could see that the site was set back and unlikely to be spotted from below.

"Can you believe our good fortune?" one of the men said as he dismounted.

"Our waiting paid off. She was sitting there waiting to be plucked," the leader answered, looking toward Isabel. "Hardy, help our guest from her horse."

The leering young man who had laughed at Marianna's words came to help Isabel. He raised his hands toward her, and she had all she could do to keep from cringing.

"I can get down," she said with as much dignity as she could manage, but he leered at her and put his hands on her waist. Repelled by his dirty clothes and bad smell, Isabel pushed away his hands and got down quickly.

"We have a wild one here," he said with an unpleasant laugh. Grabbing her arm, he pulled her roughly toward the shelter. "She should be fun to tame."

He was not a large man, and Isabel managed to shake out of his hold on her. But her action made him angry, and without warning he swung at the side of her head with the flat of his hand. He hit her so hard that her head covering came off and she fell to the ground. She scraped the skin off her hands on the stones as she tried to break her fall, but she forced herself not to cry out.

"Hardy, leave her be." The leader spoke sharply to the young outlaw, then turned to address Isabel for the first time. "If you want to rejoin your party, you'll do as I say. Otherwise I'll give you to my young friend here. I don't think you'd like that."

The leader grabbed her arm and pulled her to her feet, then pushed her toward the cave. Isabel had all she could do to keep from falling again. Then he barked an order: "Sit still or I'll tie you up."

⁓

BACK ON THE TRAIL, IT HAD TAKEN MARIANNA ONLY a few minutes to catch up with the rest of the party. The noise of the river had covered any sound the bandits made during their abduction. She knew time was important, and she rushed directly to Chetwynd at the head of the line, ignoring the stares of the other riders. When he turned to listen to her, she explained quickly what had happened.

The color drained from Chetwynd's face, but that was the only outward sign of the fear that gripped him. Jerome and Ingram had moved close enough to hear Marianna's words.

Before anyone else could reply, Jerome said, "Let me follow, my lord." He was straining to get started and only waited for permission.

"They might spot you," Chetwynd said, as he wondered if there was anything they could do.

"Not if I'm on foot. If I climb along the top of the canyon, I might see where they are camping."

"They threatened to kill Lady Isabel if anyone follows them," Marianna warned.

Chetwynd stared at the frightened woman for a second. He didn't want to alarm her further, but he knew there was no reason to believe the men would free Isabel, even if a ransom were paid.

Ingram spoke up. "Jerome is small and skilled at remaining concealed. He'll be careful. The bandits are not likely to go far. They probably have a hideaway prepared."

Chetwynd knew he had to decide quickly, as valuable time was slipping away. Jerome had already jumped from his horse.

"Go, but make sure you're not seen. We don't want to put Lady Isabel in danger. If you find them, come to the convent and report to me. Don't try to do anything on your own, Jerome. We will leave a horse and one man here to wait for your return."

His squire had moved away as soon as he'd said *go* and was already scrambling up the side of the canyon as Chetwynd shouted the last words.

Although Chetwynd feared there was only a slight chance Jerome would spot the bandits, he knew that if anyone could find them, it was his squire. He was fleet of foot, and his young eyes were sharp.

From the worried look on Ingram's face, Chetwynd knew they both shared the same fear for Isabel's safety. If anything happened to her, he wasn't sure how he could live with himself. He had brought her along on the journey and then tried his best to ignore her. It hadn't worked for a minute, and now he might lose her.

"Perhaps we'll learn something at the convent that will give us a clue as to who the bandits are." Chetwynd spoke to encourage himself as much as to give hope to Ingram.

⁓

WRAPPING HER ARMS AROUND HER KNEES, ISABEL sat close to the entrance of the cave. Her cheek was throbbing from the blow she'd received from the young man they called Hardy, and the top of her head felt like it might explode. But she refused to feel sorry for herself because she knew her capture was her own doing. She shouldn't have lagged behind the others. The bandits must have been following the caravan, waiting for an opportunity to snatch someone. As they said, she had made it easy for them.

From what the leader had said to Marianna, it was clear he knew Lord Chetwynd. She wondered briefly if Chetwynd would be angry at her carelessness. But she knew better. He would be concerned for her safety. The only comfort she could take from the situation was that Marianna had not been taken as well.

To keep from surrendering to despair, Isabel decided to plan her escape. From their ruthless handling of her, she suspected they would not release her even if a ransom were paid. She had to at least try to free herself.

Except for the young outlaw called Hardy, the men did not pay much attention to her. But Hardy kept a close watch, and she stayed perfectly still so as not to give him an excuse to put his hands on her again.

At the back of the cave, she could see that the leader was changing his clothes, discarding his tattered outfit and putting on finer garments. Once he was better dressed, he reminded her of a merchant she had seen a few times on their journey. She had noticed him because he seemed to be keeping an eye on their party, and at the time she had wondered if he was interested in one of the serving women. Now she realized she should have alerted Chetwynd or Ingram about his interest. The bandits must have been following their caravan for some days, getting ready to make their move.

Isabel chastised herself again for how easy she had made it for them. She sat with her head lowered to her raised knees, her hair hanging over her face and eyes. She hoped the bandits would not realize she was observing them through her thick curtain of hair. The leader was obviously going to be the one to deliver the ransom instructions to Chetwynd at the convent.

There were several ways he could deliver the message that would not bring suspicion upon himself. The convent would be busy with travelers, and one more merchant would not be noticed. She must try to make an escape tonight, under cover of darkness. The thing she feared most was that they might tie her up and make an escape impossible. She would act docile, which should not be hard, she told herself. Then they might not deem it necessary to bind her.

As it turned out, there was no need to worry about being tied up. After the merchant left, Isabel observed Hardy pouring wine. Looking over at her to see if she noticed, he added some powder to the cup. Since her eyes were still covered by her hair, he had no way of knowing he had been observed. When he headed toward her, carrying the cup, Isabel was sure he planned to drug her. If she was correct, she could pretend to fall asleep and wait for a chance to slip away.

"Maybe a cup of wine will make you feel friendlier." Hardy smirked, holding the cup out to her.

Isabel pretended he had startled her from sleep. "I am thirsty," she murmured.

The bandit watched her closely, so Isabel made it seem she was drinking his offering. Fortunately, he could not see the cup was still full, and she took as long as possible, making sipping sounds. When Hardy was distracted by noise from one of the horses, Isabel checked to make sure the others weren't watching her and emptied the contents into the sand beside her, covering the damp spot with her skirt. When Hardy returned from checking on the horses, he looked to confirm the cup was empty.

Isabel began to wonder how soon the drug was supposed to take effect. She decided she could take her cue from Hardy, waiting to see when he expected her to fall asleep. She just hoped he did not have other ideas for her while she slept. The leader had warned him to leave her alone before he left, but Isabel was not sure how seriously Hardy would take that warning.

Although the outlaws had taken a devious route to reach their hideaway, hoping to mislead anyone who might follow them, she judged that they hadn't traveled far from the aqueduct. If Isabel could find her way back to where they had captured her, she could hide and hope someone would look for her. Since she had no idea where the Convent of Saint Ives was located, it seemed best to head for a place that was familiar.

Of course her plan depended upon her escape, Isabel reminded herself, and she shivered at the thought of making a move. What she really wanted to do was curl up and pretend she was somewhere else.

Although it was getting dark, the bandits had not lit a fire. Hardy came to stand over her. "Move farther into the cave," he said, pointing to where they had set their bedrolls.

When Isabel replied, she slurred her words and acted sluggish. "I can't breathe in close places. Please don't make me move," she begged, acting as pathetic as possible. It was not hard to do.

Hardy looked back to where the other men were huddled together, eating and drinking, and must have decided he preferred to have her away from the group. He touched her hair, and she had to force herself not to pull away.

"Sweet dreams, my lady," he whispered, and moved to join the others.

Isabel sighed with relief and vowed to do whatever was necessary to escape the disgusting bandit.

At first Hardy glanced over at Isabel a few times, but she pretended to be asleep, and he soon became engrossed in the game the men were playing. They had lit some candles, which Isabel hoped made it more difficult for them to see her in the dark beyond their circle of light. She managed to noiselessly arrange her heavy cloak, propping it up with a few sticks and hiding behind it. If they did glance over, she hoped it would look like she was lying under the cloak.

The game they played involved loud cheering after a successful throw of wooden cubes. Isabel planned to make her move during the next cheer. When it came, she prayed the noise would cover any sound she made. The first time she crawled only a short distance, staying close to the ground and leaving her propped-up cloak behind her.

There was a patch of ground near a tall bush a short distance beyond the cave. She made it her first goal. Isabel knew she had to steady her nerves and only move short distances until she was far enough away so that she needn't worry about being heard. She prayed they would continue to play the game until she was a safely away.

When she was finally huddled behind the tall brush, Isabel wanted to stand up and run, but fear of discovery kept her patient. She would never be able to outrun Hardy. Although it was dark, she could see quite well and was sure they would be able to find her quickly once they discovered her gone. Hopefully, the time it took for their eyes to adjust to the dark would give her a little extra advantage.

Forcing herself to go slowly, Isabel finally managed to crawl far enough away that she didn't need to worry about being heard. Although she wanted to head down the bank toward the river, she figured that was what they would expect her to do. Instead she stood up and climbed uphill, hoping to find a hiding place above their cave where she could wait until they discovered her missing. If they could not find her quickly, they might head for the convent to warn their leader that she had escaped. Then she could make her way to the aqueduct.

To move faster, she lifted her skirt and wrapped it around her legs, frantically searching around for cover. There were many large rocks and stubby trees, but none gave her the protection she hoped for. She feared the bandits would discover her missing before she found a hiding place, and she began to shiver violently. They were sure to punish her attempt to escape.

Suddenly Isabel froze. Something was moving silently along the ridge toward her. She feared it might be an animal, and her heart began to beat wildly. When a shadow appeared in her path, she fell back in terror.

"It's me. Keep coming."

Isabel recognized Jerome's voice, but shock kept her from moving toward him.

There were shouts from below, and Isabel knew her disappearance had been discovered. The sound was enough to set her in motion, and she rushed to Jerome. Without a word, he took her arm and guided her along the ridge into a crevice behind some rocks. Since there was no room to stand, Isabel bent over and sat with her back against the wall. Jerome squeezed in beside her and arranged a covering of branches over them.

"How did you find me?" she asked in a breathless whisper.

"I was on the other side of the river searching for signs of a trail. From there I happened to see the sun shining on metal and caught sight of movement. I crossed the river, climbed to this spot above the cave, and have been waiting for dark. I built this little blind in case the outlaws looked about.

"Lord Chetwynd said not to try anything on my own. I planned to find him and tell him where you were. I was just about to leave when I spotted you moving up the hill. I couldn't believe my eyes. How did you get away?"

Before she could reply, Isabel heard rustling noises outside their hiding place. They shrank back into their small shelter. Isabel could see through the covering Jerome had devised, and spotted two men searching. The outlaws must have divided into pairs, one pair going toward the water and the other pair up the hill. Isabel feared the men outside would stumble into the blind. She shut her eyes, not wanting to see it when it happened.

"The little witch couldn't have got this far. She must have gone to the river." It was Hardy who spoke. He sounded like he was right on top of their hiding place.

"I thought you drugged her, you lout. How did she get away?"

They had moved away and Isabel couldn't make out Hardy's muttered reply, which was followed by a long string of curses.

Neither Isabel nor Jerome said anything for a long time after the men hurried away. When it had been quiet for a while, Isabel relaxed a bit and realized she was practically on top of Jerome. The crevice was situated between a rock and a steep part of the bank. "Sorry," she said as she moved as far away as possible in the tight enclosure.

"That's better." Jerome moved his cramped arm and laughed softly. "My arm has lost all feeling."

"I know what you mean. I think my whole body has lost all feeling. What do we do now?" Isabel asked, cheered to have someone to share her dilemma.

"They may be back. It's safest to stay put for now. This spot is well hidden."

"I think you're right. I'd hate to have to stumble around in the dark. We'll have a better chance of keeping our footing in the daylight."

"Tell me how you got away?" Jerome asked, unable to contain his curiosity another minute.

Isabel listened to make sure there was no sound from outside and then started her story. Jerome was an appreciative audience, gasping when she mentioned the drugged wine, and making a whistling noise when she described sneaking away under the cover of their boisterous game.

When she had finished, Jerome patted her arm. "You are clever as well as brave, my lady."

Isabel smiled at his words. "Coming from someone who was quick enough to follow the outlaws on foot, that's quite a compliment."

"That was luck. You were smart. Lord Chetwynd's always telling me how I need to use my head."

"From what I can see, you use your head very well. This is an excellent hiding place."

There was a long pause, and Isabel suspected Jerome was blushing. When he did speak, he ignored her praise. "Maybe we should take turns sleeping. We need our rest for tomorrow."

The blood was still pulsing through her veins. "I don't

think I can sleep. I'll take the first watch," she replied, encouraging him to sleep if he could.

Jerome had made himself as comfortable as possible when they heard more rustling noises outside. At first Isabel suspected animals, but then she heard a rock roll down the hill and a soft curse. The hunters had returned, and this time they were being as quiet as possible, hoping to fool their game into making some sound. Isabel prayed her young friend was right in his optimistic assurance that the searchers would not stumble upon the crevice where they hid.

This time the bandits were not close when they passed by, and Isabel breathed a sigh of relief. Once it was quiet again, Jerome fell asleep leaning against her side. His weight was light and his warmth a comfort, as she had left her cloak behind. Calming down, she began to notice that her head throbbed and her scraped hands were burning. Although she knew they had to stay put, she longed to climb down to the river to dip her hands in the cool water and treat herself to a long drink.

To get her mind off her discomfort, Isabel thought about what daylight would bring. She was confident Jerome would have a suggestion about what they should do. She grinned when she remembered how impressed he had been by her escape. He had no idea how frightened she had been.

Her thoughts drifted back to Chetwynd, as they always seemed to do. She had caused him nothing but trouble. He had sent Jerome to find her, and she knew he would be worried sick about the two of them.

CHAPTER NINE

ORCED TO OBEY THE INSTRUCTIONS OF THE kidnappers or risk harm to Isabel, Chetwynd led his men toward the Convent of Saint Ives. Unwilling to lose a minute in attempting to work out measures they could take to gain some control of the situation, Chetwynd and Ingram conferred anxiously as they rode.

"One of the bandits will deliver the ransom demand, Ingram. I'll arrange for the porter to note new arrivals that look suspicious." Chetwynd was hoping the porter would be an experienced observer of travelers. "You can seek out the local sheriff," he said.

Ingram nodded. "I know Sheriff Willem. A thorough man," he assured Chetwynd. "He may have information about similar abductions on the road. Perhaps there have been other kidnappings for ransom."

The Convent at Saint Ives was a teaching convent run by the sisters of the Holy Cross. Young girls came to the convent to study, some staying to become nuns and others returning home to marry.

Chetwynd's sister, Gilda, was one of the nuns, and he had been looking forward to seeing her. He had worried about how he would introduce Isabel, and he could take no satisfaction in the delay of this task. He would give anything to be able to ride through the gates of the convent with Isabel at his side and announce that she was his wife. His only consolation was that his familiarity with the nuns would make the task of enlisting their aid easier.

As Chetwynd gave his horse over to the convent porter, he requested an interview with the abbess. The porter agreed to see if she was available, but before he had a chance, Gilda, her veil and brown habit flapping behind her, ran across the courtyard.

"I saw you approaching," she cried as she flung herself into Chetwynd's arms. When her brother squeezed her so tight her ribs ached, she pushed back to look at his face. "Whatever is the matter?"

"My wife has been kidnapped," he answered, wiping a hand over his eyes.

"You're married?" was the first question that Gilda asked, then, "Dear lord, when was she kidnapped?"

"I have to see the abbess. I'll tell you both the details at the same time. I need help, Gilda."

"Of course. Come with me," she said, taking his hand and leading him to the chamber where the abbess spent most of her time working on the convent books. Although Gilda knew the abbess didn't like to be disturbed, that fact did not deter her.

When Gilda knocked loudly, they heard an impatient one-word reply: "Enter."

As soon as Abbess Ermguerrd saw Lord Chetwynd's face, she rose and came around the table to greet him, taking his hands in hers. "It's good to see you again, Lord Chetwynd. Has something happened?"

After a hasty greeting, and without taking the seat offered him, Chetwynd paced as he told them about Isabel's kidnapping in as much detail as he could remember. Both women listened intently, their faces solemn.

When Chetwynd had finished, the abbess was quick to reply. "Ralph is a conscientious porter, and he will take note of everyone who arrives. It seems likely we will be looking for a single man, or perhaps two. Any information Lady Isabel's maid can give Ralph about the appearance of the outlaws will be helpful."

Relieved by her quick grasp of the situation, Chetwynd nodded. "I know Marianna will be more than happy to do all she can. She is an observant woman, and although she wasn't in their company long, I'm sure she'll be able to help with a description of the bandits. As you can imagine, Marianna is very upset at being forced to leave her mistress."

As Chetwynd remembered the look of distress on the servant's face, he paused a moment before going on. "We left two of my men behind, and they should be arriving sometime tonight with further news. My squire is going to search on foot for any trace of the bandits, and the other man is waiting at the aqueduct for him to return. Please have the porter direct them to me at once, no matter what time they arrive."

"Of course. Hopefully they will have good news."

"I can't thank you enough for your help and understanding, Reverend Mother."

"No need for thanks, Lord Chetwynd. Please let me know if I can do anything more. You have done all you can for now. It's time to ask for the Lord's help. Go with your sister to the chapel and renew your strength with prayer."

On their way to the sanctuary, Chetwynd finally took time to give some attention to his sister. "You're looking well," he said, managing a smile as she took his arm.

Gilda was the only family member with whom he remained close. Although she and Isabel were about the same age, Gilda was more delicate in appearance, a fact that belied the strength of her character. In spite of her austere habit and

small stature, her lovely face shone with health and contentment. Being in Gilda's company had always been a restful
and revitalizing experience for Chetwynd.

"I wish I could say the same for you, dear brother."

"To tell the truth, I feel helpless, and I don't much care
for the feeling."

"You can depend on the abbess, Chetwynd."

"I know she'll do all that's possible to help us."

Gilda nodded and then asked him the personal question
she had abandoned when she heard of the kidnapping. "How
is it that you are suddenly married? The last I heard you were
still vowing to avoid such a fate."

Since he had mixed emotions about the event, Chetwynd
wondered where to start. "It's a complicated story. Isabel is
Lord Justin's sister. You've heard me speak of him. I hadn't
planned to marry Isabel, but when I arrived at her father's
manor at Narbonne. . ." Chetwynd paused. How could he
explain how the match came to be arranged without sounding ridiculous for the role he had played?

"You fell madly in love with her," Gilda filled in for him.

Chetwynd was shaken by her comment, realizing it was
close to the truth, but it was closer to lust than love. As soon
as he'd seen Isabel swimming in the pond, he had wanted her
for his own.

"Not exactly," he mumbled. "I hadn't meant to marry. The
match was arranged to make it easier for Lady Isabel to
travel with us."

Gilda's raised eyebrows told Chetwynd that she questioned his abbreviated version. But he didn't elaborate, and
she didn't press him. "I'm eager to meet Lady Isabel," was all
she said.

The thought that the meeting might never happen was
like a knife in Chetwynd's heart. To hide his pain, he turned

his face away from his sister. But Gilda had always been able to read his moods, and she squeezed his arm.

"Come, my dear. We will pray for Lady Isabel's safe return."

Inside the small chapel, brother and sister knelt together. Chetwynd abandoned the usual prayers he had repeated by rote for so many years. Instead he pleaded silently for God to watch over Isabel and keep her safe. Although the presence of Gilda and the quiet of the chapel calmed his anguish, the relief was fleeting.

Later, in his room, Chetwynd was again tormented by thoughts of Isabel, his beautiful and spirited wife, alone with the outlaws. The possibility that she might be hurt terrified him. To ease the distressing images the situation brought to his mind, he paced back and forth in the narrow space between the small bed and the door, wondering what more he could do. Ingram had been dispatched to speak with the sheriff. The porter, briefed by Marianna, was on guard at the gate. The good sisters had taken charge of Marianna and were praying for Isabel's safe return. All he could do now was wait, and the lack of activity was difficult to bear.

As the night wore slowly on, Chetwynd moved to lie on his bed and stare at the ceiling. He had wasted so much precious time. Instead of avoiding Isabel, he should have been getting to know her better. It was clear she desired him, as he did her. Unfortunately, he had made mistakes in his life and there were matters to settle before he could think about marriage.

If Isabel were returned to him, he'd make it right. He'd explain to her his relationship with the queen, and then seek Justin's blessing on their marriage. He suspected that he would have trouble convincing Justin, who knew of the mistakes he had made, that he would be a suitable husband for his sister. He couldn't even convince himself.

There was a soft knock on his door. Chetwynd leapt

from his bed, hoping to hear some news of Isabel. Pulling open the door, he found Matthew, the soldier he had left at the aqueduct to wait for Jerome. It took only a second to see that Matthew was alone. Chetwynd's heart sank.

"What news?" he asked.

"Jerome didn't come back. I waited longer than you asked me to, but there was no sign of him. I thought you should know, my lord."

Matthew was his youngest soldier, not many years older than Jerome. He looked as dejected as Chetwynd felt. "It's all right, Matthew. You did the right thing."

"I just thought you should know he didn't return," he repeated, pushing his hand through his already tousled hair. "I can go back to the aqueduct and wait longer."

"Not tonight, Matthew. Get some rest and we'll see what tomorrow brings. Perhaps there will be some news by then."

Ingram arrived at the door just as Matthew was about to leave. He spoke without preamble. "Marianna insisted on staying in the dining hall to watch all newcomers, and I sat with her. She thinks she recognized a newly arrived merchant."

"Where is he?" Chetwynd asked, already heading through the door.

Ingram grasped his arm to stay him. "Hear me out, Chetwynd. I sent Marianna away so the merchant wouldn't know we spotted him. I was keeping watch on him as he had some supper when a curious thing happened. Another man arrived.

"I learned later from the porter that the second man didn't even unsaddle his horse, but hurried into the great hall and spoke to the merchant I was keeping an eye on. They left the hall together and rode away. I thought about sending a man in pursuit, but I was afraid of putting Lady Isabel in danger."

"Why didn't you come to me directly?" Chetwynd roared. But even as he shouted his frustration, he knew he was wrong and rushed to apologize. "No, I'm sorry, Ingram. You did the right thing. My presence would have alerted him, and it would be too difficult to follow them in the dark without being seen. You did right."

Unable to stay still, Chetwynd paced back and forth, thinking out loud as Ingram and Matthew pressed themselves against the wall to stay out of his way in the small room.

"There has been no ransom message, but our suspect has left. What could it mean? Perhaps Marianna was mistaken and he's not connected to the outlaws."

"Or perhaps he left a ransom message to be delivered after he left," Ingram said.

Chetwynd nodded. "If we don't receive a message by morning, something has probably gone wrong with their plan. We can try to pick up their trail then. We have to wait until morning to do anything," he concluded reluctantly. "Damnation, I may go crazy by then."

"Morning is almost here, Chetwynd," Ingram reminded him.

Chetwynd nodded again, then remembered Ingram's errand. "Did you learn anything from the sheriff?"

"Not much. There have been many incidents along the roads from the south. The routes that follow both the Rhone and the Rhine Rivers have been plagued by robberies. The sheriff says there are many poor men who can't make a living any other way.

"But in spite of that, the sheriff believes Lady Isabel's kidnapping, by outlaws who know you by name, is different from the usual robberies along the road. He asked if you have any enemies who might wish revenge. I didn't respond, but it's something we should consider, my lord."

At this suggestion, Chetwynd sat on the bed and put his head in his hands. Remembering that Matthew hadn't eaten,

Ingram sent him off to get some food and then sat down beside his friend.

Chetwynd finally lifted his head. "I have also thought about that possibility, Ingram. The help I gave the queen has earned me some powerful enemies." Chetwynd paused and added, "And now Jerome may have been taken as well."

"Or there could be another answer," Ingram was quick to remind him. "Jerome may have found something and thought it best to keep an eye on things. You know the lad can take care of himself. He's been doing that since he was a child."

"I told him that if he found something to return and tell me about it, Ingram."

"That's the other thing about Jerome; he has a mind of his own. You're always telling him to use it. If he thought it best, he might not obey your order."

Ingram's assessment of Jerome's character brought a trace of a smile to Chetwynd's face. After Ingram left him, he spent what remained of the night mulling over different scenarios of what could have happened to Isabel and Jerome.

At first light, Chetwynd and Ingram discovered Gilda and Marianna seated together in the dining hall. Both women looked up with hopeful expressions on their faces.

"Any word, my lord?" Marianna asked.

"Nothing. There is still no sign of a ransom note. We suspect the kidnappers have changed their plans. That may be good news," Chetwynd said to cheer Marianna. "We will be leaving soon to search the area. Jerome may have returned to the aqueduct or left a message for us."

"I'll get ready to accompany you, my lord," Marianna replied.

"I think it's best you stay here with Gilda." Then to discourage her from arguing, he added, "We can travel faster on our own."

Although Marianna was clearly disappointed, she didn't object. "I'll do as you think best. Just bring her back safe." She turned away, and Chetwynd could tell by her trembling shoulders that she was weeping.

IN THEIR HIDING PLACE ABOVE THE OUTLAW'S CAVE, Jerome and Isabel had passed a fretful night. Each had slept for a short period, but it was cold, and there was not enough space for them to lie down. To pass the time while waiting for daylight, they whispered to each other.

"I can't believe you managed to find me," Isabel said.

"It was just luck, my lady," he replied.

Isabel was positive there was a great deal of skill involved. Ingram had told her that Jerome was twelve years old, yet the young squire seemed to possess an innate cunning, as well as an innocent and energetic nature.

"Tell me about your duties as a squire, Jerome," she said, eager to learn more about the exceptional young man.

"My most important duty is caring for Lord Chetwynd's horse, my lady. War horses are bred to do battle. They must be strong enough to carry a soldier in full armor. The care of such an animal is a great privilege, and Chetwynd's horse is the best."

Jerome spoke about the horse in a respectful voice that reminded Isabel of her own appreciation of the large war horses. "How long have you been in the service of Lord Chetwynd?"

"Since I had seven years. It was then he found me."

"What do you mean, found you?"

Jerome was silent for a few seconds, and Isabel detected a reluctance to speak for the first time. She was also silent, not wishing to push him further than he wanted to go with his story.

"My parents and sisters died from a fever, and I was given to a farmer." Jerome paused for a minute, as though making a decision; then the story poured out of him. "The farmer had too many mouths to feed. His oldest son was always stealing my share of what food there was. He beat me when his father wasn't around. I finally ran away to the forest."

Jerome paused again and wiggled about for a minute before continuing. "I tried to steal food from Chetwynd's troop, and Ingram caught me. They planned to leave me at one of the monasteries that take in orphans. Until then they fed me and gave me duties to perform. At first I planned to run away when I got a chance, but they were good to me—the first kindness I'd known since my family died. So I stayed and tried to be useful."

Jerome spoke thoughtfully, as though he hadn't considered his history in some time. Isabel found it hard to reconcile his story with the joyful lad she had come to know.

"I wasn't much use at first," he told her. "But I kept at it and learned to do chores. The talk of leaving me at a monastery died. When I was ten, I became Chetwynd's squire."

Isabel could hear the pride in his voice as he continued. "You may think Lord Chetwynd's troop is small, my lady, but all the men are skilled. And he is the most skilled knight in the kingdom. King Louis has sent him on many campaigns and granted him a fine manor. Until this spring he had his choice of campaigns."

Jerome went suddenly silent. Isabel knew from Justin that King Louis, as well as his father before him, used private armies rather than maintaining a large army of his own. The king rewarded his knights for their service by granting them land so that they could support their men. She remembered that Chetwynd had mentioned receiving a benefice from the king when her grandmother had talked of Isabel's dowry.

Isabel respected Jerome's reluctance to speak further about whatever had happened between Chetwynd and King Louis. Jerome's loyalty to and enthusiastic praise of Chetwynd did not surprise her, as she knew he was devoted to his master. It occurred to her that Chetwynd probably felt the same about his young squire. They clearly had a long history together, and her carelessness had put the lad in danger.

"I'm sorry I dragged you into the mess I made, Jerome." Isabel was embarrassed when she heard her voice crack as she spoke. She hoped Jerome couldn't tell she was fighting tears. It was one thing to endanger her own life by her carelessness, but the fact that she had done the same to Jerome was unforgivable.

"I wasn't dragged, my lady. I begged Lord Chetwynd to let me search for clues. You escaped from the outlaws, and together we'll find our way to the convent."

When Isabel was silent, he said, "Tell me something about your life, my lady."

Isabel smiled at his obvious ploy to distract her, but she couldn't think of anything in her life that would interest Jerome. Then she suddenly remembered that there was one story that might appeal to him.

"There is one tale I can tell you. It happened when I was your age, and like your story, it had to do with the first time I met Lord Chetwynd."

"You met my lord when you were twelve?"

"Maybe *met* is not the correct word." She wondered if Chetwynd had told anyone that he knew her. It was unlikely, since it hardly qualified as a meeting. She had been unconscious at the time.

"Lord Chetwynd was a soldier with Lord Malorvic, and they were coming back from a tour of duty on the Spanish

March, just like this time. He was fairly young himself then. Do you know Lord Malorvic?"

"No, my lady. Ingram told me Chetwynd formed his own troop shortly before they found me."

"Well, Lord Malorvic had some unruly soldiers in his company, and four of them came upon my friend Emma and me when we were gathering flowers in the meadow. Emma was smart enough to run away, but I was too stubborn to see the danger."

Isabel suddenly wondered why she had started this story. She certainly didn't want to tell Jerome about being attacked by soldiers. All she had planned was to relate an adventure and maybe have an excuse to talk about Chetwynd. Now it was too late to stop, as Jerome was clearly intrigued.

"Two of the soldiers started teasing me." She had hoped to play down the horror of the attack by her use of words, but she could tell by Jerome's gasp that he suspected what really happened. The lad had seen more of cruelty than she had.

"You were attacked by those soldiers," he said, clearly shocked.

"Yes, but just by one. He hit me when I tried to escape and knocked me to the ground, but Lord Chetwynd came to my rescue before anything could happen. My vision was blurred, perhaps by the blow, and all I could see was his long, golden hair shining in the sunlight. It seemed like there was a halo above his head, and I thought he was an angel come to save me. I passed out, and Lord Chetwynd carried me to Emma's cottage so her mother could tend my wound."

"Is that how you got the scar on your forehead?" he asked in an awed whisper.

"That's right. I didn't see Chetwynd again until you arrived at my father's manor. In fact, I never even knew his name or what happened to him. And all this time he was a good friend of my brother's."

"I'm glad Lord Chetwynd was there, my lady."

Jerome's solemn tone told her he understood what could have happened to her. "Yes, I was fortunate. But I wish I had met him then. He was gone by the time I recovered. All I remembered was seeing an angel. I made the mistake of telling my friend Emma about it. She teased me for years."

Jerome laughed then. "I'm sure Lord Chetwynd never told anyone you called him an angel."

"I suppose not." Isabel was pleased that she had succeeded in making Jerome laugh. Then she noticed that she could actually see him smiling. They had made it through the night.

Since they hadn't heard anything more from the outlaws, Jerome suggested they venture outside. "I'll see if their horses are tethered by the cave," he said. "They may be gone," he added hopefully.

Jerome carefully removed the branches while Isabel held her breath, imagining that the outlaws were waiting outside for them to make a move. She had visions of the outlaws jumping out of the bushes to ambush Jerome. But all remained quiet.

When Jerome moved out of sight, Isabel suddenly panicked. She didn't want to be alone. It was all she could do to stay in their hiding place. Fortunately Jerome was back in a matter of minutes, and she gave a huge sigh of relief.

"Their horses are gone. They may be searching for you." He reached for Isabel's hand. Stiff from being in the cramped space, Isabel was happy to have his help.

Looking Isabel full in the face for the first time in the daylight, Jerome's mouth fell open. "What happened to you?"

Isabel realized he was staring at her cheek, and she

touched the sensitive area where she had been struck by the outlaw. "Does it look that bad?"

"The whole side of your face, it's discolored and swollen. You didn't tell me you fell." Then he looked more closely and asked, "Did someone hit you?"

"One of the outlaws. We should be going," she urged.

"I'll cut his heart out!" he roared. "Which one did it?"

"Jerome, I don't need you to cut anybody's heart out," she said, trying not to laugh. "I need you to help me get away from here. I'm sure it's not as bad as it looks."

He was still fuming about her injury, muttering to himself. Isabel tried again to persuade him to focus on the present problem.

"Lord Chetwynd may be looking for us already. We need to make our way to the other side of the river where I was kidnapped. Since we don't have horses, it won't be easy to get across. Can we cross on foot somewhere, or do we need to wade through the water?"

Her question succeeded in turning his mind to strategy. "We don't need to cross the river until we get to the aqueduct. We can travel along the riverbank until we reach it, cross over it, and climb down on the other side. With the outlaws on horseback, we'll hear them if they return. We must stay close to cover as we move."

They spent most of the day making their way carefully along the rugged terrain. The need to make sure there was always a place to hide nearby meant they had to take many detours, slowing their progress.

A soft rain began to fall. The rain kept them from becoming too thirsty, but they were both hungry. As Isabel grew tired, it became harder for her to keep her footing on the uneven slope of the canyon. Although neither one complained, their progress slowed even further.

Isabel was trying to keep pace with Jerome when she twisted her ankle and fell to her knees. Jerome was immediately at her side. "Sit down and rest, my lady."

She almost laughed because she knew there was no way she could have done anything else. "Maybe you should go on alone, Jerome," she suggested, although she dreaded the thought and was relieved by his answer.

"No. We stay together. We both need a rest." Then he sat down as well.

After what seemed a short time to Isabel, Jerome stood up again and offered her his hand. Isabel wasn't sure she could stand, but she found that her ankle, although sore, supported her. In silence she followed Jerome. "It's not far now," he promised.

When they finally reached the aqueduct, the familiar landscape lifted Isabel's spirits. Aches, hunger, and fatigue were almost forgotten.

"It's beautiful, isn't it?" she remarked, sitting down to stare at the structure.

"It's a bridge," Jerome replied, obviously wondering how a bridge could be considered beautiful. "When we cross it, we're going to be in plain sight of anyone watching."

Isabel acknowledged the problem with a nod. They were sitting about halfway up the steep slope. "Perhaps we should climb down to the river and wade across," she said, though she didn't believe she could take another step.

"I don't think so. The river flows rapidly in the middle where it's deep. It would be risky."

They sat resting, pondering their predicament. It was late afternoon, but they still had plenty of daylight hours to find their way to the convent. Finally, Jerome made a suggestion.

"I'll go across the bridge alone. If anyone is watching, I'm just a peasant crossing the aqueduct. The bandits don't know I'm with you. I'll be able to have a good look around from up there. If it's safe, I'll come back for you. You can hide behind these bushes, and you'll be able to see me when I'm on the aqueduct."

The ledge they were sitting on protected Isabel from view from below. She wondered if the plan was as safe as he made it sound. "Don't take any chances," she warned him.

Jerome nodded, then started his climb up the steep bank, going slowly so as not to disturb the rocks and start a landslide. He had a distance to go before he could climb onto the aqueduct and start across. Although Isabel hated being alone, she told herself she would be able to see him when he reached the aqueduct.

Jerome had only been gone a few minutes when Isabel heard a rock rolling down the hill below her. From the sound she guessed someone was climbing up the bank toward her. Isabel pulled back on the ledge. Whoever it was must have spotted Jerome and was following him. If she were correct, the climber would not expect anyone to be so close. Determined to protect Jerome, Isabel picked up a large rock with the idea of stopping the climber.

There was no further sound. Isabel tried to see if anyone was below, but the ledge made it impossible to see beyond it without leaning out over the rim. If the climber came close, she would have a good chance to attack him from above. She weighed the large rock in her hand, hoping it was big enough to do the job.

The next sound she heard came from directly below her. She jumped up, caught a glimpse of a figure where she expected to see him, and threw her weapon at his head. The rock had just left her hand when she realized the climber had golden hair. She screamed a warning, but Chetwynd had already ducked. Still the rock landed on his shoulder with enough force to knock him over.

Appalled at what she had done, Isabel scrambled down to where Chetwynd lay. He was struggling to get up, and she moved so quickly she bumped into him, knocked him over, and landed on top of him.

Recognizing that his attacker was Isabel, Chetwynd ceased struggling and lay back to stare at her. "Saints preserve us," he muttered.

"Are you all right, my lord?" Isabel was sickened by what she had done. As soon as the rock left her hand she was sure it would kill him.

Without waiting for him to answer, Isabel began imitating the check he had done on her when she fell from her horse. She had little idea what she was feeling for, but she took comfort from running her hands over his well-formed limbs. Surely she would be able to tell if he had broken any bones.

Stunned by Isabel's sudden appearance more than the attack, Chetwynd pushed her hands away and struggled to sit up. "I'm fine, Isabel. Just relax a minute. Don't help me."

"I could have killed you. I'm just trying to see if you're hurt." Upset that he refused her help and afraid he was angry, she couldn't stop the tears from pouring down her cheeks.

Chetwynd didn't say another word. He stood up and gathered her into his arms, holding her tightly while she soaked his doublet with her tears. Her whole body was shaking from the force of her sobs, and he had to practically drag her to a safe spot under the ledge.

Isabel became aware that Chetwynd was kissing her forehead and holding her tight against him as he ran his hands up and down her back. She stopped crying and lifted her face, hoping to taste his lips.

His kiss was sweet, and Isabel was glad he was holding

her tightly, as she knew she could never stand on her own. Unable to get enough of his taste, her arms circled his neck and she returned his kiss with increasing eagerness.

Suddenly rocks were crashing around them and someone was shouting. At first Isabel was impatient at the noise that interrupted them, then frightened when Chetwynd pushed her behind him.

Jerome was rushing down the slope, sending rocks flying in all directions. He had heard Isabel scream and when he didn't find her on the ledge, he began shouting her name.

At the same time, Ingram and Matthew were scrambling up the hill, dodging rocks and shouting for Chetwynd. Isabel, hidden behind Chetwynd's back, listened to him calling to his men.

"I have Lady Isabel. She's safe." He pulled Isabel from behind him to prove his words, but he kept her tucked safely under his arm.

Ingram, Matthew, and Jerome all stared at her, but only Jerome was smiling.

"What happened to your face?" Ingram asked.

Chetwynd frowned at the question and turned to have a look. "Damnation," he whispered.

Suddenly self-conscious, Isabel knew she must look like a wild woman. Her hair had been uncombed and uncovered for two days, and her clothes were dirty and torn. She put her hands to her face, to hide the swelling.

Chetwynd gently pulled her hands away. When he saw they were scraped raw, he examined them tenderly. "My god, what happened to you?"

Jerome was watching Chetwynd examine Isabel. When she hesitated, the squire answered for her.

"One of the outlaws struck her so hard she fell to the ground," he said. "I didn't see her injuries until this morning.

All night long, she never complained. If the devil had been in the cave, I would have gone after him. Well, that's what I thought at first. But of course the smart thing to do was to speed Lady Isabel away from there."

Chetwynd silenced Jerome by putting a hand on his shoulder. "Take a deep breath," he ordered gently. "Now, tell us how you rescued her."

Jerome's eyes went wide at Chetwynd's assumption. "I didn't rescue her. She escaped during the night. She tricked them. They tried to drug her, but she figured out a plan. She climbed up the hill to where I was hiding. The outlaws were out looking for her. We hid together until daylight. I have to tell you, it was cold in that hiding place. Did you catch the outlaws?" he asked, out of breath again.

All the time Jerome was speaking, Chetwynd stared at Isabel as her amazing courage began to sink in. She might appear helpless now, but she had fought against great odds and used her head to save herself.

"No, we thought you were the outlaws," Chetwynd answered Jerome, his eyes still on Isabel. "We've been searching the area all day."

"I'm so sorry I attacked you," Isabel said, and even in her own ears her voice sounded pathetically weak.

Being careful of her injuries, Chetwynd pulled her back into his arms. "Hush. I know you were trying to protect Jerome. I'm sorry you had to go through this ordeal. We'll hear more of your tale at the convent. Now we need to get you and Jerome patched up and fed."

Over Isabel's head, he looked at his squire. "You were there when Lady Isabel needed you, Jerome. I'll never forget all you did."

CHAPTER TEN

ARIANNA AND GILDA WERE PHYSICAL opposites. Marianna, tall and large boned, towered over the small, delicately featured nun. Despite their physical differences, they shared an open and friendly nature. When Chetwynd left the convent to search for Isabel, Marianna had been frantic with worry over what he might find. Gilda, who was used to helping women in distress, offered comfort. A bond of concern and caring quickly united the two women. By evening, they were strolling the courtyard arm in arm, telling each other they needed the exercise, but in truth keeping watch for new arrivals.

It had become dark when they finally spotted Lady Isabel, riding in front of Chetwynd on his large war horse, coming through the gate of the convent. Chetwynd was reluctant to release his hold on his wife, but Marianna reached out with such eager tenderness that he passed Isabel into her care. Although greatly relieved by the sight of her mistress, on closer inspection Marianna was shocked to find her bruised and disheveled.

In a large bedchamber reserved for special visitors, the two women worked together to bathe and feed Lady Isabel. Once the dirt was gone from her face and hands, her bruises showed up even more vividly.

"These will fade in a few days," Gilda pointed out to reassure Marianna as much as Isabel. "But they may blossom into some vivid colors before that happens."

Although dazed and sleepy upon her arrival at the convent, Isabel was revived by the thick soup Marianna brought for her, as well as her curiosity about Gilda. Chetwynd had introduced them when they arrived, but then she was rushed away to a bedchamber.

"I didn't know Chetwynd had a sister," she said. She guessed that Gilda was about her own age and was eager to learn more about her.

"And I didn't know he had a wife," Gilda said with a sparkle in her eye. "You should rest now, my lady, and we'll talk later."

"Please, don't go. I need to talk."

Gilda nodded. "Sometimes it helps to talk. Tell us what happened," she urged, assuming Isabel wanted to tell them about her capture.

The two women listened intently while Isabel gave them a quick outline of her capture and escape. But Isabel soon made it clear that she didn't want to talk about herself.

"How long has it been since you've seen Chetwynd, Gilda? Are there other brothers and sisters?"

Although Jerome had given her a few details about Chetwynd as a leader of men, Isabel was hungry for more information about her husband. By turns he infuriated her by the distance he kept between them, and stirred her desire for him by some tender act.

"I can't believe you're not collapsing with fatigue, Isabel. Are you sure you don't want to lie quietly for a while? We can talk tomorrow."

"I'm too wakeful to settle down. It might help to talk a little," Isabel pleaded. What she didn't say was that she hoped

Chetwynd would come to her, and she didn't want to be asleep.

The two caretakers exchanged looks. Marianna shrugged her shoulders to indicate they should indulge Isabel. Gilda began speaking in a soft voice, hoping to lull Isabel into sleep.

"Chetwynd and I didn't spend much time together growing up. But we have become close in recent years. Aachen is not far from here, and Chetwynd often stops at Saint Ives to visit. We have two brothers older than Chetwynd. They remain in Aquitania with my father to help with the estate they will inherit one day. Neither Chetwynd nor I have returned home for many years."

Marianna adjusted the blanket around Isabel's shoulders and urged her to drink some water, while Gilda described the home she had left at an early age.

Isabel watched Gilda as she spoke, looking for a resemblance to Chetwynd. As far as she could tell, they shared the same coloring. Although Gilda's hair was covered by a dark veil, her skin was fair and her eyes a deep shade of blue. But she noticed that while Gilda had a serene countenance, Chetwynd's expression was usually tense and alert.

Closing her eyes, Isabel wondered if it was her vocation that gave Gilda her air of serenity. If she had listened to her father's advice, she might also be living in a religious community. Gilda stopped speaking, hoping that Isabel had gone to sleep.

Opening her eyes, Isabel said, "At one time my father urged me to become a nun."

"I'm not surprised. Marriage and the veil seem to be the only two options that fathers think about for their daughters."

"I might have considered it, but I was by nature opposed

to any idea my father had for my future," Isabel admitted. "How did you come to join the sisters of Saint Ives, Gilda?"

"When I was ten years old, I came here to be educated. Chetwynd had been sent to a noble household for his education, but my father thought I would be safer in a convent, taught by nuns, until I was ready to marry. He was rather distressed to find I liked it here and wished to stay. When I was twelve, my father proposed a match with a wealthy landowner, but I was not the least bit interested."

Coming to a sitting position, Isabel interrupted her. "The same thing happened to me. I was supposed to marry when I was twelve."

"My lady sabotaged the match," Marianna interjected with a beam of approval. "The man was old. Nowhere near as comely as Lord Chetwynd."

Gilda nodded her understanding. "The man my father chose for my future husband had lost his wife and needed help raising his young children. I begged to stay at Saint Ives for a few more years. Then at fourteen my father again tried to persuade me to marry. By that time I knew I never wanted to leave the convent. There was a terrible row, but my father finally accepted my decision."

"Did you experience a spiritual calling?" Isabel asked, thinking about her own lack of such feeling.

"I don't recall any divine revelation, if that's what you mean. I was more attracted by the way of life at the convent. We're not as isolated from the world as you might think. Since we're near Aachen, the location of the king's favorite palace, we have visitors almost every night.

"Many of the children who come to us to be educated have families in various parts of the empire. From them we hear stories of family life in places as far away as Rome and Bordeaux. Children are very observant, and they love to tell each other tales. Their openness is delightful, and it's a great joy to work with them."

Gilda's expression became more serious. "There is also satisfaction in being a refuge for women who have no other place to go. In some cases their husbands have died; in others the wives have been abandoned."

Gilda stopped her story abruptly. "I'm talking too much. You really should rest, Lady Isabel."

"No. Please, go on." Isabel was fascinated by Gilda's tale. She had never met anyone like her. "Why are the women abandoned by their husbands?"

"All right. Lie down. I'll talk for a few more minutes if you promise to go to sleep."

Isabel thought those might be the words Gilda used often with the young girls she taught, and she nodded agreement.

"The most common reason for abandonment is failure to bear children. We also shelter women who have been accused of adultery. Husbands are sometimes quick to seek a divorce for either adultery or barrenness, especially if they have concubines who have borne them children.

"In the cases where the husband obtains a divorce, the women are often set adrift. Through my acquaintance with these women, I have become somewhat of an ally in divorce cases. Last year when the bishops were deciding one particularly involved case, I was called to Aachen to give evidence."

"What happened?"

"The count received his divorce. But I was able to secure a settlement for the wife. It worked out for the best, because it wasn't a good marriage."

"Is it difficult to obtain a divorce?" Isabel asked.

"Yes. The church doesn't allow them often."

"How about an annulment?"

Gilda paused, no doubt wondering if Isabel had a personal interest in the matter. "An annulment is fairly easy to obtain if the marriage has not been consummated."

Isabel nodded and rushed to change the subject. "Your vocation is certainly different from what I imagined, Gilda. I thought it would be a quiet life, spent in prayer. The opposite seems to be true. My life has been very sheltered by comparison." When Gilda raised her eyebrows, Isabel smiled and added, "Well, at least until recently."

"Saint Ives is almost too worldly at times, especially for the nuns who seek a more spiritual vocation. But for me it's exciting and satisfying. I suspect I have more independence than most wives."

Isabel thought about her marriage to Chetwynd. If it was annulled, life as a nun seemed a better alternative than making another match. She had begun to suspect that Chetwynd cared for her, but she couldn't be sure how strong his feelings were, and he had made it clear he didn't wish to be married.

"I'm not sure how much Chetwynd has told you about our marriage, Gilda. It's not a conventional match. I wished to leave Narbonne, and we married so that I could travel with the caravan." Isabel decided not to speak further of Chetwynd's reason for marrying her. "The marriage is to be annulled when it has served its purpose." Isabel noticed Gilda's eyes widen at her words.

"I suspected there was something unusual in your hasty match, but I admit I wouldn't have judged your marriage to have been based on convenience alone."

Isabel smiled and stared at the fire to avoid Gilda's eyes.

"I think exhaustion is taking its toll, Isabel. Things will look better in the morning. Just let me suggest that you not give up on Chetwynd. He was hurt by the first woman he loved, a situation that would make any man cautious."

Isabel was tired, but she couldn't let Gilda's casual comment go unquestioned. "What do you mean, Gilda?"

"We'll talk tomorrow."

"Please tell me."

Gilda sighed, sorry she had brought it up. Of course Isabel would want to know what happened. "Last story, Isabel. When Chetwynd was very young, he was in love with Theresa, a young woman who came to be educated at my father's manor. I was only about ten and was still living at home. When Chetwynd went away to join the household of Count Jonas, he thought he had an understanding with Theresa that she would wait for him. While Chetwynd was away, my mother died. My father had his eye on Theresa, and he asked her father for her hand in marriage.

"I expected Theresa to refuse the match, but she was young and ambitious. Chetwynd was a third son and not likely to have much of an inheritance. Theresa married my father. Maybe you can understand why he is slow to trust his feelings."

Isabel nodded and closed her eyes.

"I think we have talked enough for one evening. Now it's time for you to sleep, my dear. Marianna and I will sit by the fire in case you need anything."

"Thank you for telling me about Theresa, Gilda."

Although Isabel was bone-weary, she still couldn't fall asleep. Gilda had urged her not to give up on Chetwynd, but Isabel knew his reluctance to take a wife went beyond his memory of Theresa. There was also the beautiful Queen Judith.

Isabel wondered if Gilda knew about Chetwynd's involvement with the queen. If she did, she hadn't given any hint of that knowledge. Gilda had made it clear that her life at Saint Ives was not an isolated one, a fact that gave Isabel reason to suspect she knew about her brother's latest love affair.

Isabel had expected Chetwynd to come see her, which was one of the reasons she had fought going to sleep for so long. After finding her at the aqueduct, Chetwynd had been tender and loving, practically carrying her down the steep riverbank. When he judged her to be too tired to ride the horse they had brought for her, he mounted his and instructed Ingram to lift her up to ride in front of him. Isabel had almost objected to being declared too feeble to ride, but then realized she wanted to be as close as possible to Chetwynd.

Isabel remembered the feel of Chetwynd's arms around her waist and his strong thighs against the back of her legs. Although she had been cold at first, his body heat soon warmed her. In the saddle he was only slightly taller than she was, and he leaned his face against her hair. She had relaxed against his body, taking comfort from his heat, the dusty smell of his clothes, and the beat of his heart.

They had traveled in silence, the motion of the horse soothing them while the growing darkness seemed to wrap around them, protecting them from the rest of the world. The sensation was so private and glorious that Isabel wanted their journey to go on forever.

They had arrived at the convent much too soon to suit her. Although Chetwynd left her in the care of the women, she had been sure he would come by to see her. But perhaps she'd misjudged him, making more of his tenderness than he meant to convey. She pushed away the thought and concentrated on her memory of his body.

UPON THEIR ARRIVAL AT THE CONVENT, CHETWYND experienced a strong urge to ride away with Lady Isabel. The hour he spent holding her close was the most contented hour he had spent in a long time. Nothing else seemed to matter but the woman he held cradled in his arms. As long as he held her, Isabel seemed safe and a part of his life.

Although he hated giving up those feelings, he knew her injuries needed to be cared for, as she was both hurt and dirty. He would have preferred to tend to her himself, washing her body with warm water, feeding her some fresh fruit, and kissing her bruises. But he knew he had no right to indulge his fantasies. He had duties to attend to, and he could hardly deprive Marianna of the pleasure of nursing Isabel.

Chetwynd had reluctantly released his hold on Isabel, promising himself he would get to the bottom of the danger which had threatened her life, and might still threaten her. Once separated, he felt like a part of him was missing, the part that gave him warmth and contentment.

He consoled himself by turning to the other person he cared for and was concerned about. Like Isabel, Jerome was bruised and dirty, but he was also alert and hungry. It was quiet in the communal dining hall, as most of the nuns and their guests had retired. But food was quickly found for the returning men. Chetwynd and Ingram watched Jerome attack the meat and bread in front of him, while they picked at their own food, holding back the many questions they wanted to ask.

Finally, Chetwynd could no longer restrain himself. "Tell me exactly how you found Lady Isabel."

"It was by chance, my lord," Jerome replied, taking a long drink of cider to prepare himself to relate the story.

"From atop the canyon, I was looking for a sign of the outlaws when some movement on the opposite hill caught my eye. I crossed the river and climbed the bank. I was careful to circle far away and above where I saw movement, my lord. From there I worked my way along until I was above the outlaws. I could hear one of them talking to Lady Isabel, so I knew she was there."

Once started, Jerome needed no further encouragement. "I planned to do what you said. Return to tell you."

Jerome knew Chetwynd expected his men to follow orders. He rushed on. "Before I could get away, I saw one of the men was leaving. I didn't want to meet up with him. I had found a hiding place, so I waited until he had a good start. By that time it had become dark. I was ready to leave when I heard something. I was afraid I had been found out. Imagine my surprise when I spotted Lady Isabel climbing toward me." He shook his head as though he still couldn't believe it.

"You already told us how she managed to free herself. Why didn't you try to return then?" Chetwynd prompted.

"The outlaws were searching for her. I pushed her into the hiding place. The outlaws came nearby several times. We hid in the dark hole and prayed they wouldn't stumble on us. They didn't know Lady Isabel had help. Maybe they thought she fell in the river and drowned."

Jerome must have observed Chetwynd's involuntary grimace at this possibility, so he hurried on. "Lady Isabel knew better than to head for the river. We stayed hiding during the night, waiting for daylight. I would have returned as you ordered me, but I didn't think it best. I'm sorry you had to be worried about her for so long."

Chetwynd was aware that Jerome was watching to see what his response would be. "I was worried about both of you. But you did right, as I'm sure you know. To do otherwise would have put Lady Isabel in danger. No one with any sense obeys orders when it's obvious that circumstances have changed. Now go on. Can you tell us anything about the out-laws?"

Jerome relaxed and continued. "They were dressed poorly, almost in rags. But I suspect that was a disguise. Their horses were tied outside the cave, and I saw that they were strong and in good shape. I crawled close enough to see that the saddles were of fine leather and well-made. I doubt they were poor men, my lord."

"What about their age or other distinguishing marks?" Ingram asked.

"I didn't get close enough to see the men as they re-treated to a cave. Lady Isabel can tell you more. Nothing gets by her. She figured out the wine was drugged and didn't drink it." His eyes were shining with admiration as he spoke.

Then his face darkened. "The man who struck her did it before I got there. It's a good thing I wasn't there. I would have given myself away by rushing to her rescue as you did all those years ago, my lord."

The words had slipped from Jerome's mouth. While In-gram looked puzzled, Chetwynd's face tightened noticeably. Jerome must have known he had said more than he should have. He rushed on, "Neither one of us could sleep, and we talked to pass the time. Lady Isabel told me the story."

"What else did you talk about?" Chetwynd snapped, fear-ful of the confidences that might have been shared.

"Just my own story, my lord. About how I joined your troop. Lady Isabel asked how I became your squire. It was after that she told me how you rescued her when she was just about my age."

Chetwynd relaxed. It was foolish to think Isabel would give Jerome intimate details or that he would spread tales. He knew he owed the young squire a huge debt of gratitude.

"You did well, Jerome. Your observations may help us

discover the outlaws. And I'll never be able to thank you enough for what you did to help Lady Isabel."

Although Ingram must have been puzzled by the exchange between Chetwynd and Jerome, he didn't inquire about it. Instead he asked, "Do you have any idea which way the outlaws went?"

"No, I believe they left in the night. If I had been on my own, I would have tried to pick up some clues at their cave, but I didn't want to delay moving Lady Isabel to safety. It took us a long time to travel, as she was hurt and we were both tired."

"You acted wisely," Chetwynd assured him. "They will be long gone by now, Ingram. From what Jerome has told us, I think we can assume the kidnappers were not common bandits stealing to feed their families.

"Marianna recognized the merchant, and he left here in a suspicious manner. If the outlaws were soldiers hired by my enemies, we do have someone to watch for. He may not suspect we are on to him."

Chetwynd moved restlessly in his seat, eager now to look in on Isabel. "In the meantime, I think we should delay our departure for a day to make sure Lady Isabel is rested and healing properly. Then I will persuade her to stay here while we go on to the palace."

When both Jerome and Ingram looked surprised at his words, Chetwynd defended his decision. "The convent is the safest place for Lady Isabel until we know more about the kidnappers. After her experience, I'm sure she will want to rest in a safe place."

"Lady Isabel does not frighten easily," Jerome commented. Then when he saw the frown Chetwynd directed at him, he added, "I'm sure you know best, my lord."

Chetwynd ignored his words and turned toward Ingram.

"Perhaps we should send the rest of the men on to their homes. If Lady Isabel stays here, we don't need them for protection. After resting a day, the three of us can travel to the palace on our own."

Ingram delayed his answer until Jerome had left for his bed. Then he spoke up. "I think you should wait until you speak with Lady Isabel before you make a final decision about leaving her behind, my lord. You promised to take her to her brother."

Although Chetwynd resented being reminded of his promise to Isabel, he knew Ingram was right. If there was one thing they had all learned about Isabel, it was that she had a strong will and a mind of her own. He would have to be careful how he approached the subject of leaving her behind. He nodded to acknowledge Ingram's warning, but didn't comment further.

"I'm curious, Chetwynd. What's the story Jerome was talking about? You never mentioned that you knew Lady Isabel before we arrived at Narbonne."

"I didn't know her. Not really. Eight years ago, I kept four soldiers from attacking a young maiden in a meadow. It turned out to be Lady Isabel. When we arrived at Narbonne, she remembered me."

"And you, did you remember her?"

Chetwynd raised his eyebrows. "I remembered a feisty little maid who fought off one of the soldiers, giving him a vicious bite on the hand when he dared to touch her."

"She hasn't changed much," Ingram said.

Chetwynd nodded. "I suppose you're right."

After wishing Ingram a good rest, Chetwynd went directly to Isabel's bedchamber. Marianna and Gilda were dozing in front of the fire, but they awoke when he entered the room.

"Thank you for watching over Lady Isabel. Go to your beds now. I'll stay with her," he said, pointing to a bench along the wall. "I can sleep there."

The two women looked at each other, and Chetwynd was afraid they might insist on staying. He wanted to have Isabel to himself for a while. But neither woman objected, and Marianna was indiscreet enough to smile her approval.

Alone at last with Isabel, Chetwynd knelt beside her bed. She lay on her back with the blanket pulled up to her chin. In spite of the discolored cheek, her face, surrounded by a mass of curly hair, looked peaceful. He breathed in the lemon scent of her hair and closed his eyes at the pleasure it gave him. He had planned to rest on the bench, but he couldn't move away. Settling into a more comfortable position kneeling at the edge of her bed, he rested his head on his arms. With his face close to hers, he listened to her breathing and couldn't imagine a more reassuring sound.

WHEN ISABEL TRIED TO MOVE IN HER SLEEP, SHE felt something holding her head in place. She opened her eyes and discovered Chetwynd had his arm on her hair. He was asleep, slumped beside her bed. She thought about how tired he must have been to fall asleep in such an awkward position. She held her head still so as not to wake him.

His head was buried in his arms, his golden hair mingled with her own dark curls. Although she did not wish to disturb him, Isabel could not resist touching his hair with her free hand. While her hair was made up of tight curls that gave resistance when you tried to pull your fingers through them, his tresses were rose-petal soft. There were no tangles to keep her fingers from sliding through the silky locks.

At her touch, Chetwynd turned his head to look at her. It was early morning, and there was just enough light for Isabel to see his face. His expression was still soft and relaxed from sleep.

"Would you come into bed and hold me?"

Her voice was a whisper that pulled at Chetwynd's very soul. He halfheartedly tried to decline. "I don't think it's a good idea, my lady." In spite of his words, he laid his hand on her throat and felt the pulse beating there.

"I'll turn my back. You are fully clothed, my lord."

Because Isabel turned away from him and moved over in the bed, she missed seeing his smile. She pulled her knees up, hoping to remind him of how he held her on the horse. She gave a sigh of relief when she felt him raise the blanket and move onto her bed.

Chetwynd positioned his body behind hers and moved one arm around her. As his hand rested below her breasts, he became very aware of the fact that her night shift was much thinner than the clothes she had been wearing when they were on his horse. Her rounded breasts rested on his arm, and he couldn't help cupping one of them. When she snuggled back against him, Chetwynd was afraid he might go mad. He was fully awake now.

To distract himself from the soft body that was arousing his own, he whispered in her ear, "You told Jerome I rescued you from soldiers."

"Yes," she murmured, her voice husky with satisfaction. "We talked through the night. He told me how you and Ingram rescued him from life as a robber. You are a very chivalrous man, my lord."

He didn't feel like a chivalrous man. In fact, all he could think of was turning the woman he held so tenderly onto her back and burying himself deep inside her. He reminded himself that she was a virgin. If he did what he wanted to do, it would give her more pain than pleasure.

As his own tension grew, he could feel Isabel relaxing. He willed himself to do the same. If he could lull her to sleep again, he could back out of her bed. He moved his hand away from her breast and gently rubbed her stomach. He had seen mothers do this to put their babies to sleep.

But Isabel was not a baby, and Chetwynd could tell she was far from being lulled. She moved her own hand on top of his and pressed it against her. She might be a virgin, but she was aware of the erotic potential of her body. When she directed his hand lower, he knew where she wanted him to go. Through her shift her mound felt hot and moist.

Pushing that thin bit of clothing aside, he rubbed her gently, tantalizingly, until she was moving against his hand in a more desperate and increasing rhythm. She turned her head into her pillow to bury her moans. Unable to refuse her the release she sought, Chetwynd increased the pressure of his caresses. It wasn't long before he felt the small contractions against his hand.

Isabel lay still for a long time. She was too embarrassed to take her face out of her pillow. She had talked him into her bed. He had given her pleasure, but taken none for himself. She tried to keep him from turning her face to look at him, but she wasn't strong enough.

"What's the matter?" he asked, although he thought he knew.

"I shouldn't have talked you into my bed. You can go now." Her voice was a whisper, and she wouldn't meet his eyes.

"Isabel, you have nothing to be ashamed of. You have a lovely, sensual body. It's a pleasure just to touch you."

"But you don't desire me." She looked at him then, and her eyes were incredibly sad.

"Is that what you think?"

Chetwynd pulled her against him, allowing her to feel his aroused body. His mouth found hers, and he kissed her with all the passion he had held in check. His mouth moved on hers until she opened her lips, giving him the access he desired.

It was a long time before he stopped making love to her mouth, tasting her and tangling his tongue with hers. Isabel felt her desire for him growing again and groaned when he pulled back and looked into her eyes.

"I want you, Isabel. I've wanted you from the moment I saw you moving in the pond. But you're a virgin, and there are things I must settle before I can change that. We need to wait."

Her eyes shone. "You desire me." It was a statement, not a question, and she tried to move closer again.

"Yes, I do." He held her away. "Did you hear the rest? We need to wait," he repeated.

"How long?" she asked as she placed her hand on his chest and felt his heart beating wildly.

He rolled his eyes and grimaced. "I hope not too much longer."

CHAPTER ELEVEN

ISABEL WATCHED CHETWYND LEAVE HER bed. He kept his back to her as he straightened his clothes. Although Chetwynd had made a point of showing that he desired her, she couldn't help but wonder if she understood his meaning. She hoped he wanted to be her husband in every sense, but perhaps he only wished to satisfy his physical need. Isabel longed to ask him a question that would clarify his intent, but she was embarrassed by what had just happened. She had practically begged for his caress. Feeling self-conscious, she decided to wait until he left the room to leave her bed.

"Will we be leaving Saint Ives soon, my lord?" she asked.

When Chetwynd turned to face her, Isabel was sitting up with the blanket pulled up to her chin and her hair a wild tangle that reminded him how good it felt when he grasped a handful. He knew he'd have to move much farther away, preferably to another room, if he wished to avoid being tempted back into her bed.

Chetwynd had meant to tell her they were delaying their journey, but when Isabel awoke and pleaded with him to join her in bed, he had forgotten everything else.

"We are staying here for a day to make sure you're rested." His voice was a little hoarse, and he cleared his throat. "I meant to tell you earlier."

"I don't need to rest, my lord. I'm ready to travel. I know how eager everyone is to reach their homes."

Chetwynd watched her drop the blanket and start to rise. He cursed under his breath as he observed her rosy nipples and rounded breasts through the thin shift.

"We're not leaving today, so get back under the covers, Isabel," he ordered.

His terse command was enough to send her scurrying under the blanket, and he almost smiled at the sight. Thankful that she was covered, he changed his tone. "We're near to Aachen, and I'm sending my men on ahead. You aren't delaying anyone. After I complete an errand, I'll come back."

Isabel frowned. "You didn't have to shout."

Had he shouted? he wondered. No doubt he had. "No, I didn't have to shout. I'm sorry. I have a surprise for you. I'll send Marianna to help you get ready. You look much improved after your rest, and we're going for a short ride."

Isabel perked up immediately at his words. When she flashed him a smile, Chetwynd quickly left the room. Isabel wondered at his great hurry and puzzled over what his surprise could be.

Marianna arrived with fresh baked bread to tempt Isabel out of bed, only to find her mistress already searching through her clothes.

"I thought you'd want to stay in bed and rest today, my lady. I understand we aren't continuing our journey until tomorrow."

"Chetwynd is taking me for a ride, Marianna. I need to be ready when he returns for me."

"You do look much improved, but I wonder if going for a ride is wise. I understood we were delaying a day so that you can regain your strength."

"Don't worry yourself, Marianna. I suspect wherever Lord

Chetwynd is taking me is not far. I want to wear something nice today." She looked at herself in the glass and made a face. "Look how my bruise has turned black and yellow. Do we have any powder we can use to cover it?"

"I think I can find some, although I doubt anything will cover it completely. You are in good spirits, my lady. Did something happen last night?"

"Yes, I got a good rest. Now help me prepare for our ride."

"That's not what I meant, and you know it. You heard what Sister Gilda said. A marriage is difficult to annul if it's been consummated, my lady. She is an expert on these matters."

"Marianna, I told my grandmother and I'm telling you, I don't plan to trap Chetwynd."

"Of course not. But things change. I suspect your husband may be more than ready to try and trap you."

Isabel shook her head. "Nothing happened between us last night." At least nothing that you could consider consummating a marriage, she thought. "Please don't say another word about it, Marianna."

Though Isabel protested, she couldn't blame Marianna for her curiosity. But that didn't mean she wanted to confide the fact that she invited Chetwynd into her bed and made it all too clear that she wanted him to make love to her. In the future, she would have to be more careful not to forget herself. She must wait for Chetwynd to indicate he wished to be her husband.

Marianna's disappointed expression caused Isabel to soften her tone. "I know you have my best interests at heart, Marianna. If anything's going to come of our marriage, it's important that it happens because we both want it that way. Now please help me dress for our ride."

WHILE MARIANNA WAS HELPING ISABEL, CHETWYND went in search of Ingram. He found him in the dining hall.

"Is Lady Isabel well this morning?" Ingram asked.

"She is surprisingly fit. But her face has blossomed into color. I wish I could get my hands on the man who did that to her."

"When you finish with him, I'll take a turn."

The thought sobered the two men, and they ate in silence for a while. Other late risers came in search of food, but after seeing the expression on Chetwynd's face, they sat apart, giving the two men privacy.

"At least one of the outlaws knew you, Chetwynd. Have you thought about who might want to act against you?"

"Constantly. I've made enemies, as you well know. The name that springs to mind is Lothar. He is probably my most powerful enemy."

Ingram nodded. "The king's oldest son is bad-tempered, and he is furious with Queen Judith. He made it clear at the Spring Assembly that he objected to the support you gave the queen in her efforts to gain territory for Charles," Ingram said.

"I still believe the queen is within her rights to seek an inheritance for her young son," Chetwynd replied.

"I'm not saying you are wrong to support her, but you have to expect opposition from King Louis's grown sons."

"Charles is their half-brother. They should be willing to see he receives a share of the empire," Chetwynd argued.

Ingram shrugged. "There are other parties who might wish to keep you from using your influence to help the queen, Chetwynd."

"I suppose you mean the church fathers."

"Yes. The bishops had a hand in dividing the empire between Lothar, Pepin, and Louis the Younger. They worked for many years to negotiate a plan for orderly succession, hoping to keep the empire Christian and powerful. They have a strong motive for keeping the division as it is."

"I considered that. But although I have made enemies among religious leaders, I can't think of one who might organize a kidnapping. They are clerics, after all."

"You know that doesn't mean they don't take strong action when they believe it's necessary."

"You're right, and I won't rule them out. Another possibility is Bernard of Septimania. As the king's chamberlain, he works closely with the queen in managing domestic matters. I've thought about him a great deal since we left court. I suspect he was jealous that Judith sought my help on several occasions."

"He's jealous of more than that," Ingram muttered.

Chetwynd couldn't believe his ears. "What did you say?"

Ingram ignored the question. "Bernard has a reputation for conspiracy. I wouldn't put anything past him. I think he and Lothar are your most powerful enemies."

Although his friend hadn't overtly criticized him, Chetwynd couldn't help but blame himself for the mistakes he made. Lothar, Bernard, or even one of the bishops could have reasons for acting against him.

"I admit I've made mistakes, Ingram. But it is unlikely any of the enemies we mentioned know of my marriage to Isabel. We have to look elsewhere for who might be involved in her kidnapping."

"Could someone have followed us from Narbonne?"

"A possibility. In any case, it is clear that I need to do everything possible to keep Isabel safe."

"Have you informed Lady Isabel you're going to leave her at Saint Ives?" Ingram asked.

"No. And don't look at me like that. I'm taking her to the Roman bath at Mainz. I promised her a surprise. I'll have a chance to talk to her there and inform her of my decision."

"Some surprise," Ingram grumbled.

"The surprise is the visit to the bath," Chetwynd said, trying to curb his growing irritation with his friend. "You know how impressed she is by Roman ingenuity."

"You're not going to be able to bribe her with a tour of the bath," Ingram warned. "Lady Isabel will not look favorably upon being left behind."

"A bribe is not what I had in mind," Chetwynd snapped. But of course he had hoped to make her more receptive to his decision. "I just want to do something she'll like. She's been through a lot in the last two days. It should be easier to talk to her in a more relaxed setting, away from the convent."

"I think I should come along. You'll need someone to stand guard if you're going to try the waters. You'll be in a vulnerable position in several ways." Ingram smirked at this thought and added, "We can leave Jerome here to keep an eye on things."

"I was planning to ask you to come. I may need some moral support after telling Isabel I'm leaving her behind," he admitted.

Ingram raised his eyebrow. "You're asking me to help convince her?"

"Try to see my point of view, Ingram. I wouldn't be suggesting Lady Isabel stay at Saint Ives if I didn't think it necessary for her safety. She was lucky to have escaped from the kidnappers, but they may try again. And then there are my enemies at court. Gilda often protects and hides women. She will make sure Isabel is well cared for while we work on discovering who is behind the plot."

Ingram hesitated, clearly considering his answer. "Lady Isabel has already proven she can take care of herself. Are you sure her safety is the only reason you're abandoning her?"

His patience at an end, Chetwynd slammed his hand on the table, causing several heads to turn in his direction. "I'm not abandoning her!"

Ingram merely shrugged at the outburst. "Perhaps that's too strong a word. But I fear that's how Lady Isabel will view your decision." Ingram paused again. "I shouldn't be giving you personal advice, but I have become very fond of Lady Isabel. Just be sure you know what you're doing and why you're doing it. Then tell Isabel the whole truth."

Ingram's advice startled Chetwynd. In all the years they had been together, he couldn't remember him ever advising him about personal matters. Although he suspected Ingram had not been happy about his involvement with Queen Judith, his friend had never said a word.

"It seems everyone has grown fond of Lady Isabel. First Jerome was smitten; now you stand up for her. I understand what you're saying, Ingram. I promise I'll do the best I can to make things clear to Isabel."

Chetwynd knew Ingram had a point. He couldn't put off telling Isabel the truth for much longer. She had already heard gossip about Queen Judith and himself.

"Tell the men they're free to leave, Ingram. Then wait for me at the stables."

Feeling the need for a quiet place to think, Chetwynd headed for the chapel. He and Isabel had missed the morning service. Kneeling, he said a prayer of thanks for Isabel's safe return and sat back on the bench. When Ingram advised him to consider his true reasons for leaving Isabel behind, his friend was hinting that his involvement with Queen Judith might be influencing his decision.

Whatever Ingram might think, Chetwynd no longer had any feelings for the queen beyond the sympathy he felt for her situation. She was a young and beautiful woman married to a much older man who had deserted their marriage bed. The king spent his time and energy on religious retreats, leaving Queen Judith on her own to protect her young son's birthright. When she sought Chetwynd out, he had been eager to help, and later flattered when she invited him into her bed. Even then he had known he wasn't the only one she had granted this boon.

In the garden at Narbonne, he had told Isabel that he had an attachment, when in fact his relationship with Judith was over. But rumors died hard, and his career had been hurt by his involvement with the queen. He had selfishly believed that having a wife would put an end to the gossip. What Chetwynd hadn't thought about was the danger from enemies he had made while helping the queen.

If he had cause before the kidnapping to suspect he had done Isabel a disservice by marrying her, it seemed a certainty now. It was all the more reason to do everything in his power to protect her. Contrary to Ingram's advice, Chetwynd still believed it was important to leave Isabel in a safe place, at least until he knew what he was dealing with at court. But Ingram was right about one thing; he had to tell Isabel the truth about his relationship with the queen.

As Chetwynd arose from the hard pew, he spotted his sister seated at the back of the chapel. Gilda smiled at him, and they left the chapel together.

"You seemed deep in prayer, or perhaps thought. I waited for you to finish," she explained. "How is Lady Isabel today?"

"She's recovering quickly," he replied, thinking about the energy she'd displayed in bed. "I'm taking her to the Roman bath at Mainz."

Chetwynd took Gilda's arm and guided her to the walkway around the cloister garden. There were few people around, but Chetwynd kept his voice low and his eyes alert for eavesdroppers.

"As I'm sure you've heard, we've delayed our journey for a day. I believe Isabel should stay at the convent with you until I can assess the situation at court. I fear she may still be in danger."

When Gilda halted, he had to turn to face her. "Are you sure that's the best plan?" she asked. "I think she would prefer to be with you."

"Yes, I think it's for the best," he replied with a patience he didn't feel. "There are too many people who could have reason to harm Isabel just to spite me."

Gilda shrugged, and they started walking again. Both were quiet while two nuns passed them by. Then Gilda said, "We had a long talk last night, Chetwynd. Isabel told me you plan to have your marriage annulled. I found it hard to believe. When you came to her room last night, I saw the expression on your face. Marianna and I left you alone to care for her."

Gilda didn't continue, but Chetwynd knew the question she was asking. "I'm surprised Isabel told you about us, although I guess I shouldn't be. She is very frank, and I know you're a good listener. Our marriage is still not consummated, Gilda."

His sister nodded. "I'm already fond of Isabel. I wouldn't want her hurt."

Chetwynd interrupted her before she could continue. "Please believe me, I don't want that either."

"I do believe you, Chetwynd. But you didn't let me finish. I don't want you hurt either. Be sure you don't do anything to destroy what you have found with Lady Isabel. She is not Theresa, you know."

Moved by her concern for him, Chetwynd embraced his sister. "I'm well aware of the fact that Isabel is nothing like

Theresa. I will come back for her. Remember that, and reassure her if you think it's necessary."

When Chetwynd finally returned to her room, Isabel couldn't hide her relief. He had been gone for so long that she had been afraid he had changed his mind about their outing.

"Sorry for the delay, Isabel. You look fresh and rested. I see you have managed to hide most of the bruise on your face." He grinned at her as he leaned forward to take a closer look.

"Marianna found what she calls powder. I suspect it's baking flour. Where are we going?"

"There's a Roman bath nearby. I believe you mentioned you'd like to see one."

Isabel's mouth fell open, but no sound came out. She rushed forward, about to throw her arms about his neck, then almost as quickly pulled back.

Sorry that he had made her feel self-conscious about touching him, Chetwynd smiled to put her at ease. "Ingram offered to accompany us. Although it's not far, it's best to be cautious."

Isabel had hoped they could be alone, but she understood Chetwynd's concern for safety. Later, as they rode away from Saint Ives, she felt like a falcon set free to soar across the sky.

"The bath is on the outskirts of Mainz, straight ahead and up that slope," Chetwynd said.

"I'll race you," she answered. Without waiting for a reply, she urged her horse in the direction he had pointed.

Isabel had not exaggerated her ability to ride a horse. Chetwynd remembered how outraged she had been that first night when he suggested she would slow the progress of their journey.

Chetwynd rolled his eyes and spoke to Ingram. "So much for safety. Keep guard at our backs."

It only took a minute to catch up with Isabel, and Chetwynd had to smile at the determination on her face as she leaned over her horse's head, urging him on.

They galloped their horses like children who had been released from their lessons. When Chetwynd pulled ahead of her, Isabel laughed at the sight of his golden hair flying out behind him. She'd noticed he seldom wore a helmet to cover it. They soon left the discreet Ingram far behind.

Only upon approaching Mainz did they slow their horses and stop at the impressive stone building that housed the bath. Chetwynd helped Isabel from her horse, and they climbed the wide stairs to enter on the top level. Once the heavy wooden door closed behind them, it was dark inside.

When Isabel's eyes adjusted to the dim interior, she saw that the upper floor was a walkway around a square opening. Over an ornate railing, they could look down upon the pool of water located below them.

Leaning over the railing, Isabel stared down at the dimly lit green bath. She found it difficult to see the bathers. Clouds of steam swirled above the waters, and figures moved in and out of view. Light flickered from torches mounted on the walls. The steady murmur of pumping water added to the flickering light, and rising steam gave the impression of a mysterious underworld. Isabel was mesmerized, and Chetwynd had to grasp her arm to pull her along.

"The changing rooms are this way. Would you like to try the waters?"

"Are women allowed in the bath?" Even as Isabel followed Chetwynd, her eyes were still glued to the scene below. She couldn't tell if the bathers were men or women.

"Usually women have their own bathing hours, but I doubt anyone will object. We'll stay in the darkest corner."

In a small dressing closet, they stripped down to a single

layer of clothing. Isabel's shift was long, but Chetwynd wore a lightweight shirt that only reached his knees. He took her hand and led her down a narrow staircase to the floor below where they approached the shadowy bathing area.

Still overwhelmed by the steamy atmosphere, Isabel hesitated, but Chetwynd pulled her along toward the bath. True to his word, he led her to the darkest corner, and with the hum of the pump, and the fact the other bathers discreetly ignored them, it felt as though they were alone.

When Chetwynd lowered himself over the side and into the warm water, Isabel saw it just covered his shoulders. She sat on the edge of the tiled pool moving her legs in the water. Impatient to have her with him, Chetwynd reached up, placed his hands on her waist, and pulled her down, causing her body to slide against his own.

By now he should be used to the thrill of holding her, Chetwynd told himself. But each time it happened, he seemed more aware of each soft curve and found it harder to let go. It was Isabel who pulled away and turned her back to him. She paddled through the water, putting a short distance between them.

From the way she moved away whenever he came near, Chetwynd realized that Isabel was determined to keep her distance. He had planned to do his best to resist the temptation to take her in his arms, but Isabel wasn't giving him a chance to practice restraint. For some reason that irked him.

"Do you like the water?" he asked very softly.

"What?"

He spoke even softer. "I said, do you like the water?"

Because the noise of the pump drowned out his words, Isabel moved closer to Chetwynd. "I can't hear you, my lord."

Chetwynd reached out and pulled her against him. For a moment she laughed and struggled, then went still in his arms and whispered, "You tricky knave." She moved her body against his to tease him. The trick backfired when it aroused her as much as it did him. She wondered how she imagined it could be otherwise.

"Do you know what you do to me, Isabel?" he murmured into her ear.

She wrapped her arms around his neck then. "Perhaps we could be very good friends. It would be all right for friends to kiss, I would imagine."

He obliged her, and in her enthusiasm, she wrapped her legs around his waist. The kiss lasted a long time while they leisurely reacquainted themselves with each other's mouths. Isabel returned the thrusts of his tongue. When he seemed to enjoy that, she bit his bottom lip.

Chetwynd groaned into her mouth. Isabel wondered if she had hurt him and stopped the kiss to stare at him. "Are you all right?"

"Not really. We need to talk."

"Right now?" she asked, making her complaint clear by her frown. The last thing she wanted to do was talk.

He reluctantly unwrapped her arms from around his neck and pushed her away. "Yes. Right now, but not in the bath. I'm getting out. You swim for a few minutes more, then follow me to that massage room over there."

Isabel looked where he was pointing and nodded. She didn't have much choice but to do what he requested. When she entered the massage room, she found him wrapped in a large flannel. He held one out to her. She turned her back, slipped out of her wet shift under the dry cloth, and wrapped herself in it. When she turned around, Chetwynd was sitting on a high table against the wall.

As Isabel moved toward him, he separated his legs and made room for her to stand between them. His flannel had slipped to his waist and she stared at his bare shoulder where a large bruise had turned black and blue. "Good lord, I did that," she said, remembering the rock she had aimed at him when she thought he was a kidnapper. Without thinking, she leaned forward to kiss the bruise.

Chetwynd shivered in response to her tender gesture. "We have matching bruises," he said softly. "We've both been marked by this journey."

And not all the marks are visible, Isabel thought as she realized how much her life had changed in the last two weeks. He might have been thinking the same thing, because his face took on a serious expression. "We need to talk."

At the tone of his voice, alarm bells started to go off in Isabel's mind. He clearly had bad news. She pulled back from him, and he let her go. She moved to sit beside him and stared down at his bare feet, waiting to hear what he had to say.

"I'm worried about the kidnapping, Isabel. We haven't made any progress in finding the outlaws responsible."

Isabel interrupted before he could say more. "Perhaps it was just an accident that they happened upon me. It was my fault for lagging behind. Can't we forget about it?"

"They knew my name, Isabel. It was no accident. I've made some enemies at court by siding with Queen Judith and supporting her ambitions for her son. I used my influence to help her and spent a great deal of time in her company." He paused, knowing it was time to tell the truth. "The queen and I were close for a short time. But it ended before I left court."

Isabel's stomach rolled. She realized she had hoped the rumors were false. He hadn't said they were lovers, but the message was clear.

When Isabel kept her head down and didn't reply, Chetwynd continued. "It seems unlikely my enemies at court were responsible for your kidnapping. But that doesn't mean they won't try to injure you to spite me."

Isabel still wouldn't meet his eyes, and Chetwynd was impatient to be done with his explanation, so he rushed ahead. "I want you to stay at Saint Ives with Gilda when I leave tomorrow."

Isabel jumped off the high table. "No!"

"Let me finish, Isabel." She was pacing the floor, but he gripped her arm and held her in front of him. "It's for your own safety. I'll come back for you as soon as I can make arrangements to ensure your protection. I need to talk to Justin."

Unable to pull away, Isabel stared up at him, her eyes blazing. But her voice was steady as she asked, "How long will that take?"

"I can't say."

"That's what I thought. Will I stay here forever? Did you ever mean to take me to court? No, don't shake your head, Chetwynd." Isabel's mind was churning furiously. "I know you think I'm an unreasonable bother. Let me ask you this. Whose side is Justin on in this political situation?"

"Justin tries to stay neutral. As an advisor to the king, he feels it's his job to mediate conflicts."

"And Justin wishes to have me with him, you said as much. You could have accomplished that without marrying me. Well, now you can bring me to Justin, and I'll be safe with him."

Though he knew she was angry, Chetwynd still hoped she would listen to reason. "Isabel, you're still my wife. Bringing you to Justin isn't going to change that. You'll still be in danger."

Isabel was outraged that he would use that argument. "No, I'm not really your wife. You can get an annulment right away on those grounds. You can make it clear to everyone that you have no concern about me, and I'll be safe. In fact, you can take up with Queen Judith again. That will make your position with me very clear to everyone."

Chetwynd shook his head. Both Gilda and Ingram had warned him. Even Jerome had something to say on the matter. Why had he thought she would suddenly become reasonable and willingly accept his judgment?

Chetwynd stared into the fiery brown eyes that were daring him to try and reason further. Then he started to laugh. He was as surprised at his outburst as Isabel was. As he watched her eyes widen and her mouth open, he laughed harder. That was when she made a fist and struck him on his sore shoulder. He stopped laughing to gasp in pain.

Isabel was immediately aghast at what she had done. "Saints alive, that's your sore arm."

Chetwynd wiped a tear from his eye. It was from laughter, not pain. "What am I going to do with you, Isabel?"

His face had softened, and Isabel hoped he was relenting. She moved between his legs and placed her hands on his chest. He watched her fingers move into the pale hairs below his stomach and thought he might stop breathing. Because of the strange roar in his ears, it took him a minute to realize someone was calling his name. He recognized Ingram's voice.

"What is it?" he called out impatiently without taking his eyes off Isabel's face.

"Chetwynd, it's urgent," Ingram called from the other side of the curtain that was pulled across the entrance.

Chetwynd paused another few seconds as he looked at Isabel, then sighed deeply and gently pushed her away. At the entrance he whipped open the curtain and faced Ingram.

Before Chetwynd could say a word, Ingram made a blunt announcement. "Queen Judith has arrived at Saint Ives with her entourage. She has been accused of witchcraft by Bishop Agobard and banished to the convent."

While Isabel struggled to grasp the meaning of his message, she noticed that Ingram was carrying their clothes. He sent an apologetic look in her direction. Behind Ingram she saw Jerome, his eyes directed toward the floor, and realized he must have brought the message from Saint Ives.

Chetwynd grabbed his clothes and addressed his squire. "Jerome, wait for Lady Isabel to dress, then bring her back to the convent."

Before Isabel could say a word, Chetwynd looked at her with a warning scowl. "Don't say anything, Isabel. Just this once, do what I ask of you without argument. Jerome will bring you along as soon as you're dressed."

Chetwynd had no need to worry. Isabel was too startled to object to being left behind. In stunned silence she watched as he strode from the room, still wrapped in a flannel. He closed the curtain behind him so she could dress in private. She wondered vaguely if he would take time to dress, and almost laughed at the thought of his arriving at Saint Ives in his flannel. Then she heard Jerome clear his throat outside the curtain, and hurried to put on her clothes.

CHAPTER TWELVE

*A*N UNEASY SILENCE HUNG BETWEEN JEROME and Isabel as they rode back to Saint Ives at a leisurely pace, neither one of them eager to reach the convent. For the first time, Chetwynd's squire seemed to have trouble meeting her eyes, and his withdrawal hurt and puzzled Isabel. They had been through a great deal together and had become close confidants while escaping from the outlaws.

Determined to break the silence without referring to the present situation, Isabel asked, "Have you ever seen a Roman bath, Jerome?"

"No, my lady."

Since baths were no doubt not open to squires, Isabel was not surprised by his answer, but she hoped to at least spark some interest. "The Roman bath was glorious. The water was warm and steamy. It seemed to support my body so that I could float much easier than in the pond back home. Perhaps it's the minerals in the water. I could smell them and didn't like the smell at first. But I got used to it soon enough."

There was still no trace of the chattering lad she had come to care for. Jerome kept his horse at a slow and steady pace and stared straight ahead.

Isabel became even more determined to elicit a response

from the young squire. "But there was one thing I didn't en-joy. Lord Chetwynd told me he was leaving me at the con-vent while he continued on to Aachen. I lost my temper at the news and struck him with my fist, on his sore shoulder just below the big black-and-blue bruise from when I hit him with a rock. You should have seen his face."

Isabel succeeded in getting Jerome to look at her. With wide eyes and an open mouth he was searching her face to see if she was serious. "You struck him?"

"I did. I might have done it again, but Ingram arrived in time to rescue Chetwynd from further attack."

Jerome shook his head from side to side, his smile back in place. "I told Lord Chetwynd you weren't afraid of any-thing, my lady."

That wasn't quite true, Isabel thought. She was afraid of being abandoned. But events had taken a drastic turn with the appearance of the queen. Would Chetwynd still leave for Aachen as he had planned? Isabel had overheard Ingram tell Chetwynd that the queen had been banished to the convent. It was hard for Isabel to believe she had heard correctly.

"Jerome, can you tell me exactly what happened after we left Saint Ives?"

Jerome thought about her question for a minute, perhaps wondering if his loyalty to Chetwynd would be compromised if he gave her the information she sought. He must have de-cided it wouldn't because he signaled his horse to move closer to hers.

"It was shortly after the noon meal. Two messengers gal-loped wildly into the courtyard. I could tell by their speed that something was afoot. They asked to see the abbess. It wasn't long before word spread that Queen Judith was on her way."

After looking about, Jerome slowed his horse even more

and continued his story. "You should have seen the nuns running about. They were buzzing like a hive of bees.

"I stayed close to the porter, offering to help cool the horses of the messengers. They are especially bred to race long distances, you know. You should have seen them, my lady. Not big like war horses, but thinner and lighter. It must be heaven to ride such a horse."

Isabel nodded. Of course he would notice the horses. "Did you learn anything about why the queen was arriving unexpectedly at Saint Ives?"

There was a slight pause as Jerome shifted his mind from horses to people. "A messenger came to the stable to check on the horses. I overheard him confide that one of the bishops, I forget his name, had banished the queen from court. When the porter questioned him, the messenger said King Louis was on a religious retreat. The bishop acted while the king was away."

"I can see that you have a talent for being in the right place at the right time, Jerome."

She needn't have worried about him going silent again. Jerome was now into his tale.

"In no time, rumors about the queen were flying about. Suddenly there was a great noise in the courtyard. The clatter of horses and clinking of armor brought everyone to attention. A special troop of guards led the way, mounted on giant war horses. They were the queen's escorts."

Isabel stared ahead and tried to picture the scene. If the queen had been banished, would the soldiers be guarding her to prevent her escape, or were they protecting her?

"What about the queen, Jerome? Did she ride a horse?" she prompted. Everyone who had seen the queen always mentioned how beautiful she was. Except for Chetwynd, but then he had said little about her.

"The queen rides in a litter decorated with fancy draperies she can pull for privacy. There were also dozens of servants and many wagons loaded with furnishings. I heard a nun say the queen always brings her own tapestries for the walls and serving dishes for the table. I even saw some fancy chairs tied on top of one of the wagons. You had to see it to believe it."

Jerome painted quite a vivid picture. "Was there any talk of why Queen Judith was banished? Did you hear anything about that?"

"I did hear the word *witchcraft*." Jerome whispered the word, looking around again. Witchcraft was never spoken of casually. "I'm sure it had something to do with witchcraft."

Isabel appreciated the fear the word evoked. The charge of witchcraft, used mostly against women, was a dangerous accusation because it was difficult to defend yourself against it. She shivered at the thought, remembering women in Narbonne who had been accused of performing the devil's work. It was hard for her to believe the charge would be brought against the queen.

On the other hand, Isabel had no doubt the queen had angered religious leaders with her ambitions for her son. Her grandmother, who fancied herself knowledgeable about royal affairs, had explained that the bishops' main concern was keeping the Christian empire united under the king's three grown sons. Still it was hard to imagine they would retaliate so strongly.

"Do you think the queen has done something recently to anger the church fathers?" Isabel asked.

He shook his head and shrugged his shoulders. "I heard no rumors. Didn't really have time. Queen Judith spotted me in the crowd at Saint Ives and called me to her."

As soon as the words left his mouth, Jerome seemed to

regret he had spoken them. But he hurried on, avoiding her eyes. "Lord Chetwynd is well-known by everyone at court. The queen asked about him, and told me to find him." Jerome seemed embarrassed by the part he had played.

The queen had recognized Chetwynd's squire. In spite of the information Isabel had already received through gossip, as well as from Chetwynd himself, the intimacy that recognition implied startled Isabel. Now her husband was rushing to be at the queen's side. Isabel reined in her horse, upset enough to think about not returning to the convent.

Jerome rode a short distance until he realized she had stopped; then he turned and rode back to her. "I didn't mean to upset you, my lady."

"You didn't upset me, Jerome," she lied. "Thanks for telling me about the queen's arrival."

Because his unhappy face made it clear that he didn't believe her, Isabel smiled at him. "I'm not going to kill the messenger."

"Good," he replied simply.

Isabel urged her horse forward. "Let's get back to Saint Ives so I can see for myself what's happening." As appealing as not returning to the convent seemed at the moment, she knew it wasn't a real possibility.

Jerome nodded, but he remained silent for the rest of their ride. Isabel was relieved, as she had heard enough.

As soon as they entered the gate, the porter informed Isabel that Gilda was waiting for her in her bedchamber. Lord Chetwynd was nowhere to be seen, but the courtyard was full of activity. There were many newly arrived servants unloading wagons. One of the women greeted Jerome and turned to study Isabel.

Ignoring the woman's open appraisal, Isabel stared at the chairs and tables that awaited placement. Jerome's description had been accurate, but it had not prepared her for the number of people and volume of goods. She wondered if there were enough rooms at the convent to lodge the queen and her followers.

Rushing to her room, Isabel found Gilda and Marianna packing her things. Before she could ask what they were doing, Gilda embraced her warmly, then stood back to peer at her face.

"I can't believe how much better you look today, Lady Isabel. Of course your bruise is still quite colorful. Did you enjoy your visit to the bath?"

"Very much. I wish we could have stayed longer."

"We need more powder for your face, my lady," Marianna remarked.

"I imagine the water washed the powder away," she answered as she looked around the room. "What are you doing here?"

Gilda wrinkled her nose in distaste. "I'm sorry for the confusion. We need this room for some of the queen's party. You can share my chamber for now. Chetwynd asked me to fill you in on what's been happening here. He's busy at the moment, or he'd talk to you himself, I'm sure."

Busy with Queen Judith, were the words Gilda omitted. Isabel nodded to indicate she understood. "I'll help you pack."

Gilda suddenly waved her hand at the disruption in the room and turned toward a bench. "The queen has us all scurrying about. I'm going to sit for a minute so we can talk in peace," she explained.

Isabel smiled, remembering Jerome's description of the nuns. Clearly Gilda didn't enjoy buzzing about like a bee.

"I'll finish up here while you talk," Marianna offered.

As soon as they settled side by side on the bench, Gilda sighed and said, "I'll tell you what I know, Isabel. The queen has been banished from court and is to be cloistered at our convent. Bishop Agobard claims Judith has been bewitched by Gerberga, a nun I have met a few times. The bishop has either persuaded the king, or taken it upon himself—I'm not sure which—to banish the queen. The deed has taken us all by surprise, as you can imagine."

Isabel shook her head. "I don't understand how this could happen. Why would the king agree to the queen's banishment?"

"We don't know for sure that he did, but I can guess at one reason. King Louis is getting old. All he wants to do at this stage in his life is enjoy a little peace and prepare to meet his maker. I have no doubt the king wishes to retire to a monastery himself and leave his grown sons to govern the empire. It's not uncommon for noble men and women to spend their last years in a monastery or convent."

"That may be true, Gilda, but the queen is young."

"Ah yes. That's where the witchcraft charge comes in. No doubt it's meant to force her into a convent.

"Bishop Agobard wishes to rid the court of a powerful queen who upsets his hopes for a united and strong empire. This isn't his first attempt. About a year ago, Bishop Agobard tried to convince the king that Judith had committed adultery with Bernard of Septimania and that Charles was Bernard's son. If his accusation had been believed, Charles would have lost all rights to a royal inheritance."

For the first time, Isabel was beginning to feel sympathy for the queen. "I had heard rumors from my grandmother, but nothing specific. What happened?"

"Fortunately for Judith, Charles bears a strong physical resemblance to the king's grown sons. The queen was able to convince the king the charge against her was false. This latest maneuver to remove her is dramatically different, but the goal is the same."

"Does the bishop have a chance of making this accusation any more believable than the first one?"

"There is background to support the charge. The queen and Gerberga, a nun who resides in Aachen, are close allies. For many years there have been rumors that Gerberga practices black magic and witchcraft. These accusations may have started because she uses her skills as a healer to help women with health problems of various kinds. The most dangerous advice she gives is how to prevent pregnancy and space children. It's a practice the church opposes, as do some husbands."

Isabel nodded her understanding. "There was a woman in our village who was branded a witch for similar practices. My grandmother supported her and saved her from her accusers."

"Yes, unfortunately it's a common story. For the most part, the good that Gerberga does works in her favor. She is very popular among women who fear having children one after the other. Even a few church officials support her work."

Isabel was puzzled. "What does this have to do with Queen Judith?"

"The queen has always supported Gerberga. Bernard of Septimania is the king's chamberlain, and Gerberga is his sister. I imagine he brought them together. I suspect Judith had advice from Gerberga when she wished to conceive a child with an elderly husband. Having a child was important to Judith. It was a way of assuring her position as queen."

Isabel couldn't help being curious. "Are there means of helping with conception?"

Gilda shrugged and smiled at her interest. "So some women believe. But I've never had much faith in potions. The latest rumor is that Gerberga has predicted that Charles will one day take his father's place as Holy Roman Emperor.

Of course the bishops are outraged at this, as is Lothar, the king's eldest son."

"Why would Gerberga make such a dangerous prediction?"

"She probably believes it. Considering this, Charles is a lot younger than his three brothers and may indeed one day be emperor. The abbess knows Gerberga well, and she says the nun is getting old and is unconcerned about her own safety."

"How does her prediction result in the charge of witchcraft?"

Gilda rested her head on the wall as though the story tired her. "Gerberga has been accused of reading the entrails of chickens. It's an old Roman ritual for predicting the future. Of course the church frowns on such practices, but they never really died out completely. Whether Gerberga has been doing this is uncertain, of course, and I myself doubt it."

"So the bishops are using the queen's connection with Gerberga to drive her from court," Isabel said.

"That's the way it seems to me. It's unlikely they will be able to force Queen Judith to take the veil, but they can keep her here for a long time. It has happened before. When Charlemagne died, and King Louis became emperor, the first thing he did was send two of his sisters to a convent. Each had consorted with several men and had several children out of wedlock. It was behavior encouraged by Charlemagne who they say was fond of having grandchildren. But Louis the Pious has different ideas about how women should conduct themselves."

Gilda stood up and brushed at her dark habit. "I have wandered with my explanation, Isabel. Queen Judith will be with us for a while, although I somehow doubt it will be for long. I'm sure she has plenty of resources to call upon for help.

In any case, being sent to a convent is not the worst thing that can happen to a woman."

Isabel nodded, remembering Gilda's own story. "I noticed the queen has brought a great many of her belongings with her. She intends to be comfortable during her stay. Is there room enough at Saint Ives to accommodate her?"

"We'll have to move some people around, including you. But there's also a large guesthouse reserved for royalty when they come on retreats. Queen Judith will be afforded the best accommodations, although I suspect she is already making plans for her return to the palace."

Just as Gilda was preparing to help Marianna move Isabel's belongings, Chetwynd appeared at the door. Isabel noticed that he didn't look in any better humor than when he had demanded that she stay at the bath and return with Jerome. The scowl on his face deepened as he looked at the small stack of Isabel's things that Marianna had piled by the open door.

"What's all this?" he asked.

Gilda spoke up. "We're moving Isabel to my chamber. This is a large room, and it's needed for some of the queen's people."

He nodded abruptly. "You can move her things to my bedchamber," he said.

Chetwynd's reply caused all three women to stare at him. When he saw their reaction, he added, "I'll sleep elsewhere."

As Chetwynd watched Isabel's eyes narrow, he wondered why he never managed to say the right thing.

Lifting her chin in the air, Isabel said, "I prefer to stay with Gilda."

Before Chetwynd could respond, his sister took Marianna's elbow and headed for the door. "We were just leaving. We'll come back later to help with Isabel's things." The two women disappeared quickly.

Staring at each other, Chetwynd and Isabel hardly noticed their departure. Finally, Chetwynd spoke. "That came out wrong, Isabel. I want you near me. I said I'd sleep elsewhere for the benefit of Gilda and Marianna."

As he spoke, Isabel watched weariness replace impatience on his face. She remembered that except for a few hours kneeling at the side of her bed, he hadn't slept the previous night. But she felt too vulnerable to let herself soften. "Did you tell the queen that you are married?"

"No. There is a crisis in progress, in case you haven't noticed." He closed his eyes then, and for a moment there wasn't a sound in the room. "I'm sorry I don't know why I can't get this right. Please allow your things to be moved to my bedchamber. I have a lot of explaining to do. But please believe me, right now is not the time. Did Gilda fill you in on the details of what has happened?"

"Yes. I think I know most of the story."

"Good. Did she tell you about Gerberga?"

"Gilda said she's a nun and a friend of the queen's. I know she has been accused of witchcraft in the past."

Chetwynd nodded. "In this case, she has been accused of bewitching the queen, encouraging her to believe that Charles will inherit his father's empire. We just received word that Gerberga has been executed."

Isabel could see the anger in his eyes. "Does Gilda know? She was just telling me about Gerberga," she asked.

"The abbess will speak to the nuns later. She wants to handle telling them in her own way. The queen doesn't know either, but the abbess confided in me. I'm telling you because I want you to understand how serious this matter is."

She moved a step closer to him. "Is the queen in danger?"

"I don't think so. I'm sure Gerberga's fate was meant as a warning for the queen, but the poor woman is dead, and her execution is a terrible shock to the many people who knew her. It shows how desperate Bishop Agobard has become. Although I doubt anyone would dare harm the queen, he has kept Charles at court as an added threat."

"How terrible. The queen must be frantic at being separated from her son."

"The queen believes Charles is safe, and she's probably right. He is with his nurse, who also happens to be a close relation of the king. The nurse adores Charles and will take good care of him. From the queen's point of view, it's best that he remain at court with his half-brother Lothar. She reasons that if any harm comes to Charles, Lothar would be blamed. He can't afford to have anything happen to the queen's son." Chetwynd spoke as though he might not agree with her view.

"What do you think, my lord? Is the boy safe?"

"I hope so. I wish the queen would at least pretend to give up her determination to advance Charles. But she remains defiant, believing that Lothar wouldn't believe her in any case. I suppose she's right."

They had been standing in the middle of the room, but Chetwynd moved to lean against the wall as though he suddenly needed support. The action emphasized his weariness, and Isabel moved closer to put her hand on his cheek. She felt his body relax at her touch.

"I'm deeply involved in this matter, Isabel." His words were full of regret.

Isabel answered softly and simply, "I know."

The compassion in her voice and on her face loosened something inside Chetwynd, and he reached out to pull her against him, wrapping his arms around her. He had always desired Isabel, but what he felt at that moment was more comfort than erotic craving. It was peace and support and perhaps love. Amazed that he could experience such emotions with a woman, he groaned when Isabel tried to pull back.

"Not yet, not yet. I need you in my arms a little longer," he murmured, kissing her forehead, afraid to break the spell.

Isabel stayed in his embrace. As much as she enjoyed the sweet closeness, Isabel was frightened by the despair with which he spoke of his involvement. Finally, she whispered against his cheek, "What happens next, my lord?"

Her question dragged him back to the present, but he didn't loosen his embrace. "I need your help, Isabel. The queen has asked to see you."

Her eyes widened. "Why would she want to see me? Does she know I'm your wife?"

"She knows."

"But you said you didn't tell her."

"I didn't have to. By the time I arrived, she knew of our marriage and that you are Justin's sister. The queen is good at discovering things," he said. "Especially if there might be some advantage to her in the knowledge," he added.

"Is Justin somehow involved in this affair?"

"I doubt it very much. But the queen views him as someone who can help her. She's probably right. Justin's reputation for bringing parties together is greatly respected by both sides in the struggle to ensure an orderly succession to the throne. I tried to put her off, but she insists she wants to see you."

"But why?"

"No doubt she wishes to use you in some way, perhaps to gain Justin's support. I'm going to do my best to keep you out of it, Isabel. But I can't very well refuse to present my wife to the queen."

Anxiety made Isabel's throat tighten. Whatever she might

think personally, Judith was still queen and a powerful woman. "When does this happen?" she managed to ask.

"As soon as possible. She's holding a reception in the dining hall, and it may have already started. You should get ready."

"Get ready? I'll never be ready for this meeting."

Chetwynd smiled at her. "You were so eager to reach the palace. Don't you wish to meet the queen, Lady Isabel?"

"No. Do I have to go?" she asked in a pleading voice.

Chetwynd sobered. "I'm afraid so."

The fact that the queen knew about his marriage had Chetwynd wondering if she might pose a threat to Isabel. The idea haunted him. "I'm very sorry that our marriage has involved you in this matter, Isabel. I vow to do my best to keep you out of harm's way."

"Are you referring to your intention to leave me at the convent while you travel to Aachen?" She put some space between them so she could watch his face.

"No. We're going to stay together, Isabel. I gave up the idea of leaving you behind when you struck me at the Roman bath. Lord, that hurt."

"I really had forgotten about your bruise, my lord. I must have been blinded by anger. I'm so sorry."

"I deserved it. Everyone warned me against trying to leave you behind. I should have listened."

"They did?" Isabel couldn't help being cheered at this news.

"I won't leave you, Isabel. You're my wife and you stay with me."

Isabel wasn't sure how much to read into his answer, but she hugged him tightly and buried her face on his chest to hide the tears that sprang to her eyes at this happy news.

"No tears, my lady," he said, lifting her face and gently

wiping the tears away with his fingers. "Now listen to me. I have no idea what the queen will ask of you. Try to follow my lead in answering her request. Whatever happens, we stay together. I promise you that."

As though to emphasize his point, he kissed her. Chetwynd finally forced himself to gently release his hold on her. "We can't delay any longer, Isabel. Do you want to change your gown and perhaps put some powder on your bruise?"

Isabel had forgotten everything at his vow that they would stay together. Now she was startled back to reality. She remembered Jerome's description of the luggage the queen had carried with her and imagined her many fine gowns "I can't go like this."

Isabel looked down at herself. At the bath she had thrown on her clothes, and they were already wrinkled and smelly from riding a horse. She had no intention of appearing before the queen in her soiled riding clothes.

"I'll find Marianna, and you can get changed. But don't take too long, Isabel."

At the worried expression on her face, he wove his hands into her thick hair and made her look at him. "You're going to do fine, Isabel. Just remember this. The queen wants something from you. She believes you, and your connection with Justin, can be useful to her. You have an advantage over her because you know that. We'll deal with this together."

Isabel gave him a tentative smile. "I like the sound of that, my lord."

"Just one word of warning. The queen is good at using people. Be careful, my love."

At hearing his use of the endearment, Isabel felt like her heart could fly. She would have thrown her arms around him, but he was already headed out the door. If he truly loved her, she knew she would be able to do anything.

CHAPTER THIRTEEN

*L*ADY ISABEL, PLEASE STAND STILL. IT'S difficult to help you into your gown when you keep moving out of my reach."

"Marianna, this gown will never do. Let's try another one."

"You already tried on the only six gowns you have. Dark red is an attractive color on you, and the silk's a fine quality. Sit down and let me adjust the covering for your hair."

"Now that I think about it, I don't believe red is an appropriate color for meeting the queen. I don't want to wear a color that will offend."

Marianna's patience came to an end. "This is a deep red, darker than a ruby and almost brown. There is nothing wrong with the color. You're making a fuss to delay meeting the queen."

Isabel plopped down on the bench. "What do you suppose she wants of me? I suspect she's eager to have a look at Lord Chetwynd's country-bred wife. I'm not eager to be inspected."

"You were nervous the first time you faced the soldiers in your father's dining hall, then again when in the company of lords and ladies at the first manor we visited. Remember those occasions? You charmed everyone, including Lord

Chetwynd." Marianna struggled to confine Isabel's hair under her head covering.

"I don't think you can compare meeting lords and ladies with the queen, Marianna. What am I supposed to say? How should I act? I don't think I can do this."

Marianna took Isabel's face in her hands and turned her head upwards so she could look directly into her eyes. "My lady, in my mind you are worth a dozen queens. I can't give you advice, for I know nothing about royalty. But you, my lady, are resourceful. You figured out how to foil a band of kidnappers. You will figure out what to say and how to act when you meet the queen."

Isabel stood up and hugged Marianna, kissing her on both cheeks before Marianna could pull away. "Now look what you've done, my lady. I'll have to start over on your head covering." In spite of her complaint, Marianna couldn't hide her smile.

There was a brief knock, and Gilda rushed into the bedchamber. "Chetwynd is worried about you. I think he's afraid you might not come. Isabel, you look lovely. That gown is a good choice."

Marianna grinned and nodded at her words.

"Are you sure? I have a forest green gown I could change into if this is the wrong color."

Marianna sighed loudly and Gilda chuckled. "Are you stalling, Isabel? The gown you have on is just fine."

"That's easy for you to say, Gilda. You don't have to worry about how to dress. I'd feel more comfortable in a plain brown habit."

"It does have its advantages. No decisions to make in the morning. Come along, Isabel. Your husband awaits you."

Isabel followed Gilda into the great hall where Queen Judith was receiving visitors. A long line of people waited their turn to greet the queen, and the two newcomers joined in at the end. Isabel was relieved to see her gown was not much different from those worn by the other noblewomen. The last thing she wanted to do was stand out in the crowd.

"We could move to the head of the line. After all, the queen expressed a wish to meet you, Isabel," Gilda reminded her.

"I'd rather wait my turn." She was in no hurry for the meeting. Maybe if she delayed long enough, Queen Judith would become tired and decide to take a rest. The possibility cheered her, and she took time to examine the crowd of people in front of her.

The large group was made up mostly of women. Although they were quietly talking among themselves, Isabel sensed an excited anticipation. Even the nuns were not immune to the flutter. It was hard for Isabel to reconcile their excitement with the fact that the queen had been banished to Saint Ives. Under the circumstances, the festive atmosphere seemed out of place.

Although Isabel could not catch a glimpse of the queen through the crowd, she saw that people at the front were being ushered over to a canopied area. She could hear introductions being made, and a soft, cultured voice speaking in reply. Some people stayed under the canopy only a minute, others longer, then each moved on to make room for the next person in line. Isabel hung back as long as possible, standing a little behind Gilda.

When she was finally close enough to see the queen, Isabel was unprepared for the sight of Chetwynd standing a little behind her. The fact that they shared the same fair coloring and handsome features made them seem like a matched pair. Isabel imagined Zeus and Hera could not have looked more royal sitting atop Mount Olympus. The thought made Isabel's stomach knot uncomfortably.

Chetwynd stood still, his face expressionless and his body at attention. His eyes were the only things that moved, and Isabel pulled back a little so he wouldn't notice her. She concentrated on watching the queen.

In contrast to Chetwynd, Queen Judith was animated, greeting each person warmly as though they were the only one in the room. Isabel could not tell if they were old friends or new acquaintances, as each received the same gracious smile. When Isabel moved nearer, she realized the queen said something personal to each one, asking about their circumstances or inquiring about a member of their family.

The queen came from Saxony, where the women had a reputation for fair complexions. Seated on a raised chair, her regal bearing was displayed to full advantage. Except for a small gold tiara, her blond tresses were uncovered and hung down her back. A vivid-blue, low-cut gown showed off perfectly shaped white shoulders. There was no indication that the royal beauty who dominated the room with the brilliance of her smile had recently been banished from court.

As the line moved nearer, Isabel noticed there were several attendants on the far side of the queen. They seemed to be in charge of making introductions, supplying the queen with information on each person. They also moved the visitors along without giving the impression of hurrying anyone.

Perhaps aware of the charming picture she and Chetwynd presented, the queen turned to favor him with one of her smiles, a little extra sparkle in her eyes to indicate the special connection they shared. At the sight of that smile Isabel closed her eyes, afraid to see if Chetwynd would respond.

Although Isabel had been hiding behind his sister, Chetwynd finally spotted her as she neared the queen. Isabel hung back, clearly unaware of how appealing she looked as she peered around like a curious child with eyes wide and her white teeth chewing her lower lip. Chetwynd grinned as he moved along the line to stand beside her.

"I've been searching the crowd for you. I was afraid you weren't coming," he whispered to Isabel. "You could have moved to the front of the line."

Isabel didn't look at him or bother to answer. In her mind she still saw Chetwynd as he looked standing beside the queen. Although the queen had a reputation for being a great beauty, Isabel still hadn't been prepared for her radiant presence.

While Gilda was being introduced, Chetwynd put his hand under Isabel's arm just above her elbow. She ignored him until he gave her a little shake. She twisted about to glare at him.

"That's better," he said without freeing her arm. "Relax. You're not Daniel entering the lion's den."

Isabel tried to free her arm, but realized she could not dislodge his firm grip without making a scene. At the same time, she was relieved to be rescued from the paralyzing tension she had been experiencing. Her anger at his jest had displaced the dread of coming face-to-face with Queen Judith.

When Gilda moved on, the queen turned toward Isabel. Lord Chetwynd was introducing her, and his words were ringing in Isabel's ears, making her a bit dizzy.

"Your Majesty, may I present Lady Isabel, daughter of Lord Theodoric of Narbonne. Lady Isabel recently did me the honor of becoming my wife."

It took a few seconds for his last words to register with Isabel. She was staring at Queen Judith, who was even more striking up close. But if Isabel was surprised by Chetwynd's words, she was even more surprised by the queen's smile. It was the same gracious smile she bestowed on the many who had gone before Isabel and gave the impression that the queen was hearing pleasant news.

While Isabel bowed her head, Queen Judith spoke in a voice that projected sincerity. "How very nice to meet you, Lady Isabel. I trust your journey from Narbonne was a pleasant one?"

"Yes, thank you, it was," Isabel replied automatically, completely forgetting that she had been kidnapped by a group of outlaws. She congratulated herself on the surprising fact that she managed to say these few words without a stutter or croak.

"At court Lord Chetwynd was a great favorite with the noblewomen, Lady Isabel. I urged him to marry, and I'm happy to see he has finally followed my advice. My best wishes to you both."

Isabel had no idea how to reply to this information, and wondered if it could possibly be true. She knew little of life at court, but it seemed unlikely to her that a woman would urge her lover to marry. Fortunately, the queen didn't seem to expect her to reply, as she hardly paused before continuing.

"I would like to know you better and hear how you managed to capture the elusive Lord Chetwynd. Would you be kind enough to wait behind the others so we can become better acquainted?"

Although it sounded like a request, Isabel suspected it was a command. "Of course, Your Majesty," Isabel agreed, pretending she had a choice, and hoping her expression didn't reveal the anxiety she felt.

"Lord Chetwynd will take you to my chamber. I should not be much longer, Lady Isabel."

The queen spoke as though she were genuinely concerned about keeping them waiting. As Chetwynd led her away, Isabel's spirits lifted. It was over and she hadn't disgraced herself. But upon entering the queen's chamber, Isabel remembered how Chetwynd had looked standing behind the queen. Her sense of relief was short-lived.

"The queen certainly had a great deal to say about your popularity at court, my lord."

Chetwynd ignored her reference to the queen's words. "You're doing fine, Isabel. I knew you would."

Isabel suspected he was patronizing her. "I must say I was surprised at how graciously the queen accepted my introduction as your wife. But then I guess it was her idea that you marry."

"Don't believe all you hear, Isabel. The queen manages to turn every event to her advantage. It's her specialty."

"Yes, I can see that she does. I had the impression she was on a grand tour of convents. She gave no sign she had recently been banished from court."

Isabel remembered the intimate smile the queen had sent Chetwynd's way, and couldn't help resenting the clear signal of their relationship. "The queen's control of her emotions is remarkable. Imagine meeting your lover's new wife, and giving her a gracious smile and best wishes," Isabel commented tartly.

Her words shattered the patience Chetwynd had been working hard to maintain. "I can understand why you're surprised at her control, Isabel. As long as I have known you, I can't remember a time when you made any effort to control your emotions."

Isabel blushed at his remark, but still managed a sharp reply. "You, like the queen, have been a master at controlling your feelings."

Chetwynd rolled his eyes toward the ceiling, searching for strength from above. She was correct, of course. Since he met her he had fought hard to control his desire to lie between her legs.

"I don't want to argue with you, Isabel. I didn't mean that

the way it sounded. In fact, one of the many things I admire about you is the fact that you are so open about how you feel. I enjoy being able to read your emotions on your face. I can't tell you how reassuring I find that trait."

His words surprised her. "Truly?"

"Truly," he replied with a wide smile.

Isabel turned her head away to hide her own smile. She wasn't sure she should forgive him so quickly, so she studied the large room.

"Look at this place," she muttered, waving her hand to indicate the furnishings

Intricate tapestries of rich colors hung on the walls and warmed the room. Placed beneath a lively harvest scene was a chair made of dark wood, its seat padded and its arms decorated with elaborate carvings. Clearly it was the queen's chair, as there were benches arranged on either side. There was no doubt where the attention of visitors would be directed.

"All the comforts of the palace," Chetwynd replied. "The queen doesn't go anywhere without them."

Isabel was still studying the decor when one of the queen's attendants entered the room, followed by the queen herself. Queen Judith's fixed, regal smile was still in place, but to Isabel's eye it was beginning to look a bit strained. She decided to imitate the queen's gracious countenance. Returning the queen's smile with a broad smile of her own, Isabel hoped it looked more sincere than it felt.

After the queen passed by them, headed for her chair, Isabel noticed Chetwynd had raised one eyebrow at her in a questioning manner. She turned her version of the regal smile on him. In response he shook his head and looked heavenward once again.

While the queen's attendant helped her to her seat, adjusting her long skirt and making her comfortable with extra pillows, Judith's demeanor underwent a subtle change. She was as poised as ever and the smile was still in place, but it had become wistful. "I enjoy meeting people, but I'm afraid the circumstances are not as pleasant as I would wish. I'm sure you know, Lady Isabel, that I am not here by my own will."

It was the first sign the queen had given that all was not right with her world. At the mention of her unhappy fate, Isabel was chagrined that she had made fun of the queen's brave smile. She didn't know how she should reply, so she waited for the queen to continue.

"There has been a terrible misunderstanding, but I'm sure that once I'm able to speak with the king, it will be straightened out. Please forgive me if I get right to the point, Lady Isabel. I'm a bit tired from my long journey and meeting so many people.

"You are no doubt wondering why I asked to speak to you in private. Let me be frank. I know your brother, Lord Justin, is one of the king's most trusted advisors. I have a favor to ask of you, Lady Isabel." She stared straight into Isabel's eyes as she continued.

"I beseech you to use your influence with Lord Justin to assure him a mistake has been made, and persuade him to arrange for me to see the king as soon as possible. I know King Louis has begun a religious retreat, but Justin will certainly be able to contact him. I will do everything possible to make your trip to meet your brother easier. Guards will escort you to ensure your safety and speed your journey."

For a minute Isabel was puzzled by the request. Surely the queen could reach Justin without her assistance. Then it occurred to her that Judith had proposed the mission to separate her from Lord Chetwynd. There had been no mention of him. Perhaps she meant to keep Chetwynd by her side. Isabel wanted more than anything to reach Aachen and

Justin, but she hoped the queen wasn't implying that Chetwynd stay behind.

Before Isabel had a chance to form her reply, Chetwynd spoke up. "Your Majesty, may I suggest you send me on this mission. It was only two nights ago that outlaws abducted Lady Isabel. I planned to leave her in the protection of the convent until I can be sure she is no longer in danger. I can travel more quickly to seek out Justin and deliver your message."

Although Queen Judith was still very much in control of her emotions, Isabel could see by the way she narrowed her eyes that she was not pleased by Chetwynd's suggestion. "I appreciate your offer, Lord Chetwynd, but I need you here. I am, of course, most distressed to hear about Lady Isabel's abduction. But she is here, so the incident must have been resolved successfully.

"I do not wish to put Lady Isabel in danger, and I would not ask her help if this were not an urgent matter. I feel confident the guards I employ can protect her. Perhaps much better than she has been protected so far."

Isabel's eyes widened as she realized this comment was meant as an attack on Chetwynd's ability to do the same. She had been right about one thing, the queen intended to keep Chetwynd with her.

Chetwynd's reply was uncompromising. "I know this is a serious matter, Your Majesty. But Lady Isabel has not been to court before, and I think I can be more effective in this situation. You can trust me to serve your interests."

"I know you wish to help, Lord Chetwynd. The best way you can do that is by staying here where I need you."

The queen and Chetwynd were staring intently at each other, engaged in a battle of wills. Isabel was suddenly furious at being discussed as though she were not present.

"Your Majesty, I'm sure your guards can protect me from

any danger. I will be pleased to carry your message to Lord Justin." Isabel spoke boldly, strengthened by the anger she felt at Chetwynd for ignoring her and reverting to his plan to leave her behind.

Chetwynd and the queen looked at her in surprise. Then, clearly satisfied that her will had prevailed, the queen's regal smile was back in place. Chetwynd kept his face expressionless, but his narrowed eyes had turned dark. Isabel quickly looked away from him.

Queen Judith spoke up before Chetwynd had a chance to argue further. "You are very brave, Lady Isabel, and I appreciate your offer. I am sure you are looking forward to seeing your brother again. I know you will be successful in your mission. Since it is too late for you to leave tonight, I will make arrangements for you to leave early in the morning. This has turned out very well, indeed. Lord Chetwynd is fortunate to have found you, Lady Isabel. My best wishes to you both."

Isabel realized at once that she had been manipulated. Chetwynd had warned her about the queen and asked her to follow his lead. Instead she had let her anger get the better of her. Now she couldn't look at Chetwynd because she knew she hadn't given him the trust he had asked for.

"I will speak to the leader of my guards immediately, and he can arrange your trip to Aachen, Lady Isabel. Thank you for your cooperation in this matter." The queen made it clear the interview was over.

Isabel bowed her head and hurried from the queen's chamber. She had thought Chetwynd might stay behind with the queen, but he was right on her heels. She continued on to her room, eager to be alone and think about what had happened. But Chetwynd followed her into her bedchamber, and she jumped when he slammed the door behind them.

Knowing that she had betrayed him in some way, Isabel

reluctantly turned toward him. She was surprised to see that anger had disappeared from his face and resignation had taken its place.

"I'm sorry, Chetwynd. I should have followed your lead as you asked. Instead I allowed the queen to lead me along the path she designed."

"Don't blame yourself, Isabel. You were manipulated by an expert," he said, his voice sounding weary.

"Were you planning to leave me behind as you told the queen?"

"No, I promised I wouldn't. You're going to have to trust me in the future."

Isabel nodded. "I could tell I'd made a mistake almost at once. It was the fact that you both seemed to forget I was there that made me react as I did. I was sure you meant to leave me."

Chetwynd nodded his understanding. "We were both manipulated, Isabel. I got drawn into a battle of wills with the queen. And I should have known better. If I had gone along with her request, we could have left the room and worked out a reason why you couldn't go. So much for hindsight."

"What do we do now? Have I ruined everything?"

Chetwynd began to pace. "No, of course not. We'll think of something."

He was still pacing when they heard a soft rap at the door. Chetwynd signaled her not to answer. He didn't wish to be disturbed until he had a plan.

But there was another rap, and they heard Ingram's voice. "Lady Isabel, I must speak with you."

When Isabel opened the door, Ingram didn't look surprised to see Chetwynd. "I thought I might find you here."

"I'm glad you came," Chetwynd answered. "We need your help."

"I had a purpose in seeking you out, my lord. Marianna

spotted the leader of the kidnappers again. He must be very bold to have returned to Saint Ives. He has shaved his head and is elegantly dressed, but I'm sure it's the same man she pointed out to me earlier. He must not be aware of the fact that we spotted him the first time. His reappearance has complicated matters."

"What do you mean? Did you seize him for questioning?"

"No, my lord. That was impossible. You see he belongs with the queen's party."

"Damnation." Chetwynd's face clouded with anger. "Are you sure?"

"I'm afraid so. That was one connection we didn't consider."

Chetwynd shook his head. In spite of this news, he didn't see how Judith could have been involved in the kidnapping.

"There could be some other explanation, Ingram. The same agent might be employed by someone else and is keeping an eye on the queen."

Chetwynd knew he couldn't rule out the possibility that the queen had been involved somehow in Isabel's kidnapping. But it was hard to imagine her motive or how she could have known of his marriage. They had been lovers only briefly, and he never had the impression that she was the jealous type. On the other hand, it seemed important to Judith to surround herself with strong, admiring men who might help her, and the queen had just proved that she was determined to keep him with her.

Isabel put her hand on his arm, and he realized he had been staring into space. "We can't be sure what the kidnapper's association with the queen means," he told her, then turned to Ingram.

"We have another problem. The queen has asked Lady Isabel to approach Lord Justin on her behalf. The reason she gave for her request is that she desires Justin to contact the king and convince him to give her a hearing. Judith wants me to stay here while Isabel goes to Aachen, protected by some of her guards, of course. They are supposed to leave tomorrow morning."

"What are you going to do? You can't let her go with the queen's guards," Ingram said.

"I know. The queen means to separate us. She leaves me no choice. I must get Isabel away from here as soon as possible."

"Do you want me to accompany Lady Isabel?" Ingram asked. "It might be hard for you to get away if the queen is determined to keep you here."

Isabel had been looking from one to the other as they spoke. She thought about objecting to Ingram's suggestion, but instead held her breath, waiting for Chetwynd's answer.

"Thank you for your offer, Ingram, but I have no intention of being separated from Isabel again. We'll leave together. If you and Jerome stay behind, you can pretend ignorance of our flight and keep your eyes open for further developments."

Ingram nodded. "Jerome will want to go with you."

"Convince him we need him here."

"Where will you go?"

"Home, Ingram. Aquis is located between here and Aachen, and we can reach it quickly. Only my most trusted friends know its location. When you feel it's safe for you and Jerome to get away, you can seek out Lord Justin and bring him to Aquis. When we are all together and have more information, we can make further plans."

"Are you sure you won't need Jerome? It's not as close as you make it sound."

"Two people leaving the convent will be less conspicuous than three. You and Jerome can make your presence known and be a distraction. No one will think anything is amiss if Isabel and I don't appear for the evening meal. We are newly married and about to be separated. If we do this right, no one will know we are gone until morning and we'll be at my manor by then."

Hearing that Chetwynd had no intention of leaving her behind, Isabel was glad she had kept her silence. She spoke up for the first time. "What about Marianna? She'll want to come with me."

Chetwynd put his arm around her shoulders. "As with Jerome, it's better if she stays here. We need to move quickly and travel as far as possible before we are missed. Ingram can cover our disappearance for a longer time if Marianna stays here. He will see that nothing happens to her and will bring her with him. Will you trust me in this?"

Although concerned about her maid's reaction to being left behind, Isabel nodded, and Chetwynd gave a sigh of relief before he turned back to Ingram.

"One more thing. I'll write a letter for the queen, telling her that upon much consideration I decided it would be best not to wait until morning to seek help from Justin, and to speed delivery of her message, I must leave immediately with Isabel. I'll point out we must keep our departure a secret to protect the queen from any spies in her party, adding that we can make better time alone, and stressing our desire to serve her quickly. Words to that effect."

"I'm sure you can make it sound sincere. I almost believe you," Ingram said with a smile.

"You can delay discovering the letter in my belongings as long as possible. That way when she finds we're gone, she'll think we're on our way to Aachen."

Isabel's eyes widened as he spoke of the letter. "Will the queen believe you?" she asked.

Chetwynd shrugged. "I doubt it very much. But she'll pretend she does to save face."

"I hope you're right. How do we get away without being seen?" Isabel asked.

"We'll leave while everyone is at chapel."

As Isabel listened to the two men work out the details, she appreciated how well they worked together.

"Shouldn't we talk to Gilda, Chetwynd?" Isabel asked. "We can enlist her help to ensure that those we leave behind are safe?"

Both men turned to her, and Chetwynd grinned as he embraced her. "Good idea, Isabel. Bring Gilda here immediately, Ingram. We don't have much time."

CHAPTER FOURTEEN

By the time Gilda and Marianna rushed into the bedchamber, Isabel had tossed together a few necessities for their journey, and Chetwynd had written a letter for the queen. The anxious expressions on the faces of the two women made it clear they knew something was amiss.

"Ingram said you wished to see us," Gilda said.

Marianna caught sight of the small bag Isabel had packed. "Are we going somewhere, my lady?" she asked.

Isabel took her maid's hand and drew her to the bench to sit beside her. "Something's happened, Marianna. The queen wants me to go to Aachen tomorrow morning with some of her guards as escorts. I'm supposed to contact Justin for her, and she wants Chetwynd to stay here. In order to stay together, we decided to leave this evening before anyone can discover we are gone."

"I can be ready in minutes, my lady," Marianna assured her.

Isabel looked up at Chetwynd, wondering if he'd changed his mind. He knelt in front of Marianna so he could look into her face.

"We need you to stay here, Marianna," he said.

Marianna opened her mouth to respond, but Chetwynd

continued before she could speak. "Isabel may be in danger, and I must get her away as soon as possible. I need your help. In order to fool people into thinking we are staying in my room, I'd like you to ask that food be prepared for our supper. Pretend we are closeted for the night."

Marianna's eyes were wide as she looked from one to the other. "Are you going to Aachen, my lord?"

Chetwynd paused only a minute before trusting Mariana with the information. "I'm taking Isabel to my manor. It's not far away, and few people know its location. Ingram will bring you there as soon as it is safe."

"Is it really necessary that I stay behind?"

When Chetwynd nodded, Marianna sighed. Then before he could say another word, she said, "The cooks love to spread tales. I'll tell them you are surprising Isabel with a private supper, and no one is to disturb you."

Chetwynd grinned. "Excellent. Thank you."

Marianna turned to Isabel. "I trust Lord Chetwynd knows best, my lady." When tears appeared in Isabel's eyes, she added, "He will take good care of you."

Gilda, who had been watching the exchange, spoke up. "What can I do?"

"I've written a letter for the queen, Gilda," Chetwynd said. "I was going to have Ingram deliver it, but perhaps you would be a better person to give it to her. That way Ingram won't be implicated in our flight. But I want you to wait until our absence has been noticed. Hopefully, that will be long enough to give us a good lead on anyone who might pursue us. If too many people leave at one time, we will surely attract attention and raise suspicion. Ingram and Jerome, like Marianna, are staying behind."

Chetwynd placed the missive in her hand. "This letter explains that I have joined Isabel on the mission the queen requested she undertake. The queen promised to send guards along with Isabel, but since one of the kidnappers was spotted in her party, I distrust her intent."

Marianna gasped when she heard this news, but Gilda remained calm. "I agree you must get away," Gilda said. "I can use the excuse of being cloistered with a group of nuns as a reason for not delivering the letter right away. I will explain that the nuns are praying for the queen's safe return to her rightful position at court. I think she'll like that."

Looking from one to the other, Chetwynd gave Marianna and Gilda approving nods. "You are both resourceful. I suspect the queen will have met her match in the two of you."

Managing a little laugh, Isabel wiped her eyes, and the other two women smiled, clearly pleased by Chetwynd's praise.

Isabel stood up to embrace Gilda. "Take good care of Marianna," she whispered. She had come to respect Gilda, and she knew in her heart that the competent nun would not only keep her safe but also give her moral support.

"I always wanted a sister, Isabel, and I'm sorry to be saying goodbye to you so soon. But I'm sure I'll be seeing you again before too long. No doubt the circumstances will be happier. If you ever need a sanctuary, you'll always have one here."

Marianna clung to Isabel for a minute as they prepared to part. It occurred to Isabel that only a few days ago Marianna had to leave her with the outlaws, and she regretted leaving her maid behind again.

"We'll be together again soon, Marianna," Isabel promised.

"I hear the bells for chapel. We'd better be going," Chetwynd said, gently taking Isabel's arm.

As she followed Chetwynd from the room, Isabel glanced back and was comforted by the sight of Gilda and Marianna standing together arm in arm.

Outside, the walkway was crowded with people headed to chapel for vespers. Chetwynd and Isabel walked in the same direction, but at the last minute they turned away toward the stables.

Jerome intercepted them. He was frowning, and Chetwynd was sure he was going to object to being left behind. Instead he said, "I spoke with Ingram. I'll distract the stable guard while you mount your horses. They are ready for you."

Chetwynd nodded and was about to speak with his squire when Jerome turned toward Isabel. "Godspeed, my lady," he whispered.

She reached out to touch his shoulder. "Thank you," she mouthed.

As they rode away from the stables, Isabel pulled the hood of her cloak around her face. They kept their horses at a slow pace so as not to attract attention. However, once out of sight of Saint Ives, they increased their speed. Earlier in the day they had raced playfully on their way to the bath, but this time they were fugitives. Both of them were aware of the difference.

When they were far enough away so that it was safe to slow the horses, Chetwynd said, "Jerome is not happy with me for leaving him behind. You have won his affection."

"I've come to care for him, as well. Perhaps sharing danger brings people close." She thought about the time she had spent with the young squire and how he had spoken about Chetwynd. "I wouldn't worry, my lord, Jerome holds you in high regard."

"It's good to know I have two men that I can trust to watch out for you if need be."

Isabel frowned at the reminder of the danger facing them. "Will those we left behind be safe, my lord?"

"Yes, I'm sure they will. The queen is in no position to alienate anyone. She needs all the help she can obtain."

Isabel nodded, and silence fell between them as they concentrated on the trail. Since Chetwynd was used to leading and Isabel to following, they settled easily into the pattern that had been established on their long journey from Narbonne.

The trail, one that Chetwynd had followed many times, was a fairly easy one until they reached the mountains. The familiar route gave Chetwynd an opportunity to ponder the decision he had made after their interview with Judith. As a soldier, he often had to react quickly to a dangerous situation and trust that his action was the correct one.

From the moment the queen invited Isabel to a private meeting, he suspected Judith would try to manipulate Isabel in some way. In reviewing the exchange, he didn't believe he had overreacted to the queen's request that Isabel deliver a message to Justin. At the very least, her purpose was to separate him from Isabel. The worst possibility was that Judith posed a threat to his wife. In view of this latter possibility, he believed he had made the right decision.

During the interview, he had a chance to compare the two women. The queen was a skilled tactician, but Isabel had been quick to see beyond her gracious manner and concerned expressions of interest. He grinned when he recalled how his wife had imitated the affected smile Judith beamed at everyone.

Although Isabel hadn't trusted him as he had asked, he could hardly fault her for that. From the beginning he had been less than honest.

Unlike Judith, Isabel never used her feminine wiles to influence him. In fact, he had found her to be stubborn, argumentative, and more than willing to fight for what she desired. Although these traits had at times driven him to distraction, he also admired her directness and determination. During their short time together, she had become important to him, and he made a silent vow to do everything in his power to keep her safe.

They had traveled late into the night when Chetwynd turned to signal they should stop to rest the horses. Used to the routine of traveling with him, Isabel slid unassisted from her saddle. Chetwynd checked his horse, then hers, while she walked a short distance to stretch her legs. They had reached a meadow, and the full moon was so bright it cast shadows of the surrounding trees.

Isabel sat in the tall grass and leaned back on her elbows to contemplate the stars. When Chetwynd approached her with the waterskin, she took a long drink.

"How much farther to Aquis?" she asked.

"Not far in distance. But we have to cross those mountains." He was pointing to a dark formation that loomed on the western horizon. "Aquis is on the other side."

Isabel could not help but groan at the sight of the high mountains.

"It's not as bad as it looks from here. There's a pass we'll go through. The moon is bright, and there is not much vegetation. It will be light enough to see our way. Once we reach Aquis, we can spend the night in the comfort of my manor house. It will be more restful than trying to sleep in this meadow. Do you think you can continue riding long enough to reach a soft, clean bed?"

"When you put it that way, I'm sure I can." The thought of sleeping on the ground did not appeal to her. But she lay back to rest, making a pillow of her hood.

Chetwynd stood towering over her, unwilling to get too

comfortable. But when Isabel patted the ground beside her and asked what Aquis was like, he crossed his legs and sat down. They had traveled far enough that they didn't have to worry about being followed.

"It's a fairly large estate, about the size of your father's manor. The main source of income is the vineyard, although the farmers also raise other crops. There were already tenant farmers in place when the king granted me the land. I've been there several times for short visits, but never spent a long stretch of time there. I think you'll like it. The manor house is comfortable, and it overlooks a valley where the grapes grow."

"I've always wanted to see a vineyard in operation."

"Bosco, my chief steward, looks after the place. He's an excellent manager, and the estate makes a good living. More than enough to support my small army. Bosco's wife oversees the running of the household. The woman makes the best bread you'll find anywhere."

As Chetwynd spoke, he reached out to pull her cloak tighter around her. "Aren't you cold?" he asked.

Isabel shook her head no. "It's a lovely night. Is there a swimming pond on your land?"

Chetwynd smiled at her question. He didn't want to start thinking about Isabel in a swimming pond, so he stood up and extended his hand to help her up. "I'm not sure whether there's a pond, but you can investigate. You're just asking me questions about the estate to put off crossing the mountain."

"You're getting to know me too well, my lord," she complained mildly. But Isabel let him help her up. She climbed onto her horse willingly enough, thinking of the soft bed on the other side of the mountain.

The ride up the pass was like a dream sequence. The moon lit the way through huge, dark shapes looming on either side of the trail. Isabel found it comforting to imagine that the moon was a beacon set in the sky to guide them to safety.

As they descended into the valley, the trail became steep. Isabel remembered her fall on a similar descent and used every muscle in her body to hold herself in the saddle. It seemed to take forever to move downhill. By the time they reached level ground, Isabel's muscles were screaming for a rest.

Chetwynd glanced back at her, then pointed ahead to give her encouragement. She could see a building on a hill in the distance. She nodded, indicating she could make it, and used all her remaining strength to keep from falling out of her saddle. Although it was very early morning, it was still dark when their horses stopped in the courtyard of Aquis.

To Isabel's surprise, a man appeared to greet Chetwynd and then disappeared again into the main building. She was so tired it was an effort to keep her eyes open. When Chetwynd came to help her dismount, she practically fell on top of him. He gently held her up until two women appeared to help her into the house. They were making comforting sounds, but she was too exhausted to pay much attention to their words. At one point she knew they were offering to help her change her clothes, but when she saw a bed she fell onto it, her face buried in the covers. Ignoring everything else, she surrendered to her need for sleep.

When Isabel awoke, she found herself still facedown on the bed. She felt rested but in need of a wash. The room was large, and the small bag she had packed was on the floor. Although the bed was of ample size, there was no sign of Chetwynd or his clothes.

Using the water basin that had been left for her, Isabel cleaned off as much of the travel grime as possible before changing into fresh clothes. Once she had made herself presentable, she felt ready to explore. She took a deep breath and left her room.

Since there was no one in the dining hall, she took a few minutes to look around at the pleasant but simply decorated room. Someone had taken good care of the hall, as the tapestries were well aired and the rushes under the long tables smelled sweet.

The sound of voices came from a connecting room Isabel guessed to be the kitchen. Through the doorway, she discovered two women cutting up chickens, chatting steadily as they worked. They were so absorbed in their conversation about the arrival of Lord Chetwynd and his bride that they didn't notice her for a minute. When they did, an embarrassed silence followed. Then they both curtsied in her direction.

"Good day," she greeted them. "Something smells wonderful. Lord Chetwynd told me the best bread baked anywhere is to be found in this kitchen."

The older woman beamed, and replied, "Good day, my lady. I'm Gertrude, and this here is Irma. What you smell is that very same bread Lord Chetwynd likes so much. Sit yourself down, my lady, and I'll get you some, along with a bowl of Irma's soup."

Isabel smiled her appreciation, happy to be accepted into the warm intimacy of the kitchen. It was much like the kitchen where she had grown up, a place where the women of the household spent a great deal of time preparing meals. The large table in the middle of the room was high so the women could stand while they worked. Isabel sat on a tall stool at the end of the table to await her soup. The many baskets filled with vegetables sitting on the floor reminded her of what Chetwynd had said about the farmers and their crops. The fresh smell of the vegetables filled her senses.

Gertrude wore her abundant gray hair in a plait that circled her head. The color was the only clue as to her age, for her face was unlined and cheery. She served Isabel a tankard of ale with her soup. "I hope you slept well, my lady."

"Very well indeed. I see by the sun that I've missed all of the morning and part of the afternoon." Isabel remembered that she had not even undressed the night before. "Are you the women who helped me to my chamber?"

When they nodded, she continued, "I'm afraid I was too tired to be introduced. But I do thank you for leading me to a bed."

Gertrude smiled again, and Irma, a young woman who couldn't be more than fourteen years old, gave a hoot of laughter and said, "You dropped onto the bed like a tree felled in the woods, my lady. We didn't do much."

If the women were curious about why she had arrived at such an hour after riding all night, they didn't show it. Instead they answered her questions about what they were preparing. When Isabel commented on the amount of food they were cooking, they informed her that the grape harvest was in progress, and there were workers to feed.

"It's a very good year, my lady, and the grapes are weighing down the vines," Gertrude said. "Tomorrow the workers will arrive early, and we'll need food to feed the lot."

By the time Chetwynd returned from a tour with his steward, he found Isabel kneading bread at the kitchen table. The women were chatting easily, and he was pleased at how quickly Isabel had made herself at home. Irma was the first to notice him watching them, and Gertrude followed her eyes and fell silent.

"Good day, my lord," Isabel called cheerfully when she, too, noticed his presence. She hadn't put on a head covering, and she brushed the hair from her forehead to see him better.

Dressed casually in what were clearly his country clothes, Chetwynd appeared relaxed. His tunic was longer than the one he wore riding and his boots of much softer leather.

When Chetwynd smiled at her and nodded to the other women, it was clear to Isabel that they must be acquainted. The women didn't seem at all shy about having the lord of the manor in their kitchen.

Isabel was unaware of the flour that dusted her nose, but Chetwynd found the sight irresistible. "There's some flour right here," he said as he raised his hand to brush it away.

It was a surprisingly affectionate gesture that made Isabel's eyes shine. Rather than dropping his hand, he moved it across her cheek and down to her neck. Irma giggled, and Gertrude turned to glare at the young woman. But neither Chetwynd nor Isabel seemed to notice.

There was a lump in her throat that Isabel had trouble dislodging. When she did manage to find her voice she said, "I'm afraid I slept late, my lord."

"I'm glad you did. I asked that you not be disturbed. I haven't been up long myself. Bosco, Gertrude's husband, has been giving me a tour of the manor. The grapes are being picked, so it's a busy time. If you wish, I could show you around."

"I'd like that," Isabel replied, removing the cloth that protected her dress from the flour.

Isabel was aware that the two women, who had previously pretended to be very busy with their chores, were watching them leave. Once outside, she asked, "What did you tell the people here about us?"

"Just that you are my wife and we are awaiting the arrival of your brother before proceeding to Aachen. I think Bosco wonders why we traveled through the night, but he is discreet. I gave them only the information they need to know."

They walked toward the vineyard, and the climb down into the valley was gentle. Some of the vines were still heavy with fruit, and there was a large group of pickers just finishing their day. Baskets of the purple grapes were being carried to a wagon. Although it was early evening, the sun was still warm, and the pickers wore loose clothing. The long rows of vines seemed to go on forever.

"Can we sit for a spell?" Isabel asked, indicating a low stonewall on the edge of the vineyard.

"Of course. Are you still tired from last night's journey?"

"A bit," she admitted. "But mostly I want to take time to enjoy the view."

Chetwynd followed her eyes, and was surprised at how much he enjoyed the simple pleasure of sharing the beauty of the valley with her. Isabel was changing the way he viewed Aquis. Up until this visit, he'd thought of the estate as nothing more than a means to earn funds to support his army. Now he saw it as a future home for himself, and considered the possibility that Isabel might want to share it.

"It's beautiful here, Chetwynd. How long do you think we'll stay?"

"Not long. It depends on how quickly Ingram is able to locate Justin. I doubt they will arrive as early as tomorrow, but they could be here by the next day." As they watched the pickers pushing away the loaded wagons, Chetwynd thought about what Justin's arrival might mean for them.

The sun was low in the sky and the shadows long. When Chetwynd's chief steward approached them carrying a basket of grapes, Chetwynd introduced him to Isabel. In spite of his advanced years, the steward lowered himself to the ground in a graceful, easy motion.

When Bosco handed Isabel a perfectly formed bunch of grapes, she smiled her thanks and immediately popped one into her mouth. She found it surprisingly sweet and continued eating grapes, savoring the flavor, as the men talked.

"If the weather is good, we should finish up tomorrow," Bosco told Chetwynd. "Gertrude, who is a good weather prophet, thinks we will have a fine day. She is already preparing food for the grape-pressing fete, my lord. You have never been here for a fete, and it's the highlight of the year. I think you'll enjoy it."

"What happens at the fete?" Isabel asked. Both men laughed when they turned to her. Isabel was puzzled until Chetwynd pointed to her mouth and indicated by drawing his finger under his own lips that she had juice on hers.

As Chetwynd watched her rosy tongue dart around her lips, he had a vision of himself licking away the sticky syrup. There was a slight catch in his voice when he said, "Those grapes seem juicy."

The expression in his eyes as he watched her lips made Isabel blush. She turned away to find the steward watching them with interest. "Tell me about the fete, Bosco," she said to distract herself from the heat that was flooding her body.

"It's the last day of the harvest, my lady. When all the picking is done, the farmers gather to press the grapes. They are piled in large vats, and we stomp on them to release the juice we use to make wine. To attract as many people as possible to this task, we end the workday with a feast. The pressing is a messy job. Once the pressing is done, if it's not too cold, many of the workers jump in the fish pond and then eat and drink their fill."

"There's a pond?" Isabel interrupted before he could continue.

"Indeed, my lady. It's just beyond those trees," Bosco replied, pointing to where the sun had just set.

Chetwynd and Isabel smiled at each other, both remembering another pond.

Bosco excused himself. "Tomorrow will be a busy day, my lord. I need to prepare the vats and casks."

Neither Isabel nor Chetwynd said anything as they watched Bosco walk away. As the silence between them lengthened, Isabel thought about their flight from Saint Ives. She still had a lot of questions about Chetwynd's relationship with the queen. "I think we should talk about Queen Judith and what happened," she said in a subdued voice.

"You're right." Chetwynd knew it was time for him to confide in Isabel. It had to be done before they could think about a future together, and he was more than eager to hear what she felt about that. "But it's late. I'll come to your bedchamber tonight."

After a late supper, Isabel retired to her room. She paced the floor wondering how long it would be before Chetwynd joined her. He had said he had to check some details with Bosco.

There was nothing but a bed in her room, and Isabel considered whether she should strip to her shift and lie in it. She decided that might look as though she expected Chetwynd to share her bed, or even worse, wished to seduce him into her bed. Although she would have liked nothing better, she didn't want him to know that.

Isabel sat on the bed, staring at the door. After a while she stood up and went to wash her face at the nightstand. Where could he be? she wondered. Perhaps he forgot he promised to talk to her. Or maybe he decided he didn't want to explain himself.

But it had only been a short time ago that he'd promised to come. Had he forgotten? He didn't forget. It was more likely he didn't want to talk about Queen Judith. Or perhaps she was exaggerating the amount of time that passed.

Isabel paced for a while longer, then stamped her foot. "This is ridiculous," she said out loud. "I'm going to bed."

But she didn't blow out the candle and lay listening to the noises of the manor. In the distance, she heard a loud male laugh, then later some footsteps outside her door. She was disappointed when the steps didn't stop. Just when she was losing the battle to keep her eyes open, she heard a soft knock.

"Come in," she said, her impatience clear by her tone.

Chetwynd stood in the doorway. "Sorry to be so long. I haven't been to Aquis in a while, and I felt I had to help Bosco get ready for the pickers. Would you rather talk tomorrow?"

Isabel sat up and spoke quickly. "No. Come in, Chetwynd."

She watched him look around for a place to sit, then decide to sit on the edge of her bed. Isabel lay back to put a little space between them. "I was afraid you'd decided not to talk this evening," she said, then bluntly added, "I want you to tell me more about you and Queen Judith."

Chetwynd nodded. "One of the reasons I was reluctant to talk to you about it sooner is that the story does not reflect well upon me."

He'd already delayed long enough, so he took a deep breath and plunged in. "When I first came to court, I had a small army and experienced some success in battle. King Louis was pleased with my service and granted me Aquis to help me support a larger army. I was feeling quite proud of my progress.

"I had been estranged from my father at an early age, so it was very important that I make my own living. Even if I hadn't been estranged, I stood to inherit little property as I have two older brothers.

"Before that time, I had been involved with a few women, but nothing serious. I had it in my mind that I didn't want to marry, so the women I sought out were widows. When Judith took notice of me, I was flattered. She is admired by many men, as you probably know."

Isabel turned her head away at his words, and he stopped speaking. Chetwynd leaned over her and took her face in his hands to force her to look at him. "I don't have to tell you about how she operates, Isabel. You met her. She is skilled at making people feel special and using them for her own ends. For a while she made me feel special, but I never loved her. I haven't loved any woman."

"Except Theresa," she replied in a soft voice.

Chetwynd drew back in surprise. "Theresa? How do you know about Theresa?" Then he answered his own question. "Gilda told you, I suppose."

He stared into space, thinking of his disastrous love for Theresa. "I was very young and thought I loved her. But I didn't know the real Theresa. When I found out that she had betrayed me, I swore never to marry."

His eyes met Isabel's again. "I had just learned about her marriage to my father the summer I first saw you. I believe now that if I hadn't been so disillusioned by that experience, I might have stayed in Narbonne and convinced your father that you should marry me."

Isabel's mouth fell open. "You're teasing me."

"No, I'm not. I didn't stay with you, but I never forgot you, Isabel."

Emboldened by his words, she threw her arms around his neck and pulled him down to her. He gathered her into his arms and laughed in her ear. She thought it was a lovely sound.

"It's true, you know. You were so brave, fighting off those men. Then after you'd been hit, you looked up and called me an angel. There was hair and blood in your eyes. I doubt you could really see me."

"I saw your beautiful, shining gold hair. I heard your voice and felt your gentle touch."

Chetwynd kissed her on the scar above her eye and was

quiet for a minute. When he spoke, his voice was husky with emotion. "Emma's mother told me you were betrothed. Early this year when Justin told me you hadn't wed, I was surprised and eager to see you again."

"That wasn't the impression you gave me when we met."

"No. The circumstance of my first sight of you was a terrible blow to my memory. I wasn't prepared for how you had matured, and I believed you had a lover. I was disillusioned and angry. Although I know I had no right to be."

"You know I never had a lover, and we're married now, my lord," she whispered into his neck.

"And do you wish to be my wife?" he asked.

When she nodded, his lips found hers. It was the sweetest kiss he had given her, beginning slowly and deepening until she felt lost in it. He was lying with her and she stretched her body against his, hungry to feel the length of him even though they were separated by a blanket and clothing.

When he released her mouth, she clung tighter to make up for the loss of his mouth against hers.

"Isabel?"

She didn't want to talk anymore, and she tried to kiss him again, but he was holding her face away from him.

"Listen to me, my love. I'm going to ask Justin for permission to be your husband. When we have Justin's blessing, I'll make you my wife."

"No," she whispered in an urgent tone. "I'm already your wife. Why do we have to wait?"

"I want to do this right, Isabel. I've made too many mistakes in my life."

"Everyone makes mistakes, Chetwynd," she reasoned.

He chuckled, then groaned when she teased his neck with her tongue. "Sweet lord in heaven. You aren't making this easy for me." He pulled away from her. "I respect Justin and want his approval for this marriage. It's important. He doesn't think well of me right now, and I need to win back his friendship and respect. It'll only be a little longer."

Isabel didn't want to waste any more time, but she could see it was important to him. "Could you call me your love again?"

"Yes, my love. Now I have to get out of your bed before I lose my resolve."

When he stood up, Isabel realized he hadn't answered all her questions. "Just one more thing, Chetwynd. That first night at Narbonne. Why did you tell me you had an attachment if you were not in love with the queen?"

Chetwynd knelt by the bed, afraid to test his resolve by being too close. "There were two reasons. I didn't think you wanted a real marriage. At that time I thought you had a lover, remember?

"Also, I was involved with the queen, even if I no longer shared her bed. I was determined to be free of that connection before I told you about it. Of course it was foolhardy of me not to realize you would hear of it. I'm truly sorry I wasn't more honest with you, Isabel."

"And do you think you're free of the connection now?"

"Yes. Even if Judith wished nothing more than to separate us, the fact that she tried to do that has freed me of any responsibility I felt toward her. She knows you are my wife."

Isabel nodded, and Chetwynd leaned toward her again to whisper, "I pledge all my loyalty to you, my love."

When he saw the tears leaking from her eyes and rolling down toward her pillow, he hugged her to him without another word. It was a while before he could release her; then he put his finger up to her lips to silence her and moved away from the bed.

Still too filled with happiness at his pledge to complain

about being left alone, Isabel watched him go. She lay awake for a long time, thinking about his words. All the years she'd spent waiting for her champion to return, he had also remembered her.

It was only much later, in rethinking the exchange, that Isabel considered Justin. Her brother could be very stubborn when he thought he had reason. Isabel wondered what Chetwynd would do if Justin, who knew of Chetwynd's involvement with the queen, refused to sanction their marriage. It was a thought that robbed her of her contented mood.

CHAPTER FIFTEEN

*E*ARLY THE NEXT MORNING, THE LONG TABLES in the great hall were filled with men and women consuming a hearty breakfast to prepare them for the day's work. The weather was fair, as Gertrude had predicted, and the mood of the workers was jolly. They chatted excitedly about the evening fete and shared stories of past harvest celebrations.

Isabel and Chetwynd, lord and lady of the manor, sat at the head table. When Isabel arrived in the hall, Chetwynd stood to greet her and announced his marriage to those assembled. The announcement was met with robust cheers and rowdy remarks that brought color to Isabel's cheeks.

Although at first almost everyone sent curious glances in their direction, they were soon forgotten in anticipation of the harvest. Isabel enjoyed her position beside Chetwynd as she watched the crowd devouring some of the food that Gertrude and Irma, with her help, had prepared the previous day.

Being at the head of a household was something new to Isabel, a role she had never sought at Narbonne. The welcome extended by Gertrude and Bosco made her feel immediately at home. As she looked around, she enjoyed the atmosphere of the hall with its high ceiling and scarred wooden tables. The morning sun filtered in through windows set high on the eastern wall. It warmed the dark areas with light. Although not as elegant as her father's great hall, she preferred its comfort to refinement.

Chetwynd watched his wife as she took the measure of the hall and its inhabitants. When her face settled into a contented smile, he asked, "Do you like what you see, my lady?"

"Oh yes, my lord. It's a comfortable place. And you're fortunate in your chief steward. Both Bosco and Gertrude enjoy the respect of your tenants. I can tell by the easy atmosphere."

Her words made Chetwynd realize he had taken the couple's competence for granted. "You're right, of course. They both took to you right away. You seem comfortable in the role of lady of the manor."

"I do like it here. I'm still eager to visit Aachen, but it's comforting to know we can return to Aquis."

Chetwynd's eyes looked away for a minute, and Isabel realized she had assumed too much. His next words brought her back to earth. "There are still some matters to settle, Isabel." After a pause he added, "But I'm happy that Aquis pleases you."

Isabel nodded, wondering if he was afraid to raise his own hopes too high, perhaps because he feared Justin's objection to their match. Unwilling to dwell on that possibility, she changed the subject. "How can I help with the harvest, Chetwynd?"

"Would you like to try your hand at picking grapes? It's such a beautiful day, I suspect you'll enjoy being outside, at least this morning. In the afternoon, Gertrude would be happy to have your help in the kitchen, I'm sure."

Pleased by his suggestion, Isabel smiled in reply. Justin wasn't due to arrive until tomorrow, and she planned to make the most of the day. She wanted to forget the fact that the future of her marriage depended upon her brother's approval. Justin loved her, but she couldn't predict how his displeasure at Chetwynd's past actions would color his perspective. It bothered her that Chetwynd set such store upon obtaining Justin's permission.

In the valley, Isabel watched the women cutting the full and fragrant cones of grapes from the vines. Irma had taken on the responsibility of introducing her to the craft. There had been no vineyards at Narbonne, so everything was new to Isabel. But she liked the smell of the grapes and the feel of the warm sun on her back. After watching Irma for a few minutes, she was eager to try her hand at harvesting the delicate orbs.

The first bunch she tried cutting turned into a mangled crush that stained her hands. She held out her hands for Irma to see, laughing at her first clumsy attempt. When she heard a few women nearby join in her laughter, she realized she was being watched. She determined to do better.

"Support each bunch gently, my lady, until you've cut the stalk completely. The grapes are very ripe. Don't try and pull them away until the cut is made."

Isabel nodded. On her next try, she held out the perfect, fat cone of grapes and declared with satisfaction, "That's better." When a cheer went up from the other women, Isabel's face eased into a satisfied grin.

Soon Isabel was cutting quickly and steadily. She knew she had been accepted when the women turned their attention from her to gossip about romances that had blossomed during the harvest. There was talk of the evening fete and jokes about the possibilities for what they referred to as *adventures*. It was clear the fete was much anticipated because of its opportunity to behave with more freedom than usual.

In spite of the gossip and teasing, the women worked

quickly. When their baskets were full of grapes, one of the men would come along to carry the baskets to a wagon. Once he disappeared, the man was commented upon, and suggestions were made about his virility. Isabel found some of the remarks surprisingly bawdy. The women remarked on everything from the likelihood of the man's endurance to speculation about the size of his private member. She could not help but think how much her friend Emma would have enjoyed the camaraderie.

The chatter was endless, and Isabel wondered how the women could talk so much and cut grapes at the same time. She found she had to concentrate on the task. But her ears perked up when they started to tease one of the younger women.

"You aren't going to get anywhere with Ewan, Matty. Perhaps you should look elsewhere."

"But I fancy Ewan," Matty complained.

"Of course you do. He's comely, I'll say that. But he steers clear of innocent maids."

"If he's afraid of marriage, maybe I should make it clear where my interest lies."

"It's not that, Matty. The man's afraid of a woman's first time. You know, hurting a woman. It's an endearing trait, but in your case not a useful one."

A few women laughingly suggested alternative men for Matty's first time, but one voice quietly defended Ewan. "I think it's because his member is so big. I'd give it another try if I was you, Matty. It might be worth the trouble."

Isabel worked hard to contain her giggle at what she had heard from the other side of the vine. Upon considering Matty's plight, it occurred to her that Chetwynd might be afraid of hurting her. Last night he had said he wished to wait until Justin approved the match before making her his wife. But she knew the reason he had hesitated earlier was because she was a virgin. She shook her head to drive out the thoughts that seemed to occupy far too much of her time.

Feeling the need for a rest, Isabel moved to sit on the grass beside a nursing mother. The peaceful sight reminded her of Emma, and she smiled at the young woman. When the mother prepared to return to cutting grapes, Isabel, whose hands were still aching, offered to watch the babe for a while. Her offer was quickly accepted, and the child was soon asleep in her arms.

When Chetwynd came by to see how Isabel was faring, he spotted her cradling the baby. Dressed in a brown gown with a large apron covering most of it, she looked like one of the peasant women. Her head covering had slipped, and her dark curls sprung free at the sides of her face. She sat with her legs crossed in front of her, staring at the bundle in her lap.

The baby had grabbed onto a lock of her hair, which Isabel had not bothered to pull free. Chetwynd remembered what it felt like to run his hands through her luxurious hair, and he envied the baby's hold on her. He was about to turn away without disturbing the charming tableau when Isabel noticed his presence. When she smiled up at him, he moved closer to kneel beside her.

"I was just checking to see how you were doing." He whispered so as not to wake the babe.

"My hands are tired, so I decided to take a rest. I haven't the skill of the other women."

They were at the end of a row of vines, on a grassy knoll. Most of the women had moved on, so it was quiet and peaceful. Chetwynd leaned back on his elbows to rest beside Isabel, but didn't say anything further. He enjoyed being in her company without the need for words.

Last night, after forcing himself to leave Isabel's bedchamber, Chetwynd had not slept well for thinking about her. Now it was hard for him to keep his eyes open. When he gave in to the need to lie back and rest for a minute, he soon fell asleep. Isabel sat watching over the two sleeping forms until the mother returned for her baby.

After the mother took the child away, there was no one nearby and it was time for Isabel to head back to the kitchen to help Gertrude. Chetwynd lay on his side with one arm supporting his head. The relaxed look on his face was one she had not seen often enough for it to be familiar. Isabel wondered if she should wake him. Because he looked so peaceful, she decided against it. Fighting the temptation to lean over and kiss his perfectly shaped ear, she got up quietly so as not to disturb him.

In the kitchen, a vast amount of food was being prepared for the evening feast. Isabel worked with Gertrude and Irma late into the day. When they heard whooping shouts from the valley, Gertrude explained that the workers were already pressing the grapes.

"The shouts are meant to encourage those doing the stomping. The very loud bursts signal that someone has slipped into the grapes. You'll see what I mean when you try it."

The idea of stomping the juicy cones did not appeal to Isabel. "I'm not going to stomp on those grapes that were so perfect, Gertrude."

Instead of answering, Gertrude and Irma exchanged knowing looks. Isabel narrowed her own eyes, but before she could question them, Chetwynd appeared in the kitchen doorway.

"You should have awakened me, Isabel," he complained. "It was very embarrassing to wake up surrounded by a group of giggling women. You left me in a vulnerable position. It seems that during the harvest they have little respect for the lord of the manor."

Just imagining the bawdy remarks the women might have made when they found him stretched out at their feet, Isabel started to giggle. Irma and Gertrude, who no doubt had vivid imaginations of their own, joined her.

Chetwynd threw up his hands, pretending disgust, and turned to leave. Then, as though remembering his errand, he turned back to the giggling trio. "I came to tell you we need your help crushing the grapes. Come along, Isabel. I hear you are an accomplished cutter. Let's see how you do stomping in the vat."

Isabel thought she detected a hint of mischief in his invitation. "I'll watch the stomping," she replied. "They are lovely grapes, and I don't wish to stomp them."

Chetwynd shrugged his shoulders and grabbed her hand, pulling her along with him. The two other women were giggling again.

When they arrived at the spot where the pickers were now busy pressing grapes, Isabel was fascinated to see several large vats with women jumping up and down inside them. They were stomping with their skirts tucked up around their waists. The men poured in the grapes, and a few supported the women, holding onto an arm or wrist to keep them from slipping. An explosive shout startled Isabel. She saw that a tall woman had lost her footing and sunk into a mess of crushed grapes.

Chetwynd motioned that Isabel should try it, but she held back, shaking her head. Two of the women she worked with earlier were preparing to enter the vat and noticed Isabel's refusal.

"Come along, my lady. The grapes feel good between your toes," one of them teased.

Isabel made a face and held her ground. When the women continued their urging, Chetwynd whispered in her ear, "You don't want to disappoint. It's a tradition for the lady of the manor to take a turn."

Isabel wasn't sure she believed that, but she finally removed her shoes and hose, and lifted her skirt. When she stepped into the slippery mess, Chetwynd was quick to steady her with his hands at her waist.

In spite of the fact that the women beside her were stomping with great vigor, Isabel stepped daintily up and down. However, inspired by the others, she gradually increased her own energy level. The curious sensation of wet, slippery grapes underfoot made her laugh.

"You missed a clump to your right," Chetwynd pointed out. "Now try over here." At his urging, she moved around the vat.

When Isabel accidentally splashed Chetwynd, he muttered, "Be careful. You're getting my clothes stained."

Stomping even harder, she bit her lip to keep from laughing when his sleeve became covered with a dark red stain. Chetwynd caught on to her purpose and let her slip to her knees into the pulp. A great roar went up when she managed to pull him off-balance so he tilted and had to put his hands into the pulp to steady himself.

Chetwynd scrambled to regain his balance. After that, Isabel saw the glimmer in his eyes and tried to avoid him. Before she could climb out of the vat, he swept her up in his arms and carried her away to accompanying cheers and whistles from the crowd.

As Chetwynd ran toward the woods, Isabel suspected she knew where he was headed. She clung to his neck, hiding her face in his shirt when the trees speeding by made her dizzy. She prayed he would not lose his footing and drop her to the ground. When he stopped, she let go of her grip on him and felt herself being tossed into the air. She knew enough to hold her breath.

The deep water of the pond felt icy cold against her overheated skin, and she gasped for air when she came to the surface. Chetwynd jumped in behind her and started to paddle about furiously to banish the cold. It took a few minutes for their bodies to adjust to the water temperature.

"What a trick," she complained, splashing water into his face.

"You said you wanted to see the swimming pond. Besides, I needed to wash the grape stains from my clothes. The grape stains you caused to be there."

"Here, let me help you wash." Isabel splashed him more vigorously, sparking a water fight.

Soon exhausted from the effort, they called a truce and began to paddle about slowly. Isabel finally had a chance to look around. The water was deep and clear, and the surrounding trees stood close together, providing privacy. "So this is the pond."

Chetwynd nodded. "I found it this morning. What do you think?"

"It's perfect," she declared, moving close and throwing her arms around his neck. "Everything about Aquis is perfect."

"Including me?"

"Especially you."

Chetwynd threw his head back and laughed at her words. Not used to seeing him so relaxed and happy, Isabel was delighted by the sound.

"The minute I saw this pond, I knew you'd like it, Isabel. I couldn't wait to show it to you. Will you do something for me?"

His incredible blue eyes, darkened with desire, searched her face with an intensity that made her stomach flutter.

When he looked at her like that, she suspected she'd agree to anything. "Yes, of course," she answered softly.

"I'm going to sit over there," he said, pointing to the edge of the pond. "Will you swim around on your back the way you did the first time I saw you?"

Isabel bit her lip and nodded agreement.

"But before you do, let's take off some of your clothing." Standing in the water, he helped her remove her apron and gown, then tossed the sopping clothes onto the grass.

With only a shift covering her, Isabel swam away from him. Feeling a little self-conscious, she turned onto her back and slowly moved through the water. She knew he had left the pond as she could see his blond hair out of the corner of her eye. Staring up at the sky, she moved her arms to propel herself slowly through the water.

Although uneasy at first, the water relaxed her, and the idea that her movements had stayed in Chetwynd's memory inspired her to be daring. Looking around first to be sure they were alone, she swung her hips in an erotic rhythm as she had done that afternoon so long ago. She twisted slowly through the water and moved her hands along her sides from her hips to her breasts. As she imagined Chetwynd's hands touching her, she moved them over her breasts and stomach, all the places she dreamed of him caressing her.

Carried away by her enactment, Isabel was startled when there was a splashing sound in the calm water. Chetwynd grabbed her hand and pulled her toward the shore. Isabel swallowed some water and struggled to find her footing. "What are you doing?" she managed to ask.

"What I should have done long ago," he muttered as he continued to pull her after him. They were out of the water and rushing toward the trees.

She could see that the path they were following led to

the manor house but avoided returning to the vineyard. "My gown," she panted, as she pointed back toward the pond with her free hand.

"You won't need it. You'll be in your bedchamber in a minute."

Isabel didn't allow herself to believe his intention until he shut the door firmly behind them. When he turned toward her, the intense expression on his face left no doubt of his purpose. Within seconds he had slid her wet shift over her shoulders so that it landed in a puddle around her feet. Isabel turned away, embarrassed to be naked before him.

But Chetwynd was quick to move behind her and place his hands on her shoulders. "You're magnificent, Isabel. Please let me look at you."

Although shy, she allowed him to turn her around. He stood back and stripped off his own clothes without taking his eyes from her.

Pressing her lips together, Isabel watched. She had seen a nude male body before, even one in an aroused condition, but Derek belonged to Emily and had only stirred her curiosity. Seeing Chetwynd caused her knees to go weak, and her head felt like it might float away. When Chetwynd moved toward her again and cupped her breasts in his hands, she was afraid she might slide to the floor.

"Your body's still wet," he whispered. "Do you want a flannel?"

Chetwynd had meant to give her a minute to dry off, but when she shook her head no, he backed her to the bed, rubbing his own body against hers. In spite of his impatience, he lowered her slowly onto the bed. When she opened her legs, he moved between them, fitting himself against her. He was very aware that she was still a maid, and he didn't want to frighten her.

"Wait," Isabel whispered, and the word made him groan. He didn't release her, but he pulled back to peer into her face. He had expected to see fear there, but her expression was more apologetic than fearful.

"What's the matter, my love? Are you afraid? I'll try not to hurt you."

"No, no, it's not that. But we shouldn't do this. You wanted to wait for Justin's approval. I have seduced you from your purpose."

Chetwynd stared at her, trying to understand her reasoning. "You seduced me?"

"Yes, my lord. My grandmother, and later Marianna, suggested I seduce you into making me your wife. I promised myself I wouldn't trap you, but now I'm doing just that."

Wanting to be sure she wasn't making an excuse to cover her anxiety, he asked, "You have no fear of my taking your virginity?"

"Oh no, my lord. I know it's supposed to hurt, but I'll be very glad to lose it with you. I do want to be your wife in every way."

He did his best to control his urge to grin. "Your only worry is that you are seducing me?"

Isabel bit her lip and nodded.

"Will you feel better if I seduce you, Isabel?" As he asked this last question, he moved his hand between her legs to find her already wet and hot to his touch.

After a gasp, she answered, "I think that would be . . . acceptable."

With this clear signal, Chetwynd caressed Isabel until she arched her body toward his, signaling her desire for more intimate contact. In spite of his need to plunge deeply inside her, he entered her gently until he felt resistance, then pushed quickly beyond the barrier. Once nestled within her, he thrust to his own release, calling her name as he came.

Ashamed that he had satisfied his own need without giving her pleasure, Chetwynd eased away from Isabel. She hadn't cried out, but when he looked at her face he saw blood where she had bitten her lip. He kissed her gently, tasting her blood. "I'm going to fetch you a damp cloth, Isabel. That will make you feel more comfortable."

Isabel was wondering if she should mention Emma's suggestion, and he noticed her hesitation. "What is it, Isabel?"

"Emma gave me some ointment before I left Narbonne. It's by the basin in a soft leather pouch."

When Chetwynd returned to the bed, he didn't pass the cloth to her and Isabel realized he intended to bathe her himself. He performed the intimate act of cleansing her in a loving manner that left no room for embarrassment. Then he gently applied the ointment to her swollen folds in a rhythm that soon had her breathless.

"Emma is a very clever woman, Isabel," he whispered into her ear as he continued to stroke her intimately.

It was hard for Isabel to speak as she was rapidly moving close to losing all control.

Chetwynd grinned as she tightened around his fingers and found her own release. "Tomorrow we'll try that with me inside you. Now turn on your side and let me hold you while you sleep."

Isabel moved as he suggested. Nestled with her back against him, she thought about how he had called out her name when he was moving inside her. Then with a shudder he had relaxed, hugging her tight at the same time. Although he had given her pleasure while applying the ointment, she looked forward to sharing that powerful sensation with him.

The sky was just beginning to lighten when Isabel

awoke, and it was heaven to feel Chetwynd's hands cupping her breasts. When she moved slightly to see if he was awake, he kissed her ear. "Thank you for letting me awake in your arms, my lord."

He turned her around to kiss her gently where she had bitten her lip. "My pleasure. Is your lip sore?" he asked against her mouth.

"No." She wiggled herself into a position on top of him. "I don't seem to be sore at all this morning."

"Isabel, are you trying to seduce me?"

"It's all right for me to do that now, as you have already seduced me," she pointed out reasonably. Then to emphasize her intention, she moved her hand down to his hard stomach and the nest of hair above his sex.

Now that his anxiety about hurting her had disappeared, Chetwynd relaxed and allowed himself to enjoy her exploration of his body. Her curiosity excited him, but he forced himself to remain still until her hand closed around his arousal. Afraid her soft caresses would make him lose control, he rolled on top of her and found her ready for him. He entered her gently, moving slowly in and out of her warmth.

Isabel found his slow pace heavenly and groaned her pleasure. But soon it wasn't enough. Wanting more, she used her hands on his hips to urge him deeper and faster. When she finally tightened around him, they exploded together, and Isabel shouted her amazement at the intense waves that carried her to fulfillment.

Later when she regained the ability to speak, Isabel whispered in Chetwynd's ear, "Do you think anyone heard us shouting?"

Chetwynd started to laugh, and the feel of his shaking body against hers made Isabel laugh as well. "I think everyone is probably sound asleep. But even if not, it doesn't matter.

I doubt anyone would be surprised by my enthusiastic ardor for my wife."

"Your wife. That does sound very nice."

They lay together for a while, enjoying the novelty, until Chetwynd's stomach growled. "Do you want to find something to eat?" he asked. "We missed our evening meal."

They had the kitchen to themselves, and they found plenty of food left over from the previous evening.

"I guess they were too tired to clean up last night," Chetwynd said as he cleared a spot at the table for them to sit. There was lots of bread and leftover chicken, and Isabel poured them each a tankard of ale. "No one will be stirring until noon, I'm sure."

"I do like this kitchen, Chetwynd." Isabel watched him tearing into a crust of stale bread, his white teeth gleaming.

"What are you smiling about, my love?"

"Gertrude was so proud of the fact that you like her bread." She became thoughtful. "You have a nice way with people, showing them you appreciate them. I noticed it first in the way you treated Jerome and Ingram."

"I think Jerome has shifted his loyalty from me to you, Isabel."

"Do you mind, Chetwynd?"

"It shouldn't be a problem now that we are truly man and wife. We will be as one in his eyes. I'm just glad he isn't older. He might have challenged me to a battle over you."

"I doubt that. But I have a question, my lord." She hesitated, but knew it had to be discussed. "What happened to your resolution to wait for Justin's approval of our match?"

Chetwynd took a long drink. "Somehow my desire overcame my resolve. Maybe you did seduce me, my love."

"Chetwynd! You said . . ."

"I'm teasing. I thought about Justin and my desire for his

approval after I left you that first night. I realized that if he objected to our marriage, his objection wouldn't change my determination to have you as my wife. Now it's a done deed, and I have to make him believe I deserve you."

"Hmmm. I had wondered what you would do if Justin objected. I'm glad to hear he wouldn't change your mind."

"My decision may cause us trouble, and I'm sure it won't be easy. But we'll just have to convince your brother that we belong together."

After taking a big bite of an apple, Isabel held it out for Chetwynd to taste. His bite took most of the remaining apple and filled his mouth. Since Isabel's mouth was still full, she tried to keep from laughing as he struggled to chew the huge portion. She could feel apple juice dripping down her chin.

Chetwynd couldn't help staring at her rosy mouth. When he found he was aroused again, he knew he might never get enough of his beautiful wife. Quickly swallowing the apple, he asked, "Do you wish to go back to bed for a while, Isabel?"

"Yes," was all she said as she jumped from her stool and raced him back to the bedchamber.

CHAPTER SIXTEEN

I T WAS LATE AFTERNOON WHEN ONE OF THE farmers arrived at the manor house to announce that riders were approaching. Everyone had slept late, and there was a subdued atmosphere at the manor house. Isabel was helping with the cleanup in the kitchen, while Chetwynd and Bosco, seated at a table in the dining hall, examined the account books.

The afternoon sun was burning brightly as Isabel and Chetwynd stood together in the courtyard to watch the approaching riders. Chetwynd found Isabel's hand among the folds of her skirt and held it tightly. No words were necessary to convey the nervous anticipation they both felt. Although they had not discussed strategy, there was an unspoken understanding that they would stand firm against any opposition to their marriage.

They were relieved to see that Ingram and Jerome were in the small party of men who accompanied Justin. Chetwynd held back, watching Isabel run toward her brother and greet him with a warm embrace. Justin stared at Chetwynd over Isabel's shoulder. Even from a distance, Chetwynd recognized the barely restrained fury in Justin's expression.

Chetwynd received a warmer greeting from Ingram and Jerome. They moved to stand facing Chetwynd as though to shield him from Justin. It was clear they wished a word with him first, and they used the fact that Justin was occupied with Isabel to achieve their goal.

"We got here as soon as we could," Ingram began, speaking quickly. "It took a while to persuade Lord Justin to come with us. After we filled him in on what happened at Saint Ives, he wanted us to come on our own and fetch Lady Isabel to him. He has the idea that she will be safer separated from you and plans to accomplish that as soon as possible."

"I'm not surprised, Ingram. Not long ago, I, too, believed she'd be safer away from me, as I'm sure you remember. But I have no intention of being separated from Isabel."

Both men nodded their approval, then Jerome added, "Lord Justin's very angry, my lord."

"And what about you, Jerome? Have you forgiven me for leaving you behind at Saint Ives?"

"You made the journey safely. If anything had happened to Lady Isabel, I would not have forgiven you, my lord."

The usually cheerful Jerome had spoken solemnly, making it clear how strongly he felt. Ingram frowned at the young squire's boldness, but Chetwynd's reply made it clear he didn't resent Jerome's concern. "Nor would I have forgiven myself. I appreciate your regard for Isabel's safety, Jerome."

A look of disapproval still on his face, Ingram shook his head at the exchange, but Chetwynd knew the kidnapping had formed a special bond between Isabel and the young lad who had served him for so long. He watched as his wife came to embrace his squire, and before Jerome could duck his head, Chetwynd saw that his cheeks had turned a bright shade of red.

After Isabel greeted Ingram with a similar embrace, she asked, "Where is Marianna?"

"She stayed in Aachen to prepare Chetwynd's chamber

for you, my lady. Actually we had to talk her into it, but she was tired and finally gave in. She grumbled that Lord Chetwynd's rooms needed a great deal of cleaning to prepare for your arrival."

Imagining Marianna hard at work setting Chetwynd's quarters to rights, Isabel grinned. "What happened after we left the convent, Ingram? Was the queen angry?"

"Not so you would notice, my lady. Gilda reported that she read Chetwynd's letter with some surprise, but her control was in place and she seemed to accept his explanation. The only sign Gilda could see of the queen's true feelings was that as she held the letter down at her side, she crushed it in her hand. But her regal smile was in place, and she put forward no objection to our leaving to follow Chetwynd."

Relieved to hear things had gone well, Isabel looked over to her brother. Justin had held back, speaking with his men. Ever the diplomat, he was allowing Isabel a few minutes to speak with Jerome and Ingram. When he finally approached, Justin's eyes were narrow and his face cold.

"I can't believe you would do this, Chetwynd. How could you betray our friendship in this manner?"

"Justin!" Isabel exclaimed. She knew her brother was angry, but his harsh tone and blunt speech still came as a surprise.

"It's all right, Isabel." Chetwynd took her arm. "I'm sorry you feel that way, Justin. And to tell you the truth, I understand your feelings. But come in and give me a chance to explain."

"I can't imagine what you can say to excuse your behavior," Justin answered.

Isabel took her brother's arm and urged him into the dining hall. Gertrude had already set out some food and drink. Ingram followed behind Chetwynd as though to give him support, but Jerome was clearly eager to avoid the confrontation. "I'll help the men with their horses and bring them some ale," he offered.

Once seated at the table, Justin took a long drink to wash the travel dust from his throat. Chetwynd hoped Gertrude had prepared the ale at its full strength. He'd need all the help he could get to overcome Justin's antagonism. Although Justin seldom became angry, when he did it was because he felt justified, and his anger was not easy to dispel.

Before Justin could speak, Chetwynd decided to begin with a positive suggestion. "When you asked me to stop at Narbonne and see if Isabel was happy, you said that she never married. I hoped that your request meant that you foresaw the possibility that we might make a match."

With a vigorous shake of his head, Justin responded quickly, "Don't be ridiculous, Chetwynd. Why would I wish a man who was foolish enough to become involved with . . ." He stopped abruptly and turned toward his sister. "Isabel, perhaps you should let me speak to Chetwynd alone."

Isabel noted that even angry, Justin retained his diplomatic sensibilities. "I know about Queen Judith, Justin. I'm not going anywhere. Please give Lord Chetwynd a chance to explain. He's my husband, and I expect you to treat him with the respect he deserves."

Both Chetwynd and Justin were staring at her. While Chetwynd wasn't surprised by her strong words, he had never heard anyone speak to Justin in such a scolding manner. Justin grimaced and nodded at Isabel. Chetwynd guessed that brother and sister were used to speaking frankly with one another.

"Give me your explanation, Chetwynd," Justin demanded, only slightly more politely.

"At Narbonne, it was your grandmother who first suggested Isabel and I marry, Justin."

"Of course she would. She's been trying to marry Isabel off for years. That's no reason to take her suggestion," Justin pointed out.

"Lady Winifred led us to believe your father wouldn't allow Isabel to travel with a company of soldiers unless we were married. She pointed out that Lord Theodoric was determined that Isabel enter a convent."

"My grandmother has her own reasons for wishing Isabel married. Did you try to persuade my father otherwise?" Justin asked.

Chetwynd ignored Justin's sarcastic tone and the question he didn't want to answer. "Traveling as a married couple seemed to solve several of our problems. We proposed to live together as brother and sister, with the intention that the marriage could be annulled later. Both Lady Winifred and Lord Theodoric approved the match."

"No big surprise there," Justin said.

"During our journey together, we became better acquainted. I discovered I had feelings for Isabel. As I'm sure you know, your sister is a remarkable woman, full of spirit, as well as a lively curiosity about everything. I plan to do my best to make her a worthy husband."

Justin narrowed his eyes. "Are you still living together as brother and sister?"

The question shattered Chetwynd's resolve to remain calm and reasonable, never an easy task for him. "That's none of your business," Chetwynd barked, while at the same time Isabel said, "No, we're not."

Chetwynd gave his wife a surprised glance and then echoed her answer. "No, we're not. Isabel and I are married, and we intend to stay married." Giving up on the soft approach, Chetwynd's words were meant for both Isabel and Justin.

"You intend to persist, in spite of the fact that your marriage has endangered her life?" Justin asked.

His words hit a nerve, and Chetwynd grimaced. "I'm as upset about that as you are. Isabel seems to have become a target and may still be in danger. But that doesn't change our determination to stay together. We need your help and hope that you will bless our union, Justin. That's what I am seeking. Your father has already given his permission and we don't need yours, although we do hope you will give us your blessing."

Chetwynd and Justin took each other's measure in silence for a few minutes. Then Justin turned to Isabel. "Do you truly wish to be Chetwynd's wife? If not, I can seek to have the marriage annulled. I'll introduce you at court, and you can live with me. You won't have to go back to Narbonne or a convent."

Isabel smiled at her brother. "I love him," she said. "I want this marriage, Justin."

Justin stared at her for a minute; then he nodded. "As Chetwynd has pointed out, you don't need my permission. Let's talk about how we can keep you safe."

Although he didn't offer his blessing, Justin was making it clear he was going to help. He turned to Chetwynd. "I heard the story of Isabel's kidnapping from Ingram, but perhaps you should tell it to me again. Also I want to know exactly what happened with Queen Judith at Saint Ives."

Chetwynd breathed a sigh of relief and started the tale, while Isabel added details from time to time, filling in the gaps.

Justin listened closely to their story, observing how the two finished each other's sentences. It struck him that they conversed like a married couple, and for the first time he accepted the fact that it would not be in his power to separate them. Chetwynd ended the tale with their flight from Saint Ives and the reason for it.

When they finished, Justin was quiet for a few minutes before speaking. Chetwynd took Isabel's hand under the table as they waited to hear what Justin would say.

"I think you did the right thing to flee. I can inform the queen that you sought my help, as she requested, thus supporting what you told her in your letter. It will be easy enough for me to contact King Louis, as he is cloistered at a monastery not far from the palace. Hopefully the queen will be convinced by my actions that you acted in good faith."

"Thank you for your support, Justin. It means a lot to me," Chetwynd said.

Justin nodded in an offhanded manner and continued, "I wonder about the fact that one of the kidnappers was in the queen's company. Involvement in a kidnapping doesn't seem her style. Although she is a skillful manipulator, she relies on her powers of persuasion and feminine wiles to achieve her goals. I can't remember an instance where she used force. However, I can believe she wanted to separate the two of you. That would be in keeping with her methods and any possessive feelings she has for you, Chetwynd."

"I agree, Justin. What you say goes along with everything I know about her. But how would you explain the presence of the kidnapper in her party?"

"If he's an agent of the bishops or Lothar, he could be watching the queen. Spying is not foreign to any of the parties involved in palace intrigue. Since you have supported the queen in the past, it makes more sense that the bishops or Lothar wished to delay your return to the palace. The accusation made against Sister Gerberga and the queen was no doubt in the planning stage for a while. The plotters waited until King Louis was away from the palace to initiate their scheme."

"I can't believe that either the bishops or Lothar would view my return to the palace as a threat to their plans."

"You underestimate your influence, Chetwynd. You have served the king well for many years. Both he and the other knights respect your skill and honesty. You have a reputation for reading a situation and reacting quickly."

The lessening of Justin's antagonistic tone cheered Chetwynd as much as his words. But he questioned his friend's reasoning. "I think that was true once, Justin, but I forfeited my good reputation when I became involved with the queen."

"It's not that straightforward, Chetwynd. Surely you know you are not the only man to be charmed by the queen. It's not necessarily a strong mark against you.

"And there is a much stronger reason why your support of Queen Judith is viewed with sympathy. You are not alone. I know a group of powerful lords who believe her son, Charles, has a right to his inheritance. Of course they have their own motives. They are enemies of Lothar and feel he has become too powerful and headstrong. They may believe that young Charles would be easier for them to control. Personally, I think they are deluding themselves, as Judith is not about to let Charles be managed by anyone but herself."

After listening to her brother's words, Isabel spoke up for the first time. "I can see that maneuvering for power is a complicated matter."

Justin had relaxed considerably, and he smiled at his sister. "That's true, Isabel. And it has become even more so in recent years. Charlemagne was a powerful leader who built an empire, then held it together unchallenged. King Louis has never been the strong leader his father was.

"Without a strong leader, the future of the empire is in danger, or at least that is the fear of the church. The bishops hoped to secure its future by dividing the empire among the king's three sons, with Lothar at its head. But then Louis married Judith. Now there is another son, plus an ambitious queen." Justin shrugged. "As you say, it's complicated, and the problem will not be solved easily. Maybe not for many years to come."

Chetwynd appreciated Justin's ability to take the long view, but he was more concerned with the present. Hoping to return to the immediate problem, he asked, "Since we don't really know who was responsible for Isabel's kidnapping, how do you suggest we proceed?"

"I think you should come with me to the palace at Aachen, Chetwynd. I don't believe the queen will be banished for long, and the king may need you to maintain peace. The best thing would be for Isabel to stay here at Aquis until things settle down and we can discover who was behind the kidnapping plot."

"No," Isabel said quietly, appealing to Chetwynd with her eyes. "I want to go with Lord Chetwynd."

"I promised Isabel we would stay together, Justin. I can't break that promise."

Justin looked from one to the other. In spite of his frustration with Chetwynd, they were the two people he loved most in the world. He was surprised he had never thought of them together. He spoke to Isabel. "I take it you are determined to remain in this marriage?"

Isabel nodded. She knew her brother well and prayed he would recognize and accept the inevitable. She did not wish a battle between the two men she loved.

When Justin looked at him, Chetwynd held his breath.

"So be it. I suspect you'll make a good match. I'm surprised I didn't foresee the outcome of bringing the two of you together. You have my blessing."

Isabel leapt from her chair and flung her arms around her brother's neck, nearly knocking him off the bench. When he regained his balance, Justin returned her embrace, hugging her tightly. Feeling an incredible sense of relief, Chetwynd watched brother and sister as they laughed together. Then they turned to him, and he saw two sets of identical brown eyes beaming at him.

"Thank you for your blessing, Justin," he said, his hoarse voice betraying the emotion he felt. "I will do all in my power to deserve your trust and keep Isabel safe."

"I'm sure you will, Chetwynd. Now I'd like a tour of the estate that is to be Isabel's future home." Then, as though to settle the matter, he added, "Tomorrow morning we'll all leave for Aachen."

In bed that night, Chetwynd and Isabel discussed their long-awaited reunion with Justin. "It went a great deal better than I had hoped," Chetwynd admitted.

"Yes, Justin listened to reason, thank goodness. But then I guess that's his strength. It won't be long before he comes to believe our match was his idea."

"You're probably right. I wish I could be as calm and reasonable as Justin. My mind seems to work best when I have to make a quick decision in battle or in a dangerous situation. But when I saw you again in the pond at Narbonne, I lost my mind. I was ruled by another part of my anatomy."

Isabel laughed. "I assume you're speaking about your heart."

"That, too." Chetwynd pulled Isabel to lie on top of his stomach and then pushed her upright so she was straddling him. "I want to look at you, Isabel," he said reverently as he pushed her long hair away from her bare breasts.

The way he caressed her with his hands and his eyes made it hard for Isabel to sit still. When she saw that he enjoyed her movements, she didn't even try. His caresses became increasingly intimate, and she let out a small shout. Hearing herself, she quickly covered her mouth with her hand and tried to wiggle free.

"What's the matter, Isabel?" Chetwynd asked, holding her in place with his hands on her waist. "Did I hurt you?"

Isabel replied in a whisper. "Justin might hear us. You can become quite loud, my lord."

"As can you, my love." Chetwynd grinned up at her. "Don't worry. I had Gertrude fix a room for your brother on the far side of the manor."

"What brilliant strategy, my lord. I can understand why you are so good in battle."

They had Justin's blessing, and for the first time Isabel and Chetwynd came together without a touch of anxiety. Their passion seemed to increase as they made love in a carefree and joyous manner. When they finally lay exhausted, they took turns exchanging small bursts of laughter. Although Isabel was worn out and wasn't sure she'd ever be able to move again, she didn't want to lose him to sleep just yet.

"Tell me about Aachen, my lord."

"Go to sleep, Isabel," Chetwynd muttered against her ear.

"In a minute. Open your eyes and tell me one thing about Aachen." She put her hands on his face, forcing him to look at her so she could see that he kept his eyes open.

"When we reach Aachen they should put you to work in the dungeon, torturing prisoners," he grumbled.

"There is a dungeon? No, I don't want to hear about that. Tell me something good about the palace."

Chetwynd pretended to sigh, but her enthusiasm to hear more made him eager to satisfy her. "The palace at Aachen was one of Charlemagne's favorites. Although he had many palaces throughout his empire, he spent a lot of time there.

He built a church in imitation of the great Roman cathedrals he admired so much. I think you'll like it. Everyone who comes to Aachen enjoys visiting Charlemagne's burial place at the cathedral. Now go to sleep."

"Father Ivo told me that Charlemagne gathered scholars and poets from all over the empire, and even beyond its borders, to bring them to Aachen. I can just imagine those poets sitting around, reading their poems to each other. Perhaps they even composed epics in imitation of Homer. I wonder if *Song of Roland* was composed there."

"I don't know, but the story of the brave knight who served Charlemagne is a favorite with minstrel singers. Jerome is always demanding to hear the heroic exploits of Roland."

"Yes, I can imagine he would enjoy them. Does King Louis spend as much time in Aachen as Charlemagne did?"

"Probably even more. He had a monastery built nearby, and he retreats there often. Aachen also has historical significance for the king. At the time of Charlemagne's death, Louis was ruling in Aquitania. As soon as he heard that his father was dead, he journeyed to Aachen to assume power. There was some anxiety about the reception he would receive from Charlemagne's former ministers. But Louis was greeted with enthusiasm and an oath of fealty was quickly pledged to the new king and emperor. I think Louis has a particular fondness for Aachen because of the acceptance he found there."

Isabel was yawning as he finished. "Now you're sleepy and I'm wide awake," Chetwynd complained.

"I could do something to wear you out again," she murmured, but she was asleep before she could reach for him.

"Tomorrow, my love," Chetwynd whispered as he kissed her nose.

They'd had their best day since Isabel had returned to him. But Chetwynd knew the danger was not over, and he wondered if he was wise to honor his promise to keep Isabel with him. Sighing, he accepted that he didn't have a choice in the matter. Whatever lay ahead in Aachen, they would face it together.

CHAPTER SEVENTEEN

*T*HE LAST LEG OF ISABEL AND CHETWYND'S long journey from Narbonne to Aachen was different from what had gone before. Since Justin and his men now led the way, Chetwynd was free to ride beside Isabel, followed closely by Ingram and Jerome. Isabel's sense of excitement affected her three companions, and their mood was cheerful and relaxed. Not until they were finally nearing Aachen did Isabel notice that Chetwynd had sobered and become more vigilant.

Although the day was cloudy and the visibility poor, Isabel kept her eyes focused on the road ahead, eager for her first sight of Aachen. Under the trees the moisture formed a mist, but when they suddenly emerged from the forest, the path ahead cleared, and in the distance she had an unobstructed view of their destination. It was an impressive sight. There were a great number of towers reaching up to the sky, each flying a colorful pennant. Below the towers were sturdy walls topped by battlements that ringed the city. A wide drawbridge led up to the massive structure. She could see that the tall gate on the other side, although standing open, was heavily guarded.

As their party moved closer, the ramparts loomed larger and taller. "You'll strain your neck, my love," Chetwynd teased as she stared above her.

Unwilling to lower her gaze for fear of missing something, Isabel ignored him. The horses made a loud din as they crossed the bridge, and Isabel finally lowered her gaze to study the dark water in the moat. In spite of all she had heard about Aachen, Isabel was still unprepared for its size and the vast number of people milling about the keep within its walls. Outside the approach to Aachen had been exciting, but inside Isabel felt closed-in and apprehensive because of the crowds.

"Stay close to me," Chetwynd called to her as some strangers on horseback mingled with their group, and they lost track of Justin and his men. "We'll go directly to my living quarters in the palace." He had to shout over the noise in the keep.

Isabel nodded to him and guided her horse to stay just behind his. At the stables, Chetwynd helped her dismount. "It's not far from here," he assured her, and took her hand to guide her through an open market.

There were many stalls selling fine leather goods, rich fabrics, and glittering jewelry. Isabel stopped a few times, attracted by the wares for sale. Jerome and Ingram went on ahead, and Chetwynd urged Isabel along. At last they reached an alley that led them away from the busy market, and Isabel heard her name called. Marianna flew from a doorway and embraced Isabel so tightly she found it hard to breathe.

"When you left Saint Ives, I feared I'd never see you again, my lady. Jerome told me you were on your way, and I could hardly believe it. Have you ever seen such a place? I didn't know there were so many people in the world."

Marianna held Isabel away so she could see for herself that she was all right. "You look lovely, my lady," she said.

Isabel and Marianna were embracing again when Chetwynd suggested they go inside. They followed Marianna up a long, narrow staircase that took several turns and seemed to go on forever.

"It's good to see you, also, my lord. The chambers here are handy, but they needed some airing." Marianna spoke as she climbed. "They seemed very empty without someone to share them. I'm so glad I'm no longer alone. I put all your clothes in the small bedchamber, my lady."

They had entered the outer room and Chetwynd replied to Marianna. "You can put Isabel's clothes in the large bedchamber with mine, Marianna."

Her maid looked to Isabel for confirmation of what Chetwynd had said. Isabel's grin confirmed her hopes. Marianna hugged her mistress again and then wiped away a few tears. "I knew it would work out," she murmured, more to herself than to Chetwynd or Isabel.

Now that she found herself in a quiet place, Isabel was unsure what she should do next. The few connecting rooms that were Chetwynd's quarters were sparsely furnished and had the appearance of being temporary, with little decoration on the walls. The large bedchamber was also the main room, and there were a few benches and tables in addition to the bed. When Isabel moved to one of the two windows, Chetwynd came to stand behind her. As she looked down on the surrounding countryside where the fields seemed to stretch on forever, Chetwynd placed his hands on her shoulders.

"From here it's easy to forget the palace is so large," Isabel said over her shoulder.

"That's one of the reasons I like these rooms. Does Aachen meet your expectations?" he asked.

"In some ways it does. But I didn't expect to be overwhelmed. The sheer size is startling, and in the bailey the area was so crowded."

"It takes some getting used to. Most people are overwhelmed at first." He turned her to face him. "I hate to leave you so soon, but I think I should join Justin and find out the latest news about the queen. Why don't you take a little rest, and I'll be back as soon as possible. If you like, we can visit the marketplace before vespers."

"Oh yes, I'd like that." She moved into his arms, and they held each other tightly for a few minutes. Isabel felt uneasy in the strange place and was reluctant to let him go, but she knew it would be unreasonable to object. After he gave her a long and comforting kiss, she murmured, "Hurry back."

Marianna had given them some time to themselves, but as soon as Chetwynd departed, she rushed into the bedchamber. "Tell me everything that happened, my lady. What was Aquis like? Did it hurt to lose your maidenhead? Was Justin very angry with Chetwynd? Did they fight?"

"Give me a minute, Marianna. Help me remove my head covering. Then I'll answer your questions."

With her hair free, Isabel sat on the bed she planned to share later with her husband, and Marianna pulled a bench close to her. "Aquis is a lovely manor, Marianna. There is a valley with a vineyard, and the grapes were being harvested while I was there. It's well managed by a friendly couple who made me feel at home. Their names are Gertrude and Bosco, and I know you'll like them."

"I can't wait to see it, my lady."

Isabel yawned and stretched before continuing. "When Justin arrived at Aquis, he was very angry, but he and Chetwynd did not come to blows. Chetwynd suggested that Justin might have foreseen that we would make a match when he asked Chetwynd to bring me to court. Of course Justin objected to that idea and questioned us endlessly. In the end, he accepted the marriage and gave his blessing."

Isabel lay back and closed her eyes, smiling as she remembered the scene. Although Justin had been irate, she couldn't imagine the two men coming to blows.

"And what about the other?" Marianna urged impatiently.

Isabel knew exactly what she wanted to know. "Oh yes, the other. Chetwynd was very considerate, Marianna."

Her maid frowned at her words. "You don't mean to tell me nothing happened, do you?"

Isabel laughed. "Oh, something happened. Several times. I just meant he was gentle. The ointment we brought worked well, and I owe Emma thanks for supplying it and you for reminding me it was there."

Marianna nodded her satisfaction. "He'll make a wonderful husband, my lady. I can tell just by seeing the two of you together."

"I'm sure you're right." Isabel studied Marianna, and realized she had acquired a more confident air since they left Narbonne. "Now tell me about your time here, Marianna. I find Aachen rather daunting. What are your impressions?"

"I was most uneasy when I first arrived. There were so many people everywhere. But the very first night, at supper, I found Henny. Do you remember the serving woman from our journey? She works in the kitchen when she's here, and she made me feel welcome. After I met her again, she put me to work helping her so I'd learn about the place. I relaxed a bit after that."

"I'm glad you had someone familiar to show you around, Marianna."

"Would you like me to help you change out of those dusty clothes and have a wash before Chetwynd returns?"

As Marianna lovingly attended Isabel, she described the huge kitchen and the large number of women who worked there. "It's friendly enough, my lady, although Henny warned me to be careful what I say. Gossip travels fast. Of course right now the queen is the main topic of conversation. There is also a great deal of lamenting over the death of the nun Gerberga. She was popular with the women, my lady."

"Yes, Gilda said as much. Is there any hint that the queen will be returning to the palace soon?"

"I wouldn't be at all surprised. King Louis returned from his retreat and is now gone from the palace. Some say he has gone to fetch the queen home."

"King Louis is not at Aachen?" This news made Isabel uneasy. "Justin and Chetwynd have gone to report to him, Marianna."

"Well they won't find him, my lady. Lothar is here, and from what I hear he is in a foul mood. The women say that Lothar hates his stepmother, and is cross because she is due back at court. They all wish he'd return to his own palace in Rome."

Isabel marveled at the way Marianna talked so easily about the most powerful people in the empire. "You seem to have learned a great deal in a short time."

"I keep my ears open and my mouth shut. The serving women talk a great deal, but they are careful to check who is around. Henny is trusted by many, and she is open with me."

"What did you hear about Gerberga?"

"When the nun was thrown into the dungeon, everyone assumed she would be released without harm. Apparently it was not the first time Gerberga had been seized. However, this time King Louis was away from the palace, and her supporters couldn't reach him. Bishop Agobard decided to hold a trial to test whether Gerberga was a witch. She didn't pass, of course. The trials are such that not many endure them and are found innocent. She was executed secretly before anyone powerful could help."

Isabel shivered at the tale. "How terrible," she said, an uneasy feeling replacing her happiness at being in Aachen.

"No one seems to know, or will say, whether Lothar was involved in the trial. According to the women, there was no love between him and Gerberga, and he certainly wouldn't be above using her to make trouble for the queen. But most doubt he would go so far as having her put to death. She is the sister of Bernard of Septimania, the king's chamberlain, who was also away from the palace."

"What of the boy, Charles? Is there any word about his fate?" Isabel asked.

"Oh, he is safe enough, my lady. He is being well cared for by his nurse. King Louis's son is in no danger."

Isabel remembered that Chetwynd believed the boy would be safe, and Marianna's news seemed to confirm his view. That was reassuring. But the fact that King Louis was away from the palace, and Lothar was in charge, made her nervous for Chetwynd and Justin. In Father Ivo's tales about Aachen, it was a place where poets and thinkers gathered. Clearly it was also a center of political intrigue and even menace, where people who displeased the king or the powerful church fathers could be thrown in the dungeon.

As Isabel was revising her thoughts about court life, Justin arrived at their door. Although he greeted them cheerfully enough, Isabel noticed a telltale crease on his forehead and stiffness about his mouth.

It didn't take a second for Isabel to realize he was alone. "Did Chetwynd find you?" Isabel asked her brother, trying to still her growing alarm.

"He did. King Louis is away from court, but we are expecting him to return tomorrow." Justin looked around the room to avoid looking her in the eye. "I see you have made yourself at home here."

Trying not to read too much into her brother's inability to look at her, Isabel asked as casually as she could manage, "Where's Chetwynd?"

"There is nothing to worry about, Isabel," he began, and his words had the very opposite effect from the one he desired. He might be a diplomat, but Isabel knew him too well to be fooled. She waited for the rest without speaking, and Justin finally said, "Lothar has detained Chetwynd. He said he wished to speak with him."

Making a great effort to remain calm, Isabel took a deep breath. "Why would Lothar detain Chetwynd?" she asked, using the same word Justin had used, but wondering if he meant Lothar was holding Chetwynd against his will.

"They had some words," Justin admitted. "When we entered King Louis's chambers expecting to find the king, we found Lothar. Unfortunately, he was in a foul mood. I suspect Lothar has always resented Chetwynd and his influence upon King Louis. Chetwynd's friendship with the queen increased his resentment. Our timing was bad, and Lothar turned his anger on Chetwynd."

"Where, exactly, is Chetwynd, Justin?"

"Lothar just needs some time to cool off. As soon as the king arrives, Chetwynd will be released."

Isabel kept her voice even but firm. "Justin, I want to know where Chetwynd is."

Justin looked from Isabel to Marianna. "In the dungeon, but just for a short time, I'm sure."

When both women gasped, he quickly added, "Lothar wants to talk with him. As I said, Lothar was in a temper, and I suspect he wants to cool down before he questions Chetwynd."

Isabel sat down abruptly, afraid her legs would give out. Justin sat on the bench beside her and put his arm around her shoulder.

"I'm making a mess of this, Isabel. I'm not going to try and convince you that this is not a dangerous situation. You're too smart for that. But Chetwynd is a soldier, and he's used to danger. He will survive this as he has survived many other dangers. I know this is all new to you, Isabel, but you have to trust me to see that nothing happens to Chetwynd."

Isabel nodded. "I do trust you, Justin."

Justin held her tight for a few more minutes before speaking again. "I'm sorry to bring this news, then rush away, Isabel. I knew you would be concerned when Chetwynd didn't return. Now I must see if I can find out when King Louis will arrive at court. The king is our best chance to free Chetwynd before Lothar decides to question him. I am afraid the two men rub each other the wrong way. Are you going to be all right?"

Although she had dug her fingernails into the palm of her hands, Isabel spoke calmly in hope of speeding Justin on his way. "Yes, I'll be fine. Please do all you can to get Chetwynd released. Don't worry about us."

"I'm sure he won't be held long. It was a matter of being at the wrong place at the wrong time." Justin embraced Isabel again and nodded toward Marianna. "Take good care of her," he said before he rushed away.

As soon as he left, Isabel turned to Marianna. "See what you can find out in the kitchen, Marianna," she said.

"I can't leave you, my lady. Justin asked me to take care of you."

"Marianna, you can help me by finding out all you can about Chetwynd. I don't know anyone here, but I'm sure you can learn something. From what you told me, the information will be available quickly in the kitchen."

"Yes, my lady. I'm sure the serving women will know

something. Food is sent to the prisoners once a day, late in the evening."

"Do you know who takes it?"

"A woman called Herlinda, a serving woman happy for the duty. There is a guard she fancies, so she is a good source of information. She can find out which level Chetwynd is on, and how he is faring."

"What do you mean, which level he is on?"

Marianna hesitated before answering, but at Isabel's insistent look she continued. "Prisoners detained for questioning are usually on the top level, I'm told. The lower down you are, the more serious your offense. Those sent to the bottom of the dungeon are usually never heard from again." Realizing how bad that sounded, Marianna's voice trailed off at the end.

In spite of her concern for Chetwynd, Isabel could not help but marvel at all Marianna had learned in a short time in Aachen. It was going to take her a while to catch up.

"If Lothar wants to question Chetwynd, he should be on the first level. But if he just wanted to question him, why put him in the dungeon? It's not like he's going anywhere. It doesn't make sense, Marianna. I should have made Justin tell me exactly what happened. What time does Herlinda bring food to the prisoners?"

"Not until everyone else has eaten. Late in the evening, she takes the scraps. But she might know who the latest prisoners are before that time. As I said, she fancies one of the guards."

"Good, that sounds promising. You had better go, Marianna. We're wasting time. I'll go to evening worship and then join the lords and ladies in the great hall for dinner. Perhaps I'll find Jerome and Ingram at the church. I wonder if they know about Chetwynd. I forgot to ask Justin if he informed them of what happened. I should have thought to ask for more information. If you learn anything, seek me out at supper in the great hall."

Isabel had spoken quickly, and now she was urging Marianna toward the door.

"Are you sure it's wise for you to go out on your own, my lady? You don't know the city. I could find Ingram and send him to you."

Isabel couldn't imagine sitting around waiting for Ingram to appear. "If you find him, send him to the church. But in the meantime, I'm not staying here. I have to do something, Marianna. I saw the church on the way in, and I can follow the worshippers from the church to the great hall, if necessary. Don't worry about me. Please go now."

Marianna nodded encouragingly. "You'll do fine. I'll get some news for you, my lady."

WHILE ISABEL WAS FINDING HER WAY TO THE church Chetwynd had told her about, he sat in his cell and worried about her. He kept telling himself Justin would look after her, but he could not help but be concerned, not only for her safety but also about her reaction to the news that he was in the dungeon. He had no doubt that she would extract the information from Justin. When Isabel had clung to him at their parting, he knew she had sensed they were entering another period of uncertainty.

Isabel had been right to feel uneasy. In the king's chambers where Chetwynd and Justin had expected to find Louis, they had found Lothar in a raging temper. Justin knew immediately that it was a dangerous situation. He signaled Chetwynd to leave, but before Chetwynd had a chance to disappear, the pacing Lothar had turned and caught sight of him at the entrance. Lothar's thick, dark hair was disheveled from running his hands through it, and his face was red from drink and fury.

"My stepmother's partner in sin!" he shouted at the sight of Chetwynd. "What are you doing here?"

"Lord Chetwynd is with me, Your Majesty," Justin replied quickly. He tried to calm Lothar and at the same time keep Chetwynd from reacting to Lothar's insulting remark. "He has just returned from the Spanish March. Lord Chetwynd has been away from court for some time."

Justin hoped to remind Lothar of Chetwynd's distance from the recent turmoil at the palace. He stood between the two men, but Lothar strode around him and moved close enough to stare into Chetwynd's face.

Chetwynd could smell the wine on Lothar's breath as he shouted, "Yes, yes. I know all about Lord Chetwynd. The brave knight hurrying back to help the queen. And we all know the type of help he gives."

Lothar's tone of voice and the mocking expression on his face emphasized the sarcasm of his words. There were several lords and guards present, and someone chuckled at the remark.

Squaring his shoulders, Chetwynd replied with as much dignity as he could manage in the face of the vicious attack. "I have returned to Aachen to report to King Louis about the fortifications on the Spanish March."

"So you say. Are you sure it's not to warm the queen's bed? Maybe you haven't heard, Chetwynd. Judith is not here. How sad for you."

Chetwynd ignored the fake sympathy on Lothar's face. "As I said, I've come to report to King Louis."

Chetwynd's steely control only seemed to make Lothar

angrier. "Well, you have found a different king to answer to. You seem to forget that I am also a king and share rule of the empire with my father. The king standing before you is not a feeble old man to be easily duped!" Lothar roared.

"You are not half the man your father is," Chetwynd replied softly, more to himself than Lothar.

Chetwynd knew as soon as the words were out that he had made a mistake. But when Lothar demanded he repeat what he said, he did.

Lothar let out a string of curses, then shouted, "Guards, throw him into the dungeon. I'll speak with you later, Chetwynd, after a few days in the dungeon has softened your defiance. Then you can give me your report on the Spanish fortifications."

Before the guards could act, Justin tried to reason with Lothar. "Don't do this, my lord. Chetwynd was just defending King Louis to whom he has vowed an oath of loyalty. I need him with me to discuss some important matters with you."

There was a pause and Justin looked at Chetwynd, prompting him with his eyes to apologize to Lothar. But Lothar didn't give Chetwynd time to try that approach. "I want him out of my sight. Take him away!" Lothar shouted at the guards.

Sitting in his cell, Chetwynd hoped that Justin wasn't angry with him. He had been a fool to antagonize Lothar. He had known since the Spring Assembly that Lothar had taken a strong dislike to him. He should have been more careful.

At the same time, it was clear Lothar had been looking for an excuse to detain him. He couldn't help but wonder why Lothar was so angry. Hopefully Justin would figure out what was going on and be able to obtain his freedom.

In the meantime, Chetwynd had a chance to experience the dungeon, and he didn't like it. Although he had faced danger on the battlefield many times, it was nowhere near as frightening as sitting helplessly in a cell. Fortunately, he was on the top level of the dungeon, but even here the rooms were small, and the only light came through a window high on the wall. A single wooden bench sat against the wall, and the straw on the floor was filthy. From the small barred window in the door, he could see that the other cells on the top level were empty. There was no one to talk to, not even a fellow prisoner.

After pacing for a while, Chetwynd sat with his head leaning back against the wall. He wondered what Justin would tell Isabel. Even if her brother tried to sound reassuring, Isabel would sense the truth of the situation. He knew her powers of intuition were strong, and his heart twisted at the anguish he was causing her. Isabel knew the situation at the palace was volatile, and she would remember what had happened to Gerberga. It was a dangerous time to be in prison.

Wondering about how Isabel would react, Chetwynd refused to believe he wouldn't see her again very soon. She had become the most important person in his life. He ached to hold her in his arms and tell her how much she meant to him. When he closed his eyes, he imagined her face, grinning at him, challenging him. Her strong spirit had dazzled him from their first meeting.

Suddenly Chetwynd opened his eyes. Isabel had freed herself from a vicious band of kidnappers. Remembering her courage caused him to jump up from the bench. What would she do? She might even take on Lothar. Did Justin realize he had to watch her?

Placing his face at the opening in the door, he shouted,

"Guard!" He called out over and over again, only giving up when his throat began to ache, and it was clear there was no one to hear his demand to see Justin.

CHAPTER EIGHTEEN

*I*SABEL RUSHED THROUGH THE BAILEY, THIS time ignoring the stalls in the marketplace, as well as the enticing calls from merchants hawking their wares. Focused on finding the church, she paid little attention to the people milling about on foot and horseback. To avoid being trampled by horses or getting lost in the crowd, she moved along the wall. She told herself she would circle the entire bailey, if necessary, until she came upon the famous church.

Although Isabel had told Marianna she thought she knew how to find the church, now she was turned around and nothing looked familiar. She continued on, avoiding the alleys that led away from the courtyard. She was sure the church would be in plain view. Frustrated that she didn't immediately see it, she looked for someone to approach for directions. She was about to ask an old woman carrying two huge baskets filled with vegetables when she caught sight of the church Father Ivo had told her about.

Not taking time to admire the structure, Isabel rushed up the stone steps, pushed open the tall wooden door, and stepped into the vestibule. The quiet inside was calming, and she breathed a sigh of relief. Because she was early for vespers, there were few people around. Entering the main body of the church, she saw that it was an octagon with galleries set high above the nave and a raised area for the choir on the main level. Clearly the church was designed to hold a large number of people.

Sitting down on a bench, Isabel continued looking around her, forgetting everything else for a minute in her admiration of the arrangement. She could picture the galleries full of lords and ladies observing the services far below them, and she wondered if this was where the ministers had pledged fealty to King Louis after Charlemagne died.

Isabel wasn't distracted for long from her main concern. Bowing her head, she said a long prayer for Chetwynd's safety. When she was done, she raised her head and watched as people began to enter the church. Isabel had stayed at the back, hoping to catch sight of Jerome or Ingram. They finally appeared, and she could tell by the strained expressions on their faces that they had heard about Chetwynd. It took only a minute for Jerome to spot her in the crowd. Isabel watched him point out her location to Ingram.

Once seated beside her, Ingram whispered, "Marianna said you would meet us here, my lady. I'm relieved you located the church. I was worried you'd become lost in the crowd."

"I had no problem, Ingram," she said, exaggerating to put him at ease. "Do you have any news of Chetwynd?"

"Only what you already know. Justin sought us out. We were about to join you in Chetwynd's quarters, when we saw Marianna. She told us you'd be here. I doubt your brother would approve of your venturing out alone, my lady."

"I wanted Marianna to see what she could find out in the kitchen. Waiting alone in Chetwynd's chambers would have driven me mad, Ingram."

Although Ingram's uneasy expression didn't change, Isabel

noticed that the silent Jerome was nodding in agreement, and she smiled a little. Ingram must have seen the exchange as he muttered a reminder to Jerome, "Our job is to keep Lady Isabel safe."

The young squire appeared taken aback and didn't reply.

"And just what do you intend to do, my lady?" Ingram asked.

"Except for seeking information in the great hall, I have no idea," she admitted. "But maybe I'll think of something."

"This is a serious and dangerous matter. Trust Justin to do what is necessary. Please don't do anything on your own."

"I do trust Justin, Ingram. I just need to make sure Chetwynd is safe. Don't worry about me."

The two men looked at each other, and even Jerome seemed uneasy at her words. "I'll be careful," she said.

Evening worship began, and Isabel tried to concentrate on the service. But her thoughts were full of her husband. Picturing him in the dungeon had her clenching her fists. Since the service could not hold her attention, she looked around to distract herself. There was a group of nuns who had come in late and sat together on the other side of the church. Something about one of the nuns caught her eye. Isabel realized she was the same height as Gilda, and she even held her head the way Gilda did.

When the nun raised her head from prayer, Isabel pointed and whispered to Ingram. "It's Gilda. What is she doing here?"

Ingram followed her eyes and was as surprised as she was. Worried about why Gilda would be in Aachen, Isabel could barely sit still through the rest of the service. As soon as it was over, she rushed around the back and waited for Gilda to pass by. When she did, Isabel grabbed her arm and pulled her from the line of nuns filing out of the church.

Taken aback for a minute, Gilda smiled when she recognized Isabel and embraced her. Isabel enjoyed the comfort for only a moment before pulling out of Gilda's arms. "What are you doing here? Does it have something to do with Chetwynd being in the dungeon?"

The shock on Gilda's face told Isabel that she hadn't heard the news. "Oh, I'm so sorry, Gilda. I shouldn't have blurted it out like that." She looked about quickly. "I must talk with you."

Gilda's eyes were wide, but she had regained her composure. "We need a private place. Come with me, Isabel."

Ingram and Jerome had caught up with Isabel, and she explained to them that she needed to talk to Gilda privately.

"We should stay with you," Jerome insisted.

"I'm taking her to the nuns' residence, Jerome. No men are allowed. Isabel will be safe there," Gilda pointed out. "We'll seek you out later in the great hall."

Ingram insisted that they escort Gilda and Isabel to the residence. Once there, he looked at the many nuns coming and going and frowned at Jerome as though expecting him to come up with a solution.

"We'll be safe here," Gilda repeated.

"Don't be long or I'll send Jerome in there to fetch you," Ingram warned, grinning slightly at Jerome's startled expression.

Once the men were gone, Gilda led Isabel through the residence. They passed by a warren of small rooms, and then through a door into a walled garden on the other side. Gilda indicated they should sit on a bench and said, "Everyone is at early supper. We will be able to talk here without fear of being disturbed. Now tell me what happened."

"All I know is what Justin told me, and I'm not sure he gave me the whole story. Chetwynd went off to see King

Louis, and the next thing I knew he was imprisoned. Justin said that when he and Chetwynd entered the king's chambers, they found Lothar instead of Louis. Lothar was in a foul temper.

"This is where Justin wasn't too clear. Apparently because of some misunderstanding, Lothar detained Chetwynd. Justin tried his best to reassure me that he would be able to free Chetwynd, but the climate at court makes me fearful. If Lothar wished to question Chetwynd, why detain him in the dungeon?"

Isabel did not realize that tears were rolling down her cheeks until Gilda wordlessly wiped them away with the sleeve of her robe. It was a few minutes before Isabel could continue.

"When I saw you in the church, Gilda, I thought something terrible had happened to Chetwynd and that you, being his sister, had been sent for. Which doesn't make any sense, since you couldn't have gotten here so soon. I'm having trouble thinking straight right now. What are you doing here?"

"King Louis arrived at Saint Ives to escort Queen Judith back to Aachen. He was taking a day to rest and pray, but he sent a few of us ahead to make sure everything would be ready for the queen's return. The queen requested that I go with the others.

"Since you can rarely take things the queen says or does at face value, it's hard to tell why she wanted me to come to Aachen. I'm hoping she believed the story I told when I delivered Chetwynd's note and thinks of me as a friend. She has given me a great deal of attention since that time. As you know, she was very close to Gerberga. I think she feels she can trust the nuns to help her."

Isabel stared at her. "The queen could be using you,

Gilda. I hope we haven't put you in danger by involving you in our escape from Saint Ives."

"I doubt I'm in physical danger. Of course the queen will use me if she can, as she does everyone. In any case, it has given me a chance to visit Aachen."

Isabel was relieved to hear Gilda say that King Louis was returning to the palace. "Justin is convinced that King Louis will see that Chetwynd is released," she said.

"Because of my connection to Queen Judith, perhaps I can be of some help to Justin, Isabel. I've never met him, but I'd like to. Chetwynd has spoken of him often."

"I can't tell you how happy I am that you are here, Gilda. The news you bring is good, and your presence in Aachen is comforting. I hated saying goodbye to you in such a rushed manner at Saint Ives."

"I suspect a lot has happened to you since you left the convent, Isabel. Would you like to tell me your impressions of Aquis while we walk around the garden? I'm curious as to whether you enjoyed your stay at Chetwynd's manor."

Before answering, Isabel stood up and looked around for the first time. She could see the garden was laid out in a small maze made up of shoulder-height bushes. As she headed down the path, she found shrines set in some of the corners, as well as benches where strollers could rest. Following the path, Isabel told Gilda how much she enjoyed being at Aquis.

"I had no idea the manor would be so beautiful. Chetwynd was modest in his description. We were fortunate to be there during the grape harvest. It was a happy time, and I learned how to cut and stomp grapes. Everyone made me feel at home."

A good listener, Gilda let Isabel talk. When they came to the center of the maze, they turned and started back to the beginning. "This is a wonderful garden, Gilda. It's very peaceful."

"I'm glad you like it. This garden is my favorite place in Aachen. I know everyone talks about the church that Charlemagne built to imitate Roman cathedrals, but for me there is more peace and communion with God to be had in this small, walled-in garden. I hope it's not heresy to say that," she finished with a grin.

Isabel grinned back at her. "You are the most unusual nun I've ever met, Gilda."

"And do you know a lot of nuns?" Gilda teased her.

Isabel laughed. "No, I don't. I just had a notion about what nuns are like. Very serious, prayed a lot. That type of thing."

"Yes, most people make assumptions about us. Like every group of people, each of us is a little different. Perhaps I'm a little more different than most."

Gilda had observed how animated Isabel was when she talked about Aquis. "Tell me something, Isabel. Has my brother made you his wife yet?"

Isabel pretended to be shocked by her question. "Marianna wanted to know the same thing. And before that, Justin asked if we were living as brother and sister. I didn't expect to hear the same query from a nun."

"Why don't you just answer the question?"

Isabel laughed again. "Yes. Chetwynd finally bedded me. Now everyone knows."

"Good. I never saw two people better matched."

Suddenly both women were silent, as they remembered where Chetwynd was. Gilda took Isabel's hand. "Let's sit here," she said, pointing to a bench. "There is a patch of herbs planted around the seat. Today you can smell the mint, but different fragrances dominate at different times of the year." They were quiet for a few minutes, enjoying the quiet oasis.

"I don't know what I'll do if something happens to Chetwynd, Gilda. We've had so little time together."

"I'll not try to convince you there isn't any danger. But it won't be long before the king and queen return to Aachen. When they do, Justin will approach the king and I will speak with Judith. Your brother is not going to let anything happen to Chetwynd. If Lothar is wise, he won't do anything in the meantime."

"How wise is he? Several people have said he is easy to anger."

"Let's try and find out why that is," Gilda suggested. "That's something we can do. Maybe we'll see Lothar in the great hall and can judge whether he has settled down. There might be some talk to give us a clue. We should hurry along to supper, before Ingram sends poor Jerome in here."

As they stood up, Isabel said, "Marianna has gone to see what she can learn in the kitchen."

"An excellent place to hear things. As is the dining hall. But we have to be careful. We don't want to do anything to attract attention to ourselves. If Lothar discovers who you are, he can use you to threaten Chetwynd," Gilda reminded Isabel.

"Do you think he'd do that?"

"I have no idea. But if Lothar was involved in kidnapping you to delay Chetwynd's arrival at court, he won't hesitate to use you again. Let's go and see what we can find out."

"If you're with me, you're going to stand out in your brown robe, Gilda. Lothar may know Chetwynd's sister is a nun. You'd be no safer than I would."

"You're right. We'll stop in my chamber and I'll change."

In Gilda's tiny room, Isabel sat on the narrow bed and

watched Gilda remove her habit. When she took off her head covering, Isabel almost gasped at the sight of Gilda's long blond tresses. Isabel had thought Gilda's serene face was beautiful, but the sight of her golden hair, so like Chetwynd's, made her realize just how lovely Gilda was.

"Are you supposed to doff your habit, Gilda?"

"I haven't taken my final vows, and there is no rule against it. I'll tell you a secret. I keep a spare set of clothes in case I want to roam about without being recognized as a nun. I got the idea from another nun who used to do the same thing when she wanted to investigate some abuse against a woman. She confided that she was approached in an entirely different manner when she wasn't wearing her habit."

"I can believe that," Isabel muttered as she saw Gilda transformed. Her dark-green gown was plain, but even the modest neckline couldn't hide the shape of her breasts, and her golden hair showed through her veil. There was no disguising her beauty.

"There. Now we are ready to see what we can find out," Gilda said.

In the dungeon, Lord Chetwynd had worn himself out worrying about what Isabel might do. His shouts for a guard had not been answered, and his pacing was unsatisfying in the small cell. Since the dirty straw on the floor was uninviting, he stretched out on the bench. It wasn't long enough to accommodate his length, and he had to bend his legs to lie on his back. He was used to sleeping in uncomfortable places, but his active mind kept him from doing more than dozing.

Chetwynd had his eyes closed when he heard a man's

voice outside his cell. He sat up quickly hoping it was Justin. Since the voice was deep and unfamiliar, he assumed the man was a guard. Rather than call out, he listened to the conversation and wondered if this might be his chance to have a message delivered to Justin.

"Only one prisoner on this level, Herlinda," the guard was explaining. "Some unfortunate lord who angered Lothar."

"Let's leave Dacia to deliver his food so you and I can be alone, Will. She won't mind." The woman's voice had a seductive quality to it.

"Tempting as that sounds, I can't do that. Why'd you bring her along?"

Ignoring his question, she said, "Dacia's not going to let him loose. You can lock her in with him. We need a bit of time to ourselves."

"You'll get me in trouble yet," the guard grumbled.

"It'll be worth your while," she replied with a laugh.

The guard unlocked the door to the cell, and a serving maid stepped inside before the door closed. Chetwynd heard the bolt slide into place.

Although surprised to hear that a woman was being left behind, Chetwynd immediately wondered how this event might suit his purpose. Afraid that Isabel might make some attempt to seek information, he was desperate to get a message to Justin to warn him to keep an eye on her. In the past, she had shown she was willing to act on her own if she thought it was necessary. The serving woman might be easier to bribe than the guard.

Torches had been lit outside his cell, but it was still dim within. The woman stayed by the door, clutching a pail in her hands, and Chetwynd wondered if she was frightened. He stayed seated so as not to alarm her, thinking about what he would say. Only after the others had moved away did she start toward him. In spite of the poor light and drab clothing, Chetwynd recognized the shape and movements immediately and shot to his feet.

"Good lord, what have you done?" he whispered. Isabel dropped the pail when he moved toward her, gathering her into his arms in one sweeping motion. His embrace was so tight she couldn't speak.

After a minute, Chetwynd held her away. His hands were on her shoulders, and he shook her. "What in God's name are you doing? Does Justin know you're here?" he whispered.

Isabel rushed to assure him. "No, no, don't worry. No one knows."

"This is supposed to make me not worry?" He would have shouted if he could.

"I had to make sure you were unharmed," she said, raising her hands to his dear face. "I didn't tell Justin, as he would have stopped me. It was a quick decision. I was in the kitchen with Marianna when Herlinda left to deliver food."

He pushed her hands from his face. "I knew it. I knew you would try something. That was a demented thing to do. How could those women let you come in here?"

Taken aback by his fierce reaction, Isabel defended her friends. "It wasn't their fault, Chetwynd. I talked them into it. I had to see you. It's safe enough. I won't stay long. No one pays any attention to the women who bring food to the prisoners. Please don't waste our time together being angry with me."

Instead of replying, he caught her up in his arms again. He was gentler this time as he pulled her body against his own. "I'm not angry; I'm worried. I don't want you locked in a dungeon."

"You sound angry."

He shook his head. "Do you have any idea the chance you're taking, Isabel? Trust Justin to take care of this. Once you leave this cell, promise me you will not try anything else."

With tears gathering in her eyes, Isabel nodded. "I didn't mean to upset you, Chetwynd. Perhaps I should have stayed away, but all I could think of was seeing you and making sure you were not harmed. I had to come."

"Oh, Isabel," he sighed.

"Let me finish, Chetwynd. When I discovered that Herlinda was leaving for the dungeon, I persuaded her to take me along. I had to talk Marianna into it, but Herlinda thought of it as a prank. She said there'd be no danger. Now that I see you're all right, I'll do as you say and wait for Justin to free you. Please don't be upset."

In spite of his horror that she had taken such a chance, Chetwynd was moved by her words. "It's all right, my love. If I sound angry, it's because I'm frightened out of my mind. There aren't many things that frighten me this much, but clearly thinking of you in danger exceeds them all."

Isabel breathed a sigh of relief as Chetwynd tenderly removed her drab head covering and buried his face in her neck so he could inhale the sweet smell of her. For a minute he was able to forget where they were, and he moved his mouth to capture her lips in a hungry kiss.

When his kiss became tender, she whispered against his lips, "I needed to see you, Chetwynd. That's all I could think of. I'm sorry that I frightened you. I do promise to be careful from now on."

"Maybe I overreacted, Isabel. I can't bear to think of you in here. Come sit with me until they return, but as soon as we hear them, you must get ready to leave."

Pulling her to the bench, he sat her on his lap. Making

an effort to atone for his harsh words, he asked in a teasing voice, "Tell me, where did you get this fetching outfit?"

"Do you like it, my lord? I suspect it's the latest in serving-maid fashion." She kissed him tenderly, thankful for his change of mood. "I'd like to spend the time kissing and holding you, but I have a lot to tell you.

"King Louis is bringing the queen back to Aachen, and they may arrive tomorrow. I know this because the queen sent Gilda on ahead."

"Gilda is here in Aachen?"

"Yes, I saw her in the church. It seems Judith has cultivated a friendship with Gilda since we left Saint Ives. Gilda told me all about it as we walked in the garden at the nun's residence."

"You have been busy, haven't you? I'm surprised Gilda is here. She is almost as impulsive as you are. I hope she isn't getting into any trouble." Chetwynd noticed that Isabel looked away from his eyes.

"What is it, Isabel? What is my sister up to?" he demanded.

"Gilda changed out of her habit and went to the great hall with me. Her idea was to keep a low profile. But Justin found us, and he, like you, was upset that I hadn't stayed in your quarters. Gilda distracted him, and I slipped away to find Marianna. Neither one knows where I am, but Marianna can tell them if need be."

"Dear Lord in heaven. Gilda has become involved in this as well?"

"She has been involved since she delivered your letter to Queen Judith," Isabel reminded him. "Did you know that Gilda and Justin never met? She's a beautiful woman, and I think Justin took notice of that fact."

"Isabel, Gilda is a nun."

"She didn't look like a nun. You should have seen her out of her habit. She told me she stayed at the convent because she enjoys teaching the children. She could change her mind and leave if she wished. She keeps a set of clothes in Aachen so she can move about without anyone knowing she is a nun."

Chetwynd shook his head. "She's just as bad as you are. But don't even think of matching her with Justin. He's involved with Lady Lilith."

"But Lady Lilith isn't interested in marriage. You told me that. Don't you think if she loved him she would marry him?"

"There is her children's inheritance to think of. She is protecting them by not marrying again."

"Lady Lilith should trust Justin to protect her children."

"I have no idea where you get your ideas. Forget about Gilda and Justin. Tell me what you two discovered while you were deceiving everyone."

"I saw Lothar in the great hall. He didn't seem angry, Chetwynd, but we watched him and he was drinking quite a bit."

Chetwynd stiffened. "You didn't approach him or show yourself, did you?"

"No, no, of course not. Gilda and I stayed well out of his sight. Not that he would recognize us, but we didn't even take the chance that someone would point us out to him."

"Good. Isabel, these are dangerous times. One nun has already been executed, and Lothar seems determined to prove he is in control. If Justin doesn't succeed in freeing me tomorrow, promise me you'll return to Aquis and wait for me there."

"I can't promise that, Chetwynd. It would cause me such distress to be so far away while you are in here. Please don't ask me to do that."

"You are driving me mad. My God, I love you, Isabel. All right, I won't ask that of you. But stay close to Justin."

They held each other silently for a while. "Would you like me to tell you about the garden I walked in with Gilda?"

Chetwynd smiled at her attempt to distract him from his worries. "Yes, I'd like to hear about it."

"The garden is behind the walls of the nun's residence, and it's a maze with lots of paths. But the best part was the herb garden where we sat and talked as the smell of mint drifted up to us. I think I'd like to plant an herb garden at Aquis, Chetwynd. Just outside the kitchen door. I don't think Gertrude has one. I'll have a bench built and we can sit on it together."

"I'd like that, my love. Perhaps I should forget about finding the culprit behind your kidnapping. As soon as I'm free, we can return to Aquis together. Let Justin seek out the answers for us."

Isabel beamed her pleasure. "Do you really mean that?"

"Yes. We can stay there until the Spring Assembly. All I want to do is spend as much time as possible with you."

They were staring into each other's eyes when they heard voices. Isabel had promised she would leave at once, and she gave Chetwynd one last kiss. By the time they sprang to their feet, they realized it was not the guard at the door.

"What do we have here?" Lothar asked as he strode into the cell, a self-satisfied grin on his smug face.

CHAPTER NINETEEN

*I*SABEL WAS TOO STUNNED TO DO MORE than stare at Lothar. From the smirk on his face, it was clear that he found the situation amusing. When Chetwynd moved to stand in front of her, shielding her body with his own, she lost sight of Lothar.

Two burly guards crowded into the small cell, forcing Chetwynd to back Isabel up against the wall to keep some distance between himself and the guards. She tried to peer around him, but his bulk made it impossible to see what was happening. However, there was no mistaking the menace in Lothar's voice.

"I have to congratulate you, Lord Chetwynd. Even in the dungeon you manage to find a woman to service you. I wonder what the queen would think of your ability to attract women. But then I guess she already knows about your attractions."

In spite of the provoking taunts, Chetwynd knew how important it was to keep his temper in check. "This is an innocent maid who brought me some food. Let her be on her way, and I'll answer your questions, Lothar."

"An innocent maid. Did we arrive too soon? Let's have a look at the obliging wench."

Realizing there was no point in trying to hide Isabel,

Chetwynd moved aside, trusting that she would play the role he had made up for her. Indeed, she did her best, keeping her eyes down and moving in a meek manner. Unfortunately, although her clothes were drab and bulky, with her head covering removed, her luxurious hair and fine features were evident.

Clearly surprised at her appearance, Lothar examined her suspiciously. Chetwynd was disappointed to see he was not as affected by drink as he had been when they met earlier. It would be more difficult for Isabel to deceive him into believing she was a serving maid who was assigned to feeding prisoners, one of the least desirable jobs available to women.

"Well, look what we have here. I do not remember seeing you in the great hall," Lothar said to Isabel in a tone no doubt meant to sound inviting.

"I've not been serving long. I work mostly in the kitchen," she answered in a quiet voice, her eyes still aimed at the floor.

"Is that a fact? And why would a handsome wench like you be hidden away in the kitchen? I can't imagine."

Lothar moved to stand right in front of Isabel, and his caressing tone of voice made Chetwynd's skin crawl. Relying on Isabel to act her part, he bit the inside of his mouth to keep from interfering.

"Perhaps you would like to become my private serving wench?" Lothar asked.

Isabel did not answer and kept her eyes on the floor until Lothar shouted, "Look at me, girl. Do you prefer a prisoner in the dungeon to a king?"

Isabel's head jerked up, and she looked him full in his stern face.

"Such a defiant look! I doubt there are many serving wenches like you," Lothar exclaimed.

Chetwynd tried to distract him. "Let the wench go about her work, Your Majesty. You came to talk to me. I'm ready to answer all your questions," he said, struggling to keep his voice as casual as possible.

Without looking at Chetwynd, Lothar grabbed a handful of Isabel's hair and pulled her toward him. Chetwynd jumped forward, but before he could reach Lothar, one of the guards blocked his way and the other moved in to knock him to the floor.

When Isabel turned toward Chetwynd, Lothar put his arm around her waist and dragged her out of the way. It took both guards to hold down the struggling Chetwynd. One tried to subdue him by hitting him on the head. Chetwynd heard Isabel scream and managed to throw the guards off him and push himself to his feet.

But Chetwynd stopped struggling abruptly when he saw Lothar holding a knife to Isabel's throat. "You hurt her and you are a dead man," Chetwynd hissed at Lothar, just before he was hit from behind and knocked to the floor again.

"We will see who is a dead man," Lothar shouted at the downed prisoner.

Terrified at seeing the guards kick Chetwynd as he lay on the floor, Isabel pushed the knife away with her right hand. Struggling against Lothar, she almost reached her husband. But Lothar managed to grab hold of her and dragged her out of the cell. He kept a tight grip around her waist until the guards had locked Chetwynd's cell, then pushed her at the guards.

After all the shouting, the silence from the cell was even more frightening for Isabel. "Let me see," she begged the guards, pointing toward the barred opening.

"Bring her to my chambers," Lothar ordered. He turned his back and strode ahead of them.

Reluctant to be moved away from Chetwynd's cell, Isabel dug in her heels. The nearest guard whispered in her ear, "He's not dead, only unconscious. I doubt he is seriously hurt. You'll do best to follow the king's order." The kind way in which he spoke reassured Isabel about Chetwynd's condition, and she became limp with relief.

During the struggle with Lothar, Isabel hadn't paid any attention to the fact that she had cut her hand when she pushed away his knife. By the time they had reached Lothar's chambers, there was a great deal of blood soaking her apron. When Lothar saw the red stain, his expression changed from anger to shock. The blood drained from his face, and he ordered one of his guards to fetch his physician.

"Let me see your hand," he ordered, and his voice was so commanding Isabel did as he asked.

To her surprise, Lothar gently examined her hand and located the deep cut in the fleshy area at the base of her thumb.

"I know what I'm doing. I have two sons and have attended to my share of cuts," he assured her.

By the time the physician arrived, Lothar had wrapped her hand tightly in a clean cloth and seated her in a cushioned chair.

The king's physician, an ancient man with long white hair, gently unwrapped the blood-soaked cloth. He glared disapprovingly at Lothar and spoke in a harsh voice. "You stopped the bleeding. At least you had the sense to wrap it in a clean cloth, Your Majesty." He pronounced the title in a disparaging tone.

"It was an accident, Marlin. I've never hurt a woman in my life. Is she going to be all right?"

"I don't believe in accidents. Go fetch me some water."

Lothar hesitated to obey the curt order, but he and Marlin

had been through many battles together, and with a grimace he finally moved away.

The physician leaned forward and whispered to Isabel, "It's not as bad as it looks. The hand tends to bleed a lot. But no need to let the king know it's a minor injury."

"Lord Chetwynd has been beaten. He's in the dungeon. Could you see to him?" Isabel pleaded with the kindly man who was leaning close.

Marlin straightened up and turned to Lothar, who was returning with a jug of water. "What have you been up to? This serving maid says there is an injured man in the dungeon. Lord Chetwynd, she says. I've heard of the knight. Does he need my attention as well?"

"She is no serving maid," Lothar mumbled. "Go have a look at Chetwynd." Lothar waved the physician away.

"See that she drinks this potion with lots of water." The physician handed the powder to Lothar. "And have one of your servants remove her bloody apron and find her a clean one."

Surprised that Lothar followed the physician's demands, Isabel studied the dark-haired ruler, noticing that his features were well-formed and his beard neatly trimmed. Although she knew Lothar didn't believe she was a serving maid, she wasn't sure whether he knew she was Chetwynd's wife. Because her hand was starting to hurt and she trusted the physician, she drank the potion handed her and tried to think what to do next. But the throbbing pain in her hand made her feel weak. Fatigue kept her from thinking straight, and she closed her eyes for a minute.

When she had recovered a bit, Isabel saw that Lothar was staring at her from a nearby chair. "Who are you?" he finally asked, much more gently this time.

She struggled to sit up straight, looking him in the eye. "I am Lady Isabel, the daughter of Lord Theodoric of Narbonne and wife of Lord Chetwynd," she answered in a steady voice.

Lothar shook his head back and forth. "I was afraid of that. And your brother is Lord Justin, a minister and advisor to King Louis," he mumbled, as though to himself. He was still shaking his head.

Finally, he turned to one of the guards and spoke in a weary voice. "Go find Lord Justin and bring him to me."

Isabel noticed his anger had disappeared, and he too seemed tired. "Thank you, Your Majesty. Would you please free Chetwynd?" She collapsed back against the pillows and, although it wasn't an entirely calculated maneuver, she hoped it would win her some sympathy for her request.

"We'll see about that. I didn't mean for you to be hurt. You must believe that, Lady Isabel. And I really had no idea who you were." Lothar frowned and shook his head. "What were you doing in the cell?"

"I wanted to make sure Lord Chetwynd was all right. He disappeared so suddenly. I only planned to stay a minute." Isabel was too tired to say more.

"Did Chetwynd entice you to visit him?"

"No, of course not. He was most upset that I came," she answered in a small voice, remembering how worried he had been.

"You disguised yourself as a serving wench and went to visit your husband in the dungeon. You are a brave woman, Lady Isabel. But you have caused me a great deal of grief."

"I think it is you who have caused me grief," she retorted, forgetting her resolve to do all she could to persuade him to free Chetwynd.

"Hold your tongue, or I'll throw you back into a cell, and not with your husband." Although his words were harsh, he sounded like he was scolding an irritating child.

Lothar took a deep breath. "I didn't mean that, Lady Isabel. Things have been getting out of hand around here, and I don't need another martyr. I had no idea who you were when I saw you in that cell. How could I possibly know that Lady Isabel would visit Lord Chetwynd in the dungeon? In case you aren't aware of the fact, it's simply not something ladies do."

Lothar had risen to pace back and forth in front of Isabel, and she closed her eyes because his movements made her feel sick. When he pulled over a stool to sit directly in front of her, she opened her eyes and saw his concerned expression.

"Are you all right?" When she nodded, he continued. "How long have you been married to Lord Chetwynd?"

"Almost three weeks, Your Majesty."

"Almost three weeks. All that time. And did you know about your husband's involvement with Queen Judith before you married him?"

"Yes," she replied quickly, telling herself that Lothar didn't need to know that she had no idea that Chetwynd's attachment was the queen. "How is that any concern of yours?"

"I'm the one asking the questions here. I must admit I find this situation very curious." Once again he stood up to pace the floor.

Isabel wished he would stop jumping around. Her head was beginning to ache, and she leaned back and closed her eyes again. There was a buzzing in her ears, but she could still hear Lothar mumbling in the background. He seemed to be talking to himself. She tried to concentrate on what he was saying.

"Now I remember. I've heard stories of you. You're the one who escaped from the kidnappers. No wonder they couldn't hold you. My god, you are the type of woman who inspires legends. They will be writing poems about you and

singing them along with the ode to Lord Roland. His bravery on the battlefield will be compared to your bravery
against kidnappers. I do not want to become part of the legend. As I said before, I don't need another martyr. What am I
going to do with you?"

Isabel couldn't make sense of his mumbling, and wondered if he had gone mad. Why was he talking about Lord
Roland? What did she have to do with the legendary hero of
Charlemagne's Spanish war? She must have gone to sleep for
a few minutes, as the next thing she knew Gilda was leaning
over her.

"Isabel, can you hear me?"

"Yes, of course. Stop shouting, Gilda." She tried to look
around. "What are you doing here?"

"When the guard sought out your brother, I was with
him in the dining hall. Marianna had told us where you
went, and I tried my best to calm Justin down. We were both
waiting for you to return. When Justin was summoned by
King Lothar, I followed along."

Isabel saw Justin over Gilda's shoulder, and she smiled at
him. "Greetings, brother." The pain in her hand had ceased,
and she felt very relaxed.

"What did you give her?" Justin asked Lothar. "Her eyes
are glassy. She looks like she has been drugged."

"My physician gave her a healing potion. I've no intention of harming her, Lord Justin. I never did."

"Yes, yes. So you say, Your Majesty. But she has been
hurt."

Because it was becoming hard to follow the conversation,
Isabel closed her eyes. Gilda was stroking her face with a
sweet-smelling cloth, and she allowed herself to enjoy the
sensation.

"And who are you?" Lothar was saying again. Isabel was

puzzled because she had already told him who she was.

"I'm Gilda, Lord Chetwynd's sister. I'm a nun from the Convent at Saint Ives. I became acquainted with Isabel there. Queen Judith sent me to Aachen to prepare for her arrival. She and King Louis are on their way."

"You're a nun?" Isabel heard Justin's shocked voice and tried to find him in the blurry sea of faces around her.

"Yes, I'm a nun."

Clearly Gilda hadn't told Justin she's a nun. Isabel wondered if Justin was disappointed to hear this news.

"Lord Justin, you brought this woman to my chambers and you don't even know who she is?"

"I know she's Lord Chetwynd's sister, but she didn't tell me she's a nun. Look at her; she doesn't look like a nun."

Isabel decided Justin was definitely angry, and she smiled to herself. Justin and Gilda would suit each other perfectly.

"What's a nun supposed to look like, Lord Justin?"

Gilda sounded angry as well.

Lothar interrupted them. "Can we return to the problem at hand, Lord Justin? I didn't know Lady Isabel's identity, but I did, indirectly, cause her to be injured. It was an accident that happened in Chetwynd's cell."

"It's easy enough for you to make amends, Your Majesty. Release Chetwynd and let him take Isabel back to his manor. That way they will be gone by the time King Louis and the queen arrive. Why you had to put him in the dungeon in the first place is beyond me."

Isabel approved Justin's plan. But she wasn't sure he should talk to Lothar in that manner. She always assumed diplomats spoke more diplomatically.

"You're speaking to a king, Justin. I could have you thrown in the cell with Chetwynd."

"Just settle down, both of you. Why can't you just release

Chetwynd, Your Majesty?"

Good. Gilda was keeping her head, Isabel thought. Don't let them start fighting again.

"It's very simple, my dear . . ."

"She is not *your dear*."

Saints in heaven, Justin. You're supposed to be the diplomat. Isabel tried to open her eyes, but she became dizzy and gave up the effort.

There was silence for a while, and Isabel wished she knew what was happening. Finally, she heard Lothar speaking. "I don't think it would be wise to release him just yet. We need a little time for Lady Isabel to recover from her wound. Lord Chetwynd is going to take one look at her and attempt to kill me. He already threatened me in his cell. I think his words were, 'If you touch her, you're a dead man.' Since I don't want any more trouble with either of them, I think I should delay his release."

"I'm not sure that's wise, Your Majesty. If Chetwynd's worried about Isabel, there is no telling what he will do."

"The man's locked in a cell."

"He has a lot of friends. If Isabel was able to get into the dungeon, one or two of them might also succeed."

Isabel was nodding at Justin's reply. She could picture Jerome storming the dungeon.

"I see your point. I need some time, Justin. The king and queen return to Aachen tomorrow, which is no longer far off. When they arrive, I will return to Rome. Can we delay releasing Chetwynd until then? Lady Isabel should be recovered, and I'll be on my way."

Isabel heard Gilda's voice again, and she struggled to open her eyes.

"I think Chetwynd needs to see that Isabel is all right. I can bring her to the dungeon so she can talk to him."

"He will see her injury, Gilda."

"Wait, the nun has a good idea, Justin. Lady Isabel can stand outside the cell door. She will inform her husband that she is fine and has convinced me to release him as soon as King Louis arrives."

"The nun does not have a good idea. Look at Isabel. Do you think she is in any shape to do what you say?"

"I can do it," Isabel tried to shout, but even to her ears it sounded like a whisper.

"My sister has just made my point," Justin said.

"Wait. Here's the physician. Marlin, why is Lady Isabel so sluggish?" Lothar asked. "Her color is good and the wound has been tended."

"I gave her something to relax her. Just leave her be for an hour, and she'll be fine."

"What about Chetwynd?" Isabel managed to ask the physician, remembering that she asked him to check on her husband.

"Lord Chetwynd is not seriously injured, Lady Isabel. I'm sure he has received much worse treatment and survived. If you go to sleep for an hour, perhaps you can go see him."

Isabel sighed at this promise and gave in to the drowsiness she had been fighting.

The physician looked at the other three and nodded. "Move away and keep your voices down. She should have been asleep an hour ago. No doubt Lady Isabel was straining to hear what you were saying."

Even after they moved to another part of the chambers, Justin kept his voice low. "Did you know that Isabel was kidnapped on the journey from Narbonne, Your Majesty?"

"Yes, of course. People love a good story, and it has been repeated around the palace. I understand she managed to escape."

"Chetwynd is going to want to know who was behind

Isabel's kidnapping. Did you have anything to do with it?"

Gilda, impressed by Justin's daring, kept her eyes on Lothar to watch for his reaction. She wondered if he would admit it even if he were involved.

"No, Justin. I had nothing to do with it. Don't you think it's more likely to have been the queen? No doubt she was upset to learn that Chetwynd had married. She could have arranged to have his wife kidnapped."

Since Lothar and the queen took every opportunity to slander each other, Justin wasn't surprised at his accusation. "Kidnapping does not seem her style. Judith would seek to seduce Chetwynd away, or perhaps discredit Isabel in his eyes. That would be more in keeping with her usual methods of obtaining what she desired."

"And you think I would arrange to kidnap a woman?"

"Shhhhh. Keep your voice down," Gilda said, then blushed when she realized to whom she was speaking. "Sorry," she whispered.

Justin grinned. "It runs in the family," he commented to Lothar.

Gilda narrowed her eyes at Justin before directing a question to Lothar. "If not you, and not the queen, who do you think would do such a thing?"

"Couldn't it have been some ordinary bandits? I understand outlaws survive by preying upon travelers along that route."

"According to Chetwynd, the leader was later seen in the queen's party," Justin answered.

Lothar smiled smugly. "That supports my theory. I tell you that Jezebel is capable of anything."

Justin was about to give up when Gilda asked, "What about one of the church fathers? From what I understand, Bishop Agobard was behind the plot to use Gerberga to discredit the queen."

Both Gilda and Justin were watching Lothar, wondering if he would confide in them. He took his time, clearly thinking about how much he should say.

"I did know about the plot to discredit the queen. My dear stepmother was telling people that Gerberga predicted Charles would be the next emperor. The church fathers worked hard for many years to establish a succession that would keep the empire strong and were understandably upset by Gerberga's prediction.

"Several of the bishops arranged to have Judith banished, claiming she had been bewitched by Gerberga. The queen brought it upon herself, and I supported their plan. It seemed logical. As I'm sure you remember, Louis himself banished two of his sisters to a nunnery when he first became emperor. They were said to consort with many different men. In my eyes, Judith is no different.

"But I had nothing to do with Gerberga's execution. One of the bishops took matters into his own hands and had a quick trial. Gerberga was an old enemy. If nothing else, you should believe I'm smarter than to make a martyr of Gerberga. Her death defeats the whole purpose of the plot. Now there is no reason to confine Judith to a convent. She can't be influenced by a dead nun."

Lothar was pacing while he spoke. When he finished, he sat down and leaned his head back against the chair. "I think it's time for me to return to Rome. I'm truly sorry I lost my temper with Lord Chetwynd. His connection with the queen and the bad timing of his arrival pushed me beyond good sense."

Justin appreciated the frankness with which Lothar spoke. "I wonder if we will ever find out who was behind Isabel's kidnapping," he said. "I can't really believe that one of the bishops was involved. They might view Gerberga as a threat to Christianity because of some of her practices, but I doubt they would view Chetwynd as a threat to their plans, despite his connection to Judith. The more we learn, the more puzzling the kidnapping seems."

In the great hall, Marianna, Ingram, and Jerome were nervously keeping a vigil for Justin's return. Marianna had told them that Isabel had gone to seek Chetwynd in the dungeon, disguised as a serving maid. When Isabel did not return with Herlinda, Marianna blamed herself and sought out Chetwynd's men. Although Ingram had been upset that Marianna had allowed her mistress to attempt such a folly, her distress tempered his reprimand. Ingram knew that King Lothar had summoned Justin, and he guessed it had something to do with Chetwynd and Isabel.

There were a few men drinking and speaking loudly at a nearby table, but the large hall was almost empty. Each time someone entered the hall, the three turned to see if it was Justin or Gilda returning. When it happened again, Marianna's eyes widened. She recognized the new arrival

"It's him," she whispered urgently.

"Who?" Ingram asked, recognizing the man before she could reply. He lowered his head and whispered to Jerome. "It's the leader of the kidnappers."

Jerome turned away as though he had no interest in the man. Then before either of the other two could move, he casually stood up and walked toward where the man had taken a seat across the room. The newcomer stared at Jerome for a minute before dismissing the small young man as an unlikely threat. But when he turned away, Jerome jumped the outlaw from behind. Ingram had guessed his intention and was there to help by the time Jerome had wrestled the man to the floor.

CHAPTER TWENTY

CHETWYND'S HEAD ACHED. WANTING TO stay alert, he had refused the powder the physician offered him. However, he had accepted a damp cloth, and it was draped over his eyes as he lay on the bench. His ribs were sore, but other than a bump on the head and bruised ribs, the guards had inflicted no serious damage. That fact didn't make Chetwynd feel any better. He should have fought harder, overpowered the guards, and rescued Isabel from Lothar.

He groaned at the thought. He should have kept his head and done nothing, but Isabel's scream and the knife at her throat had broken his composure. It was only later he realized that she had screamed because the guards were beating him. Even the idea that she might be hurt had driven him mad, and it still did. He jumped up and threw the cloth at the wall.

The physician had sworn that Isabel was fine, but he could have been lying to protect Lothar. Although why Lothar would need to be protected from a man locked in a cell was difficult to understand. Chetwynd moved to the door and made yet another unsuccessful attempt to force it open by ramming it with his shoulder. The resulting pain made him lean his head against the bars. As he stood there, he heard a voice just out of sight of his window.

"Guard!" he shouted, but closed his eyes at the sharp pain the effort caused him. "Come here for a minute. I need to talk to you."

When Chetwynd opened his eyes, he saw Isabel moving toward him down the narrow hallway. Certain she was a hallucination, he blinked his eyes. But when he opened them again, she was still there, only closer. Although he was aware of people behind her, he couldn't take his eyes from her face.

With her hair still uncovered and her head held high, Isabel seemed to be moving in slow motion. Afraid to say a word and break the spell, Chetwynd watched her in silence. The smile on her lips kept getting wider. The realization that Isabel was truly there, and her expression of pleasure at seeing him, made his heart twist with something that was both pleasure and pain.

His hands were on the bars at the window, and Isabel lifted one of hers to touch him. He grasped her hand in both of his and whispered in a husky voice, "Are you all right?"

Isabel nodded. She could see that there was blood in his fair hair, but she did her best to ignore it. He was alive and happy to see her. She remembered that she was supposed to reassure him that she was unharmed and tell him that he would be released when King Louis arrived, but she couldn't speak. There seemed to be an obstruction in her throat.

There were questions Chetwynd wanted to ask her, but all he could think to say was, "I want to hold you."

Isabel's lips were pressed together, and Chetwynd realized she was fighting hard to keep from crying. He didn't want to make her cry until he could hold and comfort her, so he looked beyond her for help. He saw both Justin and Gilda. Relief flooded his body at the sight of the two people he had depended upon so often for support. They would take care of Isabel.

Aware that Isabel was still struggling to maintain her composure, Chetwynd spoke in a calm voice so as not to upset her. "What has happened, Justin? Can you get me released?"

"King Louis is on his way to Aachen, Chetwynd. As soon as he arrives, Lothar will be leaving and you will be released. That should be tomorrow."

Chetwynd narrowed his eyes. Why couldn't he be released now? he wondered, but he was afraid to ask. He was still holding Isabel's hand, and it was trembling. Gilda had moved to stand beside her. He couldn't be sure from his small window, but his sister seemed to be supporting Isabel. Gilda spoke to him in a reassuring voice. "It won't be long now before you'll be free and can join Isabel, Chetwynd. King Louis traveled to Saint Ives to fetch the queen, and he is on his way back to the palace. Lothar gave us permission to speak to you and give you a chance to see Isabel. He is sorry for what happened earlier."

Although doubting what she said about Lothar, Chetwynd nodded his head. "Good, good." Something was going on, and he couldn't imagine what it was. Clearly everyone wanted him to remain calm, so he would try to do that.

They had reached an awkward impasse, and Justin hesitated, wondering what to do next. They were supposed to be reassuring Chetwynd that Isabel was all right, but Justin could tell they hadn't succeeded. He had never thought of Chetwynd as overly perceptive, but he certainly shared a connection with Isabel. There was no doubt in Justin's mind that Chetwynd could read Isabel's feelings and knew that something was wrong. He would have preferred to tell Chetwynd of Isabel's injury and explain that it was an accident, but he was afraid that would make the situation worse.

"We'll take care of Isabel," Justin promised. "I think she needs some rest, so we'll take her to your chambers where she can wait for you."

Chetwynd wanted to shout, *No, don't take her away*, but he just nodded and kissed her hand.

Suddenly he heard shouting in the hallway. The commotion was out of Chetwynd's view, but he saw surprise on Justin's face, and he thought he recognized one of the arguing voices. Isabel pulled away from the door. When she was no longer filling the small window, Chetwynd could see that Jerome was being dragged down the corridor by two guards.

"Unhand the lad!" Isabel shouted, and Chetwynd was sure she would have advanced on the guards if Justin hadn't held her back.

They were the first words Isabel had spoken, and Chetwynd gave a sigh of relief at hearing them. The power in her voice told him she was all right.

Ignoring Isabel, the guards were trying to restrain a struggling Jerome. In spite of their efforts, the much smaller lad had dragged them to Isabel's side.

Gilda stepped forward to distract the guards. "Why have you taken our squire?" she asked as though she were out in the courtyard instead of in a dungeon. "He belongs with our party. No doubt he came looking for us. I know he can be impulsive, but release him into Lord Justin's custody and we'll take him away with us."

The reasonable sounding demands coming from the small, beautiful woman distracted them for only a minute. "We had instructions to let you speak with the prisoner," one of the guards answered her as though their actions needed explaining. "There were no instructions about this one. He was causing a disturbance outside the dungeon, demanding to speak with a prisoner. He refused to go away. We'll let him cool off in a cell for a while."

Although one of the guards still held his arm, Jerome ignored the conversation between the guards and Gilda. He grinned at Isabel, clearly delighted to see her, and then turned to Chetwynd. "Ingram and I spotted the kidnapper. He came into the great hall. I told Ingram I'd get a message to you."

Chetwynd's eyes were wide with surprise as he nodded at his squire. He wondered if Ingram had known Jerome would force his way into the dungeon. "You did well, Jerome. Did the kidnapper tell you anything?"

"No, he won't talk to us. Ingram questioned him, but he pretends to know nothing of the affair."

One of the guards was furious that Jerome had succeeded in his efforts to speak to Chetwynd. He tried to pull Jerome away, but Justin intervened. "Wait. This lad has information King Lothar will be eager to hear." When the guard ignored his words, Justin added, "You don't want to be on the wrong side of Lothar. He will be angry if he can't speak to this lad immediately."

The guard hesitated and Justin addressed Jerome. "Where is this kidnapper?"

"Ingram and Marianna are holding him. I left them in the great hall."

Justin turned back to Chetwynd. "Perhaps we can clear up this matter. If Lothar is innocent of any involvement as he claims, he will want to hear about the capture of the kidnapper. I'll persuade him you should be there when he questions the man. Hopefully, that will be very soon."

"And if Lothar's not innocent?" Chetwynd asked.

"I think he is," Justin said, remembering the things Lothar had said earlier. There wasn't time to fill Chetwynd in. "You'll have to trust me. It won't be long now, Chetwynd," Justin assured him.

"I do trust you. Please take Isabel out of here."

When Isabel tried to move back to the cell, Justin took her arm. "Come with me, Isabel." She paused and he added, "I need your support in persuading Lothar to free Chetwynd."

Still dazed by all that had happened, Isabel was reluctant to follow her brother until Chetwynd encouraged her. "Go with Justin, my love. I will be joining you shortly."

"What about this one?" asked the guard who still held Jerome by the arm.

"I told you, he needs to come with us," Justin answered. "You can bring him yourself if you doubt my word."

⁓

IT WAS ABOUT AN HOUR LATER WHEN CHETWYND was escorted into Lothar's chambers. Gilda had insisted that Isabel rest in a chair, but Isabel had been watching the door and she leapt up, ran across the room, and threw herself into Chetwynd's arms. He lifted her off the floor and buried his face in her hair. It seemed like forever since he had held her.

King Lothar was watching from across the chamber, and he grimaced at the sight of Chetwynd swinging Isabel into the air. "Be gentle with her," he shouted.

Chetwynd's face was buried in Isabel's hair, but his head jerked up at the words. He gently lowered Isabel to the floor, but she wouldn't release her arms from around his neck. He remembered how weak she had seemed outside his cell. "Are you injured, Isabel?"

"It's nothing."

Chetwynd looked at Lothar for an answer, but Justin had

stepped in front of him. "Chetwynd, I hope you'll remember what happened the last time you lost your temper," Justin warned. "In the struggle in your cell, Isabel's hand was cut. It's a minor wound that has been attended to by Lothar's physician."

Before Justin finished his explanation, Chetwynd was gently pulling Isabel's arms from around his neck. He saw the wrapped hand, and remembered how Lothar had been holding a knife to her neck in his cell.

"Are you hurt anywhere else?" he asked.

"No, just this small cut on my hand. It was my fault, Chetwynd," she said, pleading with him to understand. "I should never have come to your cell. It was an accident."

Chetwynd turned her hand over in both of his. "It was not your fault, Isabel. Does it hurt?"

"No. It's fine, truly."

"Good," he replied simply. When he raised his head, he didn't even look at Lothar. "Let's get this over with so I can take my wife to our chambers."

Justin nodded, and Ingram stepped forward. Chetwynd hadn't paid attention to the others in the large room, but he became aware that Jerome and Ingram were standing beside another man. Marianna was also there, and she moved to Isabel's side.

Ingram spoke quickly, as eager as Chetwynd to be done with the matter. "Marianna spotted this man in the great hall, my lord. I recognized him as the person Marianna pointed out to me earlier at Saint Ives as the leader of the kidnappers. We've tried to get him to tell us who hired him to kidnap Lady Isabel, but he pretends not to know what we're talking about. Both Marianna and I are sure it's the same man she saw during the kidnapping."

There was something familiar about the man, and Chetwynd moved closer to have a better look. Although he had aged, there was still a likeness in the uneven set of his jaw to a young soldier Chetwynd remembered well. It seemed impossible that after all these years he should show up again.

"Cecil. It's been a long time. Still in trouble, I see," Chetwynd said. He was sure he had made the correct identification when Cecil, who had stood defiantly until he was named, lowered his eyes to the floor.

"You know this man?" Justin asked.

"Yes. Cecil and I were soldiers together serving Lord Malorvic. I last saw him eight years ago in Narbonne when he attacked an innocent maiden."

Moving to stand beside Chetwynd, Isabel peered into the man's face. She recognized him as the leader of the outlaws, but beyond that she had no memory of him. Although she knew the incident Chetwynd was referring to, it had been a long time ago. "How can you be sure it's one of the men who attacked me, Chetwynd?"

Chetwynd grabbed the man's left arm, and when Cecil tried to pull away, Ingram held him steady. Chetwynd roughly turned over his hand to show Isabel the ugly scar at the base of his thumb. That long-ago day in the meadow was a blur in Isabel's mind, but she remembered that Emma had told her many times that she had bitten one of her attackers. She saw that the scar was in the shape of a crescent and could have been made by teeth.

"If you recognize him, do you know who hired him to kidnap your wife?" Lothar asked. When Chetwynd turned toward Lothar, the king took a step back and continued. "It wasn't me. I never saw the man before."

"I doubt if anyone hired him. I'm sure he believes he has sufficient reason of his own for what he did. Isn't that right, Cecil?"

"You ruined my life, damn you," the outlaw muttered. "I

lost my position with Malorvic and never got another one. It's only right that you should pay."

"You ruined your own life when you attacked an innocent maiden," Chetwynd said. "I just saw that you didn't get away with it."

Jerome had been watching the exchange attentively. When Chetwynd's squire remembered the story Isabel had told him and understood who Cecil was, he swung his fist at the outlaw, knocking him to the floor and following him down before anyone could stop him. It took Justin and Chetwynd working together to pull Jerome off the man. Ingram stood back, grinning his approval at Jerome.

Isabel had backed away from the struggle, and Chetwynd pulled Jerome over to where she stood. "Jerome, do something useful. Give Isabel your arm for support until we can finish with this matter."

After Ingram pulled the kidnapper roughly to his feet, Lothar moved forward to question him. "You had better explain yourself quickly, or I'll put you in a cell with Chetwynd's two men. They don't seem to be too happy with you."

The kidnapper looked from Jerome to Ingram. Then he began talking. "When I kidnapped Chetwynd's woman, I had no intention of harming her. My plan was to ask for a ransom. Lord Chetwynd ruined my career, Your Majesty. After he got me thrown out of Malorvic's army, I was reduced to robbing travelers to survive. He deserved to pay."

Lothar ignored his rationale. "Why were you in the queen's party?" he asked. "Were you also working for her when you took Lord Chetwynd's wife?"

Puzzled by the question, Cecil shook his head. "Taking Chetwynd's wife had nothing to do with the queen. I know a serving woman in the queen's employ. She gives me information from time to time about travelers, and I give her a share of the take."

From Lothar's expression, it was clear he was disappointed to hear the queen wasn't involved. This fact was not lost on Cecil, who said, "I have some interesting information I can give you about the queen."

Lothar looked at the man with distaste. "I don't have anything to do with men who prey on young maidens. Guards, take him away to the dungeon."

"You'll want to hear what I have to say, Your Majesty," the man shouted as he was being hustled away.

Lothar and Chetwynd found themselves standing side by side watching Cecil disappear. There was silence in the chamber, and Chetwynd sensed that everyone was nervously waiting to see what would happen next. Chetwynd turned to face Lothar. "I'm sorry I thought you were involved in the kidnapping of my wife, Your Majesty."

The look of surprise on Lothar's face made the effort it took Chetwynd to apologize worthwhile, and he relaxed.

"Your concern for your wife is understandable, Lord Chetwynd. She is a remarkable woman. I hope we can forget about our differences and get along better in the future."

The right words had been spoken, and the two men looked at each other as though wondering what to do next. Justin stepped forward, eager to separate Chetwynd and Lothar while they were still on good terms. "I think you should take Isabel to your chambers, Chetwynd. The rest of us can take care of things from here. Perhaps Gilda will help you with Isabel."

"I'm sure Chetwynd and Marianna are quite capable of caring for Isabel," Gilda pointed out to Justin. "I'd like to speak with King Lothar about sponsoring a memorial for Gerberga. I think it would be fitting to set up a fund to help the many women who will miss the services Gerberga provided them."

Justin frowned. "I don't think this is the time or place ..."

As Justin and Gilda began to argue, Chetwynd led Isabel from the room. She looked back at the pair who stood toe-to-toe and smiled at the sight. They made a striking couple, Gilda's golden locks contrasting with Justin's dark hair.

Back in their chambers, Isabel sat on the bed and watched Chetwynd washing himself. She had used her one good hand to help him wash the blood from his hair, and afterwards he had insisted she sit on the bed while he finished up. She could see bruises on his chest and back, but they didn't mar his beauty. She remembered that was how Emma had described him to her all those years ago. At the time she had protested, not realizing a man could be beautiful.

"I think Cecil was implying that he knows something about the queen that Lothar would find interesting. Do you think Lothar is going to seek him out to hear his story?"

"I wouldn't be surprised. Lothar will use anything he can against the queen. He distrusts her, perhaps with good reason. One thing is sure. Lothar has a soft spot in his heart for you, Isabel. It's one reason I managed to keep from attacking him."

"I think Lothar may be a little mad, Chetwynd. After the physician had given me a potion, I remember him pacing the floor and muttering about legends and someone writing a song about me. He even compared me to Roland."

"Did he now? He always did like a good story, and apparently the tale of your escape from the kidnappers has been widely repeated."

"Before the physician arrived, he did wrap my hand and stop the bleeding. He was quite upset at the sight of my blood."

"And so he should be. It was fortunate for him that I finally learned to curb my temper."

"With a little help from Justin," she added.

"With a lot of help from Justin. I guess I'd better see if I can teach Jerome to control himself. Although I must say it was satisfying to see him pummeling Cecil. It made it easier for me to refrain from doing it myself."

Chetwynd picked up her bandaged hand. "Do you think we should apply a new wrap?"

"No. Marianna already changed it, as you well know. I think she wanted to see if the physician did a good job. She said it was looking quite clean. Come to bed, my lord, before the sun comes up."

Happy to do as she requested, Chetwynd gently pulled her into his arms. "I have to tell you, I was scared to death when I saw you outside my cell, Isabel. You didn't say a word. It wasn't until you ordered the guard to unhand Jerome that I knew you were all right."

"It took an effort to hold myself together, but the sight of those two big men with their hands on Jerome made me forget everything else. Both Jerome and Ingram were wonderful, weren't they? We are fortunate they found the leader of the kidnappers. Justin was able to convince Lothar to release you, and we now know we don't have powerful enemies at court."

"Yes. I think Lothar is as relieved as we are. He was more than a little worried that I blamed him for being behind the kidnapping. Hmmm, you smell good."

Isabel chuckled. "After the stench of the dungeon, I imagine anything would smell good."

"Not as good as this. Your hair is heaven. And this little spot, right beside your ear, is also nice. But this spot below your breast, it's my favorite."

"Chetwynd, you have a lot of serious-looking bruises. Maybe we'd better wait until you have healed."

He pulled back a little to see her face. "I guess we're both a little tender. We should wait."

They stared at each other for a minute. Then they both started to laugh, softly at first and then more heartily.

"We'll be careful," he said as he moved her bandaged hand out of the way and pulled her on top of him.

EPILOGUE

Aachen, Spring, 826

CHETWYND SAT ON THE EDGE OF THE BED and pushed back the thick mass of hair that covered his wife's face. Isabel was lying on her stomach, and she turned her head away from him.

"You said you'd be up by the time I dressed, Isabel. I'm washed and dressed, and it doesn't appear you have even moved," he complained.

"I'm too tired to move, and it's your fault."

Chetwynd shook his head. "You were just as enthusiastic as I was. I remember you saying we had to make up for the last night we slept in this bed. Although as I recall, our cuts and bruises didn't dampen the spirit of our lovemaking much that time either."

"Go to the great hall, Chetwynd. I'll join you later," Isabel muttered into her pillow.

"I don't trust you, Isabel. The assembly starts today, and King Louis has requested an introduction. That's quite an honor. I told him I'd present you after the morning meal."

Isabel rolled over, but her eyes were still only slits. "Have some compassion for my delicate condition, my lord."

Chetwynd pushed aside the cover and laid his hand on her slightly rounded stomach. "Yesterday we traveled from Aquis on horseback. Once we arrived, you bedded your husband with great vigor. You can't make me believe you are at all delicate."

"You do have a seductive touch, my lord," she whispered as he caressed her stomach.

"Isabel, we don't have time for . . . Someone is at the door." He threw the cover over her head and went to answer the rap.

When Isabel heard Gilda's voice greeting her husband, she threw the covers off, leapt from bed, and ran to embrace Chetwynd's sister.

"Delicate condition," Chetwynd muttered. But he had to grin at the contrast of a naked Isabel being embraced by the brown-habited Gilda. "I expect to see you both in the great hall in a quarter of an hour."

The minute Chetwynd was gone, Isabel pushed Gilda toward a bench. "I can wash and dress while you talk, Gilda. I understand you spent the winter in Aachen, and I want to hear all about it. Don't leave anything out."

Gilda raised her eyebrows, watching Isabel splash water on herself. "It was an eventful winter, Isabel, but hardly as exciting a tale you as seem to expect. Each time I prepared to return to Saint Ives, there was something I was needed for here. Because of the absence of Gerberga, several of us had to step in and take over her commitments. No one realized how many women came to her for help."

Isabel pulled her dress on over her head, then asked, "And what about Justin? Have you seen much of my brother?"

"Our paths crossed. Right now we are on opposite sides of a dispute between Count Hermanne and his wife. Hermanne wishes to dissolve their marriage, claiming the countess hasn't given him an heir. In fact she has done so, but the boy is in poor health and unlikely to survive. I am making a presentation to the bishops on her behalf, and Justin is pleading the case for the count. There is absolutely no reason why the church should dissolve the marriage, and I can't imagine how your brother can side with the count." Gilda's frustration with Justin was clear by the tone of her voice as she told her story.

Disappointed to hear that two people she cared for were at odds, Isabel reminded herself that she and Chetwynd had their differences when they first met. As she struggled with her headdress, she felt Gilda's hands helping her gather her thick curls under a veil.

"Thanks, Gilda. Tell me the news about Queen Judith. Has she been rumored to have any new admirers?"

"The queen has been on her best behavior since her return to court. She has even helped me with my work a few times, although I have a feeling she will be expecting me to return the favor. She hasn't given up her ambitions for her son. I will support her if I can do so in good conscience."

"You're very wise, Gilda. But be careful. It could be dangerous to be caught between the queen and Lothar."

Gilda nodded. "As Lothar left for Rome the same day you and Chetwynd went to Aquis, you both avoided the return of the king and queen. Lothar has now returned for the Spring Assembly and so far has not caused any problems. Justin suspects this is the calm before the next storm. As much as I hate to admit it, he's probably right. Lothar is no doubt as determined as ever to keep Queen Judith from advancing her claims for her son, Charles."

With a grimace, Gilda said, "That's enough of palace intrigue. I know Chetwynd will be impatient for us to join him, but tell me quickly about yourself, Isabel. Has it been a good winter for you?"

"Better than good. Chetwynd and I have had a great deal of time to become acquainted, and we are closer than ever. I do love him so."

"I knew you'd be happy together."

"And I love our home. Bosco has been training me to keep the accounts for the manor. He says he's getting too old to do everything by himself. It's satisfying work, and I have the support of Bosco's wife. By the time Chetwynd goes off on his next campaign, I'll be ready to manage the manor, with Bosco's help, of course."

"Do you have any idea where he will go?"

"Not yet, but Chetwynd told me the armies will be getting their assignments for the summer campaigns soon."

Gilda lowered her eyes to Isabel's waist and asked, "Isn't there something else you wish to tell me?"

"You miss nothing."

"I don't have to be too observant. You didn't have a stitch on when you greeted me."

"I'm very excited, and so is Chetwynd. Even Jerome has come around. When he first heard I was with child, he scowled every time he saw Chetwynd. Jerome has always been very protective of me. But I guess he has observed that I'm healthy and happy and has accepted the inevitable

"I have been teaching him to read. Jerome is a smart lad, and when he becomes frustrated with reading the Bible, I tempt him to work harder by bringing out the tales of Ovid. Father Ivo, our family priest, would have been proud of what I'm doing with the copies of the tales he gave me. He always said I'd be a good teacher. And what about you, Gilda, are you happy with your life?"

"I'm content. Sometimes I miss the convent, but there is a great deal of work to do here."

"Have you taken your final vows yet?"

340 / I D A   C U R T I S

"No, not yet. I have been busy with my work in Aachen, and the abbess has not pushed me to take my vows. There is plenty of time to do that when I return to the convent."

Isabel studied Gilda's beautiful face, trying to read her thoughts. "Perhaps you will choose to return to the world and give up your nun's robe."

"I doubt that. I have a great deal of freedom when I wear my habit, and sometimes it gives me an advantage when I'm trying to help someone. Justin once accused me of using my vocation to influence the cases I plead before the bishops."

"And do you?"

Gilda grinned. "Sometimes. I use whatever I need to win a case. But don't tell your brother I admitted it. He can be insufferable." Quickly changing the subject, she said, "Chetwynd's waiting. Let's go to the dining hall."

~~

As Isabel and Chetwynd waited in line to greet King Louis and Queen Judith, Isabel whispered with her husband, telling him about her conversation with Gilda. "I think Justin and Gilda were made for each other."

"You keep saying that, and you are dreaming, Isabel. You said she called him insufferable. And what about him? After embracing you in the dining hall, Justin frowned at Gilda and moved away. And before you and Gilda arrived, he was telling me it was time my sister returned to the convent and took her final vows."

"Aha, I knew it. No doubt he wants her to make up her mind to leave the nunnery. In spite of what they say, I think they fancy each other."

"Forget it," Chetwynd advised. "I remember how nervous

you were about meeting Queen Judith. Aren't you nervous about meeting King Louis?"

"Maybe a little. But I already faced Lothar earlier, and that was probably the hardest thing I had to do. The last time I saw him was a very emotional time for me, and I wasn't sure how I would react when we met again."

"I admit it was a shock when Lothar went out of his way to stop by our table. I suspect he admires you, Isabel. He greeted you warmly, while he gave me only the briefest of acknowledgments."

"I doubt I will ever understand the man," Isabel said.

They had reached the royal couple, and Isabel studied King Louis as he was speaking to the noblewoman in front of her in line. Louis was shorter than the queen and looked old enough to be her grandfather. Nonetheless, his face had a serenity that suggested he was at peace with the world. It was easy to see why people called him Louis the Pious.

Isabel had been concentrating on the king and was surprised to hear the queen speak up. "Lady Isabel, how good to see you again. Your Majesty, this is Lord Chetwynd's wife. I have told you about the assistance she gave me in my darkest hour."

Isabel noticed that the queen's smile was as bright as ever. For a minute it was easy to imagine that she had indeed helped the queen, instead of fleeing to Aquis with Chetwynd.

The king's voice was soft but authoritative. "I have looked forward to meeting you, Lady Isabel. You are a fortunate man, Lord Chetwynd. Your wife's reputation for bravery and resourcefulness are legend. My congratulations to you both."

Surprised by such praise, Isabel was speechless, but she heard Lord Chetwynd reply, "Thank you, Your Majesty. I am indeed a fortunate man."

The king spoke again, as Isabel and Chetwynd started to move on. "Perhaps we can have a chat one day, Lady Isabel, and you can tell me of your adventure with the bandits. My son Lothar tells me it is quite a tale."

When Isabel looked back, she saw that the queen's smile had become stiff and it no longer reached her eyes. As they moved on, they passed by Lothar, who leaned toward Isabel and whispered, "The ballad shall be called the *Song of Isabel*."

Pulling Chetwynd along, Isabel rushed away from the crowd of spectators who all seemed to be smiling in her direction. "Did you hear that?" she whispered to him. "The queen claims I helped her in her darkest hour, when in fact we fled in the night. The king thinks I had an adventure with bandits, and Lothar makes a jest about a ballad. Their view of me seems far from reality."

"At court, stories have a life of their own, and they can change as they are repeated. Your presence is a breath of fresh air, and everyone likes that, especially me."

Chetwynd steered her around a pillar and out of public view and then took her into his arms. "You are indeed brave and clever and incredibly arousing. If someone isn't already composing a ballad about you, they should do so."

"Don't you start talking about a ballad."

He kissed her nose. "I will be hearing soon where my next assignment takes me, and I don't wish to miss a minute of the time we have left together. Why don't we return to our bedchamber and test your delicate condition."

Isabel grinned at her golden-haired champion. "I'd like that, my lord."

Born in New Haven, CT, in April 1935, Ida Curtis grew up in a small town near Hartford, CT. After marriage, she and her husband raised a family of two children, moving around the United States as his academic career dictated, living for the longest period in Vancouver, British Columbia. After retirement, they moved to Seattle to be near their son and daughter. Based on a handbook written by a ninth-century widow of a wealthy landowner to educate her sons, *Song of Isabel* captures what life was like for a young noblewoman of that period.

SELECTED TITLES FROM SHE WRITES PRESS

She Writes Press is an independent publishing company
founded to serve women writers everywhere.
Visit us at www.shewritespress.com.

A Girl Like You: A Henrietta and Inspector Howard Novel by
Michelle Cox. $16.95, 978-1-63152-016-7. When the floor
matron at the dance hall where Henrietta works as a taxi dancer
turns up dead, aloof Inspector Clive Howard appears on the
scene—and convinces Henrietta to go undercover for him,
plunging her into Chicago's gritty underworld.

A Ring of Truth by Michelle Cox. $16.95, 978-1-63152-196-6.
The next exciting installment of the Henrietta and Inspector
Clive series, in which Clive reveals that he is actually the heir of
the Howard estate and fortune, Henrietta discovers she may not
be who she thought she was—and both must decide if they are
really meant for each other.

The Great Bravura by Jill Dearman. $16.95,
978-1-63152-989-4. Who killed Susie—or did she actually
disappear? The Great Bravura, a dashing lesbian magician living
in a fantastical and noirish 1947 New York City, must solve this
mystery—before she goes to the electric chair.

After Midnight by Diane Shute-Sepahpour. $16.95,
978-1-63152-913-9. When horse breeder Alix is forced to
temporarily swap places with her estranged twin sister—the wife
of an English lord—her forgotten past begins to resurface.

In the Shadow of Lies: A Mystery Novel by M. A. Adler. $16.95,
978-1-938314-82-7. As World War II comes to a close,
homicide detective Oliver Wright returns home—only to find
himself caught up in the investigation of a complicated murder
case rife with racial tensions.

Just the Facts by Ellen Sherman. $16.95, 978-1-63152-993-1.
The seventies come alive in this poignant and humorous story of
a fearful rookie reporter at a small-town newspaper who
uncovers a big-time scandal.